QUANTUM

TIME

THEORY

JOURNALS OF A TRAVELER THROUGH TIME

A Novel by Ned Huston

Ned Huston

Book 1 of
THE NEVERTIME CHRONOLOGY

To Bonnie who makes all things possible, the star in my night sky, the sun of my planet's orbit. You have been there since the birth of this project and have been my universe ever since.

ACKNOWLEDGMENTS

Thanks to my readers, Nelson Graff and Chip Lenno, David and Carol Stevens, to my artists Kevin Cahill and Jeff McCall, to Denise Castro who helped me with the formatting of the Vann family tree, to Troy Challenger who aided me in learning how to format an e-book, and to Chris Beem and Barbara Beckmeyer who answered my questions and gave me feedback. And also to D. S. Kane who convinced me to take publishing my work more seriously. Thanks additionally to the writers in Central Coast Writers for their encouragement and comradeship. And also thanks to all of you who have read versions of this manuscript long in the past, including Robin Murray, John Guzlowski, and Michael Main.

TABLE OF CONTENTS

vi

Foreword
By Professor Simon J. Worthy
Southeastern Illinois University

The Journals of Time Traveler Dexter Vann

I never used to believe in Time Travel. Now I search for evidence of it—and hope I don't uncover any. I want to believe in the journals, but I also hope they're just made up.

The 24 transcripts that comprise this volume were found in a barn in Gallatin County, Illinois. They were discovered inside a metal box of rather odd construction. I have done little editing of them myself, but they appear to have been extensively edited by someone previously.

If the transcripts are to be believed, they were originally recordings, though it is not clear on what type of device they were recorded. It may have been a simple tape recorder. Or it may have been something called a Subvocalizer (it is unclear at present whether a Subvocalizer is a recording device or only an attachment to a recording device).

Although they purport to be a recorded journal, the transcripts display few of the natural characteristics of a recorded account. There are none of the stops and starts, the repetitions, the fumbling of actual speech. The rough edges of the spoken narratives have been smoothed, and there are traces of a literary influence. They have not merely been transcribed, which makes me wonder whether they were edited by an older, mature Dexter Vann—or someone else entirely. If they were edited by him, why hasn't he added to them or commented upon them? Why are they still unfinished?

Most of the transcripts we do have are incomplete. They end mid-sentence or mid-thought. Nor do the transcripts give us a complete account of events in any of the Realities depicted. We merely get a glance into his world and his life.

I put the transcripts in order myself, numbered them, and identified them by Reality number and Season based on inferences and details in the texts themselves. I have also supplied a title for each account. Other than that, I have made few alterations, yet the transcripts seem to tell a complete story—the story of how the Vann family Adjusted to living in a world of constant change.

The Time Travelers have their own terminology and use words in a different sense than their meaning in the vernacular. I have capitalized such terms and defined them in a Glossary at the end of this book.

I have been hunting for more journal transcripts ever since I found the fragment I have used as an Introduction here. The countryside of southern Illinois seems to be littered with them. I have been collecting as many as I can get. I find them compelling, but you must decide for yourself whether they are genuine.

Reading these journal entries is like wandering through the open door to someone's deserted home. No one's around to object, yet you can still feel like a trespasser. But you linger anyway. The furnishings are just so interesting you can't resist exploring.

I wish I could say there is no danger in perusing these accounts, but who knows who you may be running afoul of by viewing them or what Directives I may have violated by publishing them.

Read them at your own peril.

Introduction
WHY IT SUCKS TO BE A TIME TRAVELER
Reality 267
A Fragment of a Journal entry
from the Concordance Season
By Dexter Vann

I don't want to be a Time Traveler. None of us do—not even Amos and Cooper, who were already Time Travelers when we started. I hate Time Travel.

If you've been listening to these journal entries from the beginning, you understand. But in case this happens your first, let me explain why.

Reason Number One: Because I want to have a life. I want a career. I want a community. I want stability. I want to own more than I can carry. I want to live in a world that's not constantly changing.

Reason Number Two: Because you go nowhere. Only to the Void of the Fourth Dimension to escape Changes in Time. You can't Visit the Future because nothing's there. You can't Visit the Past because you could screw up History and WIPE PEOPLE OUT OF TIME. Travel to the Past is *illegal*, and only greedy scumbags do it.

Reason Number Three: If I can Travel through Time, then greedy scumbags can, too, and they don't give a damn about you or me or anyone else. They'll use Time Travel to get rich and won't care how much they screw up everyone else's lives.

Romantic, my ass. Time Travel is NOT romantic. There's nothing romantic about living in a world torn apart by constant change. Over a trillion people have died because of Time Machines. And that's just so far.

Sure, life in the Timeflow doesn't seem so dangerous at first—when the threats are only coming at you one at a time. It takes several Seasons to realize all the hundreds of ways you can die.

Because Time Travel is not just aggravating—

It's a Death World.

SHAWNEETOWN (Illinois) 37°41′54″N 88°8′13″W—
The City That Should Have Been—a boom town on the
Ohio River, founded in 1748. For years it was the largest
settlement west of the Appalachian Mountains. It had the
first bank and for years the only bank in the western
territories. Big things were expected for Shawneetown,
the only city besides Washington D.C. to be platted by
the U.S. government. But its development was set back
repeatedly by catastrophic floods. In 1830 visionary city
planner Timothy Raveller undertook a mammoth public
works project to raise the street level by sixty feet with a
drainage system beneath it, and the flood damage was
averted. The city's growth continued unchecked.
Historically, the Gateway to the West, it eventually
became the headquarters for the Intertime Government.
In the 2010 census its population had reached 3,561,239

---From *The Time Traveler's Guide to the Chronoverse*
19th Ed.

Vann Family Tree

Vann Family Tree
Shawneetown, Illinois

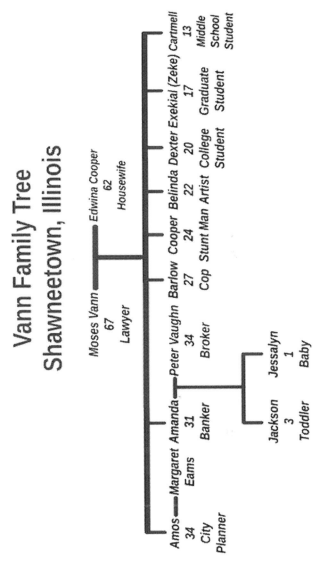

Moses Vann
67
Lawyer

Edwina Cooper
62
Housewife

Amos
34
City Planner

Margaret Eams

Amanda
31
Banker

Peter Vaughn
34
Broker

Barlow
27
Cop

Cooper
24
Stunt Man

Belinda
22
Artist

Dexter
20
College Student

Exekial (Zeke)
17
Graduate Student

Cartmell
13
Middle School Student

Jackson
3
Toddler

Jessalyn
1
Baby

1
THE BROTHERHOOD OF TIME
Reality 251
Wilderness Season

I've just got a call from Amos. Someone's made another Change in the Past, and there's a Timestorm coming our way. I've got forty minutes to get to our Safe House, or I'll I get torn apart atom by atom. If I want to Survive, I need to take Shelter..

But get this—Amos wants us to meet at the Brotherhood Lodge. His Time Machine is located *there*.

Unbelievable.

What can I say except this is how it actually happened?

If you've ever been to Shawneetown, you know I don't want to go to the Brotherhood Lodge. Nobody does. Mind you, I don't believe the stories about the Lodge. I'm not gullible. The police have been in there and have searched the place lots of times and have found nothing, absolutely nothing wrong.

It's just a house.

So what if trespassers vanish? Or go insane? So what if they're never the same afterwards? I don't believe in haunted houses. Not even a three-story Victorian mansion with a turret, eight gables, and a mansard roof. And a wrap-around porch. And a spiky black wrought-iron fence.

So people avoid it. So what? Yeah, I've heard the stories about whirring sounds and flashes and beams of light inside the house late at night. They're just stories.

They say people go in who never come out. Other people come out who never went in. Your skin crawls and your hairs stand on end if you get too near the gate—like you're about to get struck by lightning. Strangers come to visit at all hours. But Locals aren't welcome—not inside the fence.

I don't believe in all that crap.

But I still don't want to go to the Brotherhood Lodge. Would you?

Knowing Amos, I figure he's a member of the Lodge, so I guess that makes us guests and nothing bad will happen to us. Right?

But that doesn't solve anything—because when I get to the Lodge—when my ride drops me off at the curb down the block—I find another problem.

Chupacabras.

The Chupacabras are one of the dozens of gangs that have sprung up all over Shawneetown since the last Change in Time. They're like anger personified. There weren't any gangs in Reality 250, but here in glorious 251, poor people of every stripe have their gangs now. Mean, violent, nasty sadists. You get the picture.

Well, they're all over the sidewalk and the easement and the dewy grass all the way up to the fence, which is halfway to the house. There are at least two dozen of them between me and safety.

The Chupacabras like to claim territory—including anyone passing through it, and they like to cut people's faces to mark their property. And if you don't play along with them, they'll carve you up.

Amos said we probably wouldn't like these Changes that have been made in Time, but this Reality 251 is ridiculous. Seriously messed up. Someone's going to have to do something about this, set it right. But not me. This isn't my mess. I've got my own life and my own problems. I don't want any part of this.

Timestorms, gangers. It's as if someone's out to get us. But who would do something like that?

There's gun control now in Reality 251. So the gangers all have knives—switchblades. Some of them are lunging at each other in mock combat. Others are flinging their knives at a target on an old oak tree or sitting, sharpening their blades with small whetstones. Those blades are so sharp my eyes have nicks in them just from watching. The air is full of jabbing and slashing and flying knives. The glint of steel sparkles across the lawn of the Brotherhood Lodge like glitter.

The Chupacabras wear white t-shirts, baggy pants and red bandanas. Their gang mark is the scar on their face—vertical for members, horizontal for outsiders. They're a huge obstacle in my way. I don't want to have to deal with them.

But hey, I'm an engineering student. I can solve this problem. I just need to find a way into the Lodge without going through the gang.

Engineers are practical. Problem solvers. Creative but realistic. Reality's just a set of tinker toys to them. Engineering is the best career a person could have—because Engineers make a difference. They make the world a better place.

I notice a sidewalk leading from the side of the house to the fence on Jackson Street. I figure there's a gate there, and I can avoid the gang, so I walk down to Gallatin and circle around and come to the side of the house from up Jackson. I'm right about the gate, but I discover it's locked.

Give me a break! Why have a gate if you're going to keep it locked? What's worse, when I touch the gate, my short hairs stand on end like a hissy cat's, and I'm sweatin' 'cause of all those bullcrap stories. And if that's not bad enough, the gangers notice me, and a couple of them start in my direction. I've attracted their attention because I've entered their territory. They know I'm an outsider—I'm not dressed like them. I've got on my usual jeans and cowboy boots, a white shirt and a vest. I look like Wyatt Earp with a backpack.

That's right—Wyatt Earp, the gunfighter. The Marshall who got things done in the old West. The problem solver.

I notice there's an intercom with a button on the fence by the gate, so I give the button a push and wait. I'm calculating whether to run and how soon—when finally I hear something over the intercom. A high-pitched voice cackles in a strange accent. "Is what it?"

It takes me a moment to figure out the speaker means "What is it?" What kind of crazy dialect is this? How am I supposed to respond? So I say what Amos told us to say.

"Dexter Vann here to see Amos Vann."

The voice says nothing, but there's a click, and the gate swings open an inch. So I push it the rest of the way and walk up the sidewalk toward the house. I hear the gate automatically clang shut behind me like I'm in the slammer, and when I look back, I see two gangers on the other side, staring at me like I've butted in line ahead of them.

"Don't stay over there, Clyde," the tall one with the moustache says. "Come rumble with the Chupacabras."

"Yeah," says the short one. "We're not going to hurt you. We just want to mark you. Get out of there. People who cross that fence are as good as dead."

They could climb the fence if they wanted, but they stay back from it. They don't even test the gate to see if it's locked. They've heard the stories. But they're not as nervous as I am—they're still on the safe side of the fence. I turn and back away slowly and stumble over a pile of raked leaves.

I consider turning back, heeding the gangers' advice. After all, they make a good argument. But I've always had this feeling that I've got to keep plugging along. Because people are depending on me. Who, I don't know. Not my brothers and sisters. They don't need my help. No one's ever depended on me but me.

As I walk around the side of the house, I catch glimpses of faces peeping at me from curtained windows on the upper floors. They appear and disappear so quickly I end up blinking and wondering if I saw anything at all.

There's a breeze from the southwest. It's a cloudy day but warm for November, and I can smell the odor of cornbread from the vendors downtown on Poplar Street. They're getting ready for the lunch trade.

Climbing the front steps, I find there are chairs on the porch, so I take off my backpack and sit in one of the rockers to wait for my brothers and sisters. That's as far as I'm willing to go into the house alone. That seems to me the prudent thing to do. Given its track record, would *you* go in there?

I spot my younger brother Zeke across Ash Street for a few seconds, scoping things out on his motor scooter. He's smart, so I know he's noticed the side gate. So when he zips out of sight, I figure he's going to wait for the gangers to leave the side gate and enter there, which is the reasonable and rational thing to do.

The problem is my brothers and sisters are not reasonable. Or rational. They have to do everything THEIR WAY. So I know they're not going to use the side gate or listen to my advice. They're too brash to do anything in an ordinary way and too stubborn to let anyone push them around. They push back. So I know there's going to be trouble today—lots of it.

You'd think there'd be no way to get through the Chupacabras unharmed. You'd think your only option would be to go around them. But you don't know my brothers and sisters. They don't do things the ordinary way—they're extraordinary. That's the reason my middle name is "brother of" (as in "Dexter brother of [insert name of sibling] Vann").

It all started with my oldest brother Amos. He's huge. He's always been the biggest kid in his grade. And the smartest. And the most forceful. A born leader. Some people are like that.

But it ain't easy having them as your brother.

We're all smart in my family. We're achievers. We had to be. Because we've had competition. From the very beginning. All our lives we've had to compete.

My oldest sister Amanda has been fighting with Amos since birth. Vying for attention. Sharpening her weapons. Honing her skills. Is it any wonder she's intimidating? And stubborn? She won't budge an inch. You've got to understand it's not her fault she's the way she is. She *had* to become that way.

So when she shows up at the Lodge, she's not scared of the gangers. What are any of them, compared to Amos? She doesn't consider them her equals. They don't have her intelligence. They haven't developed her killer skills. She's a top executive at Shawneetown Bank. *The* Shawneetown Bank. And she hasn't risen up the ranks by accident. She's clawed her way up.

So a few low-class gangers are *nothing* to her.

She arrives in a limousine, no less. When she gets out, I see she's wearing a gray suit and sunglasses and carrying a briefcase. She looks pretty normal—at first glance. Like an ordinary mother and businesswoman. She doesn't style her hair or wear much makeup. She dresses in fancy suits like a banker. She seems like a hundred other bankers and working women. But you've got to remember Amanda is big. And she can be nasty. Once she gets riled at you, and you see those flashing eyes and hear that sharp cutting voice, there's no fire-breathing dragon you wouldn't rather be with. She'll singe you. She'll burn you to a cinder.

But she's my sister. She's family. She's a big time banker, and I'm proud of her, and I don't want to see her get sliced up by a bunch of Chupacabras.

Between her and me are two dozen ugly nasty mother huggers, and they ain't in no mood to be nice. Amanda needs to *go around* them. She needs to avoid them.

I point to the side gate and wave my arms in warning, and I make slashing and stabbing gestures and point to the gangers, but she doesn't pay me any mind. She just waves to me like she's departing on a cruise ship.

Yeah, the Lusitania.

She's not going around them—she's gonna go right through them. She's not going to let anyone intimidate her or stand in her way. She's the nerviest person you ever met. All my brothers and sisters are.

She marches right between the gangers and starts walking up the sidewalk toward the house. She's not scared. She's used to dealing with obstreperous people. I'm afraid she's going to end up with her face carved up, but the gangers keep their distance. She has the air of authority after her years working at the bank. They don't know the consequences of meddling with her, and it makes them hesitate. They seem confused.

I see a ganger step in front of her and say something, but she gives him a sharp remark, and he backs off. Amanda is used to giving orders. She knows how to motivate and persuade people—in other words, manipulate them. Sometimes she can even push *us* around, and we already know her tricks.

Gawd, I can't believe it. She's got them mesmerized. They can't understand her. They're letting her intimidate them.

Another ganger approaches her, and she barks something at him, and he retreats. She's almost to the fence when the biggest of the gangers gets in her way, but after a conversation, he too steps aside, and Amanda starts through the front gate—it's unlocked—and up the sidewalk to the porch.

Well, I'm cussin' and I'm struttin' and I'm frettin' on that porch. But I should have known she'd get by them. She's that intimidating. A whole army of Chupacabras is nothing compared to her.

"Hi, Dexter," she says when she reaches the porch. "Is Amos here yet?" She takes off her sunglasses and looks at the door to the Lodge and sits on a rocker beside me and starts checking her cell phone. She's oblivious to the gauntlet of pain she just crossed.

Okay, I'm impressed—maybe even a little jealous. I'm too upset to make a comment. So I sit down and say, "I'm the only one here so far. Zeke's going to arrive any moment."

But Houdini doesn't show up.

The person who does show up next is my older brother Barlow. He's third in line in the family, but he's never been satisfied with coming in third. It's a big family, so it's easy for a person to get lost in the crowd. That's what's made us all the biggest bunch of show-offs you ever saw in your life.

We don't show off like we used to. We're mature now. When you grow up with seven brothers and sisters, you *have to* show off sometimes, but you learn to use it strategically, so the rest don't gang up on you. But these gangers are bringing out the worst in us. Because they're shameless show-offs, and it's ticking us off. Someone needs to teach them a lesson.

My parents never paid us much attention. They expected us to excel. We had to raise ourselves, really. *You can solve that problem yourself. You're smart enough to figure it out. Don't be such a baby.* We had to earn their attention, and even then we didn't always get it.

My brother Barlow grew up with a lion and a tiger. He hasn't been safe his whole life. There was no place for him among the giants. He's larger than Amanda now, but as they were growing up, she was always bigger than him and Amos bigger still. Worst of all, he couldn't compete mentally with his older brother and sister. So he developed himself physically. He learned to dodge and elude them, outrun them, outlast them. He couldn't get any attention at home, so he got attention at school. He became an athlete. A champion. He developed physical skills—and he developed character.

He became a super show-off.

We all are in my family. We have to be. How else were we going to get any attention with all the competition? So when Barlow arrives at the Lodge, I know he's not going to avoid the Chupacabras. He has to showboat. But he's no banker. He's a cop, and the gangers hate cops.

He climbs out of a police car on Ash Street in his jeans and t-shirt like he's undercover—but he's about as inconspicuous as a fairytale giant. He's the biggest of us, after Amos. Six-eight and solid muscle. Dark-haired with chiseled features. You can tell he used to be an athlete right away, especially if you see him move, quick and smooth like a jungle cat. His knee injury doesn't show much except on x-rays, but it's kept him out of the pros. That's why he's a cop instead of in the NFL.

Does he go to the side gate? Of course not. I gesture at the side gate just like I did with Amanda, but it does no good. As the police car drives away, he sprints up between the gangers toward the fence, dodging them like the star halfback for Shawneetown U, weaving this way and that, stiff-arming the ones who try to grab him. They all begin to chase him, and he runs them to one side of the yard and then the other.

I'm out of my chair—I'm cringing because I don't want to see him get hurt. I know he can outrun them, but there are so many of them and only one of him.

As the gangers lunge at him, he hops aside or jumps over them or flips them with one of his judo moves. By the time he gets to the gate, they're all on the ground—but getting up fast. They're finding wet grass and leaves are slippery as ice.

This is more than I can take. But I'm not the only one who's had enough. Amanda's mad—mad at him for upstaging her—and she stands and starts yelling at him. "Barlow, stop fooling around and get up here. Stop tormenting those gangers."

He just grins and comes through the gate. You know the gangers want to come after him—they rush the gate—but they don't have the guts to cross through. Not after hearing all the stories. That short fence is the Wall of China to them.

As Barlow's walking up the porch steps, greeting us, I hear a noise from the side of the house, and I stand and look over the railing to see one of the cellar doors open outward, and my younger brother Zeke climbs up the steps and emerges into the light like he's risen from the grave. He's tall like the rest of us, and he wears black-rimmed glasses like Amos, but that's where the resemblance ends. He's skinny and pale like an undertaker rather than tanned and athletic. All the impressive stuff is inside his head.

His I.Q. is so high it can't be accurately measured. He had to be that smart to get by in this family. If he weren't, he would have totally disappeared. Nobody would have been able to see him with the rest of us in the way. He doesn't talk a lot or try to make a splashy scene. He knows better than to compete with us. He's kind of shy and retiring. But he knows how to show off. That's for sure.

I know he's aware of the side gate, and he's only come this way to flaunt how brainy he is. He's found the smartest way in, the safest way around the gang. He's already ahead of me in school at Shawneetown U, but now he's showed me up again. Okay, he's rubbed it in. We get it. Enough is enough. But Barlow hasn't caught on to his game yet, so he says, "How'd you get down *there*?"

Amanda gives him a look of annoyance as if to say *Don't encourage him!*

Zeke gets an ah-shucks grin on his face. "There's a passageway from the old subterranean tunnels." He has that crafty smile now, and it's making Amanda furious. He's upstaged her, just like Barlow. He sets down the bag he's carrying—a striped laundry bag with all his heart-keeps in it. Amos told us to bring our keepsakes with us—that's why I'm wearing a backpack.

Barlow frowns. "How did you know that?"

Zeke shrugs with a sly look on his face. He doesn't respond to the questions with obvious answers. He doesn't even bother to say, "Duh-uhh."

"Hello, Dexter. Hello, Amanda." He sizes up the situation and takes a seat on the porch railing and gets out his phone.

A big noise comes from down on Ash Street, and we turn to stare. It's one of those ganger cars with the big tires and the end jacked up and no muffler. It's lurching down the street, and we see some ganger chick jump out the side and come running toward the house like it's time to burn down the Alamo.

Zeke and Barlow and Amanda turn away from her to look at their phones, but I notice the newly arrived ganger is running up the sidewalk toward the gate. And then through the gate. I stop rocking and stare. What the heck? This one isn't afraid. Hasn't she heard the stories? Doesn't she know where she is? She comes all the way up to the porch, where she pauses and says, "Buenas dias" to us.

She has heavy make-up, a violet morning glory in her dark hair, a sleeveless blouse, gang signs on her arms, and a small vertical scar on her cheek. She smells of tortillas. And she's wearing one of those white Mexican dresses with an apron decorated with designs in black, yellow, and red. She's a complete stranger to me, but Barlow recognizes her and calls her name.

It's Belinda, our sister.

Holy crap! This ganger—Belinda? There's a general intake of breath on the porch, and Belinda walks up the porch steps and takes a chair and starts fanning herself like it's a hot day to her. "Ay chihuahua."

"Belinda," Amanda says, "when did *you* become a ganger?"

"Oh, muy long ago, muy long."

But it's been only two weeks since we saw her last, and she wasn't a ganger then. We're used to seeing her in a t-shirt and jeans, with a spiky butch haircut, not like this.

A ganger! I can't get over it. Why is she doing this? I want to give her the benefit of the doubt, but can there be any doubt here? She's joined a frickin' *gang*.

Okay, maybe she's got her reasons, but that's not what it looks like to us. And we're the ones who know her. This is just another in a long series of bad moves on her part. Terrible choices. Embarrassments to the family with humiliation all around.

I want to ask her why. We all want an explanation. But I know she's not going to give us any, so I don't ask. She deflects all of Amanda's questions.

Belinda had to grow up in Amanda's shadow. Amanda was class president, an athlete, on the honor roll. Belinda's never been as big as her or as popular or as smart. Amanda didn't want to share the spotlight with her brothers much less a sister. She's always been Belinda's biggest critic. Compared to Amanda, Belinda's an underachiever. She's never fit in.

Belinda's always wanted to be an artist, and she majored in that at Shawneetown U. But no one thinks that's practical, so Mom and Dad have been riding her to change majors so she'll have a fallback in case art doesn't work out. So first she switched to Anthropology (!) and then Fashion Design. But now she's sold one of her canvasses for nine hundred dollars, she's met some gallery owners, and she's going to have a show at the end of December. I can't tell you if she's any good or not because she won't show her paintings to *us*.

So when I see her with these gangers, I'm thinking she's gone back to Anthropology, only she's doing it now instead of studying it.

"Are you doing research on the gangers, Belinda?" I ask her.

She just looks at me. "No, I am one of them."

That makes Barlow mad, and he growls, "Why don't you try being one of us?"

She glances at him and says, "I've done that already." Like she's finished with us. But here she is.

Some ganger guy calls to her from the fence, so she goes down and starts talking to him and kisses him through the bars. His name's Ramon Sanchez, and he's the Latin lover type with a small moustache and hair cream. He looks all lovey-dovey, and it's clear she has some thing with him. I guess Belinda's added acting to her talents because she's really hamming it up with this ganger guy—she's known him for less than two weeks, but you'd think this was the love of a lifetime the way they're carrying on, like it's West Side Story or something.

Barlow becomes sullen and sits facing the other way as he rubs his sore knee, and the rest of us exchange glances. He and Belinda have always been best buddies like they're twins or something despite the five-year age difference. He never approves of her boyfriends. He doesn't think they're good enough for her—and they never are.

When Belinda comes back to the porch, Amanda says, "You know that guy probably won't Exist anymore when we get back from our Time Machine ride."

"I know," Belinda says. She doesn't even look at Amanda. She just sits there, staring into space, but he's still at the fence, watching her with shining eyes and holding onto the bars like he's on death row, which I guess he is.

I feel sorry for the gangers. These are part of the bunch Amos calls "Bystanders"—people who didn't Exist before the last Change in Time and won't Exist after the next. They're temporary—and therefore unimportant. They don't know how transitory they are—how could they? But I wonder if at some level they sense it. Is that why they're so mad—not because they're poor but because they're doomed?

"Hey, whatcha doing'?" my little sister Cartmell asks us, climbing up the porch steps. She's only thirteen, and she's still got her blonde curls. She's dressed in her school uniform—a new white blouse and a plaid skirt with suspenders—and wearing her Hello Kitty backpack and her red shoes, the flats with the buckles, she calls them her "ruby slippers." They're supposed to bring her luck during our ride in Amos's Time Machine.

Cartmell's different than the rest of us. She's smaller—I think she always will be. She has blonde hair instead of brown. And blue eyes like Dad. The rest of us show off by necessity, but she comes by it naturally. She has a real talent for it, and you don't even know she's doing it most the time. She's an artiste. She knows how to disappear from sight—then suddenly she's the center of attention. Everybody likes her. She's the superhero of likeableness.

We're all looking at each other in consternation because we didn't even see her get off the bus. She's too young for the stunts she pulls, and they're going to get her into trouble.

"How'd you get through the gang?" I ask her.

She giggles. "Felipe Sanchez let me through."

Felipe Sanchez? We glance at each other again, all of us except for Belinda, who's got a look of chagrin on her face.

"How do you know *him*? " Amanda demands.

"Belinda introduced me."

Amanda glares at Belinda like she wants to bite her head off. Cartmell's Amanda's ward since Mom and Dad died, so Amanda's responsible for her.

"It's not my fault!" Belinda cries. "She followed me to Ramon's. It's your own fault she doesn't have enough supervision. What was I supposed to do? Introducing her to the gang was the only way to keep her safe."

Well, we can all tell a big fight's brewing, but we get distracted by the sound of Cooper's motorcycle instead. He makes a big production out of his arrival, parks on the far side of Ash Street, and starts to stroll toward the house like he's walking the red carpet. He's got on his usual loafers and jeans and leather jacket. He's the handsome one of the family, with the high cheekbones and cologne and the perfectly styled hair. He's the most popular one in the family, too. He can charm you sockless.

Cooper had to grow up in Barlow's shadow. He's had to watch his older brother hogging the spotlight all his life. He's not as big as Barlow and not as athletic. So he's had to find other ways to get attention. In other words, he's a bigger show-off than the rest of us combined.

Barlow's always been a role model, a shining example to me of why to be good. So Cooper's done his best to be an example of why to be bad.

Several gangers are swarming around his motorcycle, because he left his keys in it, and they're fighting over who gets to steal it. Cooper doesn't care. I wonder if he's acting. He was an actor at Shawneetown U, but he mainly does stunt work in the movies now because he likes taking risks. Gambling, skydiving, drag-racing, base jumping. Anything for a kick. And he's so lucky he's usually unscathed afterwards. Usually. He's still alive, anyway.

He steps forward casually, unafraid, like he thinks he can run the ganger gauntlet by sheer luck and bravado. He knows all the rest of us have showed off on our way in, so he's got to out-do us. He's got to show off even bigger than us. He's got to show off so big it puts us to shame. Like he thinks this is a contest.

Amanda lets out a low strangled cry as the gangers line up to surround him. "Oh no, he's going to do something harebrained." She leaps to her feet, and so does Barlow. And even Zeke stands up. Daredevil Cooper has captured his audience. But whatever he was going to do gets cut short because our oldest brother

Amos arrives, wearing some weird purple suit, and Cooper halts in the street, then backs up.

You'd think, since Amos invited us and he's the one who belongs to the Brotherhood, he'd be the first one here. But he's stubborn and contrary himself, so he's got to be the last to show up.

He pulls up in a brown government car with little flags on it with a motorcycle escort. Men in suits and sunglasses climb out of the car and take up position on either side of him, but he waves them off and turns his deeply tanned face up to the house and gives us a wave. His black-rimmed glasses make him look intelligent, and his smile reveals his compassion. But if he's not smiling he's as menacing as the devil himself. And he's big, bigger than Barlow and more intimidating too.

Cooper hangs back. He knows better than to try to interfere with Amos's grand entrance.

So Amos makes his way forward, the motorcade drives off, and it's just him and the gangers down at the street. I notice the face on his wristwatch is flashing just like three weeks ago. Like Cooper, he's not carrying any belongings.

Well, everything's gonna hit the fan now.

In the distance I can see clouds gathering like some storm's brewing. It's moving in fast—suddenly everything's all gray above us, there's the feeling of change in the air, in the wind that's suddenly kicked up.

Seeing Amos all alone, the gangers like their odds. They're determined not to let anyone else pass them. It's a matter of honor. If he wants to get by, he's got to do it *their* way. He's got to give them tribute and respect—and make it clear they're in charge. He's got to let them mark him.

But Amos is the biggest of us and the oldest, and he's more stubborn too. So he pulls a revolver from under his suit coat and waves the gangers off.

A revolver! How'd he get around the gun control laws?

Most of the Chupacabras back away, but there are still a few who aren't intimidated, and they stand their ground. One in particular steps forward and says, "You aren't going to use that, and we both know it. So why pretend? You wouldn't—"

And BLAM! Amos fires, and the ganger goes *down*. The rest of them scatter, except for one who hesitates, at least for a moment. But that's not fast enough for Amos, so BLAM! Another ganger goes *down*. We jump and cringe at every gunshot. I catch a whiff of gunpowder in the air—it smells like the taste of burnt match heads.

I'm in shock. I'm totally floored. I knew Amos would make a scene. But not like this.

Amos replaces his revolver inside his coat and walks up the sidewalk unopposed. No one's even near him. They've all cleared out. As he steps over the bodies on his way up the walk, he barely looks at them—he doesn't care. They're *Bystanders*. They don't count.

Cooper falls in behind him. He's given up on the showing off contest because there's no question now who's top dog.

Barlow's all worked up and meets Amos at the porch steps and says, "Have you gone crazy, Amos? You can't shoot people down like that. When the authorities get here—"

Amos climbs onto the porch and stares Barlow down. "I *am* the authorities."

And Barlow stops in mid-sentence, his mouth hanging open. And he stops talking because he's got nothing to say. He's completely run out of words. We're all speechless. Amos has thumped the words right out of our mouths.

The wind's really picked up. It's blowing like crazy, and there's trash flying through the air. In the distance I can see an ugly black cloudbank building up with lightning bolts raining down from a knot at the front. I've never seen anything like it.

Amos surveys us and does a head count. "You're all still alive. I'm glad to see it."

Still alive? He's not referring to our narrow escape from the gangers. He's already forgotten about them. So why wouldn't we still be alive?

"Come on," he says to us. "Let's go inside." So he's the first through the door into the Lodge, with the rest of us trailing behind him. When we get inside, we discover Amanda's husband Pete and her two kids Jackson and Jessalyn are already here with their luggage, ready for another ride in a Time Machine. Maybe you think they were braver than me for coming inside the Lodge—I'd say more foolish.

Barlow's duffel bag is inside the Lodge too. He dropped it off earlier in the day. Amos told us to bring whatever we don't want to lose—all our mementos. I feel like a refugee. But why haven't Cooper and Amos brought anything with them? Have they sent their stuff ahead somehow as cargo?

A hooded Monk in a brown robe points us to the left. We continue down a long hall to an ornately carved wooden door with a small brass plaque on it, reading "999."

"What's this?" I ask.

"The Safe House." Amos does a special kind of knock on the door. And pretty soon the door opens like the hatch in a submarine, and a guy in a hooded brown robe peers out.

"Oh, it's you, Prefect. Please come in." I can smell the odors of hot tamales inside—Amos promised us lunch.

"Oh boy, this is going to be fun," Cartmell says, stepping through the bulkhead. Zeke laughs. He's almost as excited as her.

We pass through a vestibule as small as a closet and find ourselves in a rectangular space with old carpeting, a worn couch, stuffed chairs, a false fireplace, and heavy brown drapes. It looks like the living room in some old folks home and smells like it too.

My face wrinkles up like a shar pei. "I thought you were taking us to a Safe House," I say to Amos.

"Yeah, Amos," Cartmell says, "where's the Time Machine?"

Amos gestures at the room. "This is it."

I look around. My face won't unwrinkle. This dumpy room—a Time Machine? This is nothing like the space-age Timecraft we rode in on our first Trip.

"You've got to be kidding," Barlow declares,

"Nope," Cooper says. "This is the Safe House." He plops into one of the old stuffed chairs natural-like as if he owns the place.

Barlow starts to laugh. Zeke frowns, and I feel let down. Is this some stupid lesson Amos is trying to teach us? About gullibility or something? I actually believed he was serious!

"Take a seat everyone," Amos says to us, "and get comfortable." He walks over to the biggest chair in the room and sinks into its deep cushions and squeezes between its arms like an adult in an elementary classroom. The smell of tamales has vanished, replaced by the odor of musty old furniture.

"Some party this is," Amanda complains. "Aren't we going to have lunch?" She didn't want to come. She's an important banker, and she regards this Time Travel stuff as a waste of time.

"We'll lunch," Amos tells her, "after our Trip."

Amanda crosses her arms like an Indian chief.

Barlow sits on one of the chairs and bends down and looks beneath it. "Hey—this thing is bolted to the floor."

"All the furniture is attached to the floor," Amos informs him.

Cartmell sits on the couch and lets out a cry of surprise. "There's seatbelts on this sofa."

"All the chairs have seatbelts," Amos tells her. "You'll need them when we leave the Time/Space

Continuum, because there's no gravity in the Void." I can hear a hum of an engine warming up to a whine.

So maybe this is a Time Machine—just a lousy one. For lousy Trips. We already know about the Void, of course, from our last Trip. Time Travel, space travel, it's all the same thing. But this Room 999 seems a strange-ass kind of Time Machine to me.

Moving over to the wall, Amos draws the curtains aside like a game-show host to reveal a flat-screen TV between two portholes. "At first we'll be moving sideways from the Present rather than forward or backward," he tells us. "We aren't really going anywhere, just leaving the Present and coming back, after a few things have been Changed."

We're all glum and dismissive at that point. None of us want to be here. What a letdown! But when we get out into the Void, we have the time of our lives. We—Not again. Really? I've gotta go. Maybe I can finish this up next time.

2

TIME MACHINE
Reality 252
Wilderness Season

We did it! We Travelled in Time! We've actually been to the Future. Less than a Second into the Future, but still, we've Travelled through the Fourth Dimension. There's nothing there, of course, but there's no denying we're Time Travelers.

I love Time Travel! We all do—we can't help it. We all want to be Time Travelers. It's all so, well, *romantic*. So at the end of Reality 252 when we've come for our *third* ride in a Time Machine, we're rarin' to go. We're all dressed pretty much the same, except for Belinda, but our attitudes have changed. It's been over two weeks, and we're as eager as a bunch of dogs going for a ride in a car.

Amos does a head count as we scramble inside Room 999. "You're all still alive," he says. "I'm glad to see it."

Still alive! That again? We just saw him two weeks ago. What does he expect?

We take our seats in the stuffed chairs and couches same as last time. Once we're belted in, Barlow starts hollering, "Hey, let's go! What are you waiting for?"

Our pilot's one of the Monks on the other side of a partition, so Barlow bangs on the wall with his fist. "Crank her up! Bust out the jams! Voidspace, here we come!"

Zeke and Cartmell join in with the yells. I'm not yelling, but I am grinning, and so are Amanda and Pete. Jackson and Jessalyn are squealing in delight. We're ready Freddy—ready to rock 'n roll.

Cooper and Amos exchange looks. Amos is the only one of us who's not grinning—like the only adult with a bunch of out-of-control preschoolers. Our Cub Scout Pack is juiced up and ready to roll. We're about to bust out with campfire songs, start roastin' wienies and toastin' marshmallows.

We're all set to go!

So Amos gives the nod to the guy behind the partition, and the Pilot pulls his Lever and hits the thrusters. The portholes ahead of us turn black with the Void, and we're pressed into our seats. Gravity lets go of us completely once we're past the Threshold, and it's like a slingshot into the Void because it's Protospace out there, and in Protospace you have only three options—acceleration, deceleration, or rest. There is no inertia.

Viva Protospace!

Once the thrusters cut off, we're out of our seats and floating around the cabin in no time. Zeke's got his camera and is trying to take pictures through the portholes. Everyone else is turning somersaults or swimmin' through space.

The Monks have cleaned up the room since I barfed all over it last trip. I get motion sickness sometimes. I just wasn't ready for zero gravity. It doesn't seem to bother anyone else.

Cooper thought it was pretty funny when I tossed my cookies during our second flight. "Don't worry," he told me. "You'll get used to it. Newcomers get sick a lot. It's normal."

He seems to know all about it. He and Amos have been hanging out a lot recently. I don't get it. They never used to be so close, but now they act like they're in some secret club.

I'm used to my brothers and sisters having exciting private lives that I'm not part of. I've been "brother of" my whole life. It's who I am. I suppose that's why Amos has chosen me to keep this journal. I'm the spectator in the family, so I'm the natural choice. Someone has to do it, he says. And he doesn't have time for it. Neither does Amanda. Barlow's not going to do it. And Amos can't trust Belinda with it. She'd turn it into a protest. Cooper's the one who would be really good at it, but he'd embroider, "improve" on the facts, and that's not what Amos wants.

He knows I'll be fair and honest. I'll do my best. I asked him what my role is supposed to be: critic, apologist, family historian, scientific researcher? He won't say. He liked that first journal entry I made. So I guess he wants more like that. Stories of the family's adventures in Time.

This isn't a diary of my life—just of my life as a Time Traveler. So I'm leavin' out the mundane stuff: school and studying and all that and just focusing on myself and my brothers and sisters in Amos's Time World.

It's not hard, making these journals, especially with the Subvocalizer he's given me. I can record my entries without speaking out loud, while I'm in the Safe House between Realities and everyone else is clowning around. I'm only keeping this as long as I feel like it—and as long as I have a reason to. Once I'm too busy or the Changes are over, I'm done with it. Who knows—maybe I'll become important enough that I won't have time for this, either!

I keep hoping one of these mornings I'll wake up with some super talent and I'll become a stand-alone person like my brothers and sisters. But who am I kidding? I know that's not gonna happen.

What will happen is this: I'll get my college degree, and then I won't be only "brother of." I'll be Dexter Vann, engineer. I won't be at the top of my class like my brothers and sisters. I won't be Ivy League like Amos. I won't revolutionize the field of civil engineering. But I'll be somebody and not just the brother of somebody.

Of course, Time Travel makes everyone feel like somebody. We're all feeling pretty important. Even Amanda's excited for our third Trip. We don't need to trick her into coming this time. We've all been eager during the last month. This next Time Change couldn't come too soon for us. We wanted Amos to give us a ride sooner, but he said he couldn't do that. These Timecraft have been built only for a serious purpose, he says—they're not a carnival ride.

They are to us!

We're astronauts now—or Chrononauts, whatever you want to call it. Little Jackson doesn't understand that the Safe House is a Timecraft. He calls it "that floaty room" and thinks it *is* a carnival ride. In his view, what else could it be?

I think Pete likes it just as much as he does. He's a kid at heart. You should have seen him smile. He's big like a Vann but soft in the face. He's not intimidating like us.

Even Belinda—world-weary Belinda—is enjoying the Trip. She isn't a ganger anymore. The gangers completely disappeared after our second Trip. Amos says they've been Wiped Out of Time like a bunch of dodo birds.

It seems so weird to think those people are *gone*. Just like that. Vanished forever. And they didn't Exist before last Reality. Their Alternate Selves Exist, but not as gangers. They have no memory of Reality 251 or 250, where we come from. They have the same names, but they're different people. They look similar, but their memories have changed—and so have their lives.

It doesn't seem right. There's something wrong about this. Terribly wrong. But it's not my problem. I can't waste my time thinking about it. I've got textbooks to read and tests to study for. I don't have time to dwell on this Time Travel stuff. I may as well start worrying about the Mongolians as get worked up over a bunch of Bystanders.

I need to finish my degree and get a job. Then I can settle down. I don't need any detours now. I need to focus. I need to finish my junior year.

Once we maneuver onto the Plane, we can't see the Three Dimensional Earth anymore because it's behind us. All we can see is a shining star in the distance.

"What's that?" Barlow asks Amos. "Venus?"

Zeke groans. "Come on, Barlow. Get with the program. Venus is in the Three Dimensional Universe."

We're looking at Amos for an answer, but he seems reluctant to tell us. He's not wearing the same purple suit as last time. Now it's something in electric blue with oversized lapels and yellow stitching

"It's called Duration Station," he says finally. "It's one of the Time Stations in the Void."

Time Stations? Amos's Time Travel World just keeps getting bigger and bigger. The implications are staggering, but I can't let myself think about them. I've got to keep my eyes on the road. It's too easy to get obsessed with this Time Travel stuff. It can take over your whole life, but I don't want that. I want the life I've already got. I don't want to get lost in this Time Travel universe. I don't want to forget what's really important. I have goals. And they don't include Time Travel.

This is just a family outing for me—nothing more. I'm just here for the fun. I can't let myself get sidetracked. I can't let myself get distracted. I'm gonna have a good time and get back to the books. That's all. My brothers and sisters are enjoying themselves. I want to have my fun too.

So I turn away from the portholes. Barlow turns away too and starts rebounding off Belinda like they're bumper cars in free-fall. She's gone back to normal now, wearing her usual jeans and t-shirt with her jagged spiky haircut. Even the scar on her cheek is gone. Maybe she's covering it up with makeup—or maybe it was makeup to begin with.

Cooper turns on some tunes, one of his oldies, "Treat Her Right" by Roy Head and the Traits, and Barlow and Belinda start trying to dance. They've got their shoes off like this is some kind of sock hop. She's swiveling her hips to the beat, sending her twirling through the air, but Barlow's got her by the hand and pulls her back, hits the ceiling and gives her a whirl. They join hands and rock from side to side in midair.

We're all having a high old time. I don't want to make it sound like Time Travels just a big party, but—

TIME TRAVEL'S A BIG PARTY!

Jackson and Cartmell are wriggling through the air to the music like a couple wriggly eels. Barlow's yellin' the lyrics, and Belinda's doin' flips in midair. It's like one of those circuses we used to put on in the back yard when we were kids. Barlow and Belinda are the high wire act. The rest of us are clowns and acrobats and dancers.

We're twistin' and jivin'. Cooper's got his flask out and he's beltin' a few back. Even I've joined in the scene now that I've taken my motion sickness medicine.

I can see Zeke peering out the portholes and scribblin' equations on his notepad, grinnin' the whole time. A classic Vann party. Fun all around. No one goes home disappointed.

I smell pastrami, and I look over to see a picnic basket floating across the cabin. Cartmell and Zeke have discovered Amos's lunch stash, and they're in mid air, chowing down on hot pastrami sandwiches.

Then I see Jackson sail up to the flat-screen TV between the portholes and hit the "on" button, and the picture springs to life. It shows some kind of newscast. Two 'casters in silver jump suits sit behind a desk, speaking to the camera, but there's no sound. It must be muted. Their names "Myra Case" and "Red Phillips" appear briefly below them. Down the screen scrolls a list that goes something like this:

CTA Counterstrike
No More Gangs
No More Gun Control
Standard of Living Index Up
Programs for the Poor
Immigration Reform

Wilderness Season Stabilized

The two 'casters continue speaking in close-up for a minute. Another list titled "Anachronisms" appears on the screen, and I have time to spot only the top item—switchblade knives—before the camera cuts to a breaking news story.

A Wanted poster appears of some bearded guy with pale skin, gray eyes, and a white headband with Japanese characters on it. The name "Catterus" appears at the bottom of the poster "aka The Terror of the Void." Wanted for Traveling, Tampering with the Past, Violation of the 14th and 15th Directives, Assault, Murder, Piracy, and an assortment of other crimes, Bycrimes, and Timecrimes. But the kicker is the text that appears on the screen as part of the story: "Hired to kill the Vanns?"

Amos sails over and shuts off the set. He glances around, but no one seems to be paying attention but me. Everyone else is crowded around the lunch basket.

"What was that?" I ask him. "Did that mean *us*?"

"Never mind," he says. "Just ignore it."

Come again? "It looked like some sort of newscast. How can we be getting a newscast in the Void?"

Amos turns away from me. "I'll explain later," he tells me. "Just drop it and enjoy yourself—while you still can."

While I still can? He's acting like we're doomed. I look back at everyone else to see if anyone's noticed the TV, but they're too busy partying to care.

"If that was about us, shouldn't I warn everybody?"

"It wasn't about you," Amos says. "That's an old rumor. Just forget about it."

Now the music's stopped, and in between sips from the nipple of a plastic bottle of beer, Barlow's talking about buying a Time Machine of his own, but Amos tells him they're called Safe Houses, not Time Machines. Time Machines are for trips into the Past, and they cost about a billion bucks. Safe Houses Travel only into the Void. So maybe we'll build our own. Zeke's really keen on that idea. All of us want a Safe House now that we've ridden in one. I guess everyone does once they've taken their first few Trips. It makes you feel so powerful and special. It completely changes your perspective on the world.

We all want to Travel to the Past and have a look, but Amos says absolutely not. You have to have a special permit, and they're hard to get because it's so easy to cause a Change in Time by accident.

Of course, Safe Houses can't Travel into the Past anyway. You'd have to have a more powerful Machine, extended life support, provisions. Because Travelling back in Time requires a long voyage. Amos makes it sound like a real production. You have to wear a spacesuit and everything. Bring your own sources of food, water, and air. And you can't take back any souvenirs with you, because you can't remove matter from the Past.

"You say we're in the Void," Barlow complains to Amos. "But where is that? I mean, where the heck are we?" He's got this baffled look.

Amos smiles slightly. "The Future."

Barlow draws back at the answer and looks out the portholes at the darkness. "But there's nothing here."

"Exactly."

Barlow rubs his cheek. He looks like he's starting to get it. "Well then, how far into the Future are we?"

"Less than a Second."

Barlow's looking baffled again. He just can't wrap his brain around the geometry of it. There are only three dimensions in his head, and he can't translate time into space. He can't imagine a Second being a distance, especially not a long distance.

"The speed of light, Barlow," Zeke says. "Translate a Second into a distance by using the speed of light. That's the Speed of the Universe." When Zeke sees Barlow's crinkled-up face, he says. "186 thousand miles."

But that doesn't help Barlow. He just gives up. He's never liked math and science, and he's never been good at them. So he stops trying to understand his Trip and goes back to enjoying it. That's when Amos decides it's time to spoil all our fun. He unbuckles himself and rises up to the ceiling, where he can eye-stab us.

"You can't tell anyone about this," he announces, "about this Traveling in Time."

We all start to groan and protest, but he cuts us off with a chop of his hand—like his hand's a guillotine blade. The gesture makes him rebound off the ceiling, but he's ready for that and kicks like an expert to right himself. He's better at maneuvering than even Barlow and Belinda

"Not a word," he growls. "You hear me?"

We all fall silent because he's really mad, and we don't want him taking it out on us. But he can tell we're not convinced and we're gonna blab.

"Talking about this will only cause you trouble. If no one believes you, you'll be a laughingstock. If they do, it'll be worse." He's angrier than a truant officer. He looks like the librarian catching you stealing books.

"If the Bystanders believe you, you'll get detained by Homeland Security. They'll interrogate you mercilessly, and they will never ever let you go. They'll consider it a matter of national security. You'll end up Wiped Out of Time just like them."

We're all sitting or floating in stasis, trying to absorb the bad news. Ol' buzz kill Amos. He has to fire-hose our parade.

"But you're part of the government," Cartmell says. "You could get us out, couldn't you?"

"I'm a city planner!" Amos yells. "I'm not part of the Bystander government. They're beyond reasoning. They can't be saved. We don't have enough time or enough Machines to do that. There will always be Bystanders. Get used to it. And they will never understand. You can't tell them about us. They don't get it. They are our natural enemy."

So there you go. Time Travel is top secret, and you can't tell anyone about this journal or my experiences. It's just between you and me.

But I'm telling you Time Travel is a blast! We all enjoy these trips in the Time Machine—it's afterwards the problems start.

After our second trip I rush to campus for my structural analysis class. I don't want to be late. I think I'm going to be an hour early, but when I get to the classroom, I see everyone handing in tests and leaving.

"What's going on?" I ask Professor Gomez. He puts his hand up to his glasses and holds onto them for a second while he stares at me. He's short and round, not tall and skinny like the Vanns.

"Dexter, where have you been? Did you forget we were taking a test today?"

I don't know what to say. I was out getting a science lesson of a different kind. "No. That's why I'm an hour early."

He gives me this strange look. "I announced the test would be during regular class time. What made you think it would be at 1:30?"

"But that is—" And I figure out the starting time of class must have changed. Amos warned us of things like this, random changes in our lives caused by the Time Change. I'm just not expecting it to ambush me.

Professor Gomez looks at my expression and laughs. "You didn't forget when class starts, did you?"

And I hang my head like I can't believe what a screw-up I am. The last student hands in his test, and Professor

Gomez picks up the stack of tests and taps the bottom of it on his old wooden desk to even up the ends.

He looks down and thinks for a second. "Okay, come to my office, and I'll let you take it now."

So I go with him, and I'm feeling ecstatic until I see the test. It covers Chapter 12, not Chapters 10 and 11, which I studied. I do my best, but I'm not sure I've gotten more than half the answers right. I haven't heard him lecture on this material, and I only skimmed the chapter. It hasn't even been assigned yet.

I ask him about that when I hand in my test, and he frowns at me. He hands me a copy of the syllabus, and I can see Chapter 12 has already been assigned and lectured on. And I notice that class started a week earlier than before the Time Change, and I realize I'm probably a week behind in my other classes too.

Whew, that was tough! I'll just have to laugh it off, I guess, and make up for the points later in the semester. Amos says things get screwed up after Time Changes a lot, but I'll bet there'll never be another one as bad as this one! And I can't tell Professor Gomez about the Time Changes, because Amos says that would be a violation of Longtimer Law.

After our hot pastrami lunch in Room 999, my brothers and sisters trade their own stories about the mix-ups they experienced due to the Time Change between Reality 251 and 252. Everyone has a tale to tell.

Barlow got a reprimand for missing a meeting he didn't know about. Amanda missed her two o'clock and her meeting with the vice president because both got rescheduled for the hour she was on her lunch break at the Brotherhood Lodge.

Cooper's plane tickets weren't any good, which was just as well because the movie he was going to be in doesn't Exist anymore. I feel sorry for him, but I'm glad he's not leaving town because I'd miss him. We all would. Cooper doesn't seem to mind—as if he saw it coming.

Cartmell missed a party she didn't know about. And her assignments at school have changed. She says her teacher's someone different now. She thinks it's pretty funny.

Belinda couldn't find the painting she started before she left—of the Earth as seen from the Void of the Fourth Dimension. She got all bent out of shape, really had a fit, but now she shrugs and says she's going to start another one. Now she and Barlow are doing a duet in free fall. It's pretty funny to watch. Those two are always clowning around. I'm floating around this time too.

Zeke says he wants to bring his friends along next time like I did on our first Trip. But Quint didn't show up today or last time. I waited out front for nearly half an hour, but he never made it. Amos says he's a Bystander now. I guess that first Trip was enough for him. Well, maybe he'll come along next time.

Amos doesn't float around during free-fall like the rest of us, just stays in his seat. He's so *somber*. He explains things to us, but there isn't any zip in his voice. I wonder if we'll feel the same about riding in Safe Houses after a dozen trips. It's hard to imagine getting tired of this. But Amos is from the Masterpiece Season more than ten Realities ago, so I guess he's had enough. I'm afraid he's getting depressed. Cooper says he and Maggie have become separated. They've—what? Already? But I'm not finished. Okay, sure.

3

TOURISTS
Reality 253
Wilderness Season

Amos says we need to become Longtimers. We need to join the Society of Time. He makes out like it's a big deal. Not to us, of course, because, you know, we've already got lives. Still, for his sake, sure, we'll join his Society. But it's not that simple, he says. We've got to pass an exam, and before we do that we've got to Survive for seven Seasons, whatever a Season is. It sounds like it could take a whole year.

So—okay, we'll Survive. Why wouldn't we? How hard can it be?

In the meantime Amos wants to have regular family meetings to educate us. So we can pass the exam, I guess. But we don't have time for that. We have careers and lives to lead. I have classes to go to and textbooks to study and tests to take. I'm on my way to becoming an engineer.

Shawneetown U. is not the hometown fallback. It's a prestigious university, and it's not easy to get into. The engineering program is one of the best in the country. If I don't make it now, I'll never get another shot like this. This is the chance of a lifetime. I can't shuck this off for a bunch of Time Machine rides.

At our last meeting I did finally get some answers from Amos to the questions I've been asking about why we're Traveling in Safe Houses:

1) The people who cause the Time Changes are motivated only by selfishness, so their Changes benefit no one but themselves.

2) Change is not a good thing if there is too much of it. The Travelers make one change in the Past, hoping to change one thing in the Present, but there are unintended consequences. Change A causes change B, which causes change C and so on, and the result is thousands of changes: an

entire new Reality instead of just one simple Alteration.

Well, that doesn't answer all of my questions, but it does help. I still think Amos is keeping stuff from us—and now I know why. There's just too much to know. This Time Travel stuff is a lot more complicated than any of us suspected.

My life has been completely turned upside down. All of my assignments in my classes have changed. Times and places are different. I'm in a course I never enrolled in, and I'm in a frenzy trying to catch up. I don't have patience for Amos's nonsense anymore. His Time Travel World has completely screwed up my life.

It's unsettling living in this new Reality. All the little changes start to get to you. You never know when you're going to come across another one, and it gnaws at you. The environment seems like someone with dementia—angry and unpredictable and not quite sane.

I can tell Barlow's troubled too. He's always preoccupied, and his forehead is etched with fault lines. A few days ago I ran across him when I was between classes on campus at Shawneetown U. It was a sunny day with a fresh breeze. I guess he must have come there looking for me. He seems so lost, I can't tell what's going on with him.

"What are you doing here, Barlow?" I ask him when I find him on one of the benches in the Quad. He's sitting across from the library, which looks like a gothic cathedral. The other buildings on campus have imitated and updated the design so the campus is an exhibit in architectural evolution.

Barlow just shrugs at me. I don't recognize this guy. He's nothing like my brother. He's got this vacant look on his face like he's got Alzheimers.

I glance at the students hurrying past to make it to their next class. I have a class too, but I figure I can afford to be late once for my brother's sake. He's been having a tough time Adjusting to these Changes in Time, tougher than the rest of the family.

So I sit on the bench next to him and rest my backpack on the ground. "Shouldn't you be down at the precinct?" I ask him, "doing your detective work?"

He hesitates for a moment. "I decided to take a day off."

A day off? That ain't Barlow. He's had plenty of injuries over the years, but I don't remember him ever taking a day off. And he's not the type to duck out on work that needs to be done.

"What's the deal, Barlow?" I ask him. "Are you sick?"

He swallows and gets all pale. He looks like he did when his knee got whacked on the last play of the Championship Game and he found out he'd never play pro football.

"I've lost my job," he tells me. "I'm not a cop anymore."

Whoa! Not a cop? Barlow? He's gotta be a cop. That's who he is.

His face is all twisted like kneaded dough. "Losing my job's not the worst part. I can get another job." He looks at me all strange like he's seen a ghost or something.

"I've lost my karma," he tells me.

It sounds like nonsense, so I don't know how to respond at first.

"Your what?"

"My karma," he says, "the accumulation of all my acts and intentions, the determiner of my fate. It's gone." He swallows and shakes his head. "I could feel something wasn't right the first time we stepped out of Room 999, but I didn't know what it was. I couldn't sense my path like before. I couldn't feel the right thing to do. It got worse after the second Time Change. And now it's gone. Totally vanished." He turns to stare at me with that vacant look in his eyes. "My karma has disappeared. I don't have a Destiny anymore." He stares off into the distance. "And neither do you or anyone else in the family."

The throng of students around us thins out as class time approaches. When I hear the campanile bell toll, I know I'm late for class, but I decide this is more important. I can afford to blow off a class to help my brother when he needs me. These Changes have made him a castaway. He could use some company.

Karma! Of all the things to worry about, he has to settle on this? The trouble is, I think I know what he means. Things don't *feel* right anymore. Changes are lurking everywhere. You can't relax. You can't be yourself. The world is a stranger.

But why do *I* have to be the one to reassure Barlow? That should be Amos's job. He's the one who brought Time Travel into our lives.

Barlow looks up at me with his sick expression, and I remember all the times I've come to him with *my* problems, with *my* doubts, with *my* questions. He never sent me to Amos. He helped me. He gave me answers. He was a big brother to me, and he was always there when I needed him. Now it's up to me to pay back. I'm the one who needs to come up with some answers now.

"I don't feel any different, Barlow," I tell him. "I feel the same as before the Time Changes."

Barlow shakes his head. "That's because you're not as keyed in to your karma as I am. I depend upon it for guidance. It shows me the path to take. I follow it like an instinct, and it's never let me down. But now—now it's gone, Wiped Out by the Changes in Time."

He looks me in the face again, and I can see how serious he is. He knows about karma, because he studied Eastern religions back when he was a student at Shawneetown U.

I don't know what to tell him. I've never been a big believer in all that metaphysical junk like karma. Maybe there's something to it, maybe not. All I can tell is these Time Changes have spooked my brother's confidence.

"Your karma can't have vanished, Barlow," I tell him. "It builds up over an entire lifetime. These Time Changes date back only a few years."

Barlow thinks that over. His forehead creases, and he scratches at it with his thumbnail. "Maybe you're right. Maybe I've just gotten disconnected from it. Maybe it's still out there somewhere."

"You'll connect up to it eventually," I say, trying to sound confident. "You just need to give it some time."

He stares at me with that doubtful look of his. "But what am I going to do in the meantime? Ever since my karma's been gone, I haven't been able to make a decision. I've completely lost my bearings. I don't know what I'm doing." He looks around and reaches out for something that isn't there. "No one knows me down at the precinct anymore. I've lost all my friends. And that's not even the worst part."

He hangs his head and looks at the ground. "I just don't know what to do without my Destiny to guide me. I keep hoping maybe it'll come back. Maybe I can build up enough new karma in a few days to figure this out." He looks up at me. "What am I going to do, Dexter?"

He's asking me? He's the one who used to have the answers. Now he's acting like someone who's had a stroke and isn't all there anymore.

Barlow has a rugged handsomeness that makes it easy for women to fall for him and men to relate to him. I never realized before how central his confidence is to his rugged good looks. He still has the square jaw, the five o'clock shadow, and the well-arranged face, but without confidence the ruggedness is gone, and he just looks kinda pathetic.

I think of that Wanted poster of Catterus and the text "Hired to kill the Vanns?" Could that have something to do with Barlow's loss of karma?

"Come on, Barlow," I say, "let's go downtown and get us some lunch."

That usually cheers him up. Barlow's a man of action, and he's at his best when he's doing something. Sitting on a bench talking isn't his thing at all. So we take a bus downtown and eat Cuban sandwiches at some new place I've never heard of. There are plenty of those in this Reality, that's for sure. Barlow chews his sandwich like he isn't aware of what he's eating, may as well be old clothes. His mind is completely out in the Void.

"Just stop thinking about it, Barlow," I tell him. "Give it a rest. Maybe it will sort itself out."

But Barlow seems inconsolable. I've never seen him so lost. Maybe he just needs some time, I think, and he'll snap out of it. Maybe if I spend the day with him, he'll get through this and wake up normal tomorrow. That's what I'm hoping.

When the bullies came after me in grade school, Barlow taught me how to fight. He told me what to say, what to think, how to feel. How to stand up for myself. I can't pay back all he's done for me in just one day, but I can make a start. I can be there for *him*. I can help him deal with being bullied by change.

So I try to get Barlow's mind off his troubles. Maybe all he needs is to relax, take a day off, do nothing. It's worth a try. I have to keep trying, don't I? After all, people are depending on me.

After lunch Barlow and I walk down Washington Street, minding our business, and talk about how things have changed since we were downtown last. Nothing drastic—but a lot of small things, subtle differences you wouldn't usually notice, like a darker yellow on the traffic light poles. A grayer concrete in the sidewalk, a more intricate texture on the manhole covers. There's a new building going up by the Ingersol Bridge.

"The newsprint's darker on the Shawneetown Gazette," Barlow says, picking up one from a sidewalk vendor. "And it smells." He puts the front page up to his nose and squints. "Like chemicals." He drops it on the pile, and we walk on.

I try to be upbeat. I try to make Barlow feel better, but I don't want to be in this new Reality either. I want my old life back. I want my familiar world. If I wanted a change in reality, I'd take LSD. Because that's what it's like leaving your Safe House after a Change. It's like a Trip on LSD.

There are lots of things that haven't changed, but they still seem different. Because we know they have changed. They're made up of different atoms now. Same with people. They may look ordinary and have the same names, but they're different people, born a few days ago. They're made up of different atoms, and they're leading different lives. We're strangers here. Strangers in our own home town.

Dealing with all this change is like running a marathon. You get so weary—but you plod on. You have to. I guess that's why the Society requires us to Survive seven Seasons before we can be Members. We have to prove ourselves—prove we've got what it takes to live in a world of constant change, prove we're not quitters and their investment in us wasn't for nothing.

Can we do it? Can we put up with all this change and its consequences? Can we Adapt? Are we the sort of people the Society wants?

We head toward the river and turn right onto Main. The oldest architecture in town is along Main, closest to the Ohio River. The first line of buildings is like a selection of fine aged cheeses, weathered and a little brittle, their color faded. These buildings haven't changed in decades. In the center is the Bank of Shawneetown, designed to look like a Roman Temple with five doric columns, its exterior originally white as snow but now yellowed with age. Upriver from it is the Flatiron Building at eight stories the world's first skyscraper, terra cotta in color when built but now appearing rusted. In the next block downriver from it is the twelve story Riverside Hotel, the epitome of luxury and style a century and a half ago but now a strangely ornamental relic like some Greek ruin.

These old buildings are our grammy and granpappy. We have a real fondness for them. The Shawneetown Bank's our forefather. The Flatiron Building is our dear old gramps in the nursing home. This town is family to us. We've known it our whole lives.

Interspersed with the oldest buildings are a few newer, less imposing structures, designed to fit in and showcase their famous neighbors. These *are* different. Behind them rise the darkish Monadnock, the pastel Reliance, and the grayish McClernand, classic and familiar like Mom's family, the Coopers. Though not in decay, these tall buildings still look like museum pieces. It makes us feel better to be around these anachronisms. We're just like them now.

Beyond these are the white limestone skyscrapers of the 20's and 30's, our aunts and uncles, looking bright and new despite their age—like sculpted squares of cream cheese with dark indentations for windows: the Wrigley Building, the Congress Hotel, the massive Merchandise Mart, the gothic Gazette Tower, and the London Guarantee. All familiar. We feel right at home.

The buildings of the 50's and 60's rise taller still, our cousins to the northwest—the Inland Steel, the Equitable, the City Building, the Duckworth Hotel, and the Raveller, Frank Lloyd Wright's only skyscraper. Electric to the eye, the Raveller forces your gaze upward like some giant tree—inspecting and exploring the building's form. Nothing about it is static—even the grayish-green color seems elusive, shifting before your eyes, defying definition.

Now we're feeling odd again. Seeing these newer buildings is creating anxiety, even though they haven't changed. We can't tell the difference between things we never noticed before and things that have Changed.

The tallest—and most colorful—buildings are all in

Midtown, a family reunion of distant, scattered Vanns, all more than sixty stories high, none more than forty years old: the blue glass Posey Tower, the dark John Hancock, the greenish Roebuck Tower with the double antenna on top, the red State of Illinois Building, and the marble Standard Oil. These again seem familiar—but we're not sure. Some of them have moved. Switched locations. We blink and pull back and look again. The skyline doesn't look right. And we don't know if the problem is us or them.

A few residential towers follow as Midtown blends with Uptown, and the tallness of the buildings falls off quickly, ending with the rows of ritzy townhouses in the northwestern reaches of New Town. But Barlow and I can't see any of that from where we are. You can't even see the towers of Midtown from Main Street. And Barlow doesn't want to look anymore. We don't want to see any more change. We don't want to look for it. We want to ignore it and go on with our lives, but changes won't let you ignore them. They shout at you for attention.

It's the man-made things that seem to have changed the most. So we head toward Riverside Park at the western end of Main. That's the most relaxing place in town—perfect for our purposes, like a visit to grammy's.

As we try to cross Garfield, a car squeals around the corner, doin' fifty and almost runs us over. If we didn't have such quick reflexes, we'd be a couple spots on the pavement. Then when we reach the other side of the street, someone knocks a couple flower pots off her third floor balcony and they come crashing down right behind us.

"Sorry," a woman's voice comes from above. We look up but don't see anybody.

"What's with these Bystanders?" Barlow growls. "They just don't care." And I begin to wonder—are they somehow aware of their fate? Is that what's made them reckless? It's like someone's made them not care, someone out to get us. But that kind of thinking is crazy. It just goes to show how stressed out we are.

Reaching Grant Street, we cross and enter the Park. It doesn't look the same. The younger trees are in different spots. It seems like a whole new place. Of course, everything in the world actually is brand new, Spontaneously Created just a microsecond ago. Scientists used to believe all Creation was over at the big bang, but Quantum Time Theorists have concluded our universe constantly replicates itself along the Fourth Dimension, creating our illusion of motion and time passing. At first I found the doctrine of Spontaneous Creation a bit far-fetched, but then I reasoned if the universe can be Spontaneously Created once, then why not over and over again? Now a once-only Creation seems far-fetched to me.

"I could have sworn that old oak over there got taken out by lightning last year," I say to Barlow.

He shrugs. "Who knows? Maybe we're just noticing stuff because we're looking. Maybe these things haven't changed at all. How would we know? There's no way to check, and it's all small stuff, so even Amos couldn't tell us if the Time Change caused the difference. Maybe it's just you and me that are different."

It's like we've Traveled in Time to our Past, and we're rattled because it's not the way we remember it. But this isn't our Past—this is our Present.

Changes. They're everywhere. And I'm getting tired of them. They've become annoyances rather than novelties. Do all Newcomers feel this way after their first few Realities? Probably. All the little things start to eat at you after awhile, all the little Adjustments you have to make, not just with the new stuff but with familiar items that have Vanished. It's all small stuff—but there's so much of it, so much to get used to. It makes you weary.

Amos seems to think our whole environment is a danger to us—and I'm starting to see why.

"Are you excited about our next ride in the Safe House, Barlow?"

He looks off into the distance for a moment. "No," he says. "not anymore. How about you?"

I look into the treetops. "I never thought I'd say this so soon, but I'm not that excited about it either. I just wish the whole merry-go-round would stop. I'd like to get off."

"Amen," he says. "But what can we do?'

It's a mild day for mid-December, not warm but not cold either. We can smell the pretzel carts at the entrance to the park. We decide to sit on a bench over by the fountain (which is dry this time of year) and enjoy the brisk morning air for awhile. So we sit and absorb the nature around us and watch the people passing by, trying to pretend we're still in Reality 250.

We need to get away from the people too. They're not so different, really, but every time I look at them, I think *Bystanders*. It's like they're not real, just fill-ins for the genuine people.

Across from us, there's an old guy in a brown overcoat on a bench, feeding the pigeons with sunflower seed out of a paper bag. I don't pay much attention to him at first, but the longer we stay, the more different he seems to me. He doesn't sit right, not like a Shawneetowner. He's too poised. He wears his scarf oddly, like a fashion ornament rather than a neck warmer. His face is swarthy, and he has polished shoes in a moccasin style I've never seen. He smells of leather like he's just stepped out of the old West. His wrinkled face looks like it's made from a worn-out boot.

I shake my head and sigh. Maybe Barlow's right. Maybe things seem different because we're giving them a closer look.

We've changed, I think. Just as a result of dealing with change. We approach the world differently. The Time Changes haven't touched us, yet we're being molded by them.

As I think more about it, I realize subtle changes in all my brothers and sisters. Amos especially. He's never been so distant. At first I thought his aloofness was a Brotherhood custom, but now I'm convinced it's his own choice. He's changed, and I can't account for why.

And I don't like it.

As I'm mulling this over, a pale guy in a shiny silver suit walks up to the old guy on the bench and sits down next to him. The silver outfit looks like a spacesuit. This is no silver jump suit—it's the real deal. It seems more than a costume, more than a fashion—like he's from the future. I've never seen anything like it. I give Barlow a nudge. He has his arms crossed and his eyes closed and his feet stretched out in front of him. I think he must have been meditating.

He glances at me, and I nod at the stranger without looking in his direction, and Barlow takes a peek.

"So?" he whispers.

I gesture for him to be quiet, because the two guys on the bench start to talk without even noting each other's presence.

"I just heard from Catterus," the man in the silver suit declares. He's pale and beady-eyed with a short beak-like nose.

"Where is he?" the bird-feeder asks, gazing off into the distance. He doesn't look at his companion even once.

"Still out in the Void on the Shining Star."

"What's the news from Morlock?"

"Count Dracula's got some Surgery for the Cat. The Change has been moved up to Wednesday night. Spread the word. It's going to be a Deep One. This is the last you'll see of Wilderness."

The old guy tosses some more seed onto the ground. "Good riddance."

The pigeons move in and begin to peck at the seed, and without another word, the man in the silver suit stands and walks away. And after a few moments, the old man in the brown overcoat stands from the bench, leaving his bag of birdseed behind him, and walks off in the opposite direction.

Travelers. Right here in Riverside Park. They've mistaken Barlow and me for Bystanders. That's why they spoke in front of us like that. They figured we wouldn't understand what they were talking about any more than the pigeons did.

Barlow and I are stunned. We don't know what to do. I can't speak at first. I begin to feel dizzy like I'm in a Safe House in zero gravity.

"Did you hear that, Barlow? They're going to cause another Change in Time."

"I know—but what are we going to do about it?" He's asking me? Usually he's the one who's all sure of himself. He looks at me with a dazed expression like he's just gotten a concussion. "I can't arrest them. They haven't broken any laws."

I feel I've overheard someone else's bullies. This isn't my problem. This isn't my fight. But if these guys are going to Change Time, then it is my problem, and it is my fight.

"We've got to tell Amos," I say. "He'll know what to do."

Barlow hesitates, as if afraid to take action. I can't get used to him being so indecisive. It's weird.

I want desperately to stop those Travelers. But I know that won't be enough to prevent the next Time Change from happening. Only Amos will know how to do that.

As LSD trips go, this one's a bummer.

I hate to get involved in this. It doesn't seem like my problem. I'm just a college student. All I want is a normal life. I shouldn't have to deal with some Time Conspiracy. But I know Amos will want to know about it.

Barlow stares at me for a moment. "You really think

those two were—?" He swallows. "Travelers?"

"That's exactly what I think."

So I call Amos's number at the City Planner's Office. I get a secretary who tells me he's out for the day at a meeting. I ask for the number, but she doesn't have it.

"They're over at the old Flatiron Building," she tells me. "You can go there and look for him yourself, if you want, if it's a real emergency."

Frowning, I thank her and put away my phone.

"What's the matter?" Barlow asks me.

"She says he's in a meeting over at the Flatiron Building."

"The Flatiron Building!" Barlow twists his eyebrows. "That's been empty for years. I thought it was only a shell. I thought it had been condemned."

I shrug "Well, that's where she says he is." We both linger on the thought. It doesn't seem right. Usually I'd wait for Barlow to decide what to do next, but he's all bewilderment, so I tug on his arm to bring him out of it.

"Come on," I say to him, "let's go."

The pigeons continue to peck at the birdseed, oblivious to us. They're just Bystanders, and the revelation has meant nothing to them. I stand, and Barlow gets up, too, on unstable legs. These changes, they make you feel so uncertain. Your legs begin to feel like rubber. You clear your ears and rub your eyes to make sure you're hearing and seeing right. You begin to doubt your own senses. You begin to doubt your own existence.

But there's no doubt about what we just heard. And if Barlow's right about the family's losing its destiny, then anything could happen to us. Because a loss of karma is like a loss of gravity. You drift unanchored in unpredictable directions, always on the rebound, with nothing to chart your course. Now I'm feeling I'm on the deck of the Titanic, sinking into the water, everything tilted around me.

But I have to go on. People are counting on me.

I can't tell you how much I don't want to do this, don't want any part of it. I don't want to be in Amos's Time Travel World. I just want Reality 250 back. But it isn't coming back, is it? I mean, the Changes—they just lead in one direction, right? Forward. Never backward.

I'm marooned. In a hostile environment. And I'm never getting back home.

When we've walked a couple dozen yards from the fountain, the stranger's bag of bird seed blows up. Barlow and I flinch and duck—too late to have done any good. We're almost blown over by the blast, and we watch pieces of a park bench come raining down from the sky. If we'd dawdled just thirty seconds longer, that would have been us.

"Jeez!" Barlow cries. "What the truck! How many times do I have to nearly die today?"

I think of that guy in the headband, the one they call The Terror of the Void. What's he got against me and Barlow? What do any of these people have against us?

Leaving the park, we turn down Grant Street past Market to Main and head northeast toward Madison. We find the old Flatiron Building at the corner of Main and Madison. The Brownstone Skyscraper, they used to call it in the old days. It's only eight stories tall, but I guess that used to be considered high, back when the Flatiron was built.

The Flatiron Building is triangular with its rounded front pointing at the corner. It seems to recede on either side. It's the color of clay flower pots with big rounded corniced windows, tinted so we can't see inside.

Outside, the building looks just as decrepit as usual, but now there's a steady traffic of people coming out and going in the front door— including the guy in the silver suit.

Barlow and I glance at each other. What the heck is going on? I'm not sure I want to know, but we have to go in and find out. So we go in through the doors and enter a large high-ceilinged hall that branches off into two corridors that lead to the left and right. Odd-looking people are streaming in and out of the lobby as if it's some kind of terminal.

The interior of the building seems brand new. It's all shiny metal and glass, like we've entered some other building. An arrow to the left is marked "Ferry," "CTA" and "Receiving." To the right the arrow is labeled "4DTN," "Government" and "Workshops." A big man in a gold-braided gray uniform holds up a hand to stop us when Barlow and I enter. I notice the guy in the silver suit head in the "Ferry" direction.

These people in there. They're weird as hell. They're not from Reality 253, but they're not from any of the other Realities we've seen either.

"What can I do for you two gentlemen?" the guard asks as he comes up to us. He has a body that bulges like a barrel, a round chest, short fingers, and a pink face. His nametag reads "J.B."

I expect Barlow to answer, but he doesn't say anything, so I guess I'm going to have to do the talking. "We're looking for our brother Amos Vann," I say. "We have an urgent message for him."

The big man stares at us for a few moments, sizing us up. He glances over his shoulder at another guard seated at a desk behind him. "Do we have an Amos Vann in the building?"

The younger man checks his monitor. "He's in the city meeting, third floor."

The big man turns to look at us again but doesn't budge. "I'll need to see some identification," he declares. Barlow shows him a police badge, but the guard doesn't seem impressed. "Can't you do any better than that?"

So I take out the temporary Society of Time Membership card Amos has given me, and the big man smiles. "Now you're talkin'." He gestures us toward an elevator down the hall to the right. "The elevator's over there. But nobody's allowed on the third floor without a special pass. You can't go up there. You gotta get a pass." He turns his back to us to speak to the newest arrival to the building.

Nobody in the lobby demands to see our pass, so we turn to the right and head for the elevator. I can't feel I'm in danger. Everything's too strange for that. It's either all danger or none.

I'm hoping I can go left and see that "Ferry." How can they have a ferry this far from the river? It doesn't make sense. Maybe I can check on that later, I think, on my way out.

So we take the elevator to the third floor. There are only three floor buttons in the car, despite the Flatiron being eight stories tall. And there is no button for the basement. This place is weird. I feel I'm being sucked farther into Amos's Time Travel World, farther than I want to go. And I feel like a little kid, having to go to my big brother for help. But I guess that's what the Time Changes do to you. They turn you into a child, a happy child at first, and then a miserable one.

At the third floor we run into a couple more security guards in a small, tan lobby, smart aleck types in black suits and ties, one tall with dark hair and yellowish skin and the other short and stocky with short blond hair and a cowlick. We've nicknamed them Bert and Ernie. Ernie's seated at a desk. Bert stands next to it. Behind them is a big metal door, also painted tan, with an iron plate over the jamb as if to prevent lock picking. If we want onto the third floor, we'll have to go through these guys.

They just stare at us and don't say anything when we step out of the elevator. I guess they're waiting for us to speak first.

"We need to see Amos Vann right away," I tell them.

They glance at each other and won't look at us anymore. Bert, the tall man with the sallow face, pulls a headset mike forward from behind his ear. "Hey, did you guys send a couple Bystanders up here?" He seems hacked off. And his accent is nothing I've ever heard before.

"We're not Bystanders," I tell him. "We're Newcomers."

The guards glance at each other in surprise.

"It talks," the short one with the bad haircut—Ernie—exclaims in a totally different accent.

They laugh, and tucking his mike behind his ear, Bert looks us over and turns to his companion. "How much trouble do you imagine we'd get into for interrupting the meeting at the say-so of a couple Tourists?"

Ernie thinks for a second. "They'd have us down in the lobby directing traffic by lunchtime."

"But this is an emergency," I tell them. "We have vital information."

The two guards smirk at me, discounting the possibility of a "Tourist" having anything vital to say.

"Amos Vann is our brother," I tell them.

"Oh, he's your brother," Bert says. "Well, that's different."

I wait for him to open the door, but he and the short man just stand there and smirk at us.

"What's wrong with you?" I ask them. "Why can't you show us a little respect?"

Ernie, the short one, jerks his thumb at me and looks at Bert, the tall one. "The Tourist says he wants respect." Like it's a big joke or something.

Barlow frowns at me and takes a step to the side. I know what he's thinking. He figures we can take these two guys. It'd be easy, but I don't want to do it that way, because I know Amos will get mad at us, so I step over and grab Barlow's sleeve to let him know not to try anything. I don't want to see blood or feel blood or taste blood. I want to do things the clean and easy way—no showing off.

"Yeah, we're Newcomers," I say, "what's wrong with that? You two were Newcomers once."

Bert stares at me, not so amused. As if he doesn't care to be reminded of his checkered past. He sniffs and holds his nose in the air. "Do you know the average lifespan of a Newcomer?" he asks.

I don't know what to say.

"Three Seasons," he says. "I'll probably never see you again. You'll be lucky if anyone's left who even remembers you. And you want my respect? I'll give it to you when you've proven you can Survive." He crosses his arms.

I blink at him, feeling a little shocked. I hadn't realized how precarious our situation is.

"Look at these Tourists," Ernie exclaims. "They don't even know. Their Sponsor hasn't told them."

Bert rubs a finger against his nose. "He's probably waiting until they get serious to tell them. So he won't have to repeat himself. You know Tourists don't listen."

Barlow and I glance at each other to see if either of us knows what they're talking about.

The short man scoffs. "I'll bet they don't even know what a Season is."

We've heard Amos use the word, of course, but we've never asked for a definition. The short man reads the uncertainty on our faces and laughs.

"I'll bet they don't know what The Common is. Or the Time Bank. Or the *Parattak*. They probably don't even know who Dr. Morlock is."

They enjoy a huge laugh at our expense. They're Uptimers, so they have to show off. They're giving us the business. They're laying it on. Making out like we're the freshmen and they're the seniors. Hazing us. They've arrived. We just got off the boat.

Letting out a sound of disgust, Bert turns away from us and covers his nose with a handkerchief. "I can't stand the stink out here anymore," he says. "Let me through. I think I'm going to be sick." The short man gives him a curious look, then presses a combination on a pad under the desk to buzz him through the locked door, which is as thick as a vault.

I wonder if people from Wilderness really do have a unique smell all their own. It's possible, I guess. A different mixture of soaps, perfumes, street smells. Maybe even a different body odor—because a variation of diet can change the scent of your sweat. The difference would be subtle, but if the tall man comes from a time when people pay especial close attention to different shades of odor, he may have developed a very discriminating sense of smell. And if he isn't used to our scent, then we probably do stink to his nose.

The small man regards us with an unfriendly expression. He has no problem with our smell. He just doesn't like us spoiling his fun. I get the impression he doesn't like Wilderness either. Like the bird guy on the park bench. But how could someone dislike Wilderness?

It's two against one now. "We're getting in," I tell Ernie. "One way or another." But he only smirks and won't budge.

The stalemate is broken when the door behind him suddenly opens, and Amos steps into the lobby. I don't recognize him at first, because he doesn't look or act like his old self. He wears an oddly tailored suit coat and oversized cufflinks and golfing loafers. And his dark hair's cut close to the skull like a Roman citizen. He's not as soft spoken as he used to be, and his voice is a little hoarse. He's not the same Amos we've always known. I tend to forget he's not from Wilderness.

He squints at us as if he's hallucinating, even more surprised than the guards had been. "What in the Cone is this?" He glances at the guard, but the short man just raises his eyebrows and tilts his head.

Amos stares at us again and hesitates, as if having trouble recognizing us. "Dexter, Barlow?"

"We're not Bystanders, Amos," I tell him. "It's us, your brothers."

He puts his hands in his pockets. "You're still alive,"

he says. "I'm glad to see it."

Not that again! "You saw us just ten days ago," I tell him.

"Was that *this* Reality? I guess it was." He walks up to us, one hand still in his pocket. "What are you doing here?"

"We came to see you," I tell him.

His face turns at an angle. "How did you know I was here?"

"Your secretary told us."

He takes his hand out of his pocket. "But why—?"

"There's going to be a Time Change Wednesday night," Barlow says.

I nod. "We overheard a couple shady characters talking about it in the park. They've moved up their timetable."

Amos falls silent and considers the news for a moment like he's the principal trying to be fair and reasonable. He asks us to tell him exactly what the Travelers said, word for word, so I do. Then he gets a preoccupied look on his face, and he crosses his arms and brings one hand up to finger his chin. "You know, that makes sense."

Amos can tell Barlow's not quite right. I can see it in his eyes. But he doesn't say anything. He's figured out the Changes in Time are what's behind Barlow's hollowness. Taking a day off to walk around town hasn't done Barlow any good at all. And I think we've all come to the same conclusion. The next Change in Time is going to have to solve Barlow's problems by giving him his job back. That's the cause of all this. If Barlow could be a cop again, he could regain his karma and return to normal.

Normal. The word barely has any meaning.

Amos looks at us and shakes his head. "I can't get over your coming here like this. You're Adjusting faster than I expected." He smiles. "Your information should be valuable. It could mean a lot for me."

Relaxing a little, he reaches out and shakes our hands in gratitude. "Call the rest of the family and tell them to gather at the Brotherhood Lodge Wednesday afternoon. We'll have our Christmas Eve goose in Room 999. Tell everyone to bring their keepsakes, because there's going to be a Change in Time." He squeezes my shoulder and turns toward the door to return to his meeting.

"Amos," I say, "What's a Season? And who's Dr. Morlock?"

He freezes and turns to stare at me. "Where did you hear that name?"

"The Travelers mentioned it. Who is he?"

Amos adjusts his glasses. "Never mind. Just forget you

4
NEWCOMERS
Reality 254
Moonglow Season

Well, I never finished my first four journal entries, but here I am again. I just don't have time to keep up with this journal. I told Amos, but he says it doesn't have to be complete. Just do the best I can. I'm not sure who I'm doing this for, but Amos insists. Maybe he doesn't know either.

I finally got an answer from him to my question about the term *Season*. Changes in the Past cause a change in Reality. Changes Deep in the Past cause a change of *Season*. A *Season* is a culture in Time. The current Season is in the Present—the past Seasons are in the Neverbeen. There's no physical record of them in the Past. They never were. They have no Existence. Their only Trace is in the memories and records of the Longtimers.

A Light Season has a culture like past Seasons. A Dark Season has a unique culture different from other Seasons. The Dark Seasons are the ones hardest to Adjust to. So we're all wondering if Moonglow's going to be Light or Dark—and the consensus is it's something in between.

In Room 999 of the Brotherhood Lodge, we watch the Reports about the new Reality on the 4th Dimensional Television Network, weathering the Time Change in the Lodge's living room, which has begun to seem like home. Everybody's here, even Cooper and Amos, and it feels like being at Mom and Dad's for the holidays, even though Brother Samuels and a couple of the Monks are here too. Except, of course, Mom and Dad reside in the cemetery now and have for the past two years.

We were finishing a Christmas Eve dinner in the Lodge's dining hall when the Change arrived, so we've brought our pecan pie and eggnog with us into the Safe

House, and we have to eat quickly so it doesn't all float away. We have on our seatbelts so we don't float away too.

The Fourth Dimensional Television Network presents a view of the Time Change from out in the Fourth Dimension. The camera's located far enough in the Void that you can see the entire planet in Protospace, surrounded by pure blackness. It's all blue and white and brown, its features fuzzy and indistinct. The clouds of sparkles around it are reflections from the Safe Houses. They're so tiny they seem like a mist at this distance.

The Time Change begins in Sector One around Shawneetown. A dark cloud wells up like smoke from a single point and spreads over the landscape in the direction of the earth's rotation, fanning out across the circumference of the globe. The Timestorm flows over the horizon, leaving the landscape pristine behind it, and traverses the planet until it surrounds and converges on its Originating Point, where the dark clouds shrink and seem to drain down a hole until they are no more. Kind of like dunking an apple in caramel and then reversing the footage.

Then the picture on the Timecast cuts from a view of the earth to one of the Forecasters sitting behind a desk in the Fourth Dimensional Television Network studio. Myra Case, a green-eyed brunette in her thirties, is zipping up a silver Longtimer suit and sticking an earplug in one ear. We can hear the pop and buzz of feedback in the sound system like screamo music. People are rushing around in the background—this Change has taken everyone by surprise. Even the Forecasters have had to interrupt their holiday celebrations to rush to the studio.

Someone hands Myra Case a sheet of paper from off-camera, and she begins to read from it. "Our latest Reports indicate that the next Reality is the beginning of a new Season, as defined by the guidelines of the Council of Nevertime."

The Nevertime Season was the first to be named and numbered in advance and started with Reality 1. It's when the Longtimers started to get organized. Before then is Pre-History, when you had your basic Pre-Dawn Time Traveler.

"This new Season," she announces, "is called Moonglow, and it is a Light Season. Our correspondent Red Phillips has a Report on the new Season and the latest list of Anachronisms. We take you to Three Dimensions in downtown Shawneetown."

I don't want a new Season. I want the old one back. I want to go home. I'm more homesick than E.T.

The camera cuts to the Shawneetown skyline, the windows of the skyscrapers all lit up in the dusk, then zooms in on a red-headed reporter standing on a street corner with the Shawneetown Bank Building visible behind him, its stone steps leading up to a portico with five fat pillars fronting a white limestone skyscraper as tall as the Wrigley Building. There's glistening snow on the ground, and the street lights make the sidewalk bright as day against the evening sky. Red Phillips is wearing an overcoat and a conservative suit and vest with a tie and a hat. He looks like a businessman. I notice a lot of the passersby are also dressed up.

"The Wilderness Season is over, folks," he declares. His accent is sharper than ours, more nasal, and I realize this must be the Bystanders' new dialect. "We're now officially in Moonglow."

We're stunned and don't know how to react. We just lean back in our couch and stuffed chairs like we're accelerating. We've just lost our home. Wilderness is in the Neverbeen.

"The inhabitants are very businesslike, very demanding," Red Phillips declares. "You have to dress your best. Like you're going on a job interview. Nothing casual. A suit and tie. And a hat. But not a Santa hat. Nothing flip. They don't have any sense of humor here in Moonglow. This ain't Wilderness, folks. You're expected to conform. So watch your grammar and mind your manners. People will be watching. And judging you. And they expect a lot."

We're full of glum pudding and sit in silence like fans who've just watched their team lose the Superbowl. Wilderness gone. How are we going to cope?

"A lot has changed," the Reporter declares, "and you need to be careful with these new folks. I have a list of items that are now Anachronisms and don't Exist." He begins to name the various Vanished Artifacts, and the length of the list makes me wonder if this ain't a Dark Season, after all. I guess the biggest Anachronisms are casual wear and recreational items like short skirts, bikinis, floppy hats, jet skis, dune buggies. But we can get along without even noticing their absence, especially in December. It's the little things like pop-top cans and beer cozies that we'll miss. The absence of the familiar items is what can mess you up in a new Reality.

There's also a list of new technology, and I notice something called contact lenses is on the list and also pills for birth control. It's very confusing. Then Myra Case calls on analyst Eileen Von Otter for commentary.

Eileen appears in a cashmere overcoat with a fur hat and scarf. I can't tell if her clothes are Local or not. She's pretty and Jewish, but she's so bundled up I can't observe anything else about her. "Myra, all the Timers are talking about this being designated a Light Season. The Change was a thirty Range, and there's never been a Change that Deep that hasn't resulted in a Dark Season. I hear the Moonglowers are a hard bunch to get along with, they're so picky and such sticklers, just the opposite of the people of Wilderness. I know most of us have met someone like that before, but evidently they're all that way. A lot of people consider this a Dark Season."

Well, none of us like hearing that news, and we're looking at Amos, who's scowling. He presses on the crosspiece of his glasses and glances at us with his told-you-so expression. He's been warning us about a Change of Season for weeks—and now it's here, like everything he has been haranguing us about has come to pass. He's got on another crazy-looking suit, gray with a pattern of thunderbolts on it.

When our Safe House returns to the Lodge after the Change and the door opens, Amos is the first one out, and he takes off like he can't wait to get away from us. The rest of us slowly file out of the Safe House and look around. The dining table is clean and bare. Our dishes are gone—and so are the Christmas decorations we put up. All the smells of gingerbread and cinnamon have vanished too. Everything's in order like the maid just left or no one's living here. Christmas is *over*.

It's spooky to see everything so different. None of us know what to make of this. We just stand there on one leg and then the other.

A New Season. We're not going to know what it's like until we go outside and experience it ourselves. So we look at each other, then get our coats and head for the door to the Lodge like we're going sledding. We discover downtown Shawneetown on a snowy winter evening. It doesn't seem different. But that's because we haven't had to deal with the Bystanders yet.

Well, once we really get out and about in the new Season, over the next couple days, we find it's even worse for us than we'd imagined. We've all run into major problems, so we're on the phone to Amos, demanding a meeting. I know the new Reality's not his fault, but it's hard not to blame him. He's the one who got us into this.

Amos doesn't want to meet at the Lodge this time. He wants to meet in the Catacombs. Barlow and I have to take a bus from his apartment in New Town. Barlow's gotten a haircut and a shave, and he's bought a brand new suit with creases sharp as the edge of an axe. He's got on matching tie and handkerchief and even a carnation in his lapel. His hair's all slicked back.

Babe magnet.

I've bought a new suit, too, and I look like a crisp new hundred dollar bill. I've never looked so sharp in my life. So good even *I* could get a date.

We're both showing off.

But of course, we don't run into any women that count. Only Bystanders.

We're dressed to the nines in our new suits and ties when we get to the bus stop. We think we're gonna fit right in with the Moonglowers.

Like we could ever fit in with *them!*

There's no trouble when we get on the bus in New Town. Since the bus is so crowded, I figure no one will notice us. But once we're seated, it's inspection time. And when the Moonglowers get a good look at us, they turn into the Menswear Daily doing its Top Ten Fashion Faux Pas's.

Two snooty ones in expensive suits sit across from us—gray-haired guys who probably work in a clothes store. The one closest to me has thinning hair and a moustache. The other has wire-rimed glasses.

"Straighten that tie," the one closest to us says to Barlow. "And comb your hair. You look like a bum."

Barlow, who's huge, isn't used to getting criticism, and he frowns and looks at me. So I nod to get him to humor them. So Barlow straightens his tie and runs a comb through his hair. That gives the guy time to inspect me.

"Why are you wearing cowboy boots with a suit?" he demands. "Are you from Texas?"

Jeez—what's wrong with these people? They ought to be giving us the blue ribbon like we're the prize steer at the fair.

I just want to smack him. But I can't—because he has a whole busload of back-ups.

"Yeah," I snarl. "I'm from Texas."

Wrong answer. "Don't be snippy to me," the guy snaps at me. "That's not a western cut suit. Those boots don't go with it."

His companion leans forward so he can see me. He sneers at my boots, then Barlow's black dress shoes.

"When's the last time you got those shoes shined?" he asks Barlow.

Barlow looks down and blinks. His shoes look okay to us.

"I dunno," he says.

Wrong answer. We don't pass inspection. They're going to report us. Is it a crime in Moonglow to be under-shined? They act like it is. They're beside themselves in their outrage at our violation. The guy in the aisle seat ahead of us turns around and glares at us. The woman on the aisle behind us makes a comment.

Sheesh!

We look great. We really do, and we're starting to feel insulted, and it's getting our backs up. I can tell Barlow would like to bust some heads, but that's not the custom here in Moonglow. So I apologize and promise we'll improve our footwear just as soon as we can. I have to elbow Barlow to get him to apologize, too.

But apologies don't satisfy our critics. "Slob," the one across from Barlow declares.

Slob! I can't believe my ears. And Barlow—he's so frustrated and furious, there's tears in his eyes. Tears. So that's what this Bystander Reality has come to? Reducing my excellent brother to a *crybaby*? My brother the coolest guy you've ever met?

I'm restraining Barlow's arm now because I know he wants to smack somebody. I just want to yell, "Don't you know who this is? This is the star of the national championship team. This is a decorated police lieutenant." But I can't say that—because Time has

Changed. The championship never happened, and Barlow's not a cop anymore either.

You don't get credit for what's in the Neverbeen.

"Don't pay attention to them," I say to Barlow. "They're *Bystanders.*" I stand up. "Come on, let's get out of here." So we get off the bus and hike the rest of the way through the slushy streets to get away from all the hostility. But out on the sidewalk, it's the same story.

"Are you from Texas?" a passerby asks me.

"Why aren't your shoes shined?" another one demands of my brother.

Barlow tells them to buzz off, and a crowd forms around us and blocks our way.

"What did you say?" they demand.

So I apologize, and I elbow Barlow to get him to apologize too. I'm thinking we could probably take this bunch, but I'm afraid that would cause even more to join in. And we'd end up getting arrested for disturbing the peace.

It's not the fashion faux pas that gets you in Moonglow. It's the trouble that comes with it. Moonglow's a minefield.

The Moonglow Season's a fascist society. The threat of violence underlies the surface of all their petty requirements in behavior and dress. They'd love it if we gave them an excuse to take their frustrations out on us—because they're full of frustrations. They're eager to jump us and have two of them hold us down while a third one kicks us. They're bustin' at the seams to let loose and break some bones.

All the changes we had to put up with in Wilderness were annoyance enough, but Moonglow has taken things to a whole new level. The changes have become overtly hostile. The Timestorm hasn't really ended—we're still in its Aftermath. These aggravating Locals are just another violent force of the Storm.

Amanda and Cartmell meet us at an alleyway off Garfield Street. There's a metal door at the end of the alley that leads us to utility steps down into what used to be the underground labyrinth in Reality 250. But it's all deserted and dark now, except for a few utility lights. So we have to use our phones as flashlights. When we come to another metal stairway, we join Belinda, and Zeke and descend the steps that lead to the second sublevel beneath Shawneetown, where the subway used to be. We have on our suits or dresses and walk in a professional, businesslike manner.

In this Season the underground hasn't been renovated, and we can see the original stone masonry of the cavernous tunnels from a couple centuries ago when they were built under the direction of city planner Raveller. The first sublevel of the Catacombs used to consist of pedestrian tunnels and underground shopping malls. You could walk underground all the way from one end of Shawneetown to the other, if you had enough time and stamina. But no one's using the tunnel anymore, and it's empty and dark.

We're all staring around in wonder—like we really have gone back in Time to city planner Raveller's day.

The subway used to be on the second sublevel, and the canals and sewers and pumping stations on the lower levels. Nobody goes down this far these days. I guess that's why a lot of Safe Houses have been located here. Amos says some of the Longtimers have taken up residence in the lower sublevels. And a lot of government workers too. Deep underground, the Catacombs connect with a cavern. There's an underground lake, and a lot of rich Longtimers live around the lake in cabins that are Safe Houses. Amos says that some of these underground dwellers never come up to the surface.

Even on the subway platform we can hear the sound of water flowing, making it seem as if we're on the banks of a subterranean river. Amos told us to take the metal utility steps to the third sublevel that overlooks the drainage canal.

"Why did Amos have to meet us down here?" Amanda complains. "I don't like it. It's too dark."

"Everything's too dark for you," Belinda tells her. Amanda's in a fancy white dress like she's going to a party, but Belinda's all in black in a pantsuit. It's the non-conformists who wear the pantsuits in Moonglow.

The Catacombs become darker as we descend, and it takes awhile for our eyes to adjust. It's spooky down there. Above us we can barely make out the fading arabesques painted over a century ago on the arched brick ceiling. The whole thing seems bizarre to me. But even more bizarre is the feeling I'm getting that we're slowly becoming inhabitants of this underworld, as if our lives on the surface are finished. The Catacombs become darker as we descend, and it takes time to adjust. In the dimness we can see someone on a narrow walkway that overlooks a broad drainage canal.

It smells dank on these lower levels, like mud and metal and wet concrete, with just a hint of sewer. And it's getting warmer as we descend. None of us like it down here. Because of the lack of light, we can't see the far side of the canal or the end of the walkway. We just follow the gleam of light reflecting off the granite, and that leads us to Amos, a shadowy figure in the distance ahead. His features take on form as we approach. I feel like we've come to meet the Phantom of the Opera instead of our brother.

Amos is tall and massive and darkly tanned. He wears his hair cut close to the skull and the same black-rimmed glasses he had in Reality 250. Today he's got on this dark blue suit with narrow lapels and luminescent white piping. Cooper says suits like this were the fashion in Reality 238 in the Peacock Season, but how does he know? When we get close, we can see Amos's face in shadows.

"You're all still alive," he says, joining his hands. "I'm glad to see it."

"Will you stop saying that!" I growl at him.

He takes my hand and shakes it, then Zeke's. He gives Belinda and Cartmell a hug and looks out at the tunnel. We eye each other. Why such an odd meeting place?

"I've always revered Timothy Raveller for his amazing achievements." Amos leans on the railing at the edge of the walkway. "He was the greatest city planner who ever lived. He was the reason I became a city planner myself. I used to come here often." He gestures at the huge drainage tunnel. "To marvel at what can be accomplished with enough foresight."

He comes down here often? Yeah, I'd come down here often too—if I was a murderer hiding from the police.

Amos's voice sounds like it's coming from the water below, carried up by an echo rebounding across the cavernous chamber. He seems unusually talkative, which is strange since it was us, not him, who demanded this meeting. He seems to be delaying our business, and I can't understand why. It isn't like him to put us off.

"I quit my city planner's job today," Amos announces.

Quit? I'm so startled, I don't know what to say. Amos loved being a city planner. He's never had any ambition except to be another T. T. Raveller. Why would he quit his job?

"I work for the Intertime Government now," he tells us, still gazing out at the dark water rushing below us.

I didn't even know there was an Intertime Government, and suddenly I feel dizzy. Amos seems like a stranger. I've never been down on the third sublevel, and this is only the fifth Reality I've been in. It's just too bizarre.

Amos looks from one end of the darkness to the other, as if he's already forgotten his startling announcement, as if it's just leading up to something bigger. "If not for this elaborate drainage system, Shawneetown never would have become the major city it is today. It would have been flooded over and over. People would have moved away. I know the textbooks emphasize the city's natural geographical advantages: its central location on the Ohio River, its link to the Wabash Canal, its position as the gateway to the West. But the fact is that without the prodigious efforts of T. T. Raveller, the city never would have prospered to become the fourth largest in the nation."

"Fourth?" I say. "I thought it was—"

"The Time Change has made Shawneetown larger than ever. We're in the Moonglow Season. Reality has been Altered."

That's for sure. *Ruined* would be a better word.

I can tell Barlow's getting impatient with this small talk. He wants to get to the point. It's weird to see him so anxious, though I suppose he has reason to be. He's got this expression he never used to have before Time Changes. He's sallow-faced and hollow eyed like he's been up all night. Not his usual strong and confident self.

"Amos," he says, "I lost my job during the Time Change." He swallows and can't find his voice for a moment. "They don't know me down at the precinct. I'm not a cop anymore." He doesn't mention his loss of karma. He doesn't have to. It's all over his face and in every sagging muscle in his body.

Amos nods like always, and we're expecting him to give Barlow some words of encouragement and tell him everything's going to be all right. After all, Amos is our Sponsor. He understands how things work, he's got connections. He can pull a few strings, get Barlow back on the force and on the road to recovery. Set things right. But instead, he says to Barlow, "You'll never get your job back. Your days as a cop are over."

Well, that really throws Barlow. A real kick in the teeth. His whole scalp moves back, flattening the lines on his forehead, and his lips part and move slightly, as if they're trying to grasp at words but can't find any.

Amos has thrown all of us. We're looking at Barlow and him in wonder like they've been turned into a couple of goats. This isn't reasonable. This isn't the way our meeting was supposed to go.

Amanda raises her eyebrows in sympathy and squeezes Barlow's arm, but when she turns toward Amos, her face hardens. "Amos, I'm not in line for that vice presidency at the bank anymore. My bosses have completely forgotten about it, as if it never existed. All the hard work I've been doing these last few years has come to nothing." The Moonglowers have undermined her, undermined us all.

Amos turns to regard her. "Pretty soon," he says, "you won't have a job at the bank. Then after a few months the bank won't Exist anymore."

Amanda's serious look collapses, and her face gets pushed back as if struck by a shockwave from some distant blast. Her lips grow taut, and her eyes get small. She's outraged. We all are. "That's it? That's all you've got to say to me?"

"Just one more thing. Get used to it."

"Get used to it!" Amanda looks mad enough to hit him. "Is that supposed to make me feel better?"

Amos looks up, as if sighting something above us. "No," he says in a sad voice. "I doubt if anything I say today is going to make anyone feel better." He turns and looks out at the cavernous tunnel, and in our silence we can hear the flowing water below us.

I can't understand what's going on with Amos. He used to be so optimistic, a firm believer in logical positivism. He always used to cheer us up. It's not like him to undercut us like this. I'm afraid now to bring up my own problems, but what else am I going to do? There's no one else I can take them to.

I look at the shocked faces of my brothers and sisters. They're speechless, so I guess it's my turn. I take a step toward my oldest brother.

"Amos, I've got a problem." He doesn't turn or say anything, so I'm not sure what to do except go on talking. "My class schedule has changed again, and I've got a class I never enrolled in. The syllabus has changed in my other classes, too, and I'm behind. I can't pass these classes, Amos. I'm afraid I'm going to flunk out. I'm afraid they'll put me on probation."

Barlow and Amanda can get another career. They're extraordinary. They can make things happen. I can't do that. I'm Mr. Ordinary. This college degree is the only leg up I've got. I don't have any special talents. I've gotten where I am by hard work and long nights, by going to class and hittin' the books and applying myself. I'm not on scholarship. I have to pay my way. I can't start over in something else. I want to be an engineer.

Amos turns to face me slowly, almost reluctantly. He adjusts his black-rimmed glasses and chews on his thoughts.

"It's not my fault," I say.

"It never is," he tells me. I can't interpret the expression on his face. He doesn't seem evasive, but he's in no hurry either.

"You're just going to have to quit school," he declares. "Your college days are over." He turns to look at the tunnel again, and I can hear Amanda and Barlow murmuring in protest.

I can't believe it. I can't believe Amos said that. Here we've come to him for help, and he blows us away one by one.

"But this is my junior year."

Amos turns to face me, maybe he's mad this time, maybe he's upset by all of this. "It's over," he says. He looks around at my brothers and sisters. "Do you hear me? Your old lives are finished. Barlow, you'll never be a cop, Amanda, you'll never be a banker, and Dexter, you'll never be an engineer. Not as long as there are Time Changes." He takes a breath and looks at us like he's not finished. We stand there frozen on that ledge above the rushing water.

"Belinda, you'll never be an artist, Zeke you'll never be a scientist. Cartmell, you'll never graduate high school."

"But I haven't even started," she says.

Amos adjusts his glasses and licks his lips. "None of us have gotten started. But it's over. Wake up. We live in a world without continuity. Pretty soon none of you will have any job history, educational records, or references. You're going to have to start over from scratch, learn some way to Survive that doesn't depend on your background. I wish I could give you better news, but as of now your old lives are finished."

We're doubly stunned, first by the bad news and second by the messenger bringing it to us. He hasn't tried to cushion the impact at all. If anything, he's exaggerated our predicament. When did he become so blunt?

Amos is like the parent we never had. He watches out for us, scolds us, teaches us. He's our leader. I guess you could say there are different parenting styles. My parents' approach was benign neglect. Neglect because they ignored us and benign because it worked—we excelled. But one of the reasons it worked was because Amos and Amanda stepped up and covered for them (which was probably their plan all along).

In loco parentis.

Amos has always felt he has to take charge and be a parent. Because he's loco. Amanda's loco too. You can credit Ingersol with us all being atheists, but really how could we believe in god with parents like ours? We've become the gods. And sometimes it can get kind of angry and jealous up here on Mount Olympus.

Amanda tries to laugh, but she looks too grim to pull it off. "I'm not quitting my job at the bank, Amos. You can get that idea out of your head right now."

"You'll have to," Amos tells her. "You don't have a choice."

We stand there, stunned as Amos's words sink in. I feel as if the entire world has disappeared around us, and all that's left is this dark cavern. The Longtimers have a word for how we're feeling: Dischronofiliated.

"I'm not quitting my job," Amanda declares, almost laughing at the absurdity of the idea. "I've spent my entire life building up that career."

Barlow takes a deep breath and runs a hand over his scalp. "What else am I going to do but be a cop, Amos? I can't play ball anymore. Look, I'm willing to start over. I'll go back to the Academy if I have to."

Amos shakes his head slowly and leans on the railing and says nothing. There's a breeze coming from the canal, and I don't care for the aroma. None of us do.

"I don't want to quit school, Amos," Cartmell tells him. "I'd miss seeing my friends and teachers."

I know I'm not going to quit school either, but I don't say anything. I need that degree. How can I drop out after all the time and effort I've invested? How can I quit when I'm so far along? It isn't in me to give up like that.

Amos looks up at the vaulted ceiling and shakes his head. "You're not listening. You're hopelessly mired in your Past Life. Every Newcomer is. It will take months, maybe years before you can completely rid yourselves of an unhealthy attachment to the past. But you've got to start now. You've got to learn to put the past aside and start living in the present if you're going to Survive."

I don't like the direction Amos is taking us. None of us do. I don't want to change. I can't imagine quitting school now. I've already started going on job interviews, and I've got to finish my degree, or all my job offers will fall through.

Becoming an engineer means everything to me. I'll be able to make a real contribution to the world. I'll be an expert and get to work with a team. Collaborate. Travel. Advance myself. Meet challenges. I'll be able to make things happen. I'll be somebody.

"Be reasonable, Amos," Amanda pleads, "Don't take everything away from us."

"You've already lost everything," Amos tells her. "If you'll listen to me and learn, maybe you can at least Survive."

We're all glancing at each other now. So we're in some kind of Death World?

Amos is not being fair. This is not what we came for. We shouldn't have to listen to this.

Should Barlow give up getting his karma back? Give up ever being able to make a decision? Is that reasonable? Amos says he'll never be a cop again. Is that fair? Of course Barlow's going to be a cop. Doing anything else would be suicide.

Should Amanda just give up on her dreams? Give up the years of work she's put into the bank? Quit just like that? Amos is being crazy.

And should I just give up, too? Forget about getting a college degree? Chuck the last two and a half years down the well? Be brother of for the rest of my life? That won't hurt Amos—won't affect him a bit. He's already got his. But what about *my* dreams?

Amos begins to pace. "Each of these new Realities is a threat to your Existence. There are Seven Dangers you're going to face. You may run across them one at a time or in combinations or even all at once. The First and foremost is the Time Changes. Whenever you get a warning of an approaching Change, you must get to the nearest Safe House as soon as possible, and that means not only scrambling to make it on time but overcoming any obstacles in your path. You must always know where the nearest Safe House is and never wander more than twenty minutes away from it. You will always have between twenty and sixty minutes to make it to Shelter before a Time Change. The more distant the Fiddling, the longer you'll have to get to safety."

He pauses, and we're absolutely silent. Barlow's jaw is clenched so tight you can see the muscles outlined in his cheeks. He can barely get out his next question between the cuss words.

"So when are they going to end? When are these damn Time Changes finally going to be over with?"

I'm feeling startled because Barlow only cusses when he's furious.

"Oh, they'll come to an end eventually," Amos tells us. "They have to. But right now there's no end in sight. They're coming every two or three weeks. The end won't be visible until the Changes begin to slacken off."

No end in sight? That's not what we want to hear. The whole group of us begins to moan like a herd of cattle under the prod.

Amos snaps his fingers to silence us. "The authorities are doing everything they can to try to stop the Travelling and end the Changes, but it's a huge problem, and it's going to take time to solve. All we can do in the meantime is Survive."

Survive? That's all we've got to look forward to? Struggling?

"If you are Wiped Out by a Change in Time," Amos says, "I will try to Sponsor your Alternate Self in the Present, but the Society will allow me to Sponsor you only four times. If you fail to Survive four times, the Society will deem you unfit and refuse to waste any further resources on you. Of course, I won't be able to Sponsor you even a second time if I can't find you or if your Alternate Self won't believe me, or if you no longer Exist. If the Time Change commences before you were born, you might be eliminated from the Timestream altogether."

Belinda steps forward and tries to catch Amos's eye. "Amos, I don't have a show anymore. The gallery owners don't know me. That painting I sold—I still have it. Nobody ever bought it. And I can't find my other paintings. My art is gone. Amos, what am I doing to do without my art?"

Amos just ignores her. He doesn't even look at her.

"The Second Hazard you will face as Longtimers comes from the Bystanders who inhabit the new Realities you will encounter. Sometimes it's hard to take them seriously because their customs and fashions seem so silly and they Exist so briefly. But they can kill you, believe me. You never know for sure when you might be violating one of their taboos, or how serious the punishment will be. Even if they don't kill you, they can Wipe you Out of the Timestream by detaining you when a Time Change is approaching. When you need to get to a Safe House, you don't ever want to be locked in a jail cell or trapped in a crowd. The Bystanders won't understand your needs. They don't know about Time Changes, and they're not going to help you. It's up to you to anticipate and avoid their traps."

"And shoot them down," Barlow asks dryly, "if they get in the way?"

We're looking at each other, remembering how Amos dealt with the gangers back in Reality 251. "Yes!" Amos shouts at us. "Shoot them down. Why not? They're doomed anyway. You're doing them a favor. It's a better way to go than being torn apart by a Timestorm. They won't remember a thing about it once history gets Realigned. It has no bearing on whether they Exist in the new Reality. So don't hesitate to gun them down if they get between you and Survival. When the warning for the next Change comes, you can't let Bystanders get in your way. You can't let them slow you down even for a second. You've got to take whatever measures are necessary for your Survival. The Bystanders are dead already. When you take them out, you're not affecting their Survival one bit."

We stand there, staring at each other helplessly. This whole Time Travel thing has turned into a nightmare. We've had enough, but Amos just keeps going on.

"The Timecrimers, the ones who violate the Time Laws and cause the Time Changes, pose the Third Hazard to your Survival. They've made the choice to sacrifice others' safety to further their own agenda. You should beware of them and avoid them wherever you find them."

Amos adjusts his glasses, looks out at the canal, then turns to regard us. "Time Travel itself poses the Fourth Hazard to your safety—because Time Travel is susceptible to all the dangers of space travel. Safe Houses can crash or collide or depressurize. There's no food, no water, no air or heat out in the Void of the Fourth Dimension. So if your Timeship breaks down or you get lost, you're doomed."

Well, Amos goes on, and I can tell my brothers and sisters are starting to tune out. It's just too depressing. He goes into detail about all Seven Dangers: danger after danger. It's the environment versus us. I can see that plainly now. Bystanders, Timecrimers, crazed Longtimers—they're just the Time Change's wallpaper. The hostile environment is our true enemy: it's us versus the Death World.

But Surviving isn't our only problem. We also need to Adapt.

"The stress of constant threats and constant change eventually overwhelms everyone. Longtimer psychologists have identified nineteen approaches people commonly use to deal with change. I can't tell for sure which Coping Strategy each of you will choose. It will depend upon your personality and talents and skills. Amanda, for instance, will probably be a Colonizer.

She'll cope with her environment by creating a version of the old environment within the new. And Barlow will probably be a Conqueror, someone who imposes his own will on his surroundings. Conquerors make their environment adjust to them."

I watch Barlow's face as he listens to Amos, and he seems just as confused by this as me. He's no Conqueror. Amos is the Conqueror. It's just so weird, to have to completely change our lives and come up with a Strategy for Coping. It's like some strange dream.

Amos is interrupted by the sound of carousers, descending the metal staircase to the granite walkway. They wear the silver jump suits designed for the Longtimers, and they greet us boisterously as they pass. Amos knows one of them, a tall and slender brunette with delicate features. She wears the most alluring perfume I've ever smelled.

"Hello, Jordan," Amos says. "Headed for the lake?"

"Oh no," she says. "We can't go there. It's on fire."

"There was an oil spill," one of her companions explains. "And now they're burning it off."

Continuing, they descend a staircase at the end of the walkway to a boat moored out of sight on the canal. We hear its motor start up and putter away into the

5

TIME CHANGE STRESS SYNDROME
Reality 256
Moonglow Season

Well, we're still alive—no thanks to the Void Pirates or the CTA. And I've finally figured out who this journal is for. It's for me—after I get Wiped Out of Time and Amos has to Sponsor my Alternate Self. Or one of my brothers or sisters if they're the one who gets Wiped Out.

And if we don't get Wiped Out? Then it's for Posterity, I guess. Any way you look at it, basically this journal is for Bystanders. They're the ones who are going to end up listening to this.

Sorry if I've offended you. But I guess if you're hearing this, that means you're not really a Bystander anymore. Either that, or the whole thing's over now, and the Timecrimers have won or been defeated. If that's the case, I'm probably never going to meet you, so I guess I don't have to apologize or watch what I say. I'm probably dead already and long gone anyway.

Comforting thought.

Amos wants us to start living together, so we can be there for each other. We don't like the idea much, but he insists. He's the exception, though. He gets to keep living by himself in the cushy penthouse of the Roebuck Tower. One set of rules for us, a different set for him.

If I was keeping score inning by inning, the box score would go like this: when we made monkeys of those gangers in Reality 251, it was Vanns 1, Changeworld 0, but after all the surprises and dislocations of Reality 252 and 253, the score tied up at Vanns 1, Changeworld 1. In Reality 254 the Moonglowers put the Changeworld ahead of us 2 to 1. And now, after getting lost in the Void, attacked by Void Pirates, and arrested by the CTA in 255, it's looking like this is going to be a beatdown.

This isn't a baseball game at all—it's a boxing match. And we're going to lose on points. We win only if we're still standing after seven rounds, if we don't get knocked out.

I've started viewing Amos as our cut man in the corner. He's just trying to keep our bruised and battered bodies in the bout. He's trying to keep our eyes from swelling shut. He's trying to keep us off the mat. But in the ring anything can happen.

We've been staying at Amanda's Alternate Self's house in this Reality. Her house is bigger than ours since she's richer than us, being a banker and all. At least it's comfortable.

Amanda became the guardian for me and Zeke and Cartmell after Mom and Dad's tragic accident two years ago, but I'm over 18 now, so I can head out on my own if I want. Belinda was already over 18 when we lost Mom and Dad, so she's never been one of Amanda's wards, and she considers herself her own boss, but Amanda doesn't see it that way. She thinks she's even in charge of Barlow now that he's living under her roof too.

I've been thinking over the Seven Dangers Amos warned us about, and I can see they're all in effect here in the Moonglow Season. The Timecrimers are a danger because Amos warned us they might try to kidnap us so they can extort him into setting policy in their favor. He says it's happened before, to other officials. But Amos is only a Prefect. Besides, he's too stubborn to give in to extortion demands. He'd rather let us get Wiped Out of Time and re-Sponsor us next Season when we're Bystanders. So I guess that qualifies him as a danger to us—danger from a Longtimer.

My brothers and sisters aren't Longtimers, but we're all a danger to each other for sure here in Moonglow. We're driving each other nuts. We're a danger to ourselves too, because we're goin' nuts. Barlow's losin' it, Amanda's losin' it, and now Belinda's losin' it too.

So we've got dangers here in Moonglow, yeah, not the least of which is the friggin' Bystanders. They hate us, of course, but for different reasons than the gangers in Wilderness. The Bystanders of Moonglow are so damn picky, so obsessed with trivial details, so friggin' insistent on consistency and conformity and uniformity and regulations that dealing with them will make you head for hell to get some relief. They're wound so tight I'm expecting one of them to go berserk and ax-murder everyone in sight. So, yeah—they're a danger.

Of course, the Void is death itself. That's why Safe Houses need life support systems. When we're in the Void, we're only one mistake, one little slip-up from ending our lives

And those damn Time Changes—they're out to get us. They really are. And if I sound paranoid, and you think I'm crackin' up, you'd better damn well believe it and hope I'm not outside your bedroom when it happens.

Amos thinks us staying together is the answer. He thinks we're going to save each other. Well, whoop-de-doo, guess what? It doesn't protect us from the Time Change Stress Syndrome. And that's our biggest problem. He may be the expert, but he's wrong about one thing. Moonglow is not a Light Season. It's been officially reclassified as Dark.

I've got my barcalounger set up in the dining room because that's the room the family spends the least amount of time in, so I can relax in there uninterrupted and try to de-stress so I don't lose it like the rest of the family. From my chair I can cover all four entrances into the room, the kitchen to the right, the front hall to the left, the living room ahead left and the stairway ahead right. So I can make a quick exit in case I see anyone nuts coming at me.

I'm practicing my relaxation techniques, picturing myself in a peaceful place—under a tree on the Shawneetown U campus on a warm day. And I'm silently repeating my mantra.

Ah reem kin oh shee wa.

In my lap I'm holding today's Oldspaper open to one of my favorite features *Ask Dr. Clockhour*, a question and answer column about Fourth Dimensional Science. I've been anticipating it all day.

I don't know that my sister Belinda is about to run off with the Bystanders and disgrace the family and put herself in jeopardy. How could I have anticipated that? Even she never would have guessed it. Not even Dr. Clockhour could have seen this one coming, even though it developed logically step by step, like one of his explanations.

I can read Clockhour's column in peace, because Amanda and Pete aren't home from work yet, Cartmell's upstairs napping with the kids, Belinda's cleaning the kitchen, and Barlow's in the basement with Zeke. Staying indoors is the best Strategy during a Dark Season. None of us want to go out unless we have to.

The question in today's column regards our Alternate Selves in the Past, and even I could answer this one. A woman asks "Is it possible to run into your Alternate Self in the Present after a Time Change? And do we have only one Alternate Self in the Past?" Clockhour answers:

> No, you cannot run into your Alternate Self in the Present. Your Alternate Self's Extension in Time ends where yours begins—at the point you entered the Fourth Dimension before the last Change. Thus, your Alternate Self does not Exist in the Present, though all of her possessions are there, and all the Bystanders she knows still assume she Exists. Naturally, they will think you are she. You can have only one Alternate Self in the Past at a time, but that is replaced by a different one every time there is a Change in the Past. So if you remain in the Timeflow, you will have

many Past Selves but only one at a time.

Sometimes I think I could spend eternity relaxing on a barcalounger, eating snacks, and reading Clockhour's columns. Of course, I'd probably get tired of them after a millennium or two. After all, they're only my second favorite feature in the Oldspaper.

My favorite is Max Stengler's column. I've saved it for last, so after reading Clockhour's piece, I turn to Max's. This one's entitled "OLIVER AND RIA: ROMEO & JULIET—OR FATAL ATTRACTION?" and it's about this guy named Sven from Reality 231 in the Boundary Season, when they all shaved their heads, and wigs and hats were taboo, except outdoors in wintertime

Well, it seems Sven's sister Ria fell in love with a Bystander, which is shame enough, but not just any Bystander. She fell for one of the Throwbacks who hate bald people!

Well, that alone is unimaginable. Think how you'd feel if your sister became involved with a Bystander, especially one from the creepy Throwback Season. Just imagine the shame Sven must have felt.

When Sven and his family caught Ria wearing a wig of bowl-shaped hair, they went nuts. Some of her family members wanted to burn the wig and lock her away, and others wanted to throw her out on the street and disown her. She settled the matter by running off with the Bystander, whose name was Oliver, and living with his family.

I never get to find out the rest of the story, because Amanda and Pete suddenly come home from work and bust into the house without warning. I guess I don't hear them coming because I'm so focused on my reading. So now I'm caught, right in the open, and I can't get away. And you have no idea how terrifying that is unless you know how scary Amanda gets after she's had a bad day. When she's feeling like hell, you get to share that hell with her.

Pete's different. When he comes home, he's always

exhausted and only wants to plop down in front of the TV and zone out, because he's an Escapist. But today Amanda's full of pent-up rage from having to be nice to irritating Bystanders all day, and she's looking to pick a fight so she can unload on us. Unloading is Amanda's stress management technique. She has to let out her frustrations caused by the new environment so she can relax and enjoy her Colonizing.

The Moonglowers are incredibly annoying, with their neurotic obsessiveness and whiny nasal accents. They expect strict compliance with every petty aspect of their cumbersome regulations and customs, worry endlessly over details, and will pester you relentlessly until their expectations are met. To do business with them, Amanda's had to become a worry-wart like them, and for a Colonizer, accommodating Bystanders can be a real strain. She gets so fed up with the Moonglowers she has to let it out at night, and we're her dumping ground. It's her way of coping, reducing her stress. Dumping her frustrations on us works for her, but getting dumped on by her doesn't work for me. I'm going crackers living in this house. I swear to gawd I'm halfway to the Funny Farm.

This night I'm in luck because I see Amanda pulling on her white gloves, which means it's inspection time for Belinda's housework. Belinda's scrubbing all the floors. She's become this huge martyr—like she's Cinderella or something. My whole family's the same way. They think our predicament is all about *them*. This is some stupid fairytale, and *they're* the STAR.

Belinda never finished college, and with the Time Changes here, it looks like she never will. She was still living at home when Mom and Dad died and at Amanda's off and on ever since. She just hasn't been able to settle down and find herself.

Amanda walks past me into the kitchen. Belinda stops scrubbing and looks up at her as Amanda runs a finger along the top of the door frame and shows Belinda the smudge on her glove.

Belinda rolls her eyes. "This isn't the Taj Mahal," she says.

Amanda crosses her arms. "It isn't a pig sty either."

"If you don't like it, clean it yourself," Belinda says. "I'm just helping you out."

Amanda lets out a cry of outrage. "Are you so ungrateful you'll live in my house, eat my food and then complain when we expect a little in return? You're so spoiled, Belinda."

Belinda pulls off her rubber gloves and throws the scrub brush at Amanda, who ducks out of the way.

"I didn't give up my art to become your maid. I'm not your slave."

"Get in there and finish that floor!"

"Finish it yourself." Belinda stamps past Amanda and up the stairs.

"You never finish anything, do you?" Amanda yells at her. "You've always been spoiled. You're so lazy, Belinda."

I hear Belinda slam the door to her bedroom upstairs. I've seen the whole thing before, and it's so strange to me. I feel like an anthropologist studying the bizarre ritual of some primitive tribe. The Ritual of the Drama Queens. Was this fight cathartic? Do they both feel better—or worse? Should I do something? Is it over?

Then Amanda turns her sharp glance at me, and I get the feeling she isn't done unloading, and suddenly I don't feel like an anthropologist anymore. I feel like the mad doctor is coming after me to give my brain a shock treatment. So I jump up from my barcalounger and run for the stairs. Maybe I can still get away.

"Where are you going?" Amanda yells after me.

"Nowhere!" I cry, running up the stairs.

I'm out of breath when I reach the bedroom Barlow and I are sharing in this Reality. I turn the knob and start to go in to restore some normalcy to my day when I hear the sound of Belinda crying in the room next to it. I'm surprised because I haven't heard Belinda cry since she was sixteen. I guess it must be one of her new ways of reducing stress. Suddenly I don't know what to do. Should I ignore it and let her purge herself, or go comfort her? Is she in pain? Does she want sympathy? Does she need a shoulder to cry on? Or does she want to be left alone?

Life's gotten so Timewhacking complicated! This is stressing me out.

Sometimes my sisters seem more inscrutable to me than the Bystanders. They're beyond analysis. Not even Zeke's calculations can predict them. I want to go into my room, but I'm too curious. I have to find out which choice is the right one. This could be my chance to finally understand my sister. Amos told us to help each other out. So I knock on Belinda's door.

The crying sounds stop. There's silence then a voice asking who it is. I tell her, and she doesn't say anything, so I go in. She's pretending to make the bed that's already made. I enter and sit on Cartmell's bed, but Belinda doesn't look at me. She's too busy pretending to clean. She's halfway to Crazytown, if you ask me.

I feel sorry for her because I think she's been feeling low ever since Riley dropped out of the universe. And she's not disposed to the Colonizer life like the rest of us. Belinda just hasn't been able to find the right Coping Strategy for herself. So I tell her, "Amanda didn't mean any of those things she said. She was just unloading on you."

"I know that." There's a knife edge to her voice like I'm tying to accuse her of being stupid. But I'm just trying to be sympathetic.

"I know you've been having a hard time since Riley left. He never should have deserted you, Belinda. He should have stuck by you."

She gives me this irritated look like I'm being

offensive and says, "Of course he should have gone. He didn't want to be here. We were both going our separate ways eventually—we knew that. There's no reason he should have stayed. At least he was willing to pay me the compliment of believing I could Survive without him. He never assumed my life revolved around him, or that I wanted it to. None of you liked him. Why should he have stuck around? He showed a lot of respect for me by leaving like he did."

Jeez—don't bite my head off!

She's giving me this look like she wants to stick a knife in me. And for what? For that crummy loser Riley. I guess I should have figured that Belinda would defend that worthless Rejector, take his side to the last. She was always defending him because he always disagreed with everyone, but he wasn't always right. Being right didn't matter to him except in how it could strengthen his position in an argument. And sometimes it seems Belinda's taken up his contrary ways.

"None of you understand what I'm going through," Belinda tells me. We can hear the muffled voices of Amanda and Barlow, arguing downstairs. We're just one big snarling wolf pack.

"Okay, I don't know you," I snipe at Belinda. "I'm just trying to be sympathetic."

"Save it for Amanda. She's the martyr around here. I don't need it."

So there you go. I try to be nice, and she snaps at me. So I guess I've got my answer. To Belinda sympathy is an insult. And where Riley's concerned, the battle lines have been clearly drawn. It's Riley and Belinda versus the rest of us. And if you're going to cross a family battle line like that, you'd better be carrying a white flag. Otherwise, you'll become a casualty.

Belinda's always in a bad mood, which is understandable, I guess, since she never has time for her art anymore. Her art used to be the most important thing to her before the Time Changes. But she couldn't bring her canvases into the Safe House or her paints. Every piece of art she ever worked on is gone. Now she has to clean the house, do the yard work, do the shopping, watch the kids. She doesn't have time for herself. She's going Chrono, and the family's fueling up the Rocket to the Void Asylum as fast as they can.

This Time Change Stress Syndrome is no joke. Barlow's hanging off a cliff by his fingernails. And now Belinda's not much better. Amos was right—her art career is over.

So what's she gonna do? Repaint all her canvases and lug them around from Safe House to Safe House? She can't sell them to Longtimers. They can't carry around a bunch of art. And the Realities don't last long enough for her to make a reputation among the Bystanders.

So what does she do now? Go back to being a rebellious teenager? Be Cinderella and treat the rest of us like wicked step siblings? We're too stressed out to help her. She's all alone. She doesn't even have Riley to back her up anymore.

Am I going to have to watch my brothers and sisters lose everything and go to pieces one by one until it's finally my turn?

Well, that night there's a Time Change, so we all go to the Safe House down at the Brotherhood Lodge. The result of the Time Change is the Moonglowers split into two sects: the Day People and the Night People. That's what causes Moonglow to be reclassified as a Dark Season. The Day People and the Night People have completely different cultures and do not mix. The Day People of Reality 256 do not go out at night, and the Night People do not go out in the daytime. We were already familiar with the aggravating Day People but were not prepared for the Night People. You'd think we would like them since they're the opposite of the Day People, but we just can't relate to those weird Night

People, and when the Network shows us the hairstyles of the Moonglowers of Reality 256 we're astonished because the Night People wear the same sort of ugly spike cut that Belinda's had ever since she entered into her nonconformist stage. Cooper thinks it's really funny, as if this Reality is some kind of joke on Belinda.

"You're so stylish, Belinda," he says.

"Drop dead," she tells him, but he just laughs.

The Night People of the Moonglow Season start coming out at sunset after the Day People have closed their shutters and locked their doors. The Night People worship the Moon, and they hate the Day People. Night and Day are two different countries in the Moonglow Season.

Like Belinda, the Night People like to wear black. If they're not pale skinned like Belinda, they powder their faces, and some of them accentuate the effect with eye shadow.

After the Reports are finished, we exit the Brotherhood Lodge via an underground corridor that joins with a building across Ash Street. We emerge into a wide gallery, a shopping mall thronging with Bystanders. Once Belinda comes out into the open, the Night People start to crowd around her like she's famous or something.

"I love your hair," one of them says. "Where do you have it done?"

"That sweatshirt's marvelous," another says to her. "Where did you get those clothes?"

"Who does your makeup?" asks a third.

It's like Belinda's suddenly a celebrity. The Night People love her—and ignore the rest of us as if we're Day People. It reminds me of Barlow's postgame interviews when everyone wanted to talk to the star halfback and the rest of us got pushed aside.

Belinda's bewildered at first by the attention she 's getting from the Bystanders, but she likes it, I can tell. It's so complimentary. All the Night People want to be with her, hang out with her, act like her. They hang on her every word. I'm wondering if we're going to have to rescue her—grab her and run. But then I notice Belinda talking to the Bystanders with a husky Reality 256 accent, and that shocks me. I've never heard her do voices before, but this accent is perfect. She's trying to fit in! She's basking in the moon.

Amanda takes her by the arm and tries to lead her away with us, but Belinda pulls her arm free and doesn't even look at Amanda. And then the Bystanders crowd Amanda out of the way.

Amanda looks so bewildered—like some Bystander encountering an Anachronism. We're all bewildered. Belinda's never been popular before, never run in the popular circles at school like Amanda. Amanda was class president and prom queen, but Belinda's always been gawky looking and shy. She's never gotten along well with people. But now she's eating up the attention she's getting, really pigging out on it. It seems so strange.

There's no accounting for this bizarre new Reality. It seems like it was designed by some contrary fiend like Riley.

Belinda runs off with the Bystanders that night. Amanda complains about it for days afterward, like she's Martin Luther or something, how unfair Belinda's being to us, how ungrateful she is, how she's endangering herself, how unrealistic she is to take this attention seriously, how she's going to get into trouble and need us to help her out of it, and on and on. I get really tired of hearing about it and wish I could run off with the Bystanders to get away from all this complaining about Belinda. It's driving me nuts.

Sure, I've thought about leaving the family myself, getting my own life, living by my own rules. I could make it alone, I think. Being on my own would definitely have its advantages. But I couldn't do that to the family, to Barlow, to Cartmell, to Zeke. I couldn't justify hurting them or making their lives harder. Amos told us to stick together, and he knows best. So I've decided to stick it out, despite the bellyaching.

A couple days after Belinda's departure, she reappears. Amanda follows her around the house, nagging at her, but Belinda ignores her. It's like when Belinda was 17 and Mom was on her case all the time. Only, Belinda's not 17, and Amanda's not—well, anyway, Belinda's not 17.

Cartmell and I are sitting at the kitchen table eating spumoni ice cream when Amanda finally gets a response out of Belinda. They're in the dining room at the time, but their voices aren't hard to hear. They aren't exactly whispering, if you know what I mean.

"How dare you embarrass your family like this! You're disgracing us."

"I'm tired of waiting for the Time Changes to end. I want to have a life. I want to go places, meet people, have some fun. I'm tired of being cooped up with my suffocating family."

"Suffocating! We're not trying to suffocate you, Belinda. We love you."

Cartmell and I look at each other. She almost breaks out laughing. I'm shaking my head.

"I want to be around exciting, interesting people not the same old boring people all the time."

"Boring! You think your family is boring?"

"More boring than the Void."

"Belinda, if you'd just be patient for a little longer."

"I've been patient for months now, and what has it gotten me except to make me older and duller than I've ever been in my life."

Belinda runs for her bedroom and packs up her stuff and leaves us that evening. Amanda stands on the doorstep and yells at her as Belinda drags her suitcase out to the taxi and drives away.

Welcome to Crazytown, population: two.

That night, while Barlow and I lie in our beds in the

darkness, waiting for sleep, he suddenly speaks.

"You know, Belinda's right about not waiting to have a life."

I look over, but can't see anything, just starlight coming in the window. We both lie on our backs, talkin' to the darkness.

"What are you going to do, Barlow, run off with the Bystanders?"

"Bystanders." He dismisses that idea with a "pfft" sound. "I'm talking about finding some girl from Wilderness, getting something going."

"Wilderness!" I make a sound, maybe it's a kind of laugh. "Where are you going to find someone from Wilderness to go out with?"

"You don't think I can get a date?" he says. "Do you know how many dates I've had in my life? I know how to get a woman."

"You're living in the past, Barlow."

"Yeah, maybe, but at least livin' in the past is livin'."

I can smell the crisp night air and hear some faint music in the distance. The Night People have begun to party.

"Yeah," I say, "but what kind of life can Belinda have with the Bystanders? It won't last. She'll miss us, and she'll come back."

"Maybe she'll miss us," Barlow says. "But she won't be back. She's too proud to come back."

Well, I guess I was right about Belinda because she does come back two weeks later. She has a smile on her face that lingers for days, gives Amanda fits. Amanda launches into a tirade about how immoral Belinda's been. But Belinda just smiles and points out that Amanda is making assumptions and doesn't know anything about what Belinda has been doing. But there are signs, of course. Belinda is wearing Bystander clothes, and her original clothes are missing. Her shirt's a boy's shirt. And there's that smile. Belinda is so cheerful and happy it drives Amanda nuts.

Cartmell finds this empty pill bottle in Belinda's jeans the next day when she's doing the laundry. It's 2B1, a contraceptive they have in Reality 256. 100% effective, takes effect within hours of swallowing it.

Cartmell gawks at the bottle, then shows to me and says, "Well, I guess Belinda's got a life now."

"Don't jump to conclusions," I tell her. But even my mind's full of frogs after that discovery.

That night when Belinda and I are alone, she asks me, "Dexter, do you think I'm pretty?" I've noticed that Belinda has gotten less gawky looking as she's gotten older. And I can see her face would be pretty if it wasn't spoiled by that awful haircut. She has a good figure now that she's not so skinny. If she just wasn't so shy and awkward. And I tell her so. She hangs her head after that, which surprises me because I thought I was giving her a compliment.

"How am I going to become less shy?" she says. "There's never going to be another Season where everybody worships me."

Well, I can't argue with that. Maybe she'll get less shy when she gets older. She thinks about that, and all of a sudden she says, "It doesn't matter, does it, any of the things that happened back in Reality 250."

I'm not sure what she means, so I say cautiously, "Sure it matters. What do you mean?"

And then she says, staring off into the distance beyond the walls of our room, "I mean the mistakes I made, the failures, the person I was, none of that matters, does it? The people in this house are the only ones in the world who even know about it."

"I suppose."

"And when the next Season comes, nothing that happened this Season will matter either. It will be like starting over with a clean slate."

"Yeah, so?"

Belinda's smile grows. "So I can be whoever I want

to, whoever I choose to be, and if it doesn't work out, I can start over, and I don't have to worry because no one will remember."

The next day some Bystander named Shadow shows up on our doorstep and demands to see Belinda. I'm surprised to see him out in the daylight because the Night People prefer the darkness, but I notice a full moon in the sky and remember the Night People consider Daymoons a prime time for their private dealings. They schedule some of their festivals during the nights of Daymoons.

I'm not sure what to do about him, so I send Cartmell to tell Belinda he's here. The Bystander is dressed in black clothes and sunglasses (the Night People call them "Moonglasses") and has a goatee on his chin. He's big like Barlow and muscular too. Around his neck he wears a luminescent Moonball on a leather cord and on his third finger a gold ring with a moonstone setting. The emblem of the moon turns up everywhere among the Night People—in their decorations, their art, their advertisements, on their clothes.

Belinda comes down the stairs without looking at us and greets her Bystander Charming without a word. She's got on her black sweatshirt and tight gray slacks, looks just like a Night Person. And I begin to wonder just how deep into this Moonglow role she is. I notice on a leather cord around her neck is a carved wooden totem of an owl, what they call a "Moonbird." Belinda loves this Season. I think she'd stay here forever if she could. But she can't. Moonglow's a Dark Season, and it's not going to last.

Belinda's not so pleased with her Bystander Charming now that he's hunted her down. She can't run off with him, not if she wants to Survive. It doesn't matter if the glass slipper fits or not. Bystanders don't get to live happily ever after. But she's got to finish her fairytale somehow. So Belinda takes her Shadow by the wrist and leads him onto the porch.

"Who is that?" Cartmell asks me, craning her neck to get a glimpse of him as they walk out the door.

"Some Bystander."

"Well, what's he doing here?"

Cartmell and I eye each other. We both have a sudden urge to go dust the shades and curtains around the dining room window, which looks on the porch. Like we're playing the game "Maid" that Mom made up to get us to help her with the housework when we were kids. We find if we put our ears to the curtain we can accidently hear what Belinda and her Bystander Charming are saying.

"I had to see you," he tells her.

"Why?"

"You know why. After last night."

"That was last night. It's over now."

"How can you say that?"

"Be quiet. My family will hear you."

"So what? I don't care if your family hears us."

He's got a low-pitched voice like Barlow's.

"We're moving away," Belinda tells him.

"Moving away? When?"

"Any day now. We won't be back—ever."

"Can I come visit you?"

"Not where we're going."

I hate to bring up the ganger Ramon Sanchez from Reality 251 or the Void Pirate Kyb Kalim from Reality 255 or Riley from Reality 250, but this is starting to look like just another in a long line of Belinda's bad decisions. Even she admits she makes terrible choices when it comes to men. So why can't she see it now with these Night People?

When I peek out the curtain I can see she's got her eyes closed, and she's looking down. He moves closer to her.

"Take me with you," he says, pulling off his Moonglasses.

Belinda's eyes open, and her head comes up, and I have to duck behind the curtain again.

"What?" she says.

"Wherever your family's going, I want to come with you."

When Belinda doesn't answer immediately, Cartmell and I look at each other. He wants her to Sponsor him? Does he realize what he's asking? There's nothing in the fairytale about Cinderella Sponsoring her Prince. Surely Belinda's not taking this seriously. Amos has helped us all Sponsor our friends from Wilderness, but this guy's not from Wilderness—he's a stranger. She's known him for only a couple weeks. How can she even consider it?

Suddenly Barlow walks up behind Cartmell and me and asks us what we're doing and nearly scares us to death. "Nothing," I tell him. He doesn't believe me and starts to make a fuss, so we both shush him.

"What's going on?" he demands, looking from one of us to the other. When we don't say anything, he catches on to the guilty expressions on our faces and starts looking around and peers out the dining room window.

"Who's out there?" he says. "Is that Belinda?"

He heads for the front door, so we get in front of him. "Don't go out there."

We grab onto him and try to pull him back, but he just drags us out onto the porch with him. And once out there, he gets a nasty shock. Because Belinda and Shadow are in one of Amanda's sun chairs. Belinda's sitting in his lap, and they're kissing.

Barlow stops and lets out a roar. "What the hell is this?" Belinda has betrayed him. She's betrayed us all.

She breaks apart from Shadow and stands up with a guilty look on her face and tries to arrange herself and brushes back an errant strand of hair with her finger.

Shadow looks really ticked off by our interruption,

and he scowls, turns toward Belinda and jerks his thumb at Barlow. "Who's that?"

Belinda looks down. She gets really quiet. "My brother."

Shadow narrows his eyes at Cartmell and me next.

Belinda sighs. "And my family."

He's giving her a dirty look now. "You didn't tell me your family's Day People."

Belinda rolls her eyes. Now she's getting ticked off. "I told you they're not like me. And we aren't *Day People*."

Through the open front door we hear a thundering of someone barreling down the stairs. Amanda comes rushing onto the porch in her bare feet, wearing one of her suits, all red-faced and growling. She stops right in front of Belinda and shakes a finger at her. "You're NOT Sponsoring that Bystander!"

Belinda pulls back from her in shock.

"We are NOT taking that Bystander with us!" Amanda yells. "There is no way I'm going to put up with that."

Cartmell and I grab onto her and try to drag her back into the house.

"Don't do this," Cartmell pleads with her. "You're only making things worse."

But Amanda is undaunted. "I'm the oldest, and this is MY house. I make the rules, and you're going to have to abide by them."

We pull her inside until she finally relents and takes out her cellular, dials a number, and crosses her arms. "Hello, Amos?" she says. "Guess what your sister is up to this time!"

6
LIFELINE
Reality 257
Moonglow Season

Amos says he's having these journal recordings transcribed in case the technology doesn't Survive. You can never tell what the Final Season will be like. So, okay, listener or reader, whichever you are, here goes. I hope you don't mind if I address you directly. We haven't met, but I do have an imagination, and I'll bet you do, too. I can imagine who you are—and that's good enough for me. Welcome to the Time World, my friend.

When our Beepers go off at the end of Reality 256, my brothers and sisters start griping about not having a longer Warning before the current Time Change. We're outside the food court next to the merry-go-round in the Shawneetown Mall in Mitchellsville, holding our shopping bags. I can smell pepperoni pizza odors mixing with Kung Pao chicken and barbeque pork.

"I'm not done shopping!" Amanda exclaims.

"I don't want to go either," Cartmell says. "But we've got to get to Room 999." She shows Amanda her flashing Wristwatcher.

Even Barlow doesn't want to go. "Why don't they give us a longer Warning? So we don't have to rush. Why is it only sixty minutes?"

"Dr. Clockhour explained about that in his column in the Oldspaper today," I tell him. But nobody wants to listen to me. None of them are fans of Dr. Clockhour, except for Zeke, who's home watching the kids.

We leave the shopping mall and look for a cab. We finally have to call one because we're miles from the Lodge, and there's no subway. At least we can use our cell phones in this stupid Reality.

"I hope Belinda's taking Shelter," Cartmell says. "I hope she knows about the Change."

Belinda's gone back to running with the Bystanders, and we're all worried she's completely lost her Focus and started Identifying. Because if she has, this is the end of Belinda.

Does she still wear her Blinker and her Beeper? Does she even know a Time Change is coming? And does she care? Maybe she sees Moonglow as her last hurrah, her last chance to live like a human being instead of a hunted animal. Because the Time Changes are at the top of the food chain now, and we're just prey.

We're all pretty quiet, lost in mourning for Belinda, but I don't want to think about it, so I start explaining the question in Dr. Clockhour's column.

> Q: Why is the warning for Time Changes always twenty to sixty minutes? Why aren't some of the warnings one minute long—or sixty-one? Why this forty minute window?

Cartmell figures out what I'm trying to do, so she joins in. She doesn't want to think about Belinda's plight either.

"I've always wondered that," she says. "What was Dr. Clockhour's explanation?"

Barlow groans, but that doesn't stop me. I go into detail.

> A: Twenty minutes is the minimum because Changes made less than a month in the Past cannot hold. They cannot build enough momentum to surmount the Present. They bounce off the Present and reverse direction, Changing everything back.
>
> But a Change made a month in the Past gains enough momentum to surmount the Change Barrier and causes our Beacons Downtime to send out a signal that arrives twenty minutes before the Time Change. Changes made Deeper in the Past allow the Beacons more advance time to warn us, but Deep Changes gain momentum until they reach Terminal Velocity. At Terminal Velocity the Time Change is sixty Minutes

> behind the signal from the Beacons and moving at the same speed. Thus, the warning signal can never reach us more than sixty minutes ahead of the Change.

When I get to the end of my explanation, the cab arrives, and Amanda starts to launch into a tirade against Belinda as we duck inside, but I hold my finger to my lips.

"EYE-stander-bay," I say. "Utshay upay"

No one's heard of pig Latin in the Moonglow Season, so the cab driver doesn't know what I'm saying, and Amanda becomes silent because she hates talking in pig Latin. So we get the luxury of a whine-free ride.

Amanda thinks she has to re-teach us the lessons we've already learned about Survival. We have to learn from Belinda's bad example. But we already know. Amanda's just unloading on us, trying to reduce her stress. She's got the Syndrome bad. Belinda has scared her to the Threshold. First, it was Barlow, then Belinda, so maybe Amanda's next. Or will it be me? I don't want to think about it or talk about it.

We make it to Room 999 on time and enter Reality 257. That was yesterday.

My status report for this Reality:

None of us have cracked up yet, not completely. Anyway, none of us have been certified. Belinda's departure seems to have stabilized things in the house for some crazy reason—if you don't mind me using the word *stabilized* loosely.

But things have not remained stable—that's for sure—because Belinda's come home again. We're all sitting in the kitchen, having breakfast when suddenly Belinda appears in a black bathrobe. Cartmell already knows she's back because she came into their room in the middle of the night, dressed all in black like the Night People. But Cartmell doesn't say a word about it at breakfast. She just lets Belinda make her appearance.

Amanda gets quiet all of a sudden but doesn't speak

or look at Belinda. You can tell she's mad, though. We've all been really worried about Belinda because we haven't heard from her since the Change.

Belinda goes over to the coffee pot and pours herself a cup. Pete looks at her and frowns. "Since when do you drink coffee? I thought coffee was for Day People."

Belinda answers in a Moonglow accent as if it's her Alternate Self who's come back to us in her place. "All the Night People drink it, but for different Motos. The Day People drink theirs Night to Rooster them in the Sunup. The Night People shine for exotic blends. They drink to keep themselves Keen through the Velvet." Belinda seems chatty, but that's just her way of trying to ward off the criticism that we know is coming. She blows on her coffee and looks for a place at the breakfast table, but all the chairs are taken, so she leans against the countertop and sips from her cup.

Amanda has stopped eating her scrambled eggs and blueberry muffin. She puts down her fork and simmers silently, building up to her inevitable explosion. You can see all the tectonic pressures building up inside her. Her magma's really flowing down there beneath the surface.

Belinda tries to blunt the eruption by getting Amanda to vent early. "Well, I'm back," she says cheerfully, sounding more like herself and less like the Night People.

"Evidently," Amanda declares, refusing to blow. Her face turns red as the volcanic pressures grow inside her. Barlow chews on his thumbnail for a moment, trying to think of something to say. We're all pretty subdued by then, after listening to Amanda rant all night, trying to change our worrying into anger at Belinda. We had no way of knowing if she would find Shelter or not. We couldn't be sure she still Existed.

"Why didn't you call us?" I ask her, not able to restrain my curiosity. I suppose it sounds like a criticism, but I just want to know.

Belinda shrugs and takes another sip of coffee, and

that does it. Amanda blows. So loud it makes us jump. I half expect to see steam blow out her ears.

"How dare you come creeping back like this with no explanation, no excuse for your inexcusable behavior! We've been worried sick for days. We didn't know what had happened to you. Your atoms could've been scattered to the four winds as far as we knew. How dare you worry us like that! You're so involved in your escapades you can't remember to call us? Can't even trouble yourself to push the numbers on your phone?"

Belinda puts down her coffee cup, her hand shaking. She clenches her fist to still her fingers. "I left my cellular at home. I forgot it—all right? That's why I didn't call." Now Belinda sounds totally like herself. The return to old patterns has brought back the voice, the expression, the face we used to know.

Amanda's stunned. We all are. Forget her cellular? Cast off one of her Lifelines? Has she gone Chrono?

Amos gave us the lecture about Lifelines last time we were in the Catacombs. "Keep your Lifelines with you always, your Blinker, your Beeper, your phone. These are the technological devices you can never be without. Your Survival depends upon them."

Neglecting your Lifelines is clear evidence you've lost your Focus. It's the pathway to Annihilation. It means stumbling when you need to glide.

Amanda bobbles her words for a moment while her lips try to compose her outrage. "That's exactly—that's why—you've become so obsessed with yourself that you're not remembering your Lifelines. You've lost Focus, Belinda. You're losing your Direction with this irresponsible behavior. Do you have any idea how you're disgracing the family? Cavorting with the Bystanders! That's what Accommodaters do."

Belinda's jaw drops, and she lets out a huff of protest. She shakes her head at Amanda's unreasonableness. "I'm not an Accommodater. I have my own reasons for spending time with the Bystanders. Good ones. I like this Season. And they like me. I wish I could stay here permanently."

Amanda drops her chin and lets out a snort. "That's exactly what I'm talking about. You like this Season too much, so much you're entertaining Illusions now. You've succumbed to the Endurance Fallacy."

"I haven't succumbed to any Fallacy."

"Then how do you explain abandoning one of your Lifelines?"

"I forgot it, that's all."

"That's not good enough, Belinda. Longtimers don't forget their Lifelines. Ever. Not unless they've lost Focus."

"Okay, I lost Focus. Big deal. I Survived. Anyone can make a mistake."

"What mistake are you going to make next? Leave your Beeper and Blinker behind? Forget that Time Changes exist? Forget you have a family?"

"I didn't forget I have a family. I'm here now, aren't I?"

Amanda shakes her head like a hanging judge, her face red. Guilty as charged. Get the rope.

"You're not to go out alone any longer," Amanda says to her. "I'm ordering you to give up this obsession with this Season and its Bystanders. For your own good. You've gone way past the limits of acceptable behavior, Belinda. You're in so deep you're endangering yourself, and I can't let you do that."

I notice that Belinda's hair is clipped and combed now, no longer the spike cut she used to have. She's changed it to match the fashions of Reality 257. This is the first new haircut she's had since Reality 251. Is she trying to be a Chameleon? Has she finally found her Strategy?

"You're right," Belinda says, holding her coffee cup to her chest and staring at the floor. "I'll stay away from the Bystanders. I'll do whatever you ask."

I'm shocked to hear this capitulation after the long and drawn-out war she's been fighting against Amanda's control these last few Realities. To capitulate now seems completely out of character.

I didn't notice her change. It took a second change for me to realize the first.

Amos said it would happen, said we'd change eventually and need a new Strategy. Belinda's rebelling against Colonizing, turning to its opposite. So why would she capitulate to Amanda now?

"I have a request of my own," Belinda declares, putting down her coffee cup. "I want to Sponsor Shadow."

Amanda's astounded. She gasps, and all the color drains from her face. Her fingernails hit her plate, upsetting her blueberry muffin. We're all taken by surprise. We thought this crisis point was past. Belinda already turned Shadow down. She told us she had no intention of Sponsoring him. How could she return to that Nexus now? We have enough problems. We don't need her dredging up the old ones.

"No!" Amanda spouts after her trembling tongue sorts through her inventory of outraged responses. "You are not bringing that Bystander into this family. Absolutely not."

"Could I speak to you in the other room, Amanda?" Cartmell asks suddenly. We turn to stare at her as she sits, looking innocently into her corn flakes. What the heck is Cartmell trying to do? Amanda isn't one to take her advice from the youngest member of the family. She usually doesn't listen to anyone. But I guess she's so flabbergasted she welcomes an opportunity to escape and compose herself.

Cartmell walks through the saloon doors into the dining room and through the hall into the den. We can hear the sound of the TV faintly from the basement, where Barlow's taking care of Jackson and Jessalyn.

Amanda follows Cartmell out of the kitchen, and I come after her. I have to find out what this is about. I don't intend to wait to hear it from Cartmell later.

The den's the smallest room in the house, with a couch, a TV, and a couple of easy chairs. There's barely enough room for the three of us to turn around in there. Amanda frowns at me and starts to say something, but Cartmell speaks instead.

"I think you should let Belinda Sponsor Shadow."

Amanda whirls around to face her. "What!"

"Amos has let us all Sponsor someone. Now it's her turn." Of course, Amos will be his official Sponsor, but Belinda will do the work.

Amanda dismisses that argument by letting out her pent-up breath. "We Sponsored family members and people from Wilderness, not random Bystanders. I'm not letting Belinda bring a Bystander into the family just because she's lost her Direction and fallen in love."

"She's not in love with him," Cartmell declares.

Amanda squints at her. "Of course she loves him. Why else would she want to Sponsor him?"

"Because she wants to get rid of him."

Amanda squeezes her brow with her fingers, as if this is giving her a headache. "You're not making any sense."

"She told me when she came in last night. She feels she owes him, and if she can Sponsor him, she can cast him aside once he's a Longtimer. She doesn't want to stay with him any more than you do."

Amanda considers Cartmell's words for a moment. I don't relish the idea of having Shadow around. None of us like him—he's so creepy. Barlow hates his guts. So if Belinda doesn't like him, that makes it unanimous.

"Maybe she's expecting you to say no," I say to Amanda. "Maybe that's what she wants. Maybe she just needs your refusal to satisfy her conscience that she did what she could for this guy."

"I don't think so," Cartmell says. "Belinda's filed her

name as his Sponsor. She's already seen him through his first Time Change."

"What!"

Amanda and me are both blasted out of our shoes. I feel so bewildered it scares me. I half expect to hear my Beeper and Blinker go off. "She can't do that. She's not a Member. They'll never approve it. Amos will be furious. How could she make a commitment like that without consulting the family first?"

"It doesn't matter," Amanda says. "We're not going to let Belinda dictate to us. None of us want that Bystander in the family. She's disgraced us enough already."

"But he won't be a Bystander," Cartmell points out to us. "He'll be a Newcomer."

She's right about that. Longtimers can accept an involvement with Bystanders that leads to Sponsorship and Membership. They can even accept Finagling some clueless Bystander. They just can't accept Accommodation.

"If you refuse to let Belinda Sponsor this guy," Cartmell says, "she'll leave the family and try to Sponsor him on her own."

Amanda raises an eyebrow. "You may be right." She crosses her arms. "Belinda always feels she owes her friends, never feels she owes us." Amanda's lips almost smile. "Maybe that's what she needs. All this attention from the Bystanders has turned her head. I suppose all that worship would've had the same effect on us. Belinda needs a return to reality. Let her go out on her own and find out how hard it is. Maybe she'll start to appreciate us. She'll see I've been right all along. It will be bitter medicine, but she'll learn. She'll miss us, and she'll come crawling back. She'll have to. Because she'll have no choice."

"I don't know," I say. "You need to take a long-term view. Amos said the government will put an end to the

Changes. Then none of this will have any relevance. Humor Belinda this once, and maybe she'll feel she owes you. Don't drive her from the family, when the Changes are almost over. Amos says we should stick together. Don't do anything rash. We need to heal this wound, so we can return to a normal life."

Well, I suppose calling our life normal is a bit more than an exaggeration. It's like calling a Time Machine a Safe House, like calling a Traveler a Bystander, like calling the Void crowded. But there's more normal and less normal, and losing Belinda would definitely lead to less. After all, who would Amanda have to vent on without Belinda? The rest of us, that's who. And that isn't my idea of normal. Being the brunt of Amanda's frustrations could ruin any hope of things ever seeming normal for me around here.

But you're about as likely to make a Timestorm reverse direction as you are to change Amanda's mind about anything. You may as well try to navigate the labyrinth of the Brotherhood Lodge as try to steer a safe course between Amanda and Belinda. Belinda tries to act like it's no big deal, as if she can come and go as she pleases, like Cooper. But Belinda's not Cooper, and we know she can't get away with it.

I guess it was inevitable Belinda would want to Sponsor one of her Moonglow friends, after how close she got to them. We should have seen it coming, shouldn't have let ourselves get blindsided like this. That's the worst of it, the shock and the disorientation. We haven't kept pace with Belinda, and now someone's going to pay the price for that.

I don't like the mean streak I detect in Amanda. She never used to be that way. The stress of dealing with the Changes must have brought it out of her, and now she gets that way even when she doesn't have any stress to blow off.

"Dexter's right," Cartmell says. "She's our sister, not some Moon Goblin. I don't want to see her suffer."

Amanda lifts her nose in the air. "Belinda should have thought of that before she got involved in this escapade. If we're a family, we've got to cooperate with each other. We either pull together, or we pull apart."

Amanda's right. Belinda should know better than to ask us to accept Shadow. How can we say anything but no? It's almost as if Belinda doesn't want back into the family, as if she's looking for an excuse to leave us for good. But if she wants that, why has she come back? What's her motive? What does she want?

Accepting a Chameleon into the family would put a strain on our normalcy. For her also to go slumming and cavorting with the Bystanders is inviting public disgrace. Ignoring public opinion is the same as ignoring the Society, and we can't do without the Society. It's essential to our Survival. The only thing that could make it worse is if Belinda's gotten involved in the Night People's weird pagan religion. The Day People are mainly Pentacostals, but the Night People practice a kind of black magic called Jikki.

Even so, I hate to split up the family. Amos and Cooper have gone out on their own. I don't want to lose Belinda too. I'm not sure our lives can ever seem normal if Belinda leaves us. "There must be something we can do. Can't we find some way to compromise on this?"

Amanda snorts. "Compromise! Just look at the effect she's having." Amanda points to Cartmell, who's dressed all in black like one of the Night People with a Jikki charm around her neck. " Do you want to lose Cartmell next?"

Jikki's the fashion with the pre-teens now—it doesn't mean anything.

"I just want a normal life, that's all."

I can't figure out what Cartmell's up to. Usually she's indirect in her attempts to influence the family. She must really think this a crisis to come out from cover like this.

And I realize suddenly she's changed. She thinks now that she's fourteen, she's all grown up. Of course, she's so precocious she thinks she's already an adult.

Naturally, Belinda doesn't take Amanda's refusal well. So she disappears that night like we all knew she would. I don't know how Amos is going to react to this. None of us have told him, of course. So maybe he'll never find out, fingers crossed.

I'm more concerned about the impact this will have on Cartmell and Zeke. I worry about them, about how all these changes are affecting them, molding them. Especially Cartmell.

Zeke's different. He's older and less susceptible to influence, partly because he's so smart. His defining characteristic is his curiosity. He's always wondering about things, studying them, trying to figure them out.

One night about a week after Belinda's disappearance, he comes up to Barlow and me in our bedroom and says, "Come on, I want to show you something."

We glance at each other.

"Get your jackets," Zeke says. "And your boots. Some hiking is involved."

It's pretty nervy of him, supposing we'll drop everything and follow him just to look at some weird thing he's discovered, but we've never regretted doing that in the past. Zeke comes to us like this only when it's something important.

So we pull on our boots and grab our jackets, and we set off across Eddyville to a park at the edge of town and then beyond it into the woods. We end up on a ridge overlooking a hollow where there's a clearing in the trees. A bunch of weird-looking people are gathered down there—most of them dressed in all white or all black.

"Who's that?" Barlow says.

"Luneans," Zeke tells us. "It's a new religion among the Night People. They worship the moon." Zeke takes his binoculars out of his backpack to peer at them. We can hear the sound of low-pitched chanting.

Moon worshippers—that's just like the Night People. But this goes far beyond Jikki. We stare at them some more. Zeke puts down his binoculars and points.

"The ones in white are called Light Men. They worship the full moon. The ones in black are the Dark Men. They worship the new moon."

We're feeling a bit bewildered. "Okay," Barlow says. "But why'd you bring us here? Why bother us over some weird Bystander custom that won't last beyond the next Time Change?"

Good question. We both look over at Zeke. He stares back at us and presses on the crosspiece of his glasses. "Because they're not all Bystanders down there. The religion has spread to Longtimers too."

Longtimers! Following some weird new Bystander religion? I thought Contamination always went in only one direction—from Longtimers to Bystanders. I never realized it could go both ways.

We look down at the Luneans again. "What are they doing down there?" Barlow asks Zeke.

"This is one of their ceremonies. I don't understand it completely." He looks through his binoculars again. Barlow and I turn to stare some more as a man in a savage oversized mask begins to dance.

I notice some woman in white robes arrive. She's wearing a gold belt and a gold headpiece and necklace. Her robes are hemmed with colorful embroidery.

"Is that their priestess?" Barlow asks.

Zeke puts down his binoculars and shakes his head. "Nah," he says. He hands the binoculars to Barlow. "She's just some celebrity among the Night People. They defer to her and let her participate in the ceremony because she's so famous. It's a great honor to them to have her here. They call her the Queen of the Night."

Looking through the binoculars, Barlow gasps. "My

god, that's *Belinda!*" He puts down the binoculars and stares at the scene with his unaided eyes and rubs them to make sure he's not seeing things. So I grab the binoculars from him to have a look myself.

Belinda! Showing off.

Barlow begins to cuss. He cusses a blue streak. And I begin to cuss too. Zeke starts trying to smother us to get us to shut up, but we're too discombobulated. We don't realize what a ruckus we're making until we look up and see a dozen white-faced men in robes surrounding us and pointing spears at our chests.

Oh, crap.

The man in the oversized savage mask steps forward. "Take them," he says.

They bind our wrists and jab us with the points of their spears until we start moving—down the trail into the hollow. The sounds of chanting grow louder as we approach. The Light Men and Dark Men have begun to dance.

7

THE COMMON
Reality 258
Moonglow Season

Have we lost Belinda? Is that what that last Reality was all about?

Or have we lost ourselves?

Every time we venture out of our Safe House, there's some wrenching new discovery awaiting us. We're afraid to move anymore.

What does it all mean?

We're never getting Reality 250 back—that's pretty clear. But we *have to* get Reality 250 back. It can't be *gone*. It's got to be out there somewhere. We want to go *home*.

We've lost all our friends. You're all we've got left, reader. Just knowing you're out there makes everything a little more bearable. We're hanging off a cliff. We're hanging onto *you*.

The Dangers—they're hunting us down one by one, and I'm afraid we're going to start winking out of existence one by one.

Things have not gotten any easier in Reality 258. No, they've only gotten worse. We've finally encountered Catterus. Nobody has to hire him—because he already wants to kill us all. He's already made his first attempt.

We're living in a nightmare. This Reality has been even harder on us than the last. We try to imagine we're in some sane place, some durable existence like yours. We need persistence. You're the only unchanging thing in our world now, reader. Stick with us. Keep us anchored. Keep us sane with your calm predictable true-world. We need a way out of this.

Help us pretend.

I've found out that Bert, the guard from the Flatiron Building, and Amos's friend Jordan Jordan both come from a Dark Season called Dewdrop, when the sense of smell dominated the culture, and ever since learning that, I've become fixated on smells. I've discovered that every person in my life has their own characteristic odor.

My sister Belinda smells like flowers—she's wild about them. Of course, Amanda likes flowers too, but she's more likely to smell like expensive fabrics and dry cleaning fluid because of the suits she always wears. Barlow always smells like sweat or soap, like he needs a shower or just took one. Cooper smells like leather and cologne, Cartmell like bubblegum or baby powder. She thinks if she puts baby powder in her blonde hair, it looks like she just washed it.

Zeke smells like polyester. He prefers the artificial fabrics. And Amos smells like tanning oil and charcoal smoke. I don't get the smoke part, so I asked my sisters, and they say they've noticed the same thing. Maybe it has to do with the Season he's from, or maybe he just likes to grill. I don't know what I smell like, so I asked Cartmell, and she says I smell like fresh laundry right off the clothesline. I guess it all depends on when or where you catch us.

In the Brotherhood Lodge, a brown-hooded Monk leads us through the round antechamber at the front door and down a long hallway lined with doors at intervals on both sides. We pass an open door on the left that leads to a swimming pool, and I'm assaulted by the odor of chlorine. I notice an office through an open door on our right, exuding the odor of toner. I'm tempted to walk through these doors and investigate, see how far I can get. But of course that could get us in deep trouble with the Brotherhood. We'd get kicked out for sure, and Amos would be really mad.

The rest of the doors are closed and probably locked, if the Monks' behavior is any indication. They carry big rings of keys, and I never see them pass through a door without unlocking it first or come out of a door without locking it behind them. I've heard a rumor about secret rooms in the Lodge filled with gold and hidden treasure, but I don't know if there's anything to it. No intruder's ever come out of the Lodge with treasure. They come out half-insane or not at all.

At the end of the hall, where the corridor turns left, we come to another open door, and we can see Amos inside, sitting in a wing-backed chair. He stands and greets us as a hooded Monk ushers us inside.

The Monk is pale-faced, expressionless and silent, and I'm startled when she points the way and I see from her hand she's a woman. She never speaks a word; the Monks seldom do.

"The Brotherhood Monks are women as well as men?" I ask Amos, once she leaves.

"Of course," Amos says. "It's not your usual kind of religious order. We study the *Parattak*. The robes are just to offer the Bystanders something they can relate to and to hide our Anachronistic appearance."

He looks us over and does a head count, and he's about to speak when I interrupt him. "Don't say it," I growl.

He doesn't miss a beat. "I'm glad to see you all." He urges us to take a seat on the yellow vinyl couch or in one of the red or yellow vinyl easy chairs. The room is lined floor to ceiling with bookcases. The whole room reeks of books and vinyl. There's a piano in one corner, a coffee table in front of the couch. Barlow and I sit on the yellow couch against the wall, and Amanda and Cartmell sit in the red easy chairs flanking the couch, and Zeke in one of the yellow easy chairs next to Amos. Pete takes Jackson and Jessalyn in the other direction to Room 999.

Belinda's not with us. She ran off with the Bystanders weeks ago, and we're not sure if she took Shelter or not. But Amos doesn't ask us about her, and we don't want to admit to our failure to protect her. It's as if he already knows about it and knows where Belinda is, just as he knows where Cooper is.

"Our library," Amos informs us, gesturing. "With books from over two hundred different Realities."

Barlow gazes around at the different volumes. "So you're in the Brotherhood too?"

"Yes," Amos says. "The Society intended it as a refuge across Time for Travelers, so they won't be forced to cause Alterations if they get stranded in the Past, but actually everyone who reveres the *Parattak* is welcome to join."

"The what?" Amanda says.

"The *Parattak*. It's a holy book written by an anonymous Longtimer. It's part Survival guide and part revelation. I intend to present you each with a copy." A holy book! As born-once atheists, none of us are interested in some holy book.

Another Monk appears pushing a cart with a tea service on it, and Amos stands and makes a small bow. The Monk bows back.

Amos motions us over. "I ordered tea and coffee for you, but of course you may have whatever you like."

Cartmell and Amanda have tea with Amos. Barlow says he doesn't want anything, and Zeke orders a lemonade.

"I'll just have some water," I say.

We ease into our chairs and are just getting comfortable when Barlow swears in surprise like he dropped a hot fritter in his lap.

"Did you get a load of that guy?" He's talking about the Monk, whose hood is so large his face is obscured from every direction but straight ahead. I look at him as he leaves the room but can't see anything.

"He has tattoos all over his face," Barlow declares.

Amanda shudders. "These Monks give me the creeps. They are so weird."

My experiences in the Moonglow Season are fresh in my mind, and compared to the Moonglowers I don't find the Monks that odd. I guess I've changed and things don't strike me as weird to me as they used to. "I don't think they're so strange, " I tell Amanda.

"Well, hello, Belinda," Amanda says to me. She

shudders again.

Amos takes a sip of tea and puts his cup on its saucer. "Dexter's right," he says. "The Monks are Longtimers like you'll be soon. To some of them, you may appear odd."

"Us?" Amanda says. "But we're so normal."

I have something to say to that, but I hold my tongue. Amos speaks for me. "But you aren't. Not to most of the Longtimers. Garson is completely normal where he comes from, Reality 239 in the Sideshow Season. You may appear quite odd to him and to people from other Seasons." There's a strange edge to his voice, as if he considers us abnormal himself.

"In the Sideshow Season, everyone tattooed their life history on their faces in symbols, their failures, their accomplishments, their beliefs, their allegiances. You had to just look at a man's face to know him. To him, you seem like suspicious characters who are trying to hide something, who don't have the decency or courage to tattoo your past on your face for all to see."

Amanda gapes, her mouth open. "Tattoo my face?" she says. "No way." She almost laughs. "It looks so ugly." She means the tattoos. Sideshow was a Dark Season, so Garson's tattoos are pretty strange.

"What you're experiencing," Amos tells her, "is called Chronophobia, the fear of things that are different from those in your own Timeline. Believe me, Garson is quite normal for his Sociochronic Group, and he's been a tremendous asset to the Brotherhood. The Sideshow Season lasted for only one Reality, and not much is known about it. Garson has been helpful in answering our questions and filling in the gaps in our understanding of his history and culture. You'll find him quite ordinary once you get used to him. Then it's only the Bystanders who will appear odd to you." Finishing his tea, Amos places the cup and saucer on an end table. He starts to say something, but Barlow interrupts him.

"Don't tell me. Chronophobia is another manifestation of our unhealthy Attachment to Past Life."

"That's right," Amos tells him.

Barlow groans. "To you everything's a manifestation of unhealthiness. Can't Past Life ever be a good thing?"

"Of course," Amos says. "Colonizing is good. So is keeping a journal. And recording and revering your own history. There are many positive manifestations of Past Life, but the past is a powerful drug and should be indulged in only briefly and carefully."

We're getting sick of being lectured about Past Life—as if being who we used to be is some sort of crime, but Amos insists we must come to a thorough understanding of it before we can move on to a consideration of the other eight Transkarmic Elements of Being. We don't know what he's talking about, I guess it's in the *Parattak*.

Amos pauses and joins his hands. His expression softens. "But that's not why I got you together today. I've ordered a van to pick us up here. I think it's time you met some Longtimers. You need to pay a visit to The Common sometime anyway. It's one of the requirements for Citizenship."

Citizenship is the next Phase of our Adjustment after Membership, which we're working toward now. Of course, none of us know what The Common is.

The Monk Garson re-enters the room and exchanges Nods with Amos and gives Zeke his lemonade.

"Why are you always bowing like that?" Barlow asks Amos in annoyance. "Have you turned Jap on us? Why the hell do you do that?"

I can't understand why Barlow's so ticked off. I guess it's because he's Dischronofiliated and worried about Belinda. He used to be respectful of everyone's ethnic culture back in Reality 250.

Amos looks at Barlow in surprise and then at the rest of us. "I thought I had told you. It's the Longtimer Nod. It's meant to silently acknowledge the losses we have suffered as a result of the Time Changes. The losses of the Longtimers are so great they cannot pass unremarked on, so we do a short bow so we can mourn them without dwelling on them."

Barlow squints and frowns but says nothing more. Amos sits and gestures to us to take more drinks and snacks from the cart. Garson begins to gather up our glasses and cups and saucers, and this time I get a good look at his face as he bends over to pick up Amos' cup. His face looks like an engineer's blueprint. He has parallel blue lines on his cheeks with notches and little circles and arrows in them and here and there a number, red lines along his jaw, purple dots on his temples, and green designs on his forehead. He smells like cotton robes like all the Monks, but I also detect a hint of cinnamon and cloves.

"What do they mean, those symbols on your face?" I ask him, forgetting the Monks are silent.

He's so startled by the question that he almost drops the cup and saucer. He freezes, crouched over, and stares at me.

"It's all right, Garson," Amos says. "These are my brothers and sisters. They belong to the Society. You can speak freely to them."

Garson turns away from me and straightens up. "Don't the symbols anything mean," he says. "Anymore not." He places the cup and saucer on the cart. Then he pauses. "Not's true no that. Still mean they do something. You that tell they a Longtimer I'm, and everything lost I've. I home no have. I people have no. Now my life tell the story of they."

He picks up the last cup and saucer and places them on his cart.

"But what did they used to mean?" I ask him.

He glances at me. "Is Past Life that all. No it significance now has." He turns and wheels the cart out of the room.

We watch him go. Barlow looks at me and twirls his index finger around his ear.

As Amos takes a long sip of tea, another Monk enters the room in a brown robe. I see by her hands that she's female. She has her hood down, and we can see there are tattoos all over her face just like Garson's. Apparently, she thought the room was empty, so when she spots us, she freezes in her tracks.

She's nobody I recognize, and at first I think it's another refugee from the Sideshow Season, but then Cartmell says, "Belinda, have you become a *Monk*?"

I can see a flushing from her neck up through her cheeks despite the tattoos. Her mouth has dropped open, and there's a doe in the headlights look on her face.

We're even more shocked than she is. Amanda gasps, but the rest of us are struck dumb—like the Guy in the Sky just hit the mute button. We're flabbergasted. This is even worse than when she joined those gangers.

We're a wax museum tableau for about five century-long seconds.

Amanda lets out a shocked obscenity, which jolts us because she never cusses. But we're all blown away. This is even harder to take than the Night People. For Amanda especially. She's the most afraid of what the Longtimer life may do to us, and she's clearly appalled by what's become of Belinda. "What the hell, Belinda?" Amanda says, "My god. Do you know what you look like?"

Belinda turns away and raises her hood so we can't see her face. And then she runs from the room.

Now the sickened exclamations come out, especially from Amanda. This is more than Barlow can take too, but he just sits there frozen in horror. I'm in shock too. Belinda—a Monk? I can't get over it. A Monk! My own sister? This is too much, too effing much.

Of course, Amos isn't startled. He's known it all along, so all he wants is to gloss it over and move us forward. "I've arranged for you to settle into the Lodge," he tells us, distracting us from Belinda, "once this Season is over. There are rooms available now, and I think it's time you get away from your Alternate Life and start studying full time for the Society Examination."

We're so focused on Belinda, we can't worry about what we're going to do next Season when Moonglow's over. We're still obsessed with Moonglow and its fallout.

"So where is it we're going today?" Cartmell asks Amos in an attempt to distract us from our discovery about Belinda. Cartmell's the only one of us who's in recovery mode. She probably already suspected what Belinda was up to and didn't tell us. Damn that little sneak!

She can get away with it because we all have a soft spot for Cartmell. We feel close to her, maybe because she's the youngest. But sometimes I suspect it's because she's manipulated us to feel that way.

Amos stands. "We're making a visit to The Common. It's the largest Safe House in Shawneetown, more of a resort. You'll see."

Amanda blinks as if waking up from her bad dream about Belinda. "Do we have time for that? Isn't there a Change coming soon?"

Amos shakes his head.

"What!" Barlow jumps up from his chair. "You mean you called us to the Lodge for nothing?"

I give him a nudge with my elbow. "You have something better to do, Barlow?"

He glares at me. "Yeah," he says. "About 365 things. I've got to get a job, remember? And it ain't so easy now that nobody's heard of me." He turns his dirty look on Amos.

"Get a job on a Saturday, Barlow?" I say. "Come on." But still my mind is reeling over Belinda's surprise.

Amanda is looking almost as annoyed as Barlow. Her upset is double now this has exploded on top of Belinda's bombshell. "It's bad enough having to come here when we're in danger, Amos. Why do you have to waste our time on a weekend? I have work to catch up on."

Amos regards us without smiling, like the detention monitor when he had to stay after school to punish misbehavers. He walks over to a bookcase and pulls on one of the volumes. The bookcase slides aside, revealing a narrow passage. He motions for us to follow him, and after a couple of suppressed groans, we go along, after stamping our feet a couple times.

I still can't get over what Belinda's done. Not just weird—almost a betrayal. I step ahead on tottering legs. The passage leads to small parking lot behind the Lodge. We climb into a white van with a bluish-green three-dimensional globe painted on the side, the logo of the Society. Our driver Tate wears a chauffeur's cap and the grey and white uniform of the Intertime Government.

Driving through the back gate, he takes Poplar Street out to Garfield, that is, the street that used to be Garfield. Here in the Moonglow Season it's the MacArthur Expressway. Turning north, he drives through New Town, or what used to be called New Town on Treeline Avenue, until we reach the area where the fairgrounds used to be. Only, now it's some kind of park. On a meadow at the edge of the park sits a round, silver-walled, four-story building that looks like a donut-shaped sculpture. This is The Common, a Safe House the size of a stadium.

Tate lets us out at the park. The weather feels unusually warm for February, and we walk across the meadow toward The Common. A stream of Longtimers walk both toward and away from it. We're glad to get out of the Brotherhood Lodge, but none of us can work up any enthusiasm for visiting some new weird place.

"That's a Safe House?" Zeke asks Amos. "It's enormous."

The only Safe Houses we've ever been in are Room 999 at the Brotherhood Lodge and Room 999 in the

Roebuck Tower, so of course The Common doesn't seem like a Safe House to us. It's more like Disneyland. So when I see this monstrosity ahead of us, I finally forget about Belinda.

"The Common is shaped like a torus," Amos tells us, "and when it enters the Void, the floor and rooms slide onto the outer wall, and the whole structure rotates, creating an artificial gravity."

"You mean this is some kind of Space Station?" I ask.

"Time Station," he corrects me. "Space Stations are only in the Three Dimensional Universe. But this is more than a Station. It's also a Safe House and a Ferry into the Fourth Dimension."

Gawd, I feel like such an ant! This place dwarfs everything, and I'm totally out of experiences to compare it to. It's just effing unbelievable. I mean, come on. I feel like I'm in a movie.

When we reach the gate outside The Common, we have to show our Society Membership cards to the security guards and take a breathalyzer test. They inspect us closely, comparing our faces to the pictures on our I.D.s and ask us When we come from and where we've been for the past couple of weeks. We pass inspection, but the guards grab hold of the guy behind us and hustle him to a holding cell for a Scan. Amos told us that sometimes a Traveler can be identified by the trace elements in his system. In different Realities trace elements in your breath can be found in different proportions, and if someone hasn't spent the last weeks in Moonglow or Wilderness, his trace elements will reveal that. Timecrimers who've been in the Void recently will have odd proportions of trace elements in their systems, and sometimes you can pinpoint the last Reality they spent in the Three Dimensional World, and if they can't account for the time in between, they can be detained for interrogation.

One of the guards has a nose ring, which Amanda

finds repellant and whispers her complaint into Cartmell's ear. Right inside the gate, a tall man in a reptile-skin coat and hat corners us and begins to harangue us.

"I have some fine Anachronisms here, rare and precious artifacts from Vanished Seasons both near and far." He leans toward me and opens his coat, revealing a pocket watch the size of a hamburger bun. "Admire the craftsmanship of this Wonder Watch from Masterpiece Season." He's wearing this vest that seems to change textures depending on how the light strikes it, like some kind of hologram (Amos told me Hologrammic Clothing was common in the Merchant Season, where Bungee's from).

"You're wasting your time, Bungee," Amos says to him. "These are Newcomers from Wilderness. They aren't interested in Anachronisms."

Bungee closes his coat. He has a thin face with a hook nose and an odd nasal accent. "This one is," he says, pointing to me. "He's very interested."

"Not in buying," Amos tells him. "He just wants to include you in his journal."

Bungee gives me a dirty look. "Journal!" He wags his finger at me. *"Leave me out of yer damn journal!"*

He looks pretty ticked, so I pull back from him. "Uh, sure," I say. "I won't mention you." He growls under his breath like he doesn't believe me but moves on to make his sales pitch to the next arrival.

We climb the ramp to The Common's outermost section and enter a broad hall with rounded walls more than two stories high. People of all sorts walk by us in the center. Along the inner wall are two stories of hotel rooms and suites partitioned by a glass wall, and along the curved outer wall are restaurants and shops. At intervals along the ceiling are huge television screens.

I look up at them. "Why are there TVs on the ceiling?"

Amos doesn't glance at them. "Those are for the 4th

Dimensional Network Broadcast during the Interval between Realities when The Common will be in the Void. The ceiling will become the outer wall once The Common starts spinning. The outer wall will become the floor and the floor the inner wall. The inner wall will become the ceiling."

Amos keeps walking, but I'm still staring around, and I have to run to catch up. "I thought you said the Interval lasts about sixty minutes. Why do they spin this thing?"

Amos doesn't bother to glance at me. "The Common has to stay in the Void for several days after every Change while the Society finds a place for it to relocate. It's a nonstop party here in the meantime."

The Longtimers who throng the long hall look like refugees from a movie studio, there are so many different kinds of fashions and costumes, everything from spacesuits to tuxedos. Along the outer wall to our left are sidewalk cafes with umbrella'd tables and potted plants. Restaurants and cafes are identified by the Season they're from and feature Extinct dishes and cocktails, stuff you've never heard of. At the Nevertime Café the dish is something called Rockefeller Risotto. When we get too close to one of the tables, a man in tinted glasses, a straw fedora hat, a bow tie, and a white suit from the Clockwork Season begins to yell at us.

"Get those Voidsucking Bystanders away from me!"

"These are Newcomers, not Bystanders, Mr. Sun." Amos explains to him. The man draws a gun from under his coat. "They're Bystanders to me, and I'm not putting up with them. Bystanders killed my brother. Get them away from me!" Apparently, Amos isn't the only Longtimer who carries a gun.

Amos begins to back up, and we back up with him. Amos Nods to the Clockworker. "My condolences for your loss, Mr. Sun." Amos smiles at him, but the guy's not watching. He's eyeing us.

"What's wrong with him?" Amanda asks once we're out of his hearing.

"People living under great stress are sometimes difficult to deal with," Amos tells her, facing forward. "I warned you about Hazard Number Five. Sometimes it's like the Wild West in here."

We continue down the mall that circles the Common, passing people who look odd to us as well ones that look ordinary—but none of them truly ordinary. There's always something off or out of date in their choice of clothes, some unusual accent to their voices. Even some strange and alluring scents. Most of the Longtimers ignore us, but some sneer.

The floor, the walls, the ceilings are all battleship gray, highlighted with a different color for each neighborhood we enter. We pass shops and kiosks but mostly restaurants and hotel lobbies. Even a few offices for Longtimer organizations or Intervoid businesses. Above us on both sides are two stories of balconies hung with flags—some of them from Alternate Realities—like the American flag with a triangular blue field and yellow fringe on three sides. Then there are the flags of the Longtimers: the violet and azure banner of the Pilot's Guild, the red setting sun of the Hara Kiri Season, the gold and blue bars and squares of the Nevertime Season. Finally, odd flags with colored patterns and symbols I don't recognize. The scenery passes in a blur, too fast for us to take it in, everything disappearing around the bend in a never-ending right arc, like a dream on steroids.

An Asian man in a white satin robe and cap strides up to us and greets Amos. He smells of lotus blossoms. "Good Time, Prefect." They Nod to each other, and Amos introduces us to him as we come to a stop. Eyeing his white robe, I'm wondering if he's some religious nut.

"Mr. Yen, I would like you to meet my family."

Mr. Yen's eyebrows go up, and he looks at Amos.

"They do not Nod?" He joins his hands underneath his wide sleeves, and I wonder if he's got a gun in there.

Amos gives us a reproving glance. "They are still Newcomers—and don't understand." He shoots us another sideways look to let us know what a disappointment we are.

Mr. Yen's mouth assumes a mild smile. "Let us practice then." He bows to us. "Now your turn," he says.

So we look at each other and bow like we're at charm school, except for Barlow. "We know how to bow," he mutters. "We're not idiots."

"Very strong willed," Mr. Yen declares. "They must be from the Wilderness Season." He regards us. "When are you all from?" he asks us.

We look at each other and don't know what to say. "Now," we tell him.

He smiles patiently. "When someone asks you that, they mean what Season are you from."

What *Season* we're from? How many effing Seasons are there?

Mr. Yen regards us coldly. "They don't seem to realize that Wilderness isn't the center of the Chronoverse."

Amos smiles warily as we're passed left and right by scattered parties of pedestrians.

Mr. Yen faces him. "They must be quite a disappointment compared to your family in the Promise Season."

"No," Amos says, "they're all right. They just need to learn how to Adjust."

His family in the Promise Season? Amos has another family? His face is red, and he's looking away from us. That surprises me because I've never known Amos to get embarrassed.

I found out afterwards that Mr. Yen was Amos's Sponsor when he was a Newcomer. I think he'd been hoping we'd make a good impression by surprising Mr. Yen with how well we've Adjusted. But not us. We're too stubborn. Now I can't help but wonder: why didn't

Amos tell us Mr. Yen was his Sponsor? Why did he keep it a secret?

Amos never talks about himself. Maybe he didn't tell us because he didn't want to put us on the spot. But sometimes I get the impression he doesn't talk because he doesn't want to be associated with us.

Mr. Yen looks us over again. "Not every Longtimer will be as sympathetic with you as I have been. There are some who will view you with contempt."

Contempt! "Why?" Cartmell asks.

"Because you are know-nothing Newcomers." He looks at Amos. "You shouldn't have brought them here so soon."

"They have to learn sometime," Amos says. "Sometimes you have to throw someone into the water to teach them to swim."

My Yen strokes the hairs of his thin beard. "A harsh approach."

"It's a harsh Cone."

Suddenly our Beepers start beeping, and our watch faces begin to flash. We look over at Amos. His eyeballs roll upward, and he grimaces. "Time Change," he says, though we already know that. The sound of chattering voices begins to grow steadily louder around us. The television sets above us come on, displaying the Fourth Dimensional Television Network Logo, which is an infinity symbol modified to look like a reveler's mask.

The crowd around us grows thicker as people exit the shops and hotels and restaurants. Some pedestrians hesitate and stare at the ceiling while others rush by in a great hurry.

Mr. Yen bows. "Excuse me. I have much to do." He backs up and disappears in the crowd. We look at each other.

"I guess we're going to have to weather the Change here," Amos declares without enthusiasm. He takes out his cellular and presses in numbers. Turning his back to us, he speaks into the mouthpiece in a low voice.

We're standing like deer on the highway. What are we going to do now? I'm hoping that Cooper and Belinda and Pete and the kids know about the Change and Take Shelter.

"Get out of the way!" someone yells at us, "You stupid Tourists." A group of three men in long coats shove us aside as they pass us at a trot. "You damn Toddlers."

Barlow has to show off and trips one of them up, and the guy draws a weapon from under his coat, a rifle made of a gold-steel alloy, almost white, with a short double barrel coiled in a spiral.

"What do you want?" he says. "Total Death or just Temporary Death?" He has a beard, earrings, intense gray eyes, and a headband of ragged white cloth with Japanese symbols on it, a leftover from the Hara Kiri Season.

When Barlow doesn't tremble or look scared, the Longtimer asks, "Who do you think you are, the Intertime Government?" He pokes Barlow with the barrel.

Amos presses his own double-barreled handgun of gold-steel alloy to the man's head. "No," he says. "That would be me."

The man lets go of his rifle, and it slips to the floor. He gives Amos a look of panic. "Prefect! Look, I don't want any trouble."

"Then get out of here," Amos tells him.

"Come on, Catterus," one of his companions cries. "You'll get the whole CTA on us if you fire that thing in here. Let's go." Both of them have earrings, ugly expressions and one hand inside their coats.

Catterus picks up his weapon. "I'll settle with you later," he says to Barlow. The three of them turn, and they rush away from us.

"That was foolish of you, Barlow," Amos snaps at him. "You shouldn't interfere with people when you have no idea who they are. We're not in Reality 250 anymore. You could have gotten us irreversibly killed."

Barlow watches the guys in coats run off. He's totally disoriented. He doesn't know what he's doing or what he's just done. Catterus gives him one final look through narrowed eyes before merging into the thronging crowd.

"Who was that?" I ask.

Amos glares at me and looks away. "Travelers," he answers finally.

Travelers? Right here in The Common?

"Aren't you going to call the authorities or something?" I ask him.

"I already have."

Loudspeakers on the ceiling begin to announce a warning about the upcoming Time Change. I look at the television screen and see storm clouds shooting out lightning bolts and rolling across the countryside toward a city. White lettering across the bottom of the screen reads "18th Meridian, New Harmony."

"Please secure yourselves for Null Gravity in Five Minutes," a loudspeaker commands in an echoing voice. "The Common will be entering the Void in Five Minutes and counting. Five minutes to Dropout."

"We need to get over to the wall," Amos says to us. He looks for an opening in the traffic so we can cut across

I wish Amos hadn't brought us here. Because this place is not normal. It's about as far from normal as any place I've ever been. As we continue through the Common, I keep thinking we'll get back to where we started. But everything around us is constantly new, constantly different, none of it familiar even though we're walking in a circle

Barlow has a zombie stare on his face, and I realize he's so stunned he can't keep up with what's happening. He's like some dazed animal.

Amanda's face is twisted in anguish. "Get us out of

here, Amos," she pleads. She looks like she's going to be sick.

Amos regards the panicked Longtimer crowd with a sour expression and ignores Amanda.

Toddlers, I think. That's us. We're frightened and dizzy and staring around like rubes on their first trip to Shawneetown. What the hell are we supposed to do? We don't have a clue.

We're in the Big Time now—and not ready for it.

I keep thinking about what Mr. Yen said. We must look pretty strange to all the Longtimers who're passing us. None of them are from Wilderness or Moonglow. I don't have the slightest idea who these people are, but they know who we are. They can recognize Newcomers a mile away.

I look at the Longtimers passing us with intense, deliberate expressions, then at my bewildered brothers and sisters, milling about aimlessly like wind-up dolls. I look at the colorful and flamboyant fashions of the Longtimers and at our drab garb from Reality 256. The Longtimers know where they're going and how to get there. We look like hicks on their first day in the city.

Who are the freaks now?

The voice on the loudspeakers drowns out the crowd noise. "The Common will be entering the Void in three minutes. Three minutes and counting. Three minutes to Dropout."

"Now," Amos commands, signaling with his hand. He cuts across the Promenade with Zeke and Cartmell, but Barlow and Amanda are too slow. I start across but hang back to help them.

"Come on," I say, but we're too late. The gap in the throng has closed up.

"Two Minutes to Dropout," the loudspeaker declares. "The Common will be entering the Void in Two minutes and counting."

The foot traffic begins to thin out as the Longtimers

move toward the inner wall. I grab Barlow's and Amanda's hands and drag them across the Promenade to where Amos is standing, holding a strap like a commuter. I look for a strap to grab onto, but the straps on both sides of Amos are taken.

"One minute to Dropout," the loudspeaker declares. "The Common will be entering the Void in one minute and counting."

"Get away!" Amos cries to us. "Down the Promenade. Find yourself something to hang onto!"

Amanda and Barlow just stand there like retarded idiots in a coma. They look so weird the way they stare around The Common, hearing but not understanding. I grab both their wrists and pull.

"Come on!" I cry at them, but they don't want to leave Amos, and they keep dragging me back.

"What should we do, Amos?" they slobber.

"Get away!" he yells at them. "Find yourself a Perch." Finally, I get them to move, but it's slow going. It seems all of the straps along the wall are taken.

"Prepare for Dropout," the loudspeaker declares. The voice overhead booms out loudly over the chattering crowd. "The Common is entering the Void in T-minus ten seconds and counting." The voice begins to count off the seconds, and I look for something to hold onto. I reach for the nearest strap, but the Longtimer holding it, someone in Rainbow colored clothes, shoves me away from him with his boot.

"Get away from me, you freak."

Me the freak? Me?

I feel the floor beneath us begin to rumble. I try to grab hold of another strap, but Barlow's in the way. My feet rise off the floor as we enter the Void, and Barlow starts gyrating in midair and knocks into me, sending me somersaulting through The Common.

The Rainbower curls his lip as he watches me pass by him through the air. "Damn Newbies."

The floor begins to move to the side, the Promenade

and shops and hotels as a single unit, leaving the Longtimers hanging like bats from their straps along the wall, which will soon become the ceiling.

8

STRATEGY
Reality 259
Moonglow Season

Danger Number Three. Timecrimers.

As if Danger Number Two—Bystanders—wasn't enough!

And Danger Number Five—other Longtimers! It's out to get us, reader. This Death World is out to get us.

And worst of all: Danger Number Seven from ourselves. We're cracking up, reader, and I'm afraid the family is breaking up, too—we're about to go our separate ways, and if that happens, we're doomed.

But you're on our side, aren't you? You're rooting for us. We depend on that. Sometimes it seems like you're the only thing keeping us alive.

I think about you, reader. I think about you a lot. Who are you? Maybe you're me, and I'm only talking to myself. Or you're one of my brothers or sisters. I hope not. I hope we have more than just us to depend on, more than us rooting us on.

You're no stranger to me, reader. I know you. You're my confidant, my confessor. You're someone just like me. Just trying to Survive, trying to get by, get ahead in life, make a career, create relationships. Maybe you're just starting out like me—or starting over. Maybe you're lonely too. And more than a little stressed out. Thanks for listening, You can't imagine how good it feels to have a friend.

Or maybe you can—because I'm your friend, too, aren't I? You have me to depend on. I'm here for you just like you're here for me. You're not alone, so I guess you *can* imagine how good that feels. So feel it. Can you sense it now—the warmth of having a friend? Amos says it's important to appreciate the things we still have. We have each other, and we need to experience that, reader.

I'm feeling you there on the other side of this page. Can you feel me, too—on my side? I can feel the warmth of another person just out of my sight. You're there. I know you are. Because I can sense your presence.

Can you sense mine?

This is all leading us somewhere, reader, leading us to our destiny. What is it—and how can we get there?

It's taken me awhile to recover from my sprained ankle and other injuries sustained in The Common, but I've been hobbling around on a cane to classes and mending at home as much as possible. I'm not the only one who sprained his ankle. But a sprained ankle is the least of Barlow's problems. Because he was careening out of control, too. The Common Constables in jet-packs came after us, but before they could corral Barlow, he wrecked into one of the Longtimers hanging from a strap on the ceiling. And it wasn't just any Longtimer—it was the one they call Catterus.

Catterus drew his Void Rifle from beneath his coat to fire at Barlow, but Barlow was flailing around in a panic and accidently pulled on Catterus's arm, which jerked his trigger finger, and his weapon discharged, knocking one of his crew into the Void.

You can't live more than a few minutes in the Void, so this guy was a goner. Well, that caused a big stink, of course, and the Common Constables swarmed the area, and the Intertime Police showed up, too—before Catterus's weapon could recharge. He and his buddies had to high-tail it out of there. They stole a Void Shuttle and disappeared into the Deep.

I told Barlow it wasn't his fault a Traveler got Voided. It was just an accident. The Intertime Police blame Catterus—for breaking the law by bringing a dangerous weapon into The Common. Forbidden technology. Super-secret. He shouldn't even know about Void Rifles, much less have one. So it was all his fault. But I don't think he got the memo. He was pretty ticked off when he left.

Amos is waiting for us on a walkway overlooking a

broad drainage canal in the Catacombs beneath Shawneetown for our family meeting in this Reality. My brothers and sisters and I follow a path through the darkness of the manmade cavern and descend a wrought-iron staircase to the granite walkway below. Amos straightens up from the railing he's leaning on and turns to welcome us. He's wearing a tan suit with broad angular lapels from Reality 200.

Now that we know his meetings do not coincide with Time Changes, they have started to seem, well, avoidable. So I'm wondering if everyone's going to show up today.

This evening, Amos is in full drill sergeant mode. He does his head count and comes up one short, so instead of Nodding or saying "hello," his first words to us are "Where's Amanda?" A Timestorm gathers over his brow as he waits for our answer. We all know where she is, but no one knows what to say to Amos. We just stand there, listening to the dripping drainage pipes.

Amanda's husband Pete finally breaks the silence. He lowers baby Jessalyn's feet to the ground and holds her up by her hands. "Amanda said she had some important bank business to attend to."

Amos scowls and adjusts his black-rimmed glasses. "She knows better than that. Nothing is more important than these meetings. Do you think I have time for this? I have work to do the same as her." He gives us the eye. "Nobody misses these meetings from now on. You get me?"

I understand why he's so upset. Our last few meetings have not gone well, and we've have been reluctant to come back. All Amos gives us is a lot of bad news. He lectures us and scolds us and scares us so bad it makes our bones ache.

Amos squares his shoulders and takes a step toward us, menacing us with his hugeness. "Go get her, Barlow," he says. "Do whatever it takes. Just get her here."

Barlow's the only one of us who isn't physically

intimidated by Amos, partly because he's a big looming hulk himself. And partly because he's the third oldest in the family, after Amanda. Barlow lifts an eyebrow, his eyes gleaming. "Even if she doesn't want to come?"

"Especially if she doesn't want to come. Just don't get into any trouble with the Bystander police."

Barlow smiles. "Don't worry—I can handle 'em." He knows just what to say. Anyway, he used to. He doesn't blend in with the Locals anymore. He's got on his crimson and black letter jacket with the four stripes on the arm from each of his seasons with the Shawneetown U football team. It's an Anachronism. But none of the rest of us can handle Amanda, so Amos sends him.

As he leaves us to get Amanda, he looks pretty eager, because I think he'd rather wrestle with her than grapple with our Time Adjustment problems. I think he's relieved to escape Amos's lecturing. Lately, Amos has gotten as bad as Dad about criticizing us. I don't think he realized the negative impact he was having last time we met, but he's probably figured it out since. He knows he's got to win us over today or we're all likely to follow Amanda's example and stop coming to these meetings.

I didn't want to come either, but if I'd stayed home, it would have been a dead giveaway I haven't quit school like Amos advised. I've been hoping to keep my decision to stay in school secret.

My college career is back on track now. I'm on schedule to graduate next May with my degree in civil engineering. So Amos was wrong that I have to give it up. In three more semesters I'll graduate. Then I can get a good job and have a life. Be my own person instead of "brother of." So it's me versus the Time Changes now. Will I get to have a life, or will all that be taken away from me? I'm betting on the former, and Amos is betting on the latter.

Thanks a lot, Amos.

Following Amos's advice has not made my life

easier. I know it's not his fault. It's the Time Changes that have messed up everything, but it's hard not to blame him. Sure, he's right about Barlow and Amanda needing to move on. He's right about everyone in the family except me. I'm not extraordinary like them. I'm different, and Amos forgets that.

I look around and notice Belinda and Cooper aren't here either, but that doesn't concern Amos. Belinda's already given up on becoming a Monk. She turned up in the middle of the night at Amanda's Alternate Residence in some weird get-up of silver face paint and Nagaran clothes and got the rest of her stuff from Cartmell, then took off. She didn't explain a thing, of course. None of us have seen her since. And don't expect to.

And Cooper? Who knows? Probably in some bar or dive or poker game in some seedy hotel. He's a lost cause. There's no sense in trying to hunt him down.

Amanda's closest to Amos in the family, Barlow's closest to Belinda, Zeke's closest to Cartmell, and I'm closest to Cooper. We hung out a lot when we were kids. He played a lot of practical jokes on me, but he also taught me things: how to play poker, how to cheat at cards, how to pick a lock, open a locked car, hot wire the engine, do a 180, lose a pursuer. He's been the best bad influence a guy could have. I just hope he knows what he's doing now.

Once Barlow leaves on his errand, Amos seems to relax. He joins the fingertips of his hands together in front of him as he regards us. "Time before last we were discussing Coping Strategies when we got interrupted, and I want to return to that subject." He pauses and clears his throat. "As Longtimers, you're going to experience so much change you're going to need some kind of Strategy for dealing with it. I can't tell you for sure which Coping Strategy each of you will choose, but I gave you a list of the Nineteen Most Common ones last time, and I hope you've given them some thought."

Do you think you could Survive in Amos's Time

World without more training? It all comes down to that all-important item, your Strategy. What are you going to put between yourself and the changes? How are you going to process them, deal with them, make sense of them so you don't get overwhelmed?

Amos looks at us like he's teaching us the ABC's that we should have learned a long time ago. I can tell he's struggling to be patient. He's trying not to act like we're the stupidest people on the planet, but we're such a bunch of Time Morons that even kindergarten seems like postgrad study to us.

Taking a deep breath, he regards us with a smile. "Zeke, for example, will probably use his intelligence as his means of dealing with his situation. He will become what we call an 'Analyzer.' Analyzing his environment will be his way of Coping with it. He will probably have no other choice. We all have to adapt to our environment by the only method that suits us."

Zeke, who's been deep in thought, suddenly looks up at Amos and adjusts his own glasses with black rims like his brother's. "Are these Adaptive Strategies all equally successful?" he asks.

Amos shifts his weight. "No."

Zeke brushes his short bangs off his forehead. "Then shouldn't everybody pick the single most effective Strategy and use that?"

"People aren't the same," Amos tells him. His voice grows louder as he loses his patience. "Don't try to use someone else's Strategy. Stick with your own strengths."

We hear the sound of rushing water below us, as if someone's opened the floodgates. Zeke hesitates. He has to speak loud to be heard over the noise of the water. "You're implying that being an Analyzer isn't the best Strategy for these circumstances."

"It isn't." Amos turns away from us and looks at the cascading water pouring into the drainage tunnel. He joins his hands and lets them dangle over the railing.

"Analyzers do just fine—for awhile. But eventually they go Chrono because these circumstances are just too complicated to analyze."

We're taken aback by Amos's bluntness. I guess he forgets we don't already know this stuff, haven't yet Adjusted to our life in Hell. Maybe he's gotten tired of being careful around us.

Zeke gulps, and Amos turns and tries to smile. He's realized his callousness. "Of course, I've never heard of an Analyzer as smart as you, Zeke. If anyone can make Analyzing last, it's you."

Zeke mulls over Amos's words, trying to decide whether to accept his leadership. I'm sure he didn't like hearing Amos's fatal diagnosis any more than Amanda liked the bad news he told her about her job at the bank.

The sound of pouring water stops. Zeke looks up at Amos with a resigned expression, and I know Amos has won him over. "I suppose you're right," he says. "This situation allows for enormous complexity, and there's a limit to how much my mind can process. If I try to solve the entire Time Travelling Problem at once, I probably will go Chrono. The solution is to break it down into subsets and focus on each, one at a time rather than trying to grapple with the whole problem."

Cartmell and I glance at each other. Solve the entire Time Traveling problem? Zeke has taken an enormous bite.

"You think the Time Changes are just another calculation you can solve?" I ask him. Zeke's being grandiose again.

"Of course," he says, drawing in a breath as if we're out in the fresh air. "Any problem that science can create, science can solve. It's just a matter of finding the right approach, working through all aspects of the problem, one by one. Of course, that could take years."

Amos smiles, gratified that Zeke is at least taking things seriously. "I believe law enforcement will have the problem settled before then, Zeke."

Zeke looks up and adjusts his glasses. "Settled maybe but not solved. What's to stop the same problem from popping up in the future? Only a scientific solution can truly solve this problem."

Amos rubs his hands together and regards me. "Now, Dexter, you're smart, too, but you shouldn't try to be an Analyzer. Sometimes people are tempted to adopt a Strategy that doesn't fit them, and that never works."

Not an Analyzer? Me? I'm nothing but an Analyzer. What makes Amos think otherwise? I try not to take the remark as an insult—but it is what it is. "I looked at the list you gave us," I tell him, "but none of the Strategies on it stand out to me. I can see myself using any of them."

"I don't know," Amos says. "Maybe you'll be an Opportunist like Cooper. They don't try to analyze anything. They take advantage of each opportunity as it presents itself. You'll naturally settle on the best Strategy for yourself. Don't let anyone else pick yours for you."

An Opportunist? What a backhand slap! I scratch my cheek, feeling peeved at Amos for insulting my intelligence. I know I'm not a genius like Zeke, but I have an A- average in my engineering courses. I can be an Analyzer.

"What about me?" Cartmell asks Amos eagerly. "What Strategy will I choose?"

Amos smiles at her and begins to walk along the railing beside the canal. "An Assimilator, I'd guess. Assimilators use their emotions to help them cope. They connect with other people to ensure their common Survival. It's one of the most successful Strategies."

Cartmell smiles like she's won a popularity contest. Amos has made her day. She's clearly in his camp, and that gives him a total of three committed supporters so far, because Cooper has already sided with him. I can tell, because Amos never mentions him, as if he already knows he has Cooper's support.

I realize my mind has wandered, and I catch Amos in mid-sentence. ". . . should have started reading the *Parattak*. There are copies in the library of the Lodge. You should be learning and practicing Mams."

Amos regards us like he's waiting for confirmation, so we're shuffling our feet and nodding, trying not to disappoint him. Meanwhile, we steal looks at each other when he isn't watching. Mams? What is he talking about? The *Parattak*? He actually expects us to read that thing? We don't have time for that.

Barlow arrives, carrying Amanda over his shoulder like a sack of potatoes. He's grinning and whistling as he skips down the stairs to the walkway, the show-off. He plants Amanda on her feet right in front of Amos. She immediately turns to leave, but Barlow blocks her way. So she crosses her arms and stands there with a sullen look on her face.

None of us like it down here. It's so dank it's like breathing through a snorkel. It smells like a bathtub.

Kidnapping Amanda has not warmed her to the idea of becoming a Longtimer. Winning her over to Amos's point of view seems hopeless. And I realize if Amanda finds some excuse to quit Amos's Sponsoring, Barlow will probably duck out too, because things have not been going well for Barlow since Amos's Sponsoring began. And if I take their side, the family will be split down the middle, and Belinda won't be able to make up her mind what to do. She'll try to straddle the Threshold. And with the family split up, Cooper will go off on his own, and I don't know what Cartmell and Zeke will do. Maybe they'll back out too. Or maybe Amos will give up on all of us.

"Welcome back to the family," Amos says to Amanda with a conciliatory gesture. "I'm glad you're here. We need you to be here."

Amanda turns away from him and acts like she isn't listening. Sometimes I don't want to listen either because I feel like the Brotherhood of Time is some kind of cult that's trying to control us.

"My government duties are becoming more pressing," Amos declares. "And the time is approaching after your Sponsorship is over, when I'll have to go back to work full time, and I won't be here to guide you or take care of your problems."

Amos is going to leave us? I can hardly believe it. How can we get through this without him?

I have a sour taste in my mouth. "But you said we need to stick together. How can you leave us? You said we need to support each other."

"That's true," Amos admits. "But I don't have any choice. I have an entire government structure to support me. All you've got is each other." He pauses while we absorb what he's telling us.

"The person who poses the greatest threat to your Survival is yourself. You're Threat number Seven. Your own mistakes, your own bad judgment, your own Fallacies, your own illusions. Who's going to guard you against those? Chance are, you won't even notice them. Only someone who cares about you can help you fight against the Seventh Threat." He looks around at us. "And that means your family. They're the only edge you've got, and you'd better learn to appreciate that. Because you're going to experience more change and loss in the next twelve months than most people experience in an entire lifetime. And who's going to see you through that? Who's going to be there for you? Each other, that's who. That's all you've got, all that may stand between you and Annihilation."

"Naturally," he says, "once I'm no longer around, Amanda will take command of the family and will be your guide. You'll take your orders from her."

"Me?" Amanda exclaims in surprise.

I guess it makes sense. She's the oldest, after Amos. And she has leadership experience at the bank. She knows as much about the Longtimer life as any of us.

And Barlow, the next oldest, is in no shape to lead us. He walks around in a daze most of the time, like someone's whacked him in the back of the head with a board. In his current state, I don't think he could lead a pack of cub scouts. Of course, Cooper's almost as old as him, but he's never around.

"You see, Amanda," Amos says, "why you have to be here, why you all need to be here. You're not just training to be Longtimers—you're training to save each other. You need to be there for your brothers and sisters, to keep each other on track. Your participation is vital."

I can see the surprise on Amanda's face turn into thought, and thought turn into acceptance. She will be in charge of the family. She will be the one making the decisions, not Amos. We all need her, even Amos, and his plan can't work without her. She's indispensible. So it's up to her now, not me.

Amanda can't resist the power that Amos has offered, can't resist being the boss and saving the family. It like he's given her her own Time Machine and permission to use it all she wants. When she uncrosses her arms, I know she's come over to his side in this.

"I'm not quitting my bank job, Amos," she declares, letting him know who's boss.

Amos smiles, aware of his victory. "You will," he says, "once the Time Changes make you give it up," letting her know who the real boss is.

Five more Seasons. That's all we need to get through. Just five more Seasons. Then we'll be Members in charge of ourselves.

We hear a motorboat racing toward us from down the canal, but Amos ignores the sound as if people boat down the canals all the time.

"I've arranged to have you move into the Brotherhood Lodge for the remainder of your Initiation," Amos says. "The Lodge has a dormitory on the third floor. You'll be safe there and can devote your time to studying for the Society Examination."

"What!" Amanda cries out like she's just got stung by a bee. She's clearly not pleased with the new living arrangements.

"It's to protect you from your Alternate Life," Amos tells her. "Before *it* becomes hazardous to your Survival."

The sound of the motorboat cuts off just before it reaches us.

"Hazardous how?" Amanda has her arms crossed. She's clearly unconvinced. She doesn't want to move out of her cushy house into some dormitory.

We hear the sounds of the motorboat hitting the side of our overlook and footfalls up the granite steps. A figure looms up out of the darkness. Amos shines his phone light at the intruder, and we all recognize him. It's our brother Cooper. Amos has his gun in one hand and his phone in the other.

"Howdy, everybody," Cooper greets us. "I was hoping I could find you here." He's wearing his usual leather jacket, and I can smell his cologne. We're all glad to see him, but for him to show up at this meeting is a real shocker—and Amos seems the most surprised of all.

"What are you doing here?" he asks, putting away his gun.

"I just have a quick question. Maybe it's nothing." Cooper shrugs and glances around at us. "A notorious Void Pirate was spotted in Shawneetown today, hanging around an apartment complex in Junction."

A Void Pirate! We all remember when Pirates attacked us in the Void back at the beginning of Moonglow—and it is not one of our golden memories.

Cooper pauses and inspects our startled faces. "He eluded capture, but we looked up the names of the tenants." He stares directly at me. "Is there some reason a Void Pirate would call on your Alternate Self in this Reality?"

I regard him in shock. My Alternate Self? Sure, he's

different than me. But in league with the Timecrimers? No way.

Amos's face has turned dark. He seems angry. "Would the name of this Pirate be Catterus, by any chance?"

We whip our heads around in surprise—but Cooper looks more surprised than us. "Yeah," he says. "The Terror of the Void himself. How did you know?"

The Terror of the Void! We've ticked off The Terror of the Void? And now he's coming after me? Or is he only looking for Barlow?

We all turn to look at Barlow—then Amos.

"He's coming after all of you," Amos informs us, "not just Barlow. That's the way he works. The only reason you're still alive is because Catterus doesn't know Amanda's last name is Vaughn, so he hasn't been able to find her Alternate Residence." He turns to look at Cooper. "We're going to have to expunge her marriage from the Bystander records."

Cooper's beginning to catch on, and his frown turns into a grin. He wags a finger at us. "Have you guys been playing Bait the Bear with Catterus?"

We're flinching at his mention of that old childhood game of ours, the one that would always get us into trouble. We didn't know Catterus was a Void Pirate. It's not our fault he's on a vendetta against us. We're not ready to deal with him.

"That does it," Amos declares. "I'm moving you all into the Brotherhood Lodge next Season—just as soon as

9

LIGHT SEASON
Reality 260
Guidepost Season

This journal has become my refuge, my time with my best friend. It helps to have someone to talk to, even if you can't talk back. I think of you as someone who's a good listener. Someone sympathetic. The world needs people like you, reader. *I* need you. Because as I said, you're all I've got. You're the one dependable thing in my otherwise chaotic existence.

I don't know anything about you, but believe me, you're the most ordinary, sane, and steady person I deal with on a regular basis. Ironic, huh? Here you are carrying on a conversation with someone from a different Reality in time, and *you're* the normal one. Thanks for being here for me. I know my story must sound nuts—but I'm telling it to you the way it really happened. If I was going to lie, I'd make up something more believable than *this*.

Just another month and a half, and my junior year will be over. The job interviews have started. They'll all at Bystander firms, of course, but I ought to be able to parlay that into a job in the Timeflow once I'm a Citizen of Time. I'll only be a civil engineer, of course, but even the Timeflow should need civil engineers.

I've been rooming with Zeke in Amanda's Alternate Residence since no one wants to room with Barlow now. He still has no karma, and he keeps having bad dreams and waking me up. Besides, he snores.

Today, Zeke's sitting at the end of the bed, reading, and I'm at the headboard, propped up with a couple of pillows, when I say to him, "You know, no one can Sponsor someone until they become a Longtimer, and you have to Survive seven Seasons before you're a Longtimer."

Zeke glances over his shoulder at me. "Yeah, duh, Dexter. I've studied for the test too, you know." He acts like I've just told him the solution to two plus two. He thinks I'm trying to show off.

I let that go. "Yeah, well, Amos says he's from the Masterpiece Season, but that's only a few Seasons ago, and that's impossible because how could he be Sponsoring us now if he's a Masterpiecer?" I let that thought sink in. I let my words expand into the air, filling up the room. "And how can he have a Reality 238 suit anyway, if he's from Reality 242?" I pause. "And his accent—that's not a Masterpiece accent—there's no melody in it. You know they like to sing every third sentence."

Now Zeke has twisted around, and he's staring at me. So I go on. "At the very least, Amos is from the Nagara Season, but I think he's Longer than that, a lot Longer. I think he hails from way back, from one of the early Seasons. You heard him call Mr. Sun by name, and he's from Clockwork. And Mr. Sun was at the Nevertime Café, and Nevertime was the first Season. How does Amos know Mr. Sun so well if he isn't from one of the early Seasons?"

Zeke looks aside and considers what I've said. Neither of us speak for a couple of minutes. Then Zeke says, "If I didn't know you better, brother, I'd think you have a brain in your head."

I don't know if that's supposed to be an insult or a compliment—probably both—but I'm too focused on my thoughts to care. I can tell Zeke doesn't want to give me the benefit of the doubt, though, because he says, "The question is what difference does it make? And does he have a good reason for not telling us? If he wanted us to know, he'd have already told us. So we may never find out the reason."

He thinks he's got it figured out, but I've already thought of that, and I've got an answer for it.

"What if he's Sponsored us before?" I say, "and we didn't make it?"

Zeke frowns like I've caught him at a mistake in math. So I go on.

"He wouldn't want our past failure to discourage us. And naturally, if he's from one of the early Seasons, you gotta wonder why he hasn't Sponsored us before."

Zeke nods, but he doesn't say anything because I think he's catching up to the same thought I'm having, but I say it out loud anyway.

"What if he's Sponsored us not just once but multiple times—and we perished every time? He wouldn't want to tell us that, would he?"

The implications expand, and they're not very pretty.

"And if Amos is NOT from one of the early Seasons, how does he know so many Longtimers and how has he become so powerful that he's got a job with the Intertime Government?"

So the only reasonable conclusion is we're a bunch of washouts. Amos harangues us constantly because he knows—from experience—that we're not going to make it, that we don't have what it takes to Survive. Only Cooper seems to have Survived longer than Wilderness, but I don't go into that, don't follow my thoughts there or delve into the further implications of that dicey puzzle.

For once Zeke doesn't care for logical reasoning. He doesn't like the conclusions we're drawing any more than I do. He's got this look on his face like he's just found out he's adopted.

"Don't tell the others," he says. "And don't bring it up again. I don't want to think about it."

But he can't help it, of course. He can't help but wonder why we washed out and what might have happened in the Neverbeen. And he knows Amos isn't going to tell us squat. Not that we really want to know, it's so depressing. I probably shouldn't have told Zeke, but I had to talk to someone. And besides, he would have figured it out himself eventually. I was hoping he'd already figured it out and would have something encouraging to say so I won't feel so sick inside.

"We've got to make it this time," I tell him. "Because if we don't, Amos may give up on us. This may be our fourth and final chance."

And if we fail, we'll eventually get Wiped Out of the Timestream for good.

We found out from Amos that the average Timespan of a Bystander is less than two hundred Realities. After that, they're Wiped Out of Time forever. They not only Are no more, they've never Existed in the first place. They've joined the Neverbeen. Amos says the entire human race is made up of different people now than before the Time Machine was invented. The human race from the first fifty Realities is Extinct, except for the Longtimers. Billions and billions of people. The Longtimers refer to this as the Time Holocaust. And now I'm fearing the Vanns are on the endangered list.

My thoughts are interrupted by my Beeper, and I glance down to see my Blinker flashing. The face of Zeke's watch is flashing too. So we call to our brothers and sisters to hurry because we have to get to the Brotherhood Lodge pronto. It's a long drive all the way from Ledford. I can see now why Amos recommends living in the Lodge. We barely make it in time.

Amos is out on business, and Cooper's doing stunt work in California, and not even Ingersol knows where Belinda is, so it's only the five of us in Room 999 with Pete, Jackson, Jessalyn, Garson, Greta, and Brother Samuels. We belt ourselves in, pass a bottle of Chianti and get ready for the show. When we launch into the Void, everyone's a little tense and worried about what the next Reality's going to be like. Will we still be in Moonglow—or will it be a new Season like Amos said, and if so, will it be Light or will it be Dark? How much more change are we going to have to deal with? We're as nervous as brokers at the bell on Wall Street.

The Fourth Dimensional Television Network broadcast comes on, with the title "260th Time Change." We get a view of Shawneetown from the Antenna Tower atop the Posey Building. A camera slowly rotates, searching the horizon for Timestorms. It stops once it's pointed east. That means the Timestorm will come from the east and move westward across town.

Things look pretty tranquil and dull for awhile. It's a clear, sunny day, and you can see all the way down Main Street and across the Wabash River to the edge of town miles away. Nothing is happening except for an occasional bird or plane, and I'm wondering if this is a false alarm, when I catch sight of clouds gathering in the distance.

The wind picks up, blowing east, sending trash flying down Main Street. It's actually the Timestorm, sucking everything up. As the Timestorm approaches, you can see a wall of clouds from sky to ground, rumbling across the landscape. The camera begins to vibrate as the wind steadily increases in intensity. People and cars begin to scatter before it like insects. Lightning bolts trace down from the sky in jagged webs. The picture is without sound, but the noise must be deafening. People and cars are being picked up and pulled backwards. Trees are uprooted and fly across the sky. Everything is swirling like a spiral of debris being pulled down a drain, and it's getting hard to see anything. And when the camera blacks out, I don't know if it's escaped into the Void or been sucked up by the Timestorm.

The static of the video feed is replaced by a placard reading PLEASE STAND BY. Soothing music plays in the background.

I realize I feel weightless and items are floating around the room—a cup, a pen, a *Parattak*. I look around at the startled faces of my brothers and sisters. Some of them have their eyes closed. The Time Holocaust is not easy to watch. But everyone comes wide awake when the Timecast starts. We pay close attention this time. We don't want to get ambushed like in Moonglow. Zeke has a pen and a notebook ready so he can take notes.

Myra Case appears in the studio wearing her silver suit and ear-buds. She's dark-haired in her late thirties with a pale complexion and green eyes, and she's sitting behind a prop desk and being handed pages by someone off-screen, but she's staring ahead and obviously reading off a teleprompter.

"Hello, everyone," she says. "This is Myra Case reporting on the 260th Time Change." She pauses. "Early reports indicate this Change emanates from Deep in the Past—a seventeen Range—so we're expecting a complete change of Season. The new Season has been given the designation 'Guidepost'."

That doesn't sound so bad, if the name's any indication, but all of us are wary about the Season ending, not that we have any fondness for Moonglow. We'll miss Moonglow about as much as we miss Riley.

There's a long pause, and text begins to scroll down the screen, indicating the Timestorm's path across Missouri, Kansas and Colorado. It leaves everything calm and organized behind it. The swirling chaos and debris precede it. Its origin was apparently somewhere on the East Coast. When the scrolling ends, we know the Timestorm is over.

There's another pause as the Spotters send in their Reports. Data flows in from around the world, and in the background, you can see people scurry across the set like they're late to class.

"We take you now live to our correspondent Red Phillips in Three Dimensions in downtown Shawneetown."

The screen goes blank for several seconds, and all of us are holding our breath like pearl divers. Then a picture pops on the screen of Red Phillips with the blue glass façade of the Posey Tower behind him. He's tall, probably in his late forties, and has glasses and red hair, gray at the edges. He's wearing a buckskin coat and trousers and a coon skin cap with a tail, and I'm thinking I'm going to like this new Season.

We can see Bystanders thronging the sidewalks behind him, and there's a lot of buckskin and flannel shirts and bonnets and ankle-length dresses with petticoats. It looks like the old Pioneer Days we used to hold in Shawneetown when I was a kid. But this time it's not costumes. These are the honest-to-Ingersol fashions of Reality 260.

"Moonglow is over, folks," Red Phillips declares. We give that a hearty frontier cheer. The end of Moonglow is good news to us.

"The pioneer look is the fashion hereabouts. But they aren't backward in Guidepost. By golly, technically, this Season is advanced."

That's welcome news too. But we're still wondering if we can use our phones. How Anachronistic will they be? Are they compatible with the new cellular net?

"We'll have a list of Anachronisms in a jiffy, folks," Red Phillips declares. "In the meantime, say howdy to our roving correspondent Molly Waters." A full-figured black woman in a bonnet and calico dress joins Red Phillips as if she's out for a stroll in old Dodge City.

"Molly, what do you think of the new Season?"

She grins into the camera. She has a round face and large smiling eyes. "It's a friendly, neighborly downhome kind of place a lot like Wilderness, Red."

Another cheer arises from our crowd. So far the news has been terrific.

"There's nothing to be worried about in this Reality, Red. Guidepost is a pretty safe place."

Red's listening to a tinny voice on his earphone as he nods. "But how is it different from Wilderness?"

Molly grins. "Say what you will about Wilderness, Red. Those people had the pioneering spirit. Here it's all for show. It's more Wilderness Lite."

Red Phillips laughs. "It's been a spell since we've been Somewhen you don't need to worry none about offending the Locals, but it seems they're very easy here." He sounds like someone from Wilderness. Finally, a Reality without an accent!

"Very easy, Red. Almost too easy. You can get away with a lot in Guidepost. This is the Lightest Season I've ever seen."

This sounds great to us. No more black outfits. No more Day People. No more Night. We're coming out into the sunshine.

We're ready to celebrate!

Amos has stressed the importance of celebration. It's a big deal—not just to do it. You've got to feel it. Look forward to it. Bask in it. Let it motivate you. Let it lighten your stress. So when we find out Guidepost is a Light Season, we celebrate. We hoot and holler—and we relax. We congratulate ourselves on our good fortune.

When the list of Anachronisms appears, it too is good news, short compared to last Season. The new technology list is what's long. A lot of things have come back into Existence, including cell phones and the Subvocalizer I use to make these journal entries.

Notes aren't much needed for this new Season. Of course, you can't really tell about a Season until you're actually out in it. So when we return Three Dimensionward, Barlow and I can't wait to get outside. We're the first ones to leave the Safe House and reach the Lodge's front door.

There are a couple of Bystanders out on the porch, both guys. One of them has long blond hair and wears a fringed leather jacket and a cowboy hat, and the other is dark-haired in a white cotton shirt with a bolo tie and a bushy moustache.

"I've been watching this house for three days now," the blond one in the fringed jacket says. "And I've looked in all the windows. There ain't no one here. The Lodge is completely deserted."

"But you haven't gone inside, Obadiah?" the other one asks him.

"No need to. I was waiting for you, Wilbur."

"You're scared to go inside alone."

"I am not. I've been a ghost hunter for nine years now, and I've been in REAL haunted houses, and I tell you there's no spirits here."

I forget that Barlow and I are still in the dark fashions of the Night People. We have on the black clothes we bought in Reality 256, when we went out looking for Belinda, and the white face powder and the eye shadow and the gray lipstick. When the Bystanders spot us on the porch behind them, they jump about a foot in the air. I guess they aren't used to the Moonglow style.

"Where did *you* come from?" Obadiah cries.

When Barlow gestures over his shoulder at the open door to the Lodge behind us, the two Bystanders let out a shriek and go tearing off down the sidewalk as fast as their legs will take them.

Barlow picks up Obadiah's cowboy hat and wrinkles his face. "These Guideposters are a bunch of wussiepusses," he says. "They talk tough, but they ain't tough at all."

I nod. "Good runners, though."

Barlow has to assent to that. We watch them hurdle the fence and keep running until they're out of sight two blocks away.

"I guess we're going to have to change our clothes, Barlow. I don't think they like the Moonglow look in this Reality."

He utters a gruff agreement and rubs his stubbly chin. "I wonder if they still have our old clothes in the Safe House storage?"

"Good question."

So we turn and go inside the

10

INTERTIME GOVERNMENT
Reality 263
Guidepost Season

I feel like my life is completely out of control, reader, and that is *not* a feeling I like to have. I majored in engineering because it makes sense. Everything fits together, and everything has its place. But in the Changeworld, nothing holds together, and everything keeps moving around. Even the laws of physics have changed.

They've changed the frickin' laws of physics!

What is there to depend on? What is there to hold onto? Only you, reader. You and me together, seeing this through. I feel like you're right behind me, backing me up. You're by my side, willing to take things one at a time. You're dependable, reliable, confident. You make me feel confident—like I can engineer my way out of this.

Only a month to go now—and I'll be finished with the semester. My classes are going great, and I'm learning a lot. After two more semesters I'll have a job— that is, my Alternate Self will. Maybe it will last, maybe not. Who knows? But I'll have credentials—and work experience as an engineer.

Amos is picking us up in his black stretch limousine for our family meeting tonight, so I wander down to the garage a little early and discover Cooper at the workbench, fixing something, it looks like some kind of scope. He notices me enter, despite his goggles, but doesn't show it. He just keeps fiddling with wires and using a soldering iron. There's a burnt smell in the air. I hardly ever see him, he's gone so much. So I know this is a rare opportunity, maybe my last, to speak to him alone.

"I know you're not likely to tell me When you're from, but I can't help but wonder. And I know you're not a stunt man, not really. So where do you go on all those Trips of yours? To the Past? Does Amos know? He must, or why would he tolerate you?"

Is my brother a Traveler? Is that why he's gone all the time?

Cooper doesn't say anything. He just stops soldering and glances at me with a wary kind of respect.

"I know you're not from Wilderness," I tell him. "Sure, you've got the accent down, and you know everything a Wild Man would know, how I can't figure out, but it's impressive, it really is. But you're not the guy I grew up with. You're just not him. I know we've changed with all the constant Do-Overs in Time, but people don't change in the ways you've changed, so I guess my question is who are you?"

Lifting his goggles, Cooper looks at me and shakes his head. "You think too much, little brother. And it's addled your pate." He straightens up smoothly, puts his goggles back in place, and returns to what he's doing. But he's not going to shake me that easily.

"You work with the Intertime Police, don't you? Or is it with the CTA? Are you from the same When as Amos, or is he Longer than you?"

I hear sparks. Then Cooper stops what he's doing and turns around to stare at me, lifting his goggles again. "You're like a dog with a bone," he says, shaking his head. "But it's not a bone. It's a stick of dynamite. Let it go, little brother."

And lowering his goggles, he turns back around. I know I'm starting to get to him.

"How long have you known this Amos? Did you enter the Void together? Or separately? Was it your idea to keep Sponsoring us after all our failures—or his? What happened to the family in the Promise Season? How many times has Amos Sponsored us and failed? Did you talk him into it, or did he talk you into it?"

Cooper freezes for a few seconds. He turns to regard me, takes off his goggles, and puts down the soldering iron. "Answers aren't going to do you any good, little brother. You're like an ant trying to understand an empire. You've been around for—what—three Seasons? You ought to wait until you're grown up to learn about grown-up things." And he turns around and starts humming as he works on his device.

"Who Sponsored you? Was it Amos? Mr. Yen? What really happened to Maggie?"

But Cooper doesn't say anything else, and that's all I can get out of him. I don't get around to asking him about Dr. Morlock or the hundred other things I wonder about. But when we hear the others coming down the back stairs to the garage, Cooper grabs my wrist and says to me, "It's okay you kidding around with me, but when anyone else is here, I'm your big ol' brother from Reality 250, get me?"

"Sure thing," I say, "dear ol' brother from 250."

"Good," he says, letting go. "I knew I could count on you."

My other brothers and sisters appear out of the stairwell in their buckskin or skirts with petticoats. I've got on a red flannel shirt, and I've grown a beard. I look like a lumberjack. The Guidepost Season has been like four weeks of Halloween, or four weeks on a movie set, or four weeks in a western musical, or a four-week costume party, or four weeks playing characters in a wild west theme park. We're sick of Guidepost and ready to get back to normality.

We all Nod to each other, and we open the garage door, letting in a gust of wind with the odor of pulled pork sandwiches. Whatever Cooper was working on is out of sight, and he's put on a cowboy hat and a fringed leather jacket. Amos's limousine pulls into the driveway right on time. His chauffeur Tate opens the car doors for us.

Tate is a black man, slender and average in height, the same age as Amos, though he looks younger. He and Amos have been friends since high school. I know for a fact he's no mere chauffeur—he's high up in the

Intertime Government—maybe even Amos's boss, but he plays the chauffeur part like he's going for an academy award. He's got the uniform and the cap, the whole bit. He's another unsettling reminder that things are not what they seem in the Timeflow.

As soon as we're inside the limousine, we get a warning for the next Time Change. There are so many flashing Wristwatcher lights in Amos's limo it looks like a swarm of fireflies in there. Cooper sits in the front seat next to Tate. Amos and Zeke sit behind him in a seat facing the back. And Amanda, Cartmell, and I face them in the seat farthest back.

Tate rolls the limo down the driveway and eases us into traffic like we're going for a Sunday drive for ice cream cones.

"Turn this limo around, Amos," Amanda orders him. "We need to get to Room 999." But Amos ignores her, and we keep heading northwest.

I can tell something earth-shattering and nerve-wracking is on its way—and I don't mean the Time Change.

Amanda's dressed like a banker in a long gray dress even though she's supposedly given up banking. She has a worried look on her face because she doesn't like it when she doesn't know exactly where we're going.

"We just passed another Safe House, Amos. Stop the car and let us take Shelter. Why won't you stop? You're cutting this too close."

Amanda is used to giving orders, but Amos isn't used to taking them. He mastered the art of stubbornness before Amanda was even born.

Amos has the inertia of a sumo wrestler and the patience of a Buddha. His face has the wait-and-see expression of a farmer (he has the complexion of a farmer too because he tans year-round). He seldom says more than he has to, and he doesn't like to speculate or commit himself to an opinion. He does everything in his own time and on his own terms. He's just as stubborn as ever.

Amanda hasn't gotten any less stubborn in the last thirty years, either. With Amos devoting his time to his government duties, Amanda has gotten used to being in charge of the family, and she doesn't like having her authority challenged now.

Of course, this is Amos's limousine we're riding in, and he's Prefect of the Midwest Region for the Intertime Government, so you would expect that everyone in the car would follow his orders. But if you expect that, you're forgetting Amanda's his sister. She's known him all her life, and she remembers all of his mistakes. Amos is nothing but a delinquent kid to her.

Dark clouds are gathering in the sky, and there's a smell of rain in the air. Tate gets on the speaker, despite Cooper having the partition open between the front two seats and his elbow on the seatback.

"There's someone following us, Mr. Vann."

So I turn and look out the back window and spot a Rossiter 5000 in our lane a car length behind us on the Dewey Expressway. Timecrimers. Has to be. There is no Rossiter Automobile Company in Reality 263. It doesn't Exist. Besides, a Rossiter 5000 is the perfect pursuit vehicle because it's fast and powerful and it's built like a tank. That's how I know these Timecrimers mean business.

Amos doesn't show any reaction to the announcement that we're being followed. He just says, "I know, Tate."

The hairs on my arms are crawling like they did at the gate to the Brotherhood Lodge. We hear thunder and see lightning on the horizon.

"Morlock didn't have anything to do with this," Cooper tells Amos. "It looks like Deakins' bunch. They're the ones who are into kidnapping and extortion now."

And Amos, as a government official, is a prime target for ransom. We all are. Amanda has a shocked look on her face as she stares out the back window, but when she turns around, she glares at Amos and gives him the voice, the killer tone that will skewer you and chill you, freeze-dry you like a piece of fruit.

"You've got to stop at the next Safe House, Amos, and let us out before this thing escalates into something dangerous. We've got only ten minutes left before the Time Change."

Amos has a determined look on his face, but he doesn't say anything while Amanda baits him. The guys on the football team used to call him "The Monument" because he was so big and solid that nothing could faze him. He was the center and could take a hit without being moved back.

"Dammit, Amos, this is serious. Our lives are at stake here. As Second Financial Officer of the Bank of Shawneetown, I'm ordering you to stop this car."

Amanda is trying to pull rank on Amos, but that isn't going to work because we know he's the oldest, and besides, a Prefect outranks a banker, especially one from a Bystander bank. So Amanda resorts to her most common and effective strategy: building a coalition among the other kids against the oldest.

"Cooper, you agree with me on this, don't you?"

"Leave me out of this." Lifting his cowboy hat, Cooper puts on his earbuds and turns on his music. Rain begins to fall, splattering the windshield, and Tate turns on the wipers.

Another Rossiter 5000 seems to come out of nowhere and pulls alongside us in the next lane of the expressway. The other one closes in from behind, and they have us boxed in. The Timecrimers honk their horn and motion out the window for us to pull over.

Amanda is at first scared and then angry. You can see her rearing up like some irritated bear, ready to bash us with a swipe of her paw.

"I told you you should have stopped, Amos. Why don't you ever listen to me?"

Which is what Mom always used to say. Whenever Amanda gets stressed out, she starts acting like Mom (don't you dare tell her I said that). Mom really knew how to bombard us.

"If you'd listened to me, Amos, you wouldn't be in the spot you're in. You're going to be sorry, soon enough."

Someone's leaning out the window of the car next to us with a bullhorn, and he announces in a foghorn voice, "Pull over at the next exit, and no one gets hurt."

"Do what they say," Amanda urges. "We've got only seven minutes left." Hail begins to rain from the sky, popping across the limo's hood and roof.

"I'm not going to pull over," Amos declares, "And I'm not going to stop."

And there you go. It's carved in stone. Amos has spoken. Argument's over.

You would think Amanda would know that. You'd think she'd know her brother by now and could tell he's not going to change his mind and she may as well quit bugging him.

Of course, from her perspective, Amos ought to know her by now and know he's got to do what she wants because she's not going to let up until he does. Because once when Mom and Dad and Amos were away, Barlow made the mistake of saying, "If I let you have your way, will you finally shut up?" Since then, wearing down her opponent has become one of Amanda's main strategies.

"Stop the car, Amos," Amanda cries over the sound of hail. "Let them kidnap us. The government will pay the ransom, and we can get on with our lives. Don't let the Change Wipe us Out. We've got only six minutes left."

Amos adjusts his glasses. "Is your bank going to put up the ransom, Amanda?"

"You know I can't tell the bank about the Intertime

Government."

"Then you don't have any say in this, do you?" The hail begins to fall faster with bigger stones.

We've passed the next exit, and I suppose the Timecrimers have realized we're not going to cooperate with them, because they're leaning out their windows with submachineguns and firing at us. A raucous ratatat rakes the limousine. It sounds like hail except it's hitting us on the side. When the Timecrimers realize the limousine is armored, they aim at our tires.

"That's not Deakins gang," Amos says. "Do you see who's driving? That's Paul Dougherty, one of Pollard's lieutenants."

Pollard! His gang's been linked to bombings, murder for hire, and worse. Maybe this isn't a simple kidnapping, after all.

The hail has stopped, but the rain is pouring in sheets. We can hear the tires pop, and we're slowing down, and the ride's gotten bumpy and we're swerving back and forth, almost hitting the car in the next lane.

Cartmell's drawn her knees in front of her, and Zeke's got his eyes closed, and Amanda's put her hands over her face. But Cooper's relaxed and rocking to the music on his player. He's in another Dimension, doesn't care, like the time when he went out and partied all night when Mom was having her operation.

So I unbuckle my seatbelt and launch myself across the seat and knock off his cowboy hat and yell, "Take off them damn headphones and care about something for once in your life!"

He looks at me all ticked off and says, "Get off my back, Barlow." Then he puts his hat back on.

And the limo's bumping along, and I think we're done for, when Amos says, "Re-inflate the tires, Tate."

So I look over and see Tate press a switch, and suddenly the ride's not so bumpy, and it's smooth again, and we're speeding up. But the Rossiters have us boxed in, so Amos says, "Get 'em out of our way, Tate."

I see Tate press a button, and a grenade goes flying and hits the car beside us, and suddenly it's covered with streaks of lightning and steam. Then it disappears. It's gone. It has totally vanished in a cloud of vapor. Now there's only rain falling where it used to be.

"What the frack?" I say. "Where'd that car go?"

"Into the Void," Amos declares.

A Dimensional grenade. Cooper said the CTA was working on developing them.

"Switch to full armor, Tate," Amos commands, and iron plates rise in front of all the windows around the back and sides of the car. Tate speeds up, making the Timecrimers behind us scramble to catch up. We're passing sixty, seventy, eighty. The television screens over the seats come on, giving us a view of the car behind us as it tries to catch up.

"Amos, we have only three minutes left," Amanda cries. "For god's sake, get us to a Safe House."

But he's not going to stop. Because giving in to the Timecrimers is not an alternative. He's going to take us right into the Time Change and the Timecrimers with us. He's too stubborn to stop now. He can't because that would mean Amanda wins. And I'm wondering if he's made arrangements with the Society to Sponsor our Alternate Selves in the next Reality after our memories are Wiped Out. In a few minutes we'll be about as real as last week's dreams—because Amos really doesn't have any choice.

I look at Amanda and see she's got her palms together and her eyes closed and she's mumbling something. She's praying, for criminy's sake. This is a new one on me, I'll tell you. She's never done anything like this before. Get out the strait jacket. She's on the road to Chronoville.

When the limo comes to an underpass and enters the darkness, Amos says, "Now, Tate." And suddenly the darkness gets darker, and I'm rising off my car seat.

It's so confusing and unexpected I don't know what's happening at first. I start to think this must be what happens when you get hit by a Time Change. But it's too early for that.

"We're in the Void!" Amanda cries. "This limo's a Safe House!"

"Yeah, duh," Cooper says like he knew it all along. He's got his earbuds off and is packing up his music player.

I flail around in mid-air until I can get myself back to the seat and belt in. Everyone else has their seatbelts fastened.

Zeke is grinning at me like he just beat me at Earth Defender. He figured out the limo's a Safe House a long time ago. The limo's rocket engine fires, and I'm pressed into my seat until the engine reduces thrust and the acceleration of Protospace takes over.

Amanda's looking all annoyed like she would rather have been kidnapped than lose another argument. Cartmell's trying to cheer her up and distract her. "Maybe your house'll be in Gold Hill this time, Amanda."

Cartmell doesn't like there to be any bad feelings in the family. She's sensitive that way, and she likes exerting her control over us. She succeeds in distracting her sister. Amanda was probably thinking about how she could resume her struggle with Amos, but now Cartmell has her thinking about her Alternate Residence instead.

I figure the Rossiter 5000 is getting sucked into the Godhead about now, and the thought gives me a warm feeling, so I can relax and enjoy my ride in the limo. The battle's over. The debris is everywhere—but it's all psychic. We have to start cleaning up—mending our heads, recovering from the shock, applying bandages to our raw and bruised emotions.

Amos's limousine has a lush gray interior. The seats are wide enough to sit three comfortably with room for a wet bar on one side and a coffee maker on the other. I can stretch out my legs without my feet touching the seat across from me.

The windows of the limo look out on total impenetrable darkness as the front of the car noses ahead, its wheels still turning despite the absence of road. Out the back window the glowing Time/Space Continuum comes into view, the fuzzy Earth below us as if we've been blasted into orbit, which is true enough. We've left the curvature of Three Dimensional Earthspace. We're beyond gravity. The troubles of the world are far behind us.

The rocket engine cuts off, and slowly, the wrinkles on Amanda's face start to smooth themselves. Zeke opens his eyes and smiles, and Cartmell stretches out and yawns. Cooper's put away his music player and is looking around at the limo's ceiling. "Nice car, Amos. Did you buy it off the lot?"

Amos doesn't react. Pulling a glass from a rack on the ceiling, he asks for everyone's drink orders and glances over his shoulder at the front seat

Cooper leans the arm of a fringed jacket on the seatback. "Jack Daniels."

"Don't you think it's a little early to start boozing it up?" Amanda asks him.

"Not when it's free. Fill 'er up, barkeep."

I guess Amos thinks it's time for us to have that one drink we're allowed to help us deal with our stress. I'll bet Cooper never stops at one when Amos isn't around. Of course, even five don't affect him as much as one does us. He celebrates all the time. Today we're celebrating six months in the Timeflow. We're half a year and three Seasons into our Initiation.

It's time to party.

Amos opens an ice bucket built into his armrest and inserts a few cubes into the glass, then covers it with a lid. He pulls a plastic bottle of scotch from a rack below the glasses and, unsnapping the lid, squeezes out a stiff drink. Zeke takes the glass and a straw and hands it across the seatback to Cooper.

"Bet you've never drunk scotch with a straw before," Amos says to him.

"Bet he has," Amanda and I reply at the same time.

Giving us a wink, Cooper takes a sip, puckers, and pushes his cowboy hat back. He whistles like a cowpoke. "Good hooch, Amos."

"Amanda?" Amos pulls another glass off the rack.

"I'll just have coffee, thank you." She leans over and takes a styrofoam cup and lid from a dispenser next to the coffeepot and pushes out a stream of dark liquid. "I'm glad Barlow's with Pete and the kids now. Pete's good in an emergency, but I always feel better when there's two adults looking out for them." Taking a sip from her straw, she frowns. "Hey, this is Mountain Blend, my brand from 250!" She looks over at Amos. "Where did you get this?"

Amos just chuckles and inserts a few cubes of ice into another glass. "Zeke—a Tahiti Punch?" An Extinct drink from the Landslide Season.

Zeke smiles. "Of course."

Amos shoots out the drink from a plastic cocktail mixer and covers the glass. He already has some made up.

"What about you, Cartmell?" Amos caps the punch, inserts a straw, and hands it to Zeke. "A cherry fizz?"

Cartmell gasps. "You've got a cherry fizz?"

The drink has been Extinct since 250, but of course, Amos has connections. While Cartmell leans forward, he plunks a pink pellet into a glass of water, and the mixture begins to bubble and fizz, creating a carbonated cherry-flavored beverage. He adds ice to the glass, covers it, and hands it to Cartmell, who inserts a straw and begins to take greedy sips.

This limo ride has turned into a party. It's a little bit of Reality 250 out in the Void. Amos doesn't ask for my preference. He just reaches down and opens a refrigerator built into the floor and removes a brown bottle. He uncaps it and hands it to me with a straw.

I take it and frown. Slipping off my Subvocalizer, I turn the label so I can read it. Olde Tyme Draft Beer. The brand I used to drink in Reality 250. I'd forgotten all about it.

"I don't believe it." I haven't seen a bottle of this stuff since I was a Bystander. Inserting the straw, I take a sip, holding the liquid in my mouth for a moment before swallowing slowly. In some Realities you're not old enough to drink until you're 21, but everyone over 18 in Wilderness could drink 3.2 beer.

It's like sipping from a bottle of the past. The last time I drank one of these was in the student union at Shawneetown U. with my best friends Harley and Quint. I haven't seen Harley since. He's Extinct. The union isn't there anymore either. Even bottled beer is an Anachronism now.

Amos inserts a few cubes of ice into a glass for himself and squeezes out some bottled mineral water. Imagine that—they're bottling *water* now. He's the candy man for all of us, but he brings himself only water.

We haven't seen our oldest brother for a long time, not since he left the family meeting last Season, although he's been better than Cooper about keeping in touch. The job as Prefect has taken up more and more of his time. We have a thousand questions for him about what's going on with the Society and what's next for the Longtimers. We all read the Oldspaper, but it doesn't tell us much. We want to know the inside information, the kind you can't get from an Oldspaper.

"What's the latest news, Amos?" I ask. "The stuff we can't get from the 4DTN."

He adjusts his glasses. He doesn't want to answer at first, but he's showed off this far—a little more won't hurt. "If you were listening to the 4DTN now, you'd hear we're about to pass the 42nd Directive, outlawing Public

Anachronism and making it a crime to Inform the Bystanders. We've chartered the Society and the Brotherhood as legal nonprofit institutions. And we've authorized the CTA to enforce these laws and granted them martial law in the Void to fight Timecrime and Travelling. Of course, the CTA's authority was already well established and founded by the duly constituted government of the First Reality, but you and I know most Longtimers don't recognize the validity of

11

SAFE HOUSE
Reality 264
Guidepost Season

Reader, you're back—at last. Every Change brings Danger Number One, a Timestorm, but it also gives me time with you. We can dodge the Timestorms together.

You can't imagine how much I look forward to these chats of ours. Don't have much to say? Don't worry—I can make up your end of the conversation. After all, that's what friends are for, right? What's that? You want to know how my college career has been coming along? Funny you should ask.

In just two and a half more weeks, I'll be a senior. In two semesters I can start my career. I've proved Amos wrong, and that doesn't happen very often. He said I'd have to give it up!

My career as an engineer is all I've got left of Reality 250, besides my brothers and sisters—and they've all changed. If I give up my career ambitions, I won't be the same either. I'll be totally lost. I won't be Dexter Vann—just some dust whirl stirred up by the Timestorms.

I've discovered there's an "In Memoriam" section on the Society Message Boards to note the passing of Longtimers. It's a long list, so I scroll down until I find the names Junius Pollard and Paul Dougherty mixed in with a lot I've never heard of. I'm tempted to look for my own.

So I do.

I scroll back all the way to Harvest and the other six Seasons that followed Promise, and when I get to Nagara, there they are: all of our names, except for Amos's and Cooper's. That means we were Wiped Out back in the Sayonara Season, ten Seasons before Wilderness.

So I'm right. We *are* washouts.

We gather down in the Catacombs beneath Shawneetown for our meeting with Amos in this Reality.

Everybody's in their buckskin suits or long dresses: Amanda, Barlow, Cartmell, and Zeke and me. And also Amanda's husband Pete and her two kids Jackson and Jessalyn. We assemble at our usual spot in the dimness of a walkway overlooking a broad drainage canal. We've been having a pretty good time of it in this Reality. Barlow's bullied his way into becoming a cop again, and Amanda's intimidated them into making her vice president at the bank. Zeke and I talked our teachers into letting us make up the work we've missed in our classes. We're not sure what Amos can do for us, but we're here to listen to him because even though we've been in the Timeflow for fourteen Realities and are pretty much committed to becoming Longtimers. we still have a lot to learn about living in the Four Dimensional World.

I'm still dressed like a lumberjack in a beard and a thick plaid shirt, and I'm chewing on some beef jerky since I had to skip lunch to come to this meeting.

My oldest sister Amanda looks a little harried and upset, partly because she hates these meetings but mostly because she's so busy with her job. She has her arms crossed and looks around like someone standing in line. She taps her foot then shifts her posture and glares at Amos. "I don't see why we have to keep living in the Brotherhood Lodge. I know—you said it's because we have to avoid our Alternate Life. You said you would explain that to us, but you never did."

Amos looks like he's about to say something else, but he swallows it in order to respond to Amanda's complaint.

"All right," he says, "I was going to wait until later to discuss Alternate Life, but we can get a start now. But first let me caution you that just because this Season's easier than the last doesn't mean your situation has changed. If anything you're in more danger now than ever of falling under the sway of your Past Life."

Barlow wrinkles up his face and moans. We don't want to hear about Past Life. Amos has lost some credibility with us where that's concerned because he told us we'd have to give up our jobs and careers, but here in Guidepost things are better than ever, and we'd have really lost out if we'd followed his advice.

Amos is looking at us like we're delinquents, which I guess we are. We're not as grateful as we should be for all he's done for us. We couldn't have Survived without his help, and we are a bunch of stubborn backsliders. We ought to be taking his advice about how to Survive instead of doing what we want.

"None of you are taking the danger you're in seriously enough," he tells us. "I hope you've all been avoiding contact with your Alternate Life as I advised, but I realize many of you are still clinging to your Past Life and futilely trying to hang onto your former careers. So you need to know the dangers you are exposing yourselves to."

He pauses and taps his fingertips together in front of him as he looks at our faces to see who the guilty parties are. I try to look innocent, but I think he knows I've been going to classes at Shawneetown U against his advice. He knows Amanda hasn't given up her bank job, and Barlow is back on the police force. We're hopeless Past Lifers. We know we ought to follow his advice, but we just can't.

"You are well aware," Amos reminds us," how much your lives have been Altered by Changes in Time. None of the Bystanders know you. They know your Alternate Self, who has different memories than you of the past decade. Soon there will be Changes dating back farther than that. Your Past will become less and less similar to the one you used to know. Your Alternate Self will become more and more different from you, and your Alternate Life will become increasingly unrecognizable. Soon it may become so foreign that you will no longer be able to Adapt to it. There will be too many factors unknown to you, too many acquaintances who are strangers, too many commitments you are unaware of."

Amos gestures at us like a navy signalman, trying to save the fleet, but it's just calisthenics to us. "Your ignorance and failure to honor the commitments made by your Alternate Self can land you in major difficulties. You could end up in jail or committed to a mental asylum. And if a Time Change arrives while you are confined, I cannot guarantee the Society can rescue you. Without taking Shelter, you will get Eliminated from Time. Even your Alternate Self could disappear. Your Extension could be Wiped Out of the Timestream entirely, making it impossible for your Existence to be re-established."

He takes a breath and gives us a stern examination. Extinction. That's the dire fate we risk. But we're not dodo birds. We're important career people, and until the Changes actually make our old lives unmanageable, we'll continue trying to lead the lives we've chosen and worked for and invested in rather than giving up everything for some hard new life. And if Amos can't understand that, then it's just too bad for him.

"Your Alternate Life holds other dangers, however," Amos declares, "than simple problems of Adjustment. For in trying to Adapt to your Alternate's life, you may find yourself changing. You have no idea how contact with your Alternate Life might make you feel. When you learn of the different choices your Alternate Self has made, you may be intrigued by them—or appalled. You may get so involved with your Alternate Life that you are unable or unwilling to extricate yourself. And that can be a fatal error. Remember, your Alternate Self is a Bystander, untrained and unaccustomed to Surviving in the Timestream. If you get involved in your Alternate Life, you too may become unfit for Survival. You may think you know what you're doing, but I'm warning you that your Alternate Life can present dangers you've never anticipated. Leave it alone. Start a new life as a Longtimer and put the—"

Amos's words are interrupted by the sounds of our Beepers, all chiming in at the same time like contestants on Jeopardy. We glance at our Wristwatchers and note the dials are flashing.

A Time Change is on its way.

A Time Change! We don't want to go through another Time Change. We were just getting used to *this* Reality. Why do the damn Travelers have to change everything *again*? Fourteen Changes were enough. We don't want any more. We like Reality 263. Another Change is really going to mess with my classes—and it's not going to help Zeke with his classes either. Barlow will probably lose his job again and all of the karma he's regained, and Amanda's position at the bank will get all screwed up, too.

We shouldn't have to go through *this*.

Amos gestures to us. "Follow me. We need to find Shelter." It takes us a moment to react, and we have to run to catch up with him. He leads us up the stone steps to the second sublevel. We can hear the subway trains whizzing into the station down the platform and smell the crowd, wet from rain.

"You must never linger after you have noticed a Time Change warning," he tells us. "You must get to Shelter immediately, even if you believe you have plenty of time to make it to the next Safe House. Because you never know what delays and difficulties may beset you on your way to Shelter. Your lives may depend upon your quickness."

Zeke and I glance at each other. We've weathered every previous Time Change in Room 999 of the Brotherhood Lodge or the Roebuck Tower or The Common. Now we'll get our first taste of what a Public Safe House is like, not that we want to.

Amos checks his phone for a list of Safe House locations, and a readout of the open and closed Shelters scrolls down his screen. The nearest Safe House is on the subway level. It's out of order, of course. Amos won't even bother to check it. The Type Two Safe Houses at the subway stations are some of the oldest—and most unreliable—in Shawneetown.

Public Safe House Dimensionalizers are designed to stop working if not treated properly—in order to discourage anyone from cannibalizing them in order to create a Time Machine. Their Dimensionalizers cannot be backward engineered. They activate and enter the Void if fiddled with, so they are prime candidates for malfunction.

Public Safe Houses cannot Travel down the Pathway into the Past. They lack a rocket engine powerful enough, and they can't carry enough fuel or supplies. Their guidance systems are also inadequate for that purpose. They can barely carry out their main function, so again, they are never Amos's first choice for Shelter.

"I've downloaded all the latest Safe House information from the Society's web site.," he tells us. "You should do the same at the beginning of each new Reality and keep your list updated daily. You must always know where the closest Safe House is and also know the location of close alternatives."

So we're going to have to do this again? And again?

He picks up his pace, heading for the stairs at the head of the subway platform like he's in some relay race. "Hurry," he tells us. "We're going topside. There's no time to lose."

"But we have at least twenty minutes," Amanda complains. "Why are we rushing?"

"You can't always depend on the nearest Safe House. It may already be full of passengers. You need to conserve as much spare time as you can—because you might need it."

Hurry hurry hurry. It's always hurry in Amos's Time World.

We march double-time behind Amos into the

subway crowd and up the steps to the first sublevel and then up to the street above. Amanda and Cartmell have umbrellas, but the rest of us get soaked by the rain. I don't like storms. I hate getting wet and being wet and sloshing around in my socks.

Proceeding northwest on McKinley, we duck into the Blaine Building and start shaking the water off. Amos approaches a security guard in a khaki uniform, a guy in his thirties with jet black hair and olive skin, sitting at a desk near the door.

"Can you tell us the way to Room 999?" Amos asks him.

The guard is intent on meticulously recording numbers into a ledger. He looks up at us, shuts, the ledger, and puts down his pen. He stands and peers at us left and right slowly and carefully—because he's Mr. Control.

"I'll have to look that up," he says. "Stay right where you are." He keeps an eye on us as he reaches for a loose-leaf notebook behind him. But Amos has already turned and is leading us onto the sidewalk into the rain. "Don't ever waste time," he tells us, " on directions from ignorant Bystanders."

So we get soaked *again*.

At Locust Street, he turns and leads us southeast across McKinley to Grant Street. We're looking for the Crosstown Diner, but when we reach its usual location, all we find is an empty lot. So we just stand there in the rain.

"It's already launched." We stare at the indentations on the bare ground, like the ruins of a prehistoric fort, now filling with water, where the diner used to be.

"It happens," Amos says. "Come on. We need to get to the next one." I can't help but feel this frantic Safe House hunt belongs in one of my Alternate Lives rather than the life I want to be leading. I'm soaked to the skin.

The next Safe House is in the back room of

McElvoy's Pub on Poplar Street. We file inside and along the bar toward the back, passing a row of barstools. I smell cheeseburgers and notice a cutout square with a kitchen behind it. I'm as wet as a swimming dog—I could use a towel. It'll be hours before my clothes are dry. I'm going to be as damp and uncomfortable as a sponge the entire time.

Amos leads us all the way to the back, but when he knocks on the door to the back room, a voice growls at him to go away.

Amos adjusts his glasses. "We are Longtimers. We've come for Shelter."

"Go away," the man's voice repeats from inside. "Leave me alone."

Oh, keerist—what now?

Amos glances at us. "Sir," he says, "we have come for Shelter from the Change. This is a Public Safe House. You have to let us in."

"Go away!" the voice growls again. "This is my Safe House. Go find your own."

Barlow twirls his finger around his ear. "He's Chrono. He's not going to let us in."

A Chroniac! Why do we have to run into a Chroniac *now*?

Amos hesitates, then nods. "We'll have to find somewhere else." He turns and leads us onto the sidewalk and into the rain. I'm not getting any drier, I'll tell you for sure. Taking his cellular out of his pocket, he flips the mouthpiece into place and then punches in a number and holds the phone up to his face.

"This is Prefect Amos Vann," he declares once he's connected. He states his code number. "I'm downtown on Poplar and Grant and need a Mobile Safe House for a party of nine." Turning off his phone, he flips the mouthpiece up and slips the cellular back into his pocket like loose change.

Finally. Finally we're getting somewhere.

"They're making a pickup," he says, "around the

corner in three minutes." He races down Poplar to Garfield, stomping through the puddles like a third grader, and stops when he sees us hanging back. "Come on!" He waves to us. "We have to hurry. Our lives depend on it." The wind has picked up, and the rain is lashing us now.

He rushes around the corner, and the rest of us have to run to catch up. Pete picks up Jackson under one arm and Jessalyn under the other and tries to keep up. The rain's so thick we may as well be in a swimming pool.

"Run!" Amos yells to us, waving us on. "Stop dawdling."

We all run, dodging the pedestrians and umbrellas on the sidewalk. When we round the corner onto Ash Street, we're confronted with a huge crowd of Bystanders. I see Amos pull his gun out, and I lunge for him. "No, Amos, no!"

"Get out your guns," Amos commands us. I grab his arm.

"Don't shoot!" Amanda cries.

We can see the lights of a white van pull away from the curb down the block. On the side is the Society Logo of a blue-white world surrounded by darkness. Amos yells to the Mobile Safe House and waves his arms like the Titanic signaling the Californian, but apparently the people in the van don't see him. Our cries for help go unanswered.

Leaving the sidewalk, we rush down the street after the van, getting splashed by puddle after puddle, but the stoplight changes at the corner, and we see the van recede in the distance as we come to a halt by the curb.

Amos glowers at us. "Where are your guns?"

We look away.

"Well?" he says.

"They're in Society Storage," I tell him.

"Storage!" he yells, dripping with rain. "They can't do you any good in storage."

"They're too heavy," I tell him. "We don't want to carry them around."

"It falls out of my belt," Cartmell complains.

Amos thinks that over. "Holsters," he says. "That's what you need."

Amanda starts to growl. "No," she says. "We don't need holsters because we don't need guns. We don't want to shoot Bystanders, Amos. None of us do." She gives him one of her glares.

Amos wrinkles up his face at us. A peal of thunder drowns out his cuss words. "What is wrong with you?" He shakes his head. Rain dripping down his face, he pulls out his cellular and makes another call to the Society's Hotline. He identifies himself and gives his code prefix.

"We couldn't catch the Mobile that was just downtown," he tells the operator. "We need to order a Special." A flash of lightning illuminates his determined face. A crash of thunder drowns out his conversation, and he asks for a repeat.

"We're all out of Specials," the operator informs him. "But there is room in the Safe House on the 44th Floor of the Blaine Building on McKinley."

We groan when Amos tells us. Right back where we started. At least we know which floor this time. Amos thanks the operator, and we begin to run back in the direction we came from.

Is this our life now—running around frantically from Safe House to Safe House? What kind of way to live is that?

"Freakin' Bystanders," Barlow growls on our way back, rain running off his chin like sweat.

Once we reach the Blaine Building, we march by the security guard, who is carefully examining a column of numbers in his ledger. He glances at us like we're Hun invaders, drops his ledger, and races after us as we run to the elevators, leaving a trail of water, and push the button for the express. I feel like I've been through a car wash six times.

"Hey!" the guard cries. "You have to register. You need to explain the purpose of your visit, show me three kinds of I.D., and sign in. I need your names for a security check." He hurries toward us, slipping across the wet floor like a hockey player, reaching us just as the elevator arrives. "Halt!" he orders. "You can't go up there." But Barlow just decks him with a right hook.

The elevator door closes with us inside.

"Good work, Barlow," Amos says. "Don't ever let the Bystanders get in your way." The guard wasn't in our way. Barlow was just showing off. I'm still wiping the water off my face. At least we're out of the storm.

We rise quickly to the 44th floor. I keep glancing nervously at my watch. We have only five minutes to go. At the 44th floor, we get out and look down the corridor in both directions, trying to figure out where Room 999 could be.

A figure at the corridor's end signals to us, and Amos heads off in that direction. "Come along," he says.

Jackson is complaining. His ribs are getting sore, and he doesn't want to be carried anymore.

"You'll have to run," Pete tells him. "Can you do that for me?"

"Okay," Jackson says. So Pete slings Jessalyn over his shoulders, and Jackson runs beside him as they hurry down the hall. The rest of us quickly outpace them and stand inside the doorway of Room 999, urging them on like the third base coach.

The elevator door opens behind them, and the security guard steps out, holding his gun. "Halt!" he cries. Oh, meaningless universe, no! Not that fruitcase security guard!

Pete stops in his tracks, and Amos cusses. He pulls his revolver from under his coat and starts firing at the guard. "Come on," he cries. "We're almost out of time."

Pete takes off running again. The guard's gone into the elevator for cover, but soon his revolver peeks out and starts returning fire.

"Are they all in yet?" the Pilot calls from inside as bullets chip the plaster and richochet off the doorsills. He's an American Indian with a Counter Season accent, and he's wearing a baseball cap, a red and silver Shawneetown Salt Miners jacket, and a headset.

"Not yet," Amos cries between shots.

Pete scoops up Jackson with his free arm and runs like a fullback for the door. He's through the airlock and into the House with a minute to spare.

"Okay," Amos yells as the door closes, "we're all in."

I take a seat behind the Pilot and belt myself in and watch him as he pulls the lever of the Dimensionalizer forward.

Nothing happens.

"Oh crap." The Pilot pushes the lever again. No response. We can hear bullets striking the door like arrows in a target. I 'm all braced for null gravity, but it never comes. We're stuck in the Three Dimensional World.

Oh, endless Void, why? Why us?

"The Timesucking thing's not working!" the Pilot cries.

I look over to Amos. He has beads of sweat on his forehead and his phone up to his ear like he's calling the governor for a stay of execution.

"This is Amos Vann again," he says to the operator. "I'm on the 44th floor of the Blaine Building. We have a dozen people here in immediate need of Rescue."

On the televison screen in front of us I can see the black clouds of the Timestorm gathering in the east. From the protruding Godhead in advance of the storm, a network of lightning bolts spreads out, some of them striking the ground. Two pillars of debris rise ahead the storm like twin tornados, ready to be sucked into the cloudstream and rearranged for the 265th Reality.

We can hear the wind blowing outside, and we look around the cabin, wondering if the CTA will have time to create a bridge across the Void to us before the vacuuming Timestorm reaches

12

PAST LIFE
Reality 265
Concordance Season

Reader, it's you and me alone again. I feel like you're family now. Better. Because you don't judge me. Or ask anything from me. Or expect anything in return. You're just here for me, and you can't know how special that is. I hope you're getting something out of these journals, too. I try to tell is like it is, but I'm such a whack job now, it must sound screwy. Please, hang in there. This could be important for both of us.

With your help, I'm going to become an engineer.

The big day's finally come. It's the end of the semester, but there's a wrinkle in my plans. I am no longer a junior at Shawneetown U. And that means I will not be graduating in another two semesters.

Why not?

Because I'm a senior now, and I'll be graduating in two weeks. Somehow my Alternate Self has gotten a year ahead of me in school. Apparently, he racked up some AP credits in high school and took classes during the last three summers instead of working. How he managed to afford that, I'll never know.

I didn't expect to graduate so soon—and that's a problem. Because how am I going to do my civil engineer's job with an incomplete education? I missed an entire year. I don't know how to do the work. I never took Design of Steel Structures or Design of Reinforced Concrete Structures. I'm sure I could have handled those classes, but I never got the chance. Heck, I never even finished Hydrology or Soil Mechanics or Introduction to Transportation Engineering.

I don't have the background I need to pass the finals in my senior classes. I'm just gong to have to count on my Alternate Self to get me by.

Come on, buddy, I know you can do it! I believe in you.

I can't pass up this chance to graduate and get a job. That's my dream. I'll just have to learn on the job—or take my missed classes over the internet.

In Room 999 Barlow, Zeke and I get into a conversation while we're Hibernating and waiting for the Reports to end on the 265th Time Change. We're grousing like the three bears who've lost their porridge. I've got on my white shirt and vest and cowboy boots, and Barlow his letter jacket, and Zeke's wearing his buckskin shirt and pants.

"The Changes seem to come every two to three weeks like clockwork," Barlow observes. "I wonder why they're so regular."

He's got a point. "We ought to write a letter to Dr. Clockhour and ask him," I say.

Zeke presses on the bridge of his glasses. "Save your postage. I know the answer to this one."

Barlow and I turn away from the television screen to stare at him. Has he been reading Clockhour's columns? How could I have missed one?

"The Travelers have formed a Syndicate," Zeke tells us, "to coordinate their Time Changes so they don't Wipe each other Out. Or duplicate each other. Or neutralize each other's Manipulations. They could launch the next Change right after the last, but they take a couple weeks between their Travels to assess, regroup, and plan. So they don't get the Time Change Stress Syndrome like us."

I frown. I know he's showing off, but I can't help but ask, "How do you know that?"

Zeke gets this smile on his face. "I figured it out. So I asked Amos, and he confirmed it for me."

Damn busy-headed genius.

Barlow's scratchin' his scalp and looking at me. How does Zeke do it? And why didn't *we* figure it out? It's exasperating. We just shake our heads as we continue listening to the Reports about Concordance.

The Forecasters say this is a new Season, but other than screwing up my life more than usual, it hardly seems different from Guidepost. A lot of Longtimers think it's not a new Season, but the authorities have renamed it because it fits the definition of a Season as set down by the Accords of Nevertime. The Change is a ten Range, and there's a big Anachronism list, but it includes things that don't seem to affect society much like beer hats and male sex performance drugs. At least the Concordancers don't wear buckskin anymore. It's all Hawaiian shirts and sundresses like this Season's a vacation.

I'm starting to get the hang of this Longtimer thing. I think we all are. I'm getting used to damage control after every Change—it hasn't been as bad as it was in Moonglow. Everything's become easier for us since that Season ended.

This morning Zeke comes into my room like usual with a new idea he's hatched and tells me about it as I lie in bed. He's got on a Hawaiian shirt, but I'm still in my white shirt and jeans from 250.

"You know," he says, "the Brotherhood offers a course on Fourth Dimensional Science. It's pretty intensive and lasts sixteen weeks, and there's a fee, but I think it would be worth our trouble to take it."

I shrug. "I doubt if I'm gonna have time, Zeke. I've got classes to catch up on. I need to learn as much as I can before I have to start my civil engineer's job."

He frowns. "I thought Amos told you to give that up."

I give him one of my "get real" looks, and Zeke stares at me like Mom used to when she was on my case.

"Dexter, you've got to quit studying and going to school. That's Past Life. You've got to start a new life."

I've gotten pretty tired of hearing other people give me advice. Butting into other people's business is easy—but taking your own advice? Not so easy.

I look at him through lowered eyebrows and ask,

"Are you going to give up your own studies? And quit grad school?"

That zinger sets him back on his heels. He actually takes a step backward into the doorframe. He starts to say something to defend himself—I figure he's going to tell me his case is different, the same excuse Barlow and Amanda always use, but he blinks a few times, his mouth open. He swallows and takes a step forward.

"I guess you're right," he says. "I should quit. I'll have to quit eventually." He crosses his arms. "Will you quit with me?"

I don't say anything. I just pull on my socks. I don't have time for Zeke's nonsense.

"I guess Amos was right," Zeke says. "Sometimes we need someone else to help us see our mistakes. I couldn't see I needed to quit school, until you brought it up. Thanks, Dexter."

"You're welcome," I say without feeling it. I've had enough of Amos's advice. So Zeke's going to quit, and he expects me to quit with him. Yeah, right.

"I think grad school has been holding me back," Zeke says. "Or I would have enrolled in this Fourth Dimensional Science class a Season ago." He pauses. "Now the only thing holding me back is you."

I roll my eyes as I pull on my cowboy boots. "You go ahead," I say. "Don't wait for me." I'm not up for a guilt trip today.

Zeke just stares at me with those eyes, those super-intelligent eyes.

I put up my hand like a traffic cop. "All I've got to do is finish the semester." I stand and look in the small mirror on the wall while I comb my hair. "By next Reality I'll have my degree and a job as an engineer."

"But it won't last," Zeke says. "It'll end by next Season."

"Then I'll have another job."

"That's Alternate Life, Dexter. It's dangerous. It's

what Amos has been warning us against."

What if I could see my own situation as clearly as I can see everyone else's? An interesting thought—but irrelevant now.

"Don't give me a lecture on Alternate Life," I say, cinching my belt. "I've heard enough about that."

"But Amos is right, Dexter."

"Amos doesn't know everything," I say, slipping on my vest. "Neither do you."

Sure, Amos is the expert. He's right about my brothers and sisters. But he's not right about me. He says I should quit school. But he doesn't know the future. He can't be sure what's going to happen. No one can. He's looking at my situation from the sidelines and thinks he can call in the plays better than me, who's got everything at stake. But I'm the one who has to live with my choices, so I'm going to make choices I can live with.

Zeke swallows. "Do you think it's going to be easy for me, giving up grad school? I want to keep going just like you. I want to have that degree I've been aiming at. I want the old life I've been investing in for so long. But I can see now that's hopeless. These old plans are blocking me from seeing my opportunities for a new life in the Timeflow. We've got to live in the present, Dexter, not in the past."

"Go ahead," I say, "I think you should give up college. You're not as invested in your degree as I am." I stand up from the bed, fully dressed and ready to get to campus.

"You're no Conqueror, Dexter. You need to start fresh. This course on Fourth Dimensional Science could launch a new life for us."

Okay, so I'm intrigued. I give Zeke a sideways glance. "Where did you hear about this, anyway?"

"From Garson," he says. "He took the class, so he could become a Pilot for the Brotherhood and fly one of the faster than light Timecraft they've got. Did you know that the speed of light isn't an actual limit? According to

Fourth Dimensional Science, the universe is reproducing itself along the Fourth Dimension at the speed of light, so if you exceed light speed, you leave the universe. Photons do it all the time, but we can't see them because once they exceed light speed, they become unobservable to anyone in the Three Dimensional universe. Photons exit the universe in all directions, including along Fourth Dimensional vectors. That's why we can see the Time/Space Continuum from the Void. Garson says the big Voidships go many times the speed of light when they Travel down the Pathway into the Past. There's minimum resistance in Protospace, no gravity, and few particles of matter."

Garson! Zeke shouldn't be getting his science from *him*—although I'll admit he's a lot more normal than I thought at first. And I am intrigued by Fourth Dimensional Science. I marvel at the thought of Piloting one of those big Ships through the Void past light speed. Maybe the class could even tell us whether Dr. Morlock's real. I wish I could take the course with Zeke, but I know I don't have time for it. I have my own classes to go to.

Zeke can tell he has his hook in me, though, and he's determined to pull me into his boat. "Taking the Fourth Dimensional Science class can qualify us to become Apprentice Repairmen with the Society, Dexter, and we can move up from there. We'll have a full-time job, good pay, and we'll be protected from the Time Changes whenever we're at work."

He wants us to get a job as Dimensionalizer Repairmen? I've never thought of that alternative, but I can see the appeal of it right away.

But I have other things to do.

"Don't let me stop you," I say to Zeke. "I think it's a good idea for you. I'm surprised it's taken you so long to jettison the old life and find something new like Amos has been telling you."

"You should take his advice too, Dexter."

I smile at him. "No, my case is different. I've got something to gain by sticking to my goals, something important."

Sure, Zeke has a good plan, I'll admit. He has it figured out. But I'm too close to finishing my degree to give up. I've got to finish the race I've started. This is important. I didn't start college for nothin'. I have goals.

"I haven't told you the best part," Zeke says. "I haven't told you who's teaching the class."

Who's teaching it? What difference does that make?

"It's Dr. Clockhour," Zeke says.

I whip my head around. "What?"

"You can meet him," Zeke tells me, "if you come sign up for the class today."

Meet Dr. Clockhour? In person? I realize I'm salivating, and I have to swallow. Zeke doesn't lie or try to trick me like Cooper. But he does know how to rope me in.

"Damn you, Zeke." He has some fool notion he's doing this for my sake.

"So you're coming?"

"Heck, yes, I'm coming. I'll sign up for the damn class. But I'm not taking it. I'm not giving up on getting my degree—or on being an engineer."

Zeke's got that sly smile on his face again like he's showing off, and I just want to slap him. He knows I'm no quitter, and if I sign up for the class, I'm not going to be able to give it up.

"I'll go with you to meet Clockhour this morning," I say. "But that's all. I'm still going to campus this afternoon."

Barlow stops by my room next and leans on the doorjamb. "Hi, Zeke. What's up, Dexter?" He's wearing a suit in a Reality where everyone wears shorts and Hawaiian shirts. He's all gussied up to go out on the town, and he's chewing on some ham and cheese biscuit Greta made for him.

"Shouldn't you be at work?" I say. I take off my vest

and look in the small mirror on the wall.

He hesitates.

"You've lost your job, haven't you?" Zeke declares. "They don't know you anymore down at the precinct in this Season."

I glance over my shoulder and see Barlow tighten up and his face redden. "I'll get it back," he says. "Eventually."

Barlow's in Denial, like Amanda. He's still clinging to the old life, if he could only see it. But that's the problem. He can't see it. I wonder if he'll ever get his karma back. That would solve everything. His karma would show him the path to a new life. Without it, he has to cling to his old ways. Because Adjusting to the Timeflow isn't just a case of changing goals. He's got to change himself too. He's got to change his whole outlook, the patterns he's used to. He's got to approach the world in a new way, think in a new way, react in a new way. And not just any new way—it has to be Adaptive. It has to be the Longtimer way.

Instead of changing, Barlow's trying to find his way back to his old life. That would be the perfect solution, if it could work. But it can't.

"What are you doing today?" he asks me. He finishes eating and dusts the crumbs off his palms.

I shrug. "I've got a class at two. I figure I'll dig up Quint this afternoon, get him into the Timeflow."

"Quint!" Barlow looks at me in surprise. "I thought you'd given up on him."

I show him my palms. "A new Season, a new chance."

Barlow straightens in the doorway. "But he's a hopeless Rejector, Dexter. Besides, Amos told you to stay out of your Alternate Life."

"He's my friend, Barlow."

"He's a Bystander and an Alternate and a Rejector. He's not your friend."

I scowl at him. "I'm going to save my friend from Extinction. He'd do the same for me. I'm not going to let what happened to Harley happen to him."

That's my battle cry now. My "Remember the Alamo."

"Get your Seasons in order," the *Parattak* advises. Most Longtimers take that to mean you should make a list of the Seasons and memorize it. Because Longtimers know their Seasons in order by name. Others think the *Parattak* is suggesting the names of the Seasons have some special significance, and if you list their names in the right order, they spell out a secret message. But I think the *Parattak* is just telling us to get our priorities in order.

Barlow squints at me like Mom used to when I'd leave muddy tracks across the kitchen floor. "You're wasting your time," he says to me. "You know what he is. And you need to quit school."

"Yeah, I know," I say, getting annoyed. Sure, Sponsoring Quint ain't easy. But I owe it to our friendship to keep trying, even if he ain't my friend in this Reality. Just another of my new challenges. I'm ready for them. I'm nearly a Longtimer, and I'm prepared for anything. I've got a list of Safe Houses in my back pocket. I'm wearing my Beeper and my Blinker and carrying my supplies with my textbooks in my backpack.

I hate leaving Barlow behind. I've done what I can for him, but I still owe him. I know that. But I'll be in a better position to help everyone once I get my degree.

"Why don't you come with us?" Zeke says to Barlow, "and enroll in the Fourth Dimensional Science course?"

Barlow frowns. He looks over at me and then back at Zeke. "At Shawneetown U?"

"No," Zeke says. "This is different. If we pass, we can get a job with the Society of Time, repairing Dimensionalizers. Steady work. Good pay. We'll be protected from the Time Changes, and our job won't Disappear when there's a new Season."

I can read Barlow's reaction all over his face. He'd love to have a steady job—but in science? He's never been good at science.

I cringe so hard I can hardly keep my eyes open. "Why'd you have to tell him? You know he can't pass that class."

"He can with me as his tutor," Zeke says.

Barlow brightens, smiles at Zeke, and looks over at me like some dog eager to go on its walk. "I'm in if Dexter's in."

So it's up to me. I look at Barlow and then at Zeke. I'm cornered. Barlow needs this class to get him out of his rut. But if I drop out, he'll drop out, too. So Zeke's forcing me to take the course for Barlow's sake.

"Damn you, Zeke." He knows I'm in Barlow's debt. I'm ready to kick myself for getting in this spot.

Zeke just smiles his sly smile.

Maybe I can negotiate a January start date for my engineer's job and start it after the Fourth Dimensional Science course. But if I do that, a Time Change will intervene and screw up everything—and there goes my job. So I'm just going to have to find a way to do both.

So the three of us take the bus to the Flatiron Building. We show our Temporary Society of Time ID's to the guard in the lobby and head to the right in the "Workshops" direction. We follow the arrow for "Classroom." When we reach it, a woman dressed in a fancy orange dress from the Harvest Season hands us application forms at the door.

"I thought we were going to meet Dr. Clockhour," I say.

"That's *after* you apply," Zeke tells me.

So we take a seat in these purple plastic chair-desks on rollers and fill out our applications. A dozen other people are doing the same. The form requires a signature at the bottom, and I know when I sign, I'm signing away my life, signing away my freedom for the next four months.

I'm still going to get my degree and my engineering job. There's no way I'm letting anyone take that from me. Zeke has just piled extra work on top of me, that's all.

We turn in our applications, but only a few of the applicants hang around afterward to meet Dr. Clockhour. The rest will be seeing him on a regular basis soon enough. But of course, we have to show off. He stands and converses with the others first, and then it's our turn.

Dr. Clockhour's a giant of a man—a daddy long-legs spider of a man with long arms and long legs, large hands and a huge grin. He's nothing like I expected, except for the wire-rimmed glasses.

He looks us over jovially. "Three brothers, I take it. From Wilderness."

Before we can confirm, he adds, "You're college men, aren't you?" He smiles at Barlow. "You're the oldest." Then Zeke. "And you're the youngest. And the smartest."

What an Analyzer! We're all impressed.

"I'm Dexter Vann," I say. "I'm an engineering student."

"And I'm Zeke Vann. I'm in the graduate program in physics at Shawneetown U."

'I'm Barlow Vann—"

"Don't tell me," Clockhour says. "You're a police officer. Correct?"

Barlow grins. "I never was much good at undercover work."

Clockhour laughs. "Splendid. What a marvelous crop of prospects! This may be my best class yet." He puts his hands together. "Class will commence next Season. Until then, is there anything you'd like to know?"

Everyone's respectfully silent. Then I pipe up.

"Is Dr. Morlock real?" I ask.

Zeke and Barlow give me these exasperated looks, like I'm wasting the great man's time with my stupid question, but Clockhour's eyes light up. "Let's go to my office," he suggests, "and discuss the topic there."

So he leads us out of the classroom and down the hall to a warren of offices next to the 4DTN studio. His office is pretty small, and there are only two chairs besides his, so Zeke sits on the corner of his desk. Clockhour sits behind the desk and motions for us to come closer, so Barlow and I pull our chairs right up to his desk and lean forward.

He leans toward us and says in a low, confidential tone, "Of course, Dr. Morlock is a pseudonym. No one knows his real name—otherwise, they could track down his Extension in the Past and Wipe him Out of Time."

He looks at each of us. "Some people think the name is really just a title passed from leader to leader or shared by a committee of Violators. But if he's an individual, he's the most powerful man in history. He's as close as anyone's ever come to controlling all of Time."

We're breathing pretty fast in that quiet office. "So he's the head of the Time Syndicate?" I ask.

Clockhour nods.

"And the inventor of the Time Machine?"

Clockhour leans back in his chair, and we all straighten up. "No one knows," he says. "Maybe he invented it. People say he's from the First Reality, but who knows for sure. Almost everything from that When is Lost."

This is pretty intense stuff. And to hear it from a real authority! We're all trying to hold back our breath, afraid if we react too strongly, it will break the spell.

"So what does he look like?" I ask.

Clockhour shrugs. "He's a master of disguise."

I lick my lips. "Would he possibly wear a scarf and an overcoat—and have a swarthy face with the texture of an old boot?"

Barlow turns to stare at me, his eyes a pair of goggles.

Clockhour stands up from his desk, his mouth wide. "You've seen him!"

"And does he like birds?"

Clockhour nods in astonishment. He leans forward, his hands on his desk. "What do you know?" he demands. "What do you know about Dr. Morlock?"

13

ALTERNATE LIFE
Reality 266
Concordance Season

Hello again. I feel like I can finally relax now that you're here and we can talk. It's been a long Reality. I confess I wasn't sure if this journal thing was going to work out at first, but really it's been great having you to talk to on a regular basis. This time with you is always the highlight of my week. You're so patient with me and appreciative and such a good listener. I feel like I can tell you anything, things I can't tell anyone else, even things other people don't want to hear about.

It's summer session at Shawneetown U. now. I should have graduated last month, but it didn't happen. No diploma. No degree. I'm not even on the list for the next graduation, despite having eight semesters of credits. I don't get it. I don't understand what's happened. What the truck is going on? Senior year is not supposed to last until you're a senior citizen. It's not grades. Grades are fine. My Alternate Self just doesn't seem to want to graduate. I can't get my head around this. What has happened to me?

How important is it for Dexter Vann to Survive untouched by the Changes? So what if he's not a college student, not a professional, not an engineer with a bright future? What if he's nothing? Is that so bad?

It is in my opinion. People are counting on me.

So I go to my dormitory at Shawneetown U today to get some answers, and it isn't there. Just an overgrown empty lot in its place. I'm homeless again. I have to call university information to find out where Dexter Vann lives in this Reality. And they tell me: Legacy Hall on Raveller Avenue.

I know Amos has warned us to stay away from our Alternate Residence, but I can't find my course schedule in this Reality or anything else. I have to *know*. I have to figure this out. It makes no sense.

I discover this new building over on Raveller, across

from the stadium. It's all colors and shiny steel and glass. It hardly seems like a dorm at all. It has this new office smell to it. I go inside to the front desk and tell them I left my key in my room—can I borrow theirs? So they give me a loaner.

So far, so good.

A couple people greet me in the lobby. I don't have a clue who they are, and they look at me like I'm being rude, and that makes me feel pretty strange. So I take the elevator up to my room, and I unlock the door and go in.

There are two beds inside and two desks and the usual amount of stuff, but I can't tell which side of the room is mine. You'd think it would be obvious, but it's not. I look for engineering books, but there aren't any. I decide to poke around and try to find something with my handwriting on it. That's when this guy comes walking into the room, this guy I've never seen before, and he puts his backpack on a chair and goes and lies down on one of the beds.

"Oh, hi, Dex."

He's not paying attention to me. He's as nonchalant as a Bystander in Byville. He's about average height, short dark hair, glasses. He opens his backpack and takes out a book and starts to read. I figure he must be my Alternate Self's roommate, and that's *his* side of the room.

I'm not rooming with Harley, because he's Extinct. So why aren't I rooming with Quint? Why am I still living in a residence hall?

So I sit on the other bed and take a look at my side of the room. There's a big poster on the wall of some soccer player fielding a ball.

When did I become interested in soccer? And why would I be interested in it?

I look at the books on the desk and don't recognize them. Biology. World History. Modern Jazz. I've never taken those subjects. Where are the math books? Where are the physics and engineering books? I should be deep into my major. I should be getting ready to graduate. Where's the mail about job prospects? I don't even see a computer in the room.

I'm feeling anxious. What has happened to my Alternate Self in this Season? I'm starting to think coming here was a big mistake. I can't catch up on these unfamiliar classes—I never took these courses before. And I don't want to. I'm not interested in these subjects. I've become a stranger to myself.

There's a weird hollow feeling in the pit of my stomach. I feel dizzy when I stand up. And that's when I see it—a small framed picture, on the desk next to the bed, of some girl I've never seen before. I go over and pick it up. The breeze is blowing her light brown hair and the sun lights up her face, and she's smiling. She's very pretty.

I turn to my roommate, who's stretched out on the bed.

"Who's this?" I ask, holding up the picture. I can almost smell that beautiful hair. I've got this sudden electric feeling in my gut. I'm breathing harder. I can feel my skin tingle.

He glances over at me and gives me a strange look. "You don't know your own girlfriend?"

I look at the picture. I have a girlfriend? This pretty girl is my girlfriend? I start thinking about how I can meet her.

"Yeah, I know her," I say, clearing my throat. There's something caught in it. "But what's her name?"

My Alternate Self's roommate wrinkles up his face and touches his glasses with his thumb. "You don't know her name?" I've heard of early onset Alzheimers, but this is ridiculous.

"Yeah, I know her name," I say, trying to recover some credibility. "I was just wondering if you knew it." So now I'm accusing *him* of having Alzheimers?

He frowns. "Why wouldn't I know Marcy's name?"

Marcy. I look at the picture again. The name seems to suit her. She looks even prettier now—she's got personality. But how am I going to find her? I can't very well wander all over the kingdom, showing people this picture. There's a name for people who do things like that, and it's not Prince Charming.

Besides, what if I *do* find her? How am I going to meet her? Will she spot that I'm only an Alternate? How am I going to talk to her? I don't know anything about her. She'll be able to tell I'm a stranger, and that's all she'll focus on. She won't treat me normally.

"But what's her last name?" I say to my Alternate Self's roommate. I want to call him by name, but I don't want to have to ask *him* what his name is.

He blinks at me. "Are you all right?" Can someone who's twenty-one even get Alzheimers?

"Just dandy," I say. "What's her last name?" I'm starting to get angry—but I guess I'm just a little anxious.

"Is this a game?"

"Yeah, it's a game. Her name."

He stares at me for a second. "Kardashian," he says.

I frown. That doesn't sound right. Isn't that Greek or something?

My Alternate Self's roommate begins laughing hysterically. This is all a joke to him.

"Very funny," I say to him. "What's her REAL name?" This is important.

He regards me, mouth open. He pauses. "You really don't know, do you?"

"Of course I know. Do you?"

"How could you forget her name? Do you have amnesia?"

I'm starting to shake a little. My heart rate is way up there. My body feels electrified. I need to calm myself. So I sit on the bed, looking at the picture. My shaking hands take it out of the glass holder so I can get a better look at it.

"Are you all right, Dexter?" My Alternate Self's

roommate is sitting up now.

"I'm fine. Her name."

He stares at me. "I don't get it," he says.

"Her name."

He lies back down on his bed and takes up his book. "Ask her yourself. She's going to be here any minute."

I almost gasp. Marcy's going to be *here*? I take my comb out of my pocket and stuff the picture in there and look for a mirror, which I find on the wall. I begin combing my hair repeatedly. What am I going to say? I need to act natural. I have to make sure I don't do anything that will make her think I'm an Alternate of myself from a different Reality.

What is normal behavior? And how can I simulate it?

And then I hear a female voice speak my name. And my heart nearly jumps out of my chest. And I look over and see—

Amanda.

In the doorway.

With Cartmell beside her.

"See?" Cartmell says, "I knew he'd be here. I told you he can't stay out of his Alternate Life."

I'm stunned. "What are *you* doing here?" I want them to go away. They have to get out. Marcy's going to be here any minute. I can't have my sisters here when Marcy arrives. They'll spoil everything.

"The question is what are *you* doing here, Dexter?" Amanda's glaring at me. "You know Amos told us to stay out of our Alternate Life."

I stuff my comb in my pocket. I'm starting to panic. "You don't understand." My buttinski family will totally embarrass me. "You've got to leave. You're gonna screw up my big chance." My chance to finally have a girlfriend.

My Alternate Self's roommate is confused, and he's sitting up. "Who are these people, Dexter?"

"My sisters." I spit it out like snake venom from a

wound.

"He's got it bad," Cartmell says.

"We'd better get him out of here."

So they come in and each take hold of an arm and hoist me off the bed.

"No—wait. You can't—I have to stay here. She's going to be here any minute."

Amanda and Cartmell stop and stare at me. "She?"

Oh, crap, now they'll never let me alone.

"Yes," I tell them, removing my arms from their grasp. "I have a girlfriend. Now get out of here. This is private."

So they get out quickly. They start hauling ass—and I'm the ass they're hauling. Out in the hall I start to struggle. "Let go of me!"

"Don't make us get Barlow over here," Amanda says. "Don't make us call Amos."

That settles me down. A little. Amos and Barlow are not exactly the sympathy brigade. "But you don't understand. I have a girlfriend. I finally have a girlfriend. You've got to let me go. I've got to meet her."

They keep dragging me down the hall. They think I'm showing off.

"She's not your girlfriend," Cartmell says. "She's your Alternate Self's girlfriend."

"But I am my Alternate Self," I say.

"No, you're not!" they both yell at me.

How can I make them understand? "This is my chance. Don't you care about true romance at all?"

Amanda rolls her eyes. "Oh, brother!" They drag me into the elevator, and in a sudden frenzy, I pull my arms loose and grip the sides of the elevator doors with each hand while my sisters try to pull me back.

My Alternate Self's roommate has followed us out of the room, and he's in front of the elevator, staring at us. "You've got a weird family, Dexter."

"Help me!" I call to him.

He shakes his head. "Do you have a twin or

something? What is going on? Who are these people?"

Amnesiac and his weird-ass sisters.

Okay, I've gone beyond the Threshold. I get it, so I let go of the elevator doors, and they close in front of me. Amanda and Cartmell grab my arms again.

Everyone treats me like I'm still a kid and they have to look out for me. Even my kid sister. It's infuriating—because my interest in Marcy is all grown up, and it's none of their business.

I sigh. "I just want to meet Marcy," I say. "What's wrong with that?" It's bad enough being an Alternate, but to be Shanghaied by my family like this—

"She's a Bystander," Amanda growls. "In a few weeks she won't Exist anymore. She probably won't even recognize you in the next Reality."

I don't want to give up. I try to rally. "You don't know that. Amos could Sponsor her."

They let out a groan.

"You don't even know her, Dexter," Cartmell says. "She doesn't know you. You've never even met."

"So let me meet her. She's in love with me."

"Not *you!*" they both yell. Cartmell begins to pound on me with her little fists, and I have to hold up my free arm to protect myself from the rain of blows.

"Hey, stop!" It's like they're in a conspiracy with my Alternate Self to ruin my chances with Marcy.

Why does it matter, you ask, whether I meet this Marcy or not? I could claim I'm doing this for her sake, but she doesn't need me, not someone as fine as her. This is all for me—I know that. But I just can't shake this feeling. I don't believe my life is all-important, yet—well, dammit, people are depending on me.

"Stay out of your Alternate Life," Amanda growls.

"Why? My Alternate Self has a better life than I do."

Amanda rolls her eyes. "He's been Annihilated. He's been Wiped Out of the Timestream. Is that what you want?"

I hesitate.

"Well, do you?"

I slump, and they let go of me, and I sigh. "You don't understand. You all have spouses and jobs and lives, and all I have is this stupid degree I've been slaving at so I can get those things you have, and now I've lost that, and I'll never have anything."

"I don't have a spouse and a job," Cartmell says.

And she's right. But still— "You're an Assimilator, and you're only fourteen. Everything's going to work out for you. I don't even have a Strategy."

My sisters groan again. "Stop feeling sorry for yourself," Amanda snaps at me.

When the elevator reaches the first floor, they drag me out to a taxi and stuff me inside with them.

"The Brotherhood Lodge," Amanda tells the driver. And that's when I see her—Marcy—walking toward the dorm. My fantasy—in the flesh. I reach out the window to signal her and start to call her name, but Cartmell hauls me back inside the taxi. "No! No no no!"

The cab pulls out into traffic, and I look back to see Marcy disappear into the Legacy. In my memory the scene is surrounded by mist.

We could have had something, her and me—if it wasn't for my nosy, prying family.

It takes me the rest of the morning to calm down and think things through. My sisters are right, of course. It never would have worked out between me and Marcy. Three weeks in Concordance would not have been enough time to get to know her and let her know me. And we don't have three weeks because we're nearly two weeks into this Reality.

Marcy never would have understood. The best I could have hoped would have been to impersonate my Alternate Self, but even that was doomed to failure. I'm not him. I don't even understand him.

And he's *me*.

Maybe I could have kidnapped Marcy and taken her

into the Timeflow and made her love me. No, Amos would never have gone for it. It's not like I was married to her in Concordance. She was just my girlfriend. Maybe we weren't meant to be with each other.

I am such a loser!

So of course I seek out Barlow for company. He's still wearing his letter jacket from Shawneetown U, and I have on my white shirt and vest. We're stuck in Reality 250 like a couple of Travelers lost in the Deep. So we go for a walk around town. I want to go over to the campus, but Barlow won't agree to it because my sisters have gotten to him and explained my obsession.

"You've just got to let it go," Barlow explains to me as we walk down Front Street downtown, next to the levee. "I know all about fatal attractions. You can't make things work out. Relationships have a life of their own, and they go where they want, and you can't make them go where you want them to."

I am *so* disappointed. As if she really had been my girlfriend—when the fact is I'm terrible with girls, and I'll never have anybody.

"Oh, cheer up," Barlow says. "There's girls all over the place."

That's when I notice the face of my Wristwatcher flashing like some billboard in Times Square. Barlow gets a text on his phone from Amos to meet him at Room 999 of the Sisyphus Station.

So Barlow and I walk to the intersection of Washington and Main Streets and look for a manhole on the southeast corner. The cover is off, like Amos said it would be, and a wrought-iron ladder with curved handles sticks up from the tunnels below. Glancing at the pedestrians around us, we step around the saw-horse barriers and descend the ladder into the darkness. We'll have to hoof it from Lethe Station down the Hades Line.

I can understand why Amos likes to meet somewhere out of the Bystanders' sight, but

14

SPONSORSHIP
Reality 268
Concordance Season

I'm going to pieces. I think I'm cracking up, reader. And then I remember you're here, and that helps make everything better. I depend on you. It's true. I hope that's not too much to bear. It's a lot of responsibility, I know. What would happen to me if you stopped showing up? I don't like to think about that—about being all alone in the Time World with no one to talk to. Please keep reading this journal. Keep in contact. I need you.

My engineering career is still nonexistent in this Season—so I'm just going to have to focus on everyone else for a while until my Alternate Self gets his act together. He doesn't even have a major. He's a frigging senior, and he hasn't settled on a major. How did this happen to me?

Barlow still has no karma. He's as lost as ever. It's strange how different he is without it. The rest of us aren't having the same problem, though, and I can't figure out why not. I guess Barlow always did have a special elusive quality about him. A wisdom—a magic touch. Amos gave us our orders, but we took our cue from Barlow. He's the one who convinced us it's cool to do what Amos says. In a lot of ways he was the real leader of the family.

But now no one's going to follow Barlow, not even to the corner to get a pack of gum. He's a shell, a crash test dummy, an imposter of his former self. It's as if he's been reincarnated as some lower life form.

Barlow has come up with a way to measure his karmic level. He says it increases during every Reality but Vanishes with every Change in Time. If these Realities could last long enough, he could get his old self back, but that isn't going to happen.

It's the same with me. If these Realities would last, I could get my college career back on track. I could enroll in the right classes and carry a double load. Make progress toward a degree.

But the Changes won't let me do that.

Reality 268 isn't that different from 267, so when the Reports are finished, I head over to Shawneetown U to Sponsor Quint again. He's there, but my attempt is a total failure. He's still a Rejector—that Strategy is just who he is, and I'm going to have to accept it. But I'm still bummed out, and I'm sitting on a bench in the entry hall of the Lodge, all folded in on myself like Hyperspace, trying to figure things out. I just don't have the motivation to go to my Alternate Self's classes.

My engineering career is over in this Season—but what else am I going to do but be a student? I'm just a failure at everything these days. I hardly notice when someone enters the room and sits down beside me.

When I glance over, I see it's Garson. He has his hood down, but that doesn't startle me because I've gotten used to his tattooed face. I've even started to get to know him. The wavy blue lines on his cheeks suggest his connection to the Ohio River. The green designs on his forehead reflect his devotion to nature and the extent of his explorations. The purple pattern on his neck reveals his education and job experience. More private information lurks beneath his robes.

"Wrong what is, Dexter?" he asks me.

"I Sponsored Quint again," I say. "But he wouldn't take Shelter. And now he doesn't remember me. This is the third time Amos has approved me to Sponsor him, and I've failed again. I'm going to have to face it and give up. He's a Rejector."

Garson stares ahead glumly into space. "Yes, ah. Was my sister same the. Rejector." His voice slows and rises in pitch. "In the Neverbeen lost her I."

I look over. His head is hanging down. "You had a sister in Sideshow who was a Rejector?" Garson stares at a tragedy in the distance, Traveling toward him at light speed like a Voidship down the Pathway.

"Times I four Neverbeen the Sponsor tried her in. The not was person after she Sideshow. Did but still it I. Of for her in memory me."

As his recollection wrecks into him, he looks even sadder than me. He cared a lot for his sister. She'd been more important to him in Sideshow than Quint to me.

"And you failed four times?"

He shakes his head as if trying to cast off the memory. "Last the time no did not fail I. Same but not she person was. Know did her not I. My sister Sideshow from lost I. Not same the she person a stranger was. Not for me Sponsor I did her. For Sideshow sister in memory from my of."

I look down and nod. "Do you still see her?"

He grapples with the contentious memory. "Still. A same not the person, different person she is sister not my is she." There are tears in his eyes. "Her lost I."

"I'm sorry," I say. "I know how you feel."

Garson swallows. "Said I before nothing I now have. Now true not that's. A now I friend have." He looks at me.

I look back at him in surprise. Garson and I friends? I guess that's true. I guess we are friends. I hadn't thought about it, but I suppose things have changed for me too. I told Amanda last Season I have no one—but now I do. I have Garson.

"Give up don't," Garson says to me. "Examination the future in you when the pass, Member a become you. Quint again Sponsor can you. Give up don't you. Of in memory him." Garson seems stronger, more resolute, as if winning his wresting match with his past.

"But what if he's still a Rejector?"

He becomes agitated. "Very important you try still must. Fourth time yes even a. If still he Rejector is, Goodbye say must your. Chance have still you." He pauses, regaining his composure, delivering his words like swift blows. "To say Goodbye to him. Very important for you it is. Please sake for Garson's this do."

He's right, of course. I've got to try it again—maybe Quint won't still be a Rejector next time. I've got to go the distance—all four rounds. And if he Rejects me, I can say my final Goodbye to him.

Well, we talk some more that afternoon, and we've been hanging out a lot since. About a week later Garson comes running up to me and says, "Sister for you is looking your."

"Which one?"

And then Cartmell comes running down the hall after Garson. "Dexter, there you are!" She's got on a yellow sun dress just like the Concordancers.

She comes up to me and glances back at Garson, and he exits the room. They had tact, back in Sideshow.

"You need to come with me," Cartmell says. "I need to show you something." She grabs my arm and begins to tug on it like she's trying to drag an elephant into the circus ring.

"What?" I ask her. "What do you have to show me?"

This is one of Cartmell's schemes, I can tell. She doesn't try to pull practical jokes at my expense like Cooper, but still she's got something cooked up. This is some kind of set-up.

"I can't tell you," she says. "You've got to come see. If I try to explain, it'll ruin it. You just have to see for yourself." She's really keen on this, whatever it is. But I'm suspicious that she won't tell me. That suggests I wouldn't go if I knew what this was about.

"Come on, Dexter. Please? I hardly ever see you, you're always at class. Can't you just do something for me for once?" She gives me those eyes, those pleading eyes, and I can't say no. So I agree, and she starts dragging me by the sleeve right away. "Come on!" she says. "Hurry."

She leads me out of the Lodge and down the street, where we get on a crosstown bus to some neighborhood in the Saline Mines district, we used to call areas like this "on the other side of the tracks." It's literally on the other side of the railroad yards, and I can smell diesel in the air.

The place she wants to take me to is this low, ramshackle building, it's hardly more than a shack. Next to it is a billboard that's larger than the building.

Madame Bela
FORTUNES TOLD
Palm Reading. Astrology. Tarot.
See the Future Today

The bigger the sign, the bigger the con.

I groan when we get off the bus and I see it. "You know I don't go for this sort of crap," I tell her. "Why did you bring me here?"

"To get your fortune told," she says.

I stop and plant my feet. She tries to drag me on, but this mule won't budge. Not for some fortune telling scam.

"What is this about?" I ask her. "You know I'm not up for this."

She bats her eyes at me. "I can't tell you. You have to see for yourself." She grabs my arm and starts pulling again.

"See what?" I say. "What am I here to see?"

Cartmell stops and looks at me. "Your future," she says. She's got this sly grin on her face like she's the cleverest comedian on the planet.

A scheme. It's one of her schemes, for sure. I'm all suspicious again. "What about it?"

"Madame Bela can tell your future. She really can. She's really good at it."

I give Cartmell the eye. She knows I'm not buying it. "You brought me all the way down here just to have my fortune told?"

She nods eagerly.

I'm even more doubtful now. "Even though you know I'm not going to believe a word of it?"

"But you will," she says. "You don't know how good she is. She can see into the past and into the future. Come on, Dexter. Do it. Do it for me." She bats her eyes at me and sticks out her lower lip.

Echoes of Quint ring in my head when I hear that phrase. This is my chance to do something for Cartmell. While she still Exists. While we both still Exist. She's counting on me.

"Oh, all right." I'm the most reluctant sucker ever. Resentful rather than generous. I just want to get this over with.

"Okay, let's go."

"No," she says. "Only you. I'll wait out here."

We're still across the street. "You're not coming?" I ask her.

She shakes her head. "It's got to be you—alone."

Now there's no doubt this is one of her schemes. This proves it. But I'm on the hook. I agreed to do it. I have to proceed, even though I know I'm going to regret this.

So I cross the street and enter the Fortune Teller's. A bell rings when I open the front door. I'm in a small anteroom with a beaded curtain separating it from the main room. I hear a woman's voice say, "In come."

So I pass through the beaded curtain into a small dark room with colored mood lights along the walls. Scrims slowly spin, casting patterns on the ceiling of stars, pentagrams, and crescent moons. I smell the scent of strawberries and sweet incense. Madame Bela sits behind a table with a crystal ball on it. There's a crimson velvet curtain in a doorway behind her, and on my side of the table, a chair. She indicates for me to sit.

She's all decked out for fleecing in a scarf and a gypsy dress. There's a blue jewel smack dab in the middle of her forehead surrounded by concentric green lines and below it a veil over her eyes, but I can see her eyes beneath the veil because they're outlined with heavy eye-liner so they look like these two forbidding almonds.

It's spooky in there—but I guess that's the whole intention.

"Came to me you have today why?" Madame Bela asks in an accent I've never heard before, and I think I know why Cartmell's brought me here, though I still don't understand the secrecy.

I sit down in the chair. "I want my fortune told," I say.

Madame Bela regards me steadily. "But fortunes not you do believe in," she says in that strange musical accent. It's not a Sideshow accent—but of course, it couldn't be. But it's not a Masterpiece accent either. It's something else.

She's read my crossed arms and tapping foot. She can tell I think this is a bunch of BS. So I tell her, "I promised my sister I would do it for her."

Madame Bela continues to stare at me. "Sister older? Sister younger?"

"Younger," I say.

She regards me with a curious stare. For a hustler, she seems awfully reluctant to con me. "Fifteen dollars," she says finally. "Fifteen minutes. I the Tarot use will."

I pull out my wallet and put down the bills, and she takes them with one hand and produces a Tarot deck with the other. But it's not like any Tarot deck I've ever seen. It looks similar—the cards are the same size and shape, and the illustrations have that same medieval-esque style. But the things depicted on the cards are different, and I wonder if this is some one-of-a-kind deck.

"Life Your Present," she says and puts down three cards like she's playing solitaire. The first one is THE FREAK with a picture of a tattooed man in contortions. The next says FRIENDSHIP with a couple of smiling people on it, and the last reads SISTER with a picture of a maiden wearing a conical hat with a veil attached to the top.

I guess the freak's supposed to be Garson, and the sister Cartmell. I don't know how Madame Bela knows I'm friends with Garson, but it's not exactly a state secret.

I look up at her. "What does it mean?"

"For you," she says. "Interpret must yourself for you." She pauses. "You Garson friends are and?" She looks away. "Mind never," she says. "To Bela not need does know." She sighs and regards me. "Life Your Hidden." She puts down three more cards. THE TWINS with two identical people on it. Then SOULMATE—a heart with an arrow through it. And finally THE LOVERS—a man and a woman embracing.

I think of Marcy and want to speak, but my feelings have gummed up my speaking apparatus. I stutter out my confusion like a crab trying to scrabble across a slippery surface, but before I can go on, Madame Bela says, "Life Your Future." She puts down three more cards. The first is titled CHANGE. There's a cloud on it with lightning bolts coming out. The next is titled THE VOID and depicts a black square. The last is LOST with a depiction of a man in the middle of a forest.

"You're a Longtimer," I exclaim. She doesn't say anything.

"Lost in the Void? That's a death sentence."

She puts down another card. It says BROTHER and has a picture of a man on it. She follows it with a card that reads DEATH with a picture of the grim reaper.

I'm getting ticked off now. I point at the Death card. "What does THAT mean?"

She seems a little frightened herself. "Someone or something die will."

People die every time the Travelers Change the Past, but I don't like these cards. I don't like this game. I'm getting really mad, I guess. I wipe the cards off the table onto the floor with a violent gesture and stand up. "Who are you? What is this all about?"

She stares at me, taken aback. "No," she says. "Madame Bela talk does not herself about." The perfumy incense is overpowering every other odor in the room. It begins to smell like smoke.

I stare back at her, at those two outlined almonds. "Then do a reading," I say, "about *you*." I lean my arms on the table.

She draws back from me and frowns. "A reading want you Madame Bela about?"

"Yes." I sit down. When she just stares at me, I pound my fist on the table. "Do it!"

She hesitates. "Well very." She holds out her palm. "Fifteen dollars." So I pony up another ten and a five, and she produces a new Tarot deck. That's thirty bucks for these stupid fortunes. *You owe me big time for this, Cartmell.*

The first card Madame Bela puts down is the MYSTIC with a picture of a crystal ball. I can't believe I'm paying someone to turn over cards. It's like paying them to waste their time.

"Me," she says, pointing.

The next is SISTER followed by HEARTACHE with a picture of a heart with a knife through it. She puts down another card, MOON with a crescent moon on it and OUTCAST with a black sheep.

"Wait a minute," I say, "wait a minute." There's something aggravatingly familiar here. Sister, heartache, moon, outcast. Madame Bela.

Bel . . . a

"Belinda!" I cry.

I look up, but she's gone. I can see the velvet curtain in the doorway still swinging. So I jump up and run through it. The back door to the place is standing open. I run to it and see Belinda tear off down the alley on a motor scooter. I start to run after her, but she darts around a corner, and she's gone like a Traveler down the Pathway.

Those damn outlined eyes. I could have recognized her if not for those. They turned her eyes into bulls eyes. I stop and rest my hands on my thighs and catch my breath. I start to cuss. I lost her.

So I come back through Madame Bela's, and I exit out the front. Cartmell's still across the street, waiting, so I cross over.

"What did she say?" Cartmell asks eagerly. "What did you find out?"

I give her an intense stare. "You knew it was Belinda all along," I snarl.

She pulls back from me in surprise. "Of course. That's why I brought you here."

I don't know what to say to that. I'm too exasperated. "Then why didn't you go in yourself?"

She looks at me like I'm Chrono. "She wouldn't say anything to me. You're the only one in the family she'll talk to, besides Amos. And I couldn't have gotten him to come."

So that was her scheme. She wanted to find out about Belinda. What a conniver!

"What did she say?" Cartmell asks. "What did you find out?" She's nearly climbing all over me.

I just start walking toward the bus stop. I don't know if I'm mad or just really frustrated. I know I don't like being used as a cat's paw to snare my sister Belinda so Cartmell can find out more gossip about her.

Cartmell follows after me, chattering the whole way, the little show-off. "It wasn't easy finding her, you know. I went to a lot of trouble. It took a long time. And I didn't have any help. I knew none of you would help me find her."

She's got that right.

"Don't be like this, Dexter," she says. "Tell me. I went to a lot of trouble for this. I did a lot of investigating. Don't keep it from me. I want to know."

I still don't feel like talking. I wait for the bus, and when it comes, I get on it. But of course, she eventually wheedles it out of me once we're on the bus. I can't resist her manipulations forever. She's worse than a third degree. Fourth degree, I'd call her. So I tell her about the cards—reluctantly. And I tell her what Belinda said.

"Wow!" Cartmell exclaims, "She's still suffering! No wonder she became a Monk!"

We're both pondering that one. I know Cartmell's going to tell Barlow and probably Cooper and Zeke too. But not Amanda. No one's going to tell Amanda.

"But how'd she know about you and that Alternate girl?" Cartmell says. "And how did she know you're friends with Garson? It sounds like she was surprised to hear that."

I know this is going to get dissected and analyzed and poured over and regurgitated for weeks, and I'm sorry I ever agreed to be part of this. I should have kept my mouth shut. I should have

15

TIME CHANGE
Reality 270
Mystic Season

Well, I screwed up again this Reality. Big time. I must seem pretty pathetic to you the way I keep bumbling my way through this cussed Timeflow. I guess I am pathetic. I just can't stop hoping. And wanting and yearning. I want a career so bad—and someone to love me—and something to give meaning to my life. I know you understand. You're the only one who does, you and Garson.

If my college career can get off track, it can get back on—if I wait long enough. If I keep checking, I'm bound to find a Reality where I've graduated, where I'm an engineer and I've got a job. Then I'll have a foot in the door. It's worth a shot.

I'm going to wait out the Time Changes. That's the new plan. Eventually, the dice have to hit my number. I just have to be patient—and keep checking the records. In the meantime I need to find a way to stay occupied. And that's where Cooper comes in. He's the cure for boredom. He knows how to have a good time. Life with Cooper is an adventure.

So we go on one heck of a quest—a quest for the Lunean Fortune. And now here we are in the Catacombs with the priceless Relic—and a hundred Luneans hot on our trail, out for blood.

Climbing the metal utility steps up to the first sublevel, Cooper glances at his flashing Wristwatcher and meets my eyes. "Only ten minutes to the Time Change, little brother. We'd better get moving." So we take out running down the secret passageway, then up the spiral staircase at its end. The staircase ends at a locked door. We can hear our pursuers gaining on us. We're as vulnerable as a couple Voiders in Protospace.

"Oh crap. We look at each other. His eyes have a sparkle in them. He's having fun. His face has its usual unperturbable expression. Every hair on his head is in place, so fine it's easy to style. Mine is more cave-mannish like Barlow's.

"What do we do now?"

"Void it," Cooper declares. So we hunker down and charge the door with our shoulders. The doorjamb cracks, so we try again, this time breaking the door open with a splintering of wood.

We emerge into the middle of a long hallway, and I recognize where we are. The Lodge of the Brotherhood. An alarm blurts out, blaring intermittently.

I look down the long corridor to our left. Light emanates from the turn at the end of the hallway. Light from an open door.

"Not that way," Cooper says. "That leads to the middle of the Lodge."

The Inner Sanctum, the holy of holies. "I wonder what's there," I say, staring down the hall.

I've learned from Garson that there are other families living in the Lodge—on the second floor. There was a bunch from the Compass Season when we first moved in, but they're gone now, replaced by a group from Guidepost. And there are other Monks too, that we never see—and another Safe House, Room 888. (Garson says the Monks are expecting a new clan next Season—from Moonglow. Imagine that—Moonglow! "Day People?" I ask him. "No," he says, "Night People.") Is it the family of Guideposters down there where the light's coming from?

I'm curious, so I start in that direction, but Cooper drags me back. "Whoa, little brother," he says. "You're going the wrong way. We've got to get to Room 999. And fast."

The footsteps of our pursuers are growing closer.

The lights in the hallway begin to flicker, and flash red to warn us of the upcoming Time Change. We turn to the right and begin to run, flying like Time Machines as we follow the square spiral of corridors toward the outer perimeter of the Lodge.

The wooden door to Room 999 stands open. A red light is flashing above it, signaling it's about to depart. The door through the airlock is shutting, and Cooper and I have to dive through it to get inside.

We land on the floor and somersault across the carpet like acrobats. The door closes, and a minute later the Safe House launches into the Void. I never knew dodging the Time Changes could be so much fun, but that's Cooper for you. We stretch out and float in the weightlessness, laughing.

"Thank god for Safe Houses!" I cry.

"Amen, brother," Cooper says, admiring my prize, a plastic ring from a Concordance Season cereal box. I've just risked my life to gain that stupid ring. It's of enormous significance in the Lunean religion, worth millions to them, but of course, it has no significance to me. It's virtually worthless. I was just playing around when I grabbed the Lunean Relic—just showing off. So I take off the plastic ring and toss it in the waste basket, but it floats back out.

I guess my priorities are kinda screwed up, but I feel I've achieved something great. Those Bystanders never knew what hit them. Now that I'm here in this Safe House, all my problems are behind me, and I forget about the Bystanders who've been chasing us. In a few more minutes Concordance will be over and they won't Exist. Time Changes can erase a lot of problems.

The rest of the family is already inside the Safe House and belted in, so Cooper and I float over to a couple chairs and belt in, too. Amanda gives us a stern look, her arms crossed over her shoulder belt, but she knows it's no use scolding us—because we're such hopeless Wilderness types.

The commencement of the Fourth Dimensional Television Network's coverage of the latest Time Change distracts her attention from the two of us anyway. We listen to the Reports carefully both before and after our Safe House reaches Landfall. Because Amos has taught us a Dark Season can be dangerous. Many things will have Changed, and you've got to be ready for them. Of course, new Reports are always coming in, and you can't wait to hear all of them, or you'd never leave Shelter. And there are so many changes in this new Reality, that the list goes on and on. It's going to be Shawneetown version 20.0.

"That's enough," Amanda declares, minutes after Landfall. She's in charge of the family. Amos told us to take our orders from her. We've all accepted Amanda's leadership, but five minutes of Reports don't seem like nearly enough for a Dark Season. We glance at each other uneasily. No one wants to question Amanda's judgment, but—

"What's the big hurry?" Cooper asks her as she starts to pack up.

She peers at him, checking to see if he's challenging her authority. "I need to get to work at the bank," she says. "I'm already late." She's wearing a gray suit today and looks dressy but also comfortable. She knows how to wear expensive things.

Cooper squints and rubs his brow with his thumbnail. "I think I'll stick around here a little bit longer, if you don't mind."

"Suit yourself." Amanda slings the strap of her travelling bag over her shoulder. "Anyone want to come along?"

"I do," I tell her. Sure, I want to hear some more Reports about the Mystic Season, but I also want to save on cab fare. I need to get to campus and find out if I have a degree or not, even though I've given up school. Okay, so I'm in Denial. I'm so stuck in the past I ought to be arrested for Traveling. It's not easy giving up on a lifelong dream. I just want a peek, that's all. This is a new Season—so there's a chance now that my Alternate's finally gotten things right.

Zeke and Cartmell opt to stay with Cooper. They've both quit school, so of course, they don't have to get anywhere. All they have to do is babysit Jackson and Jessalyn while Pete and Amanda are at work.

Cartmell's biting her lip, and she knows she shouldn't butt in, but she can't help herself.

"Amanda," she says. "Amos told you to give up your bank job."

Amanda glowers at her. "Amos doesn't know everything."

"But—"

"It's my life, and I'm capable of making my own decisions, thank you." Amanda turns away from her and adjusts the strap on her bag.

Cartmell's face falls, and she looks at the floor. She should have known better than to criticize Amanda. Amanda's gotten tired of Amos's lecturing. We all have. She's looking forward to a vacation from that without Amos here. To bring it up now is like bringing up work during a picnic. Nobody wants to hear that stuff. We've had enough.

"Cartmell's right," Belinda says, but Amanda cuts her off. She should have known not to butt in. She's the last person Amanda's likely to listen to.

"I don't want to hear anything from *you*," she snaps, giving Belinda her death-ray stare.

We're all holding our breath. The old Amanda/Belinda feud has been Reinchronated. We were surprised to see Belinda show up at Room 999 in her white sundress. We wanted to ask where she's been, but we know she won't tell us, and she's so touchy and always feeling like we're judging her. At least she's not a Monk anymore—or a gypsy. The facial tattoos are gone, and so is the jewelry. She looks like a Concordancer now. No more spiky butch haircut. No t-shirts or jeans. She hasn't worn anything from Wilderness since Moonglow. And nothing from Moonglow since Guidepost.

Belinda's hair is darker than mine and finer, straight as string. Her pale face has a fresh inviting look when she's not mad about something, which she is most of the time, like now.

"I think I'll walk to work from here," Pete tells Amanda, heading off the confrontation. The Financial District is only a few blocks away, and Pete isn't on the clock, so he doesn't have to worry about being late. He can listen to as many Reports as he wants.

So Amanda turns to Barlow. "You coming with us, Bar?"

He's got on his jeans and t-shirt—he's not ready for a new Season. He hesitates for a second. "I guess I'll stay here awhile."

Which means, of course, that Belinda will come with us, because she avoids Barlow whenever she can. Her fortune telling racket in Concordance would be ideal for Mystic. She seems to have gotten ahead of herself, and I'm wondering what that's all about.

At least everyone is being responsible and cautious instead of trying to show off. So maybe we are making some progress for a change.

I sling my backpack over my shoulder and stand up. Belinda stands up too—she already has her knapsack ready. Amanda hugs Jackson and kisses Jessalyn goodbye, and we walk to the door to Room 999 and open it and walk down the corridor of the Brotherhood Lodge to the front door.

The Lodge doesn't change much from Reality to Reality, so we don't get a look at the Mystic Season until we get onto the porch in the wind. The Brotherhood Lodge is built on a hill in Westwood, so we can see the skyscrapers of Old Town easily from there. The shiny blue buildings stand like blocks of ocean. They've completely changed shape and size and color since Concordance, but I never looked at the skyline from this vantage point in the past Season, so I can't be sure how radical this last Change has been. Pretty radical, judging by the Reports we've heard and the wind that nearly knocks us over.

We aren't worried about drastic changes in the new Reality, even though there's been a shift in Seasons, because Amos has assured us there are limits to how far back in Time the Travelers can go, due to the great distances involved. Most Changes don't date back more than forty Calendars, because most Time Machines can't carry enough fuel to Travel farther than that. To mount a mission beyond forty Calendars is a real production, involving renewable or recycled sources of food, water, and air. The Deep Voidships are atomic powered, and that means sophisticated engineering beyond the means of the Timecrimers. Even a big ship stockpiled with supplies is limited to a range of about forty years. You'd need a Voidship to go any farther.

The Russian Voidship Potempkin made the longest voyage ever recorded, and that was a distance of just over two centuries. But no one knows for sure, because the Potempkin hasn't come back. Only the CTA has the capability of Traveling any farther, and their missions are secret.

Traveling into the Past is the ultimate status symbol. But even Travelers with the capability never Travel farther than what's necessary to turn a profit. Because Deep Trips aren't cost effective, and only the radical fringe groups like the STA will Travel for any reason except profit.

I suppose we should have listened to Amos and been more concerned about this latest Change. But Moonglow's the only Dark Season we've ever seen, so we don't know what to expect.

We don't know yet that Dark Seasons are time bombs.

There's already a taxicab waiting for us down at the curb in front of the Brotherhood Lodge, because the Monks have called one for us. So the three of us climb into the back, and Amanda tells the driver the address of the Shawneetown Bank. We head down Poplar to Gallatin and turn left and ride toward Old Town.

We stare out the tinted windows at the new Reality. The Bystanders of the Mystic Season have a penchant for the occult. We can see pentagrams and stars and crescent moons all over the place. The color blue seems to be everywhere, and the wind is full of the smell of strawberries and sweet incense. Even our cab driver's wearing a blue magician's robe and a blue conical cap with yellow stars and crescent moons on it. So we look out of place, of course. And the Bystanders' speech has a low musical sound to it that seems to jibe with their other-worldly interests. So we sound out of place too.

The cab driver must be wondering about us—after all, when was the last time anyone got a fare from the Brotherhood Lodge?

"Where are you folks from?" he asks us. "New York City?"

New York! We almost laugh. Our speech must sound pretty off-pitch to him—like Stephen Hawking to Mozart. There's something about his accent—and then it hits me. It's the same as Madame Bela's from Concordance.

"We're from farther away than that," Amanda tells him, which is true, but the wrong answer, because it just encourages him to keep quizzing us. Chatty cab drivers are a drag to Longtimers. They pose such a threat, such a pointless challenge.

"My name's Lord," the cab driver tells us. "Romick Lord. But most people call me Mick." He has graying hair and a moustache—he seems like someone who's moonlighting. He has a pale face, too, like most of the Mystics, from spending too much time indoors. The Mystics prefer cloudy weather and nighttime. Madame Bela told me she was a Mystic, so I'm wondering now why Belinda pulled the Mystic act in Concordance instead of now. And how did she know the Mystic

Season was coming? It has to be a coincidence because the Future doesn't Exist.

"So where is it you're from?" he asks. We can't very well tell him we're from the Neverbeen.

"Canada," Amanda informs him, thinking that a safe answer.

"Oh yeah?" Mick says. "I have a sister in Montreal."

"We're from the Yukon," Amanda replies, hoping to put an end to the discussion. We drive in silence for a few minutes, Belinda still motionless between us. She hasn't said a word since Amanda snapped at her back in the Safe House. She just stares out the window and won't look at us.

"Okay," Amanda says, trying to melt the snowman. "I know Amos said I should quit. But I can't do that. He doesn't realize how important this is to me." She glances at Belinda and raises her hands in a gesture of frustration. "I'm sorry if I snapped at you." Amanda reaches out and touches Belinda's arm, but Belinda draws it away. Amanda rubs the fingertips of her rejected hand.

"It's easy for Amos to tell me to quit," Amanda declares. "He doesn't lose a thing if I quit my job. He doesn't know how hard I've worked to get this far. It's no loss for him. But I've invested my entire life in this. It takes years to get ahead at a Bank like Shawneetown National. Bank managers are conservative people, and they don't trust you overnight. You've got to prove yourself, prove you're reliable, even-tempered, with good judgment, not just once but for years. I've spent fifteen years building up my reputation in the eyes of the bank managers. Fifteen years of hard work, no mistakes, no sick days. Fifteen years of self control. There have been times, lots of them, when I wanted to answer a slight with a slight, sass back at my boss, insult a customer, snap at an assistant. But I didn't. I kept my emotions under control. It was like holding my breath. I smiled when I was unhappy. I kept quiet when I wanted to say something. I stayed calm when my anger was raging. You can't imagine how difficult that was at first, but it became a habit. But now—I don't know what's happening to me. I'm constantly gasping for air. These Changes in Time—"

We both know what she means. The damn Changes have unhinged all of us.

"I'm just glad my old life is finished and I can start over fresh," Belinda declares.

Starting over fresh may be fine for Belinda, but it's not for me. I've put three years of hard work into getting this engineering degree. I've pulled I don't know how many all-nighters, sacrificed my social life, spent all the money I saved working during the summers. I couldn't do that again. And I shouldn't have to. I deserve that degree. I earned it. I'm an empty vending machine, all out of sacrifices.

"If you want to be a banker," Amanda says, "you've got to be even tempered. You can't complain all the time or fly off the handle like Mom. You've got to be quiet and dignified like Dad. They watch for that at the bank. For signs of character. Calmness. Control. You can't lose that control, even once.

Amanda leans back in her seat and takes a deep breath. "It took years, but it's finally happened. I've gotten *the* promotion. My hard work has paid off. My salary has doubled. I can relax, loosen the reins on myself. Because I have one boss instead of five. And he's at the bank less than half the time. Usually he doesn't come out of his office. I'm supervising myself really."

She looks at Belinda, then me. "My promotion happened because I made it happen. But now no one knows me—and I don't know them. I've lost my self control. I couldn't make the case for promotion. So you see, to start over would be impossible. This is my only chance. I'll never make it to the top again, not in these Bystander Realities. Even fifteen years couldn't make it happen."

Amanda sighs, and Belinda turns toward her and tries to catch her eye. "It's been tough for me too."

Amanda hangs her head. "I guess we all wish it could be Reality 250 again."

Amen to that.

Belinda fidgets beside me. "I don't," she says. She looks out the cab window.

"Don't what?" Amanda asks her. She looks over at Belinda.

"I never liked Reality 250," Belinda declares.

I notice the cab driver's frowning and glancing into his rear-view mirror, and I think about elbowing my sisters. I don't like discussing our Time Problems in front of the Bystanders.

"What?" Amanda turns in her seat to stare at Belinda. "How can you say that? Reality 250 was your home."

"I never felt at home there," Belinda declares, looking off into the distance.

Amanda gapes at her. "You mean you feel at home now? In these Bystander Realities?"

"No," she admits. "I've never felt at home anywhere, I guess. I just don't want to go back to living in Reality 250."

Both Amanda and I are nearly off our seats. Not want 250 back? What's with Belinda?

"People from 250 are so overbearing," she complains. "The whole place seemed oppressive to me. I felt intimidated all the time."

"What!" Now I'm the one who can't take what I'm hearing. Reality 250 was all that is good and true in the Chronoverse. "Reality 250 was free, Belinda. Wilderness was the freest Season there's ever been."

"Not free for me," Belinda says. "I need to live in a Reality that's nurturing, not one that's free, somewhere people help others to explore and grow and find themselves, without everyone staring at them and constantly finding fault."

Amanda and I look at each other. Belinda is being contrary again. Whatever we say, she's got to contradict it. Like Riley.

"I'm tired of people pushing me around," Belinda says, "trying to define me, control me."

"Oh, stop whining, Belinda," Amanda declares. "No one's trying to persecute you. I swear sometimes I can't believe you're from Reality 250 at all."

Belinda clams up after that, and I feel bad for arguing with her like we did. We just couldn't believe anyone would dislike Reality 250, especially someone from there. She has to be making it up, exaggerating, playing the devil's advocate like Riley. She picked up a lot of bad habits from that guy.

The cab driver turns left onto Market, which is a one-way street in this Reality.

"Are you all getting out on Main Street?" he asks us once we're stopped at a light.

"No," Belinda tells him. "I need to go back to the Brotherhood Lodge." So why did she get in the cab to begin with?

The driver looks at me. "What about you?"

I was hoping I wouldn't have to answer that question until Amanda had already gotten out of the cab. Now I'm on the spot, and there's no way I can duck it.

"I need to go to Shawneetown University."

The light changes, and the driver hits the gas. We pass some flower shop or fruit stand, and I smell the scent of roses and tangerines.

"Dexter," Amanda scolds me. "Amos told you to quit school. Why haven't you quit?" She's giving me one of her hard looks.

"Yeah, well," I say. "You're not the only one who wants to preserve their career."

"You haven't even started your career," Amanda says to me. "It's not like you've already invested fifteen years in it. You're still young and can start over."

Belinda side gazes me too. "Make a fresh start, Dexter. Listen to Amos for a change. Why can't you two listen to advice? You are so stubborn. I get so tired of being around stubborn people."

I feel like Joan of Arc bound at the stake for her crusade. All I want is a normal life. I want a normal job and a normal family. Is that too much to ask? It doesn't seem too much to me.

The driver turns the corner onto Washington and up to the stoplight at Main. The bank building stands on its own instead of fronting a taller building, and on the cornice, above the five thick pillars, where it used to say "BANK OF SHAWNEETOWN," tall letters now spell out "SHAWNEETOWN MUSEUM" like it's an exhibit from the past.

"Here we are," the driver says.

Amanda looks at the building and at me and then at the building. I'm as shocked as she is. What's happened to the bank?

It's gone.

"Where's the Shawneetown Bank?" Amanda says. "Where's Shawneetown National?"

The driver gets a funny look on his face. He pushes back his conical cap and scratches his head and twists around in his seat. "Shawneetown Bank! The old Shawneetown Bank's been out of business for years." He gestures at the bank building. "It used to be in there, before they made it into a museum."

Amanda's mouth opens, but she doesn't speak or move. She's too stunned. She sinks back into her seat, staring into space. Belinda starts to reach out for her, pulls back her hand and looks at me with a frightened expression.

I feel pretty damn weird, I tell you. I can feel the dread filling up my legs and then my gut. I can feel it rising up my spine. I worry it will overflow the top of my head, and I'll drown in it. Because if Amos can be right about Amanda's bank Vanishing, then he can be right about me too.

"Well, are you getting out or not?" the driver asks Amanda. She's slumped in her seat and staring ahead of her with a vacant look in her eyes, like a convict serving a life sentence. She can't answer, so I answer for her.

"You'd better just take us to Shawneetown University."

The driver makes a notation on a clipboard then sets it down beside him and puts the car in gear.

"Where's that?" he asks.

I squint at him. He's a cab driver, and he doesn't know where Shawneetown U is? That's about as likely as a beach lifeguard not knowing where the ocean is.

"Take Garfield north," I say. "Then turn at—"

"Garfield?" Mick says, tilting his conical hat. "I don't know that street."

"The MacArthur Expressway," I tell him. "I mean, the Dewey Expressway."

He wrinkles up his face and stares at me. "Just what town do you think you're in?"

"Okay, just head north," I tell him. "It's up past New Town."

"New Town?" Now I'm the one who can't believe what I'm hearing.

I just want to scream. Giving directions to Bystanders can be so frustrating.

"Go north on the street that's two block over." I point. "I'll let you know when we get there."

Mick Lord does a U-turn in the middle of the street and gets on Garfield—or highway 1 as they call it in this Reality. He shakes his head. "I hope you know where you're going. I've lived in Shawneetown all my life, and I've never heard of any university here."

I freeze for a second. I can feel the hairs curl at the back of my neck, and I can feel the dread top my scalp and run down my face in freezing rivulets. "They must have changed the name," I say. "It's the big college a few miles from here."

Mick Lord shakes his head. "There ain't no college in Shawneetown. Never has been. I don't know where you think you are, but it ain't here."

Shawneetown U gone? But it can't be.

Belinda gasps and stares at me and lifts her fingertips to her lips.

I shiver and try to swallow. "But it's gotta be there," I say. "I just had a class there last week."

We drive in silence for awhile. Amanda has totally checked out, and I'm too apprehensive to say anything. I feel if I speak, I may jinx the whole expedition. *It's gotta be there. It's gotta be.*

But as we head north and pull around the bend, I can see the road ahead, and there's nothing but empty fields and an old time cemetery like it's 1888.

"It's gone," Amanda says in a dreamy voice. "It's really gone. Amos said this would happen, and now it has."

It takes me a moment to realize she's still talking about the bank.

"It's over," she says. "Our Past Lives are over." She's still in shock, still finding it hard to believe. But it's not just the Bank that's gone or Shawneetown U. My chances of ever finding Marcy are gone too.

"Well, are you getting out at the cemetery?" the driver asks.

"Take us back to the Brotherhood Lodge," Belinda tells him. "That's where we're going now."

I swallow. Gone. I can't believe it. Like the dinosaurs. Like the Titanic. Like Wilderness.

16
DISCHRONOFILIATION
Reality 271
Mystic Season

Well, reader, the college dream is over. I won't be an engineer. You did what you could. We both did our best, but the Changes were too much for us. I don't know what's going to become of me now, but at least I've still got you to help me get through this.

Maybe it's for the best. Maybe giving up college is my destiny. What do you think, reader? Do I need to leave it behind and stop fighting fate? You have a say in this, too, you know. I can feel you trying to console me, and I appreciate that. It helps. Don't stop rooting for me. I depend on that.

I guess this feeling I've had, that someone is depending on me—it's been you. It's been you all along, reader. You're the one who's depending on me. So I'm not going to give up. I promise you that. But I'm pretty bummed out, as you can imagine.

Amos is mad at us—at Amanda and Barlow and me for our breakdowns at the beginning of the Mystic Season. He's been warning us all along to get out of our Past Life, and now we're paying the price for not listening. He insists we go to a support group—Longtimers Anonymous—for people with Time Problems. It meets in the basement of a church up on 45th Street.

So the three of us go there and sit on folding chairs in this drab room and stare at each other. There's a half dozen other people in the group: the Monk Garson, Amos's friend Jordan Jordan who's never gotten over the loss of the Dewdrop Season, a guy whose name I can't pronounce, also from some Dark Season—the African country he grew up in doesn't Exist anymore and he's the last of his kind like Garson, a former Monk named Reginald who used to be in the Brotherhood but had to drop out because he's got Chronophobia due to a traumatic experience in the Void (Chronophobia can mean the fear of anything associated with Time, not just fear of weird Longtimers), the Monk Greta, and most surprising of all, Max Stengler. He's a famous journalist with a column in the Oldspaper. All the Longtimers know him and respect him—and he's so busted up inside he's got to go to a *support group*? It boggles my mind.

Well, a couple of the others speak first, and then it's our turn. Amanda looks like she just wants to crawl under a rock. "Hi," she mumbles. "My name's Amanda, and I'm a Newcomer."

Hello, Amanda.

She opens her mouth and can't speak at first. "I—I lost my job!" She busts out into tears and puts her face in her hands. Greta and Jordan Jordan go over to comfort her. We're all pretty glum. They quiet her down and tell her she doesn't have to talk until she's ready. So now it's Barlow's turn.

He doesn't know what to say at first, so I nudge him and whisper, "Hello, my name is Barlow."

"Oh, right," he says. "I'm Barlow, and I'm a Newcomer, too."

Hello, Barlow.

He searches for words for a few seconds. "I lost my karma," he says. "The Time Changes stole it from me." He's looking around for sympathy but can see that people don't understand, so he tries again.

"I'm the same person as before," he tells them. "But it's like I've become unglued. My parts don't stick together anymore. There are gaps inside me now. And when I come to one of the gaps, I get lost—"

His words trail off, and he's just staring into space like he's forgotten what he was talking about. I hear a couple of the others sigh. They know what it's like to be lost. We all do.

Barlow doesn't know what to say next. He looks like he's finished with talking, so now it's my turn. Everyone lets him off the hook and stares at me.

I clear my throat. "Howdy, everybody," I say. "My name is Dexter, and I'm a Newcomer."

Hello, Dexter.

A gap. They're getting inside *me* now. I hesitate. "Uh—I used to be a college student," I stammer. "At Shawneetown U." I think they get the drift of that. They all lean back in their chairs like they're afraid I'm about to explode.

I lean forward and join my hands. "I used to have plans," I tell them. "I used to have goals. But the Time Changes have eaten them all up. I knew what I was doing. I knew where my life was going. But now—I've got nothin'." I throw up my hands in futility. "I don't know what I'm gonna do." I'm done.

Dexter Vann of Reality 250 is gone. All that remains is Dexter Vann actor and costume dummy. I'm nobody now, same as my brothers and sisters. And my prospects? Even less. The career dream is gone. What could possibly replace it? I am not an engineering student anymore, and that means I have no identity. Just brother of. And that doesn't mean anything anymore. I don't even have a Strategy. Where am I going to find an identity? Not from the past. Not from the present either. So from the future? Or something I completely make up?

I get a lot of sympathy, but I don't dare tell the group my other problem—the one nobody can understand, the one I can't mention to *anyone*.

I can't stop thinking about Marcy.

I want to find her. I want to meet her. I want her to be my girlfriend. I know it's wrong of me. I know it's a bad idea—but I just can't stop myself.

It's so hopeless. How would I even find her? There's three million people in Shawneetown, and I don't even know her last name. And even if I did find her, what good would it do?

I am so doomed.

Well, I could tell you what the others in the support group said, but it's supposed to be confidential, and besides, I think you get the drift. I don't know if I'm gonna go back. It's good to meet people and find out that you're not the only one having problems (I mean—Jordan Jordan, really? She's high society—an Eloi, for Ingersol's sake. What's she doing in a support group?), but I can't see what good it's going to do me to dwell on my problems and look at myself like I'm some sort of Chonoholic.

So I'm not goin' back, not this Season.

I've started taking the Fourth Dimensional Science course with my brothers Zeke and Barlow. It's pretty weird stuff. Weird as a possum in a Voidsuit. Quantum Time Theory states the universe exists in discrete Slices—Quanta lined up along the Fourth Dimension. Each Slice is as big as the universe in Three Dimensional terms, but its Fourth Dimensional thickness is unknown. We can't observe or measure it because we can't Travel into the Fifth Dimension.

Some theorists believe the universe's Fourth Dimensional thickness is only the width of its largest particle. Others hypothesize the thickness is negligible and the universe is the equivalent of a Four Dimensional hologram. Maybe it's entirely Three Dimensional and has no Fourth Dimensional thickness at all.

Spontaneous Creation is the mechanism behind the production of new Slices at the Present. That means there is no such thing as motion—only changes of position. Each new Slice differs from the last according to natural laws, but not the "laws of physics," which are largely laws of motion and conservation, at odds with Spontaneous Creation.

Quantum particles can seem to move through impenetrable barriers because they don't move at all. They are simply recreated in a different position in the next Slice. Schrodinger's cat is alive in one Slice and dead in the next. Its status does not become consistent in newly created Slices until it is interacted with in some way.

The physical science of the Timeflow is no less strange than the psychological environment we Adapt to. I've reached the section of the *Parattak* where it discusses Transformation and Disintegration, the two forces that operate in Newcomers. Transformation is good, and it is inevitable in Newcomers as they adapt to the Timeflow. Disintegration is bad, and it ends with a Newcomer going permanently Chrono. Both processes can operate simultaneously or sequentially in Newcomers, or a Newcomer can Stabilize temporarily and experience neither. Once the process of Transformation is complete, Disintegration stops. And likewise, once Disintegration is complete, Transformation stops. So it's a race inside every Newcomer to see which force will prevail.

I think Cartmell and Belinda are Transforming. I see evidence of it in them constantly. Zeke, I don't know. He's so private I'm not sure what's going on with him. He's so intelligent, he can mask what's happening inside. Barlow clearly has been Disintegrating, but I think he's Stabilized, which is good. He's not getting any worse.

Amos clearly finished Transforming a long time ago—from a Conqueror to a Superconqueror. There are no signs of Disintegration in him. There are also no signs of Disintegration in Cooper, which is another reason I don't think he's a Newcomer. I suspect his Transformation is complete—but to what? He shows signs of Past Life, lots of them, but no signs of stress. I can't figure him out. He's a possum in a Voidsuit.

I think I started Disintegrating when I found out about Marcy. I didn't realize it at the time. But I Stabilized once I abandoned my Alternate Life. I want to Transform, but I don't see how I can until I settle upon a Strategy.

Who I'm really worried about is Amanda. She's never moved past anger and denial, she's still stuck in Past Life, and the loss of her bank has hit her hard. She just mopes around and stares and moans. She's Disintegrating fast, and I don't know what to do about it. I fear she'll be the first of us to go completely Chrono.

This morning when we get up, Amanda doesn't want to come out of her room in the Lodge. I don't know if she's embarrassed or scared or just depressed, but we have to go in and drag her to the family meeting in the Library. Amos makes us get her—he insists on it. I swear he'll be lugging our corpses to these meetings after we're dead.

The Library's become our living room since we moved in a couple of Seasons ago. Zeke and I are seated on the yellow couch, Amanda's on one of the red stuffed chairs, Barlow on one of the yellow ones. Cartmell is curled up on the other yellow easy chair. In the far corner of the room, next to the piano, Pete watches Jackson and Jessalyn as they play on the hardwood floor. Cooper is turned sideways with his legs over the arm of an easy chair next to the wing-backed chair, where Amos is sipping tea, wearing his 238 suit with the luminescent white piping.

I'm wondering why he's called this meeting. This isn't our usual time, and there shouldn't be any Time Change coming, not so early in this new Reality.

Amos puts down his teacup and regards us. "What happened to Amanda in 270," he tells us, once we're assembled in the Library, "could happen to any of you in a Dark Season. That's why you've got to give up your Past Life."

Amanda sits in gray sweats, turned sideways in her chair, her arms crossed as if she's hugging herself. She looks down at the floor as Amos speaks from his wing-backed chair. It isn't only the bank that has Vanished from Existence in this Season. So have many of the people who worked there, including Mr. McNamara, her boss. He's Extinct now.

I never realized how much care and effort goes into Amanda's hair styling so she can achieve that natural unstyled look. But that effort is clear since she's given up and her hair's gone haywire. Untended, it does not look natural. It looks like a bomb went off.

She seems inconsolable.

"Don't assume," Amos says, "that just because you've been forced out of your past, your struggle with Past Life is over. It's not. You still haven't established a new life in the Timeflow. You haven't severed your Attachment to the past."

We sit there depressed. We're feeling pretty Dischronofiliated because of our losses. I've never felt farther from home. And here I am in my own home town.

"You need to accept," Amos tells us, "that your past is over. Forget your former plans. Make a new start in the Timeflow, begin a new career."

Amanda's not listening to Amos. She just sits there staring like she's lost Pete or something.

"You have six months after your Membership," Amos tells us, "to prove to the Society you've found gainful employment in the Timeflow. The Society wants useful Members who can contribute something, not panhandlers who'll be a drag on the resources of everyone else. They expect Members to be employed instead of begging or Living off the Land."

"Living off the Land?" Amanda's looking confused, as if she's just woken up. "What's that mean?"

"He means stealing from the Bystanders," Zeke tells her.

Amanda is floored. "What? That's what we're reduced to—being common thieves?"

"I wouldn't call it common," Zeke says. He's wearing a magician's robe today. The rest of us are in 250 clothes, except for Amos, of course.

Amanda still can't accept our predicament. I guess bankers are pretty touchy about any suggestion of a connection between them and thieves.

"Living off the Land is not what the Society wants from you," Amos tells her. "If all the Longtimers did it, the Bystanders would get suspicious. We'd be in danger of being discovered. So it's really a last resort. But it's better than perishing."

Amanda is appalled. "I'm not going to let you turn me into a beggar or a thief."

"Glad to hear it," Amos says. "Once you've passed your test and become a Member, maybe you can get a job at the Time Bank." The Time Bank is the bank the Longtimers use. The entire bank building's a Safe House that enters the Void whenever a Change is coming. Like the Common, it returns in the next Reality once a location for it has been found.

Amanda still looks pretty miserable. If Amos is trying to cheer her up with bad news, then he's seriously miscalculated. None of us want to hear a bunch of bad news.

And then he drops his first bomb on us.

"Brother Samuels informs me your rooms in the Lodge are needed for a family that's recently entered the Timeflow, and he'll be expecting you to move out by the end of this Season."

This announcement is met by a chorus of groans. Move out? Us? Now?

"But this is our home, Amos," Cartmell says. "We can't move out." None of us want to move out of the Lodge. It's so comfortable and familiar.

Amos looks askance at us. "You knew when you moved in, this was only temporary. Now that you've Adjusted, it's time for you give up your spot for other Newcomers."

We groan again. We don't want to go back to struggling in the Bystander World. And what about

Catterus? He could still be hunting us.

"But where are we going to live, Amos?" Amanda asks him. "You told us to stay out of our Alternate Lives and Alternate Residences."

So Amos drops his other bomb. "You're just going to have to solve that problem yourselves. I've recently received news that the Elder has Disappeared, and no one knows what's become of him." Amos knits his fingers together and massages his knuckles. "The Scion has asked me to take over as Elder until the elections in December. That means I'll have to be spending my time at the government offices on Communication Station. I'll be visiting the Society Station too and The Common, but I doubt you're going to see me again for another Season."

Just then, Amos's Beeper goes off, but it isn't his Time Change Alarm. It has a different sound, more like a chirp, from a small box on his belt. He pulls it off and holds its display up in front of his eyes and sighs.

"I need to be going," he says. "Amanda will be in charge, of course, and I'm sure Cooper can lend a hand in finding someplace to live." He stands and hesitates and shifts his weight. "I'll try to get together with you after you take your Society exams next Season." He surveys us and licks his lips and raises a hand for a wave but reconsiders and drops his arm and Nods. "Goodbye," he says and strides out of the room and down the hall.

We watch him go, then stare at each other. He sure isn't kidding about that not having time for us stuff. He vanishes as quickly as a Time Machine. And I'm wondering about that "Goodbye." Does he think we're not going to make it? Is this as far as we've ever gotten before in the Neverbeen?

"Well, what do we do now?" Barlow says.

We look over at Cooper, and he says, "Sorry, but I've been called away too. I have to go to California to do some stunt work. But I know a guy who can help you get some ID's so you can find a new place to live, and I'll have him get in touch with you." And then Cooper swings his legs around and stands up and walks out the door like a submarine disappearing under the sea.

Both of them gone. Just like that.

We look over at Amanda to see what her reaction will be. I don't expect she'll have any, she's been so low since her bank disappeared. But she surprises me. She gets up and walks over to the wing-backed chair where Amos always sits. She pulls a brush out of her purse and begins to brush her hair.

"There's no reason for us to go back to our rooms yet," she says. "We still have a lot to talk about."

She sits in Amos's chair and presses the buzzer that Amos uses to summon the Monks. The Monk Greta appears in the doorway after a moment. She's one of the more normal-looking Monks, a brunette in her late twenties. I haven't figured out what Season she's from. It can't be one of the Dark ones. She has her hood down, and we can see her pale face and curly brown hair.

"Yes, Brother—" She looks around for Amos, a little off-balance. She and Amanda exchange Nods.

"Could you get us some refreshments, Greta?" Amanda asks her. "Our brother was called away in the middle of our meeting. We could use some tea and coffee and lemonade. And some cakes and cornbread."

Greta Nods at the rest of us and regains her balance. "Certainly. I'll only be a moment."

Once Greta leaves us, Amanda leans back into the wing-backed chair, as if she's always sat there. She slips the brush back into her purse.

I squint in surprise. What is Amanda doing? Then it hits me: she intends to finish the family meeting, the same as if Amos was still here. She's going to supply us with the structure and leadership and support that Amos has been giving us but now is too busy for. Has she finally Stabilized? Is she going to be able to lead us? It sure seems like it.

I marvel at Amanda's boldness. She's taking an awful risk. What if we reject her leadership? She can't be in the mood for this, not so recently after her bank disaster. But she's rising to the occasion. This is a change for the good. The Titanic is surfacing instead of sinking.

"Our old identity is no good here in the Timeflow," she says. "We need to become Longtimers. That's who we are now—who we can become if we try." She looks us over one by one, and we can see she's right. Longtimers—that's an identity, isn't it? Not the same as engineer but just as good. A Longtimer is somebody.

"We need to keep our focus on preparing for the Society Exam. I think we should pair up," she suggests, "in study teams." She looks around. "Zeke," she says, "why don't you pair up with Barlow?"

"Barlow!" I exclaim. "Why does he get Zeke?"

Amanda regards me blandly. "Because Barlow needs the most help. You'll be pairing up with me."

She's right, of course, and I shouldn't mind, except I know I'd be a lot better prepared with Zeke as my partner.

"What about Belinda?" She isn't here, so who's going to help her? "And what about Cooper?"

"Don't worry about Cooper," Amanda says. "He'll be okay. He can pair up with Belinda."

Cooper's hardly ever around. His bed's never slept in. I don't know where he sneaks off to, maybe some gambling joint. I don't know how he expects to pass the Society Examination with all the carousing he does. I've been expecting Amos to chew him out and set him straight, but Amos hasn't gotten around to it, and Cooper won't listen to the rest of us. He acts like we're not on his level. Maybe we aren't, if my suspicions are correct.

Actually, I don't think the pairing of Cooper and Belinda is such a good idea. Belinda's not going to want to study with him. He's never around, and she's gone as much as he is. She's made friends with Greta, but Greta can't help her if Belinda's gone all the time.

Amanda's not taking Belinda's absence well. She tolerates Cooper's comings and goings, but Belinda is another story. Last time Belinda rejoined us, she was sneaking out at night and getting Greta to let her in before morning. But Amanda figures out what's going on and is waiting up for her one night. She appears in the doorway of Belinda's room and pushes the door open before Belinda can close it.

Amanda crosses her arms. "And just where have you been?'

I guess Cartmell must have been up too and watching them through the open doorway. She's like that, the little spy. She says Belinda is really caught off guard by Amanda's tactics. Just like when Mom would catch us sneaking into the house late at night.

"Nowhere," Belinda says. "I've just been out for a walk."

Amanda shakes her head. "I know you better than that. Don't you think I know what you're up to? You've been nosing around in your Alternate Life."

Belinda's eyes flash with anger. "So what?" she says. "What if I have?"

Amanda uncrosses her arms. Pleading guilty is not a viable defense before the hanging judge. "You know you're supposed to stay away from your Alternate Life. You know what Amos told us about the dangers of it."

Belinda sighs and turns apologetic. "I'm sorry," she says. "I know I shouldn't do it, but don't you have any curiosity at all? Don't you ever wonder what's happened to your Alternate in these new Realities?"

Amanda bristles and crosses her arms. "Stay out of your Alternate Life. Stay out. I'm not going to warn you again."

We've all had a nasty encounter with our Alternate Life, though I don't know what Amanda's was. It cures you of wanting to go back for more. Except for Belinda.

She just can't resist it for some reason. I'm glad Amanda's there to finally set her straight.

Now Amanda acts like she and Belinda are best buddies and there was no blowup between them, which is easy for her only because Belinda's not here.

"I think it would be a good idea for each study pair to come up with questions they think will be on the Exam. Each pair can quiz the other two as a way of getting ready for the test." She pauses and takes her glasses out of her purse and puts them on. "I'll get on Amos's case about sending over those study guides. I'll make sure he doesn't forget. He's become so preoccupied that he's bound to start forgetting things."

I'm impressed by how smoothly Amanda has taken over the family meeting. She's been despondent the last week after losing her job. She's been listless and crying and moping around, but you wouldn't know it now. Tonight she's crossed the Threshold like a Timeship. Is she Transforming? I'm a little worried she's trying to Replace Amos. He said you shouldn't use someone else's Strategy. But she seems better, so maybe it's not a bad thing. Maybe she's not trying to be a Conqueror. Maybe there's another Strategy at work here.

"I also think," Amanda says, "we ought to have review meetings in the Library every night to discuss each chapter of the *Parattak*. Some discussion could help make our reading clearer and help us remember it."

Again, I'm impressed. Zeke and I are the college students in the family, but you wouldn't know that from Amanda's behavior. She seems to have switched right into student mode. I never expected to see her so determined to become a Longtimer.

"We need to start working together," she says. "As a unit. Stop going off on our own. That's where we've gone wrong. Together we can be strong. We can meet the Changes head-on. Learn to become Longtimers as a group."

Amanda looks like she's having a realization. It's all

so clear now. "We need to start having contingency planning sessions, prepare ourselves for what's coming so we don't get overwhelmed. We should have anticipated having to move out of the Lodge, Amos having to leave us. We should have been ready for those eventualities."

Greta appears in the doorway and wheels in a cart loaded with our refreshments. We stand and crowd around her. Jessalyn wakes up, and Pete starts to spoon feed her. The rest of us choose our cakes and cornbread and drinks and return to our couches and chairs to eat. Amanda just has tea.

"I wonder what Amos is doing," I say. "What called him away."

"Cooper said something about the Pangeans," Zeke declares.

"The Pangeans?" I ask, but I'm interrupted by the sound of Greta dropping a cup and saucer. I look over and see her staring at us with her pale face before she bends down to pick up the broken china.

I frown. What connection does Greta have with the Pangeans? I never find out the answer to my question, because Barlow changes the subject, and Amanda cuts him off and turns to Zeke. "So what are our options for living quarters in the next Season?"

Putting down his glass, Zeke adjusts his black frame glasses and stares at the wall. "Depends on whether it's a Dark Season or not. If it's Dark, we ought to pay for Shelter in The Common or one of the Lodges."

Which will be *expensive*, more than we can afford.

"But if it's a Light Season," Zeke says, "we'll be able to stay at our Alternate Residences. We ought to stay together and just face the danger of one."

We're thinking of Amanda's house in the new Reality, of course, since her house is always the biggest and nicest, though who knows what it will be like now that she's not a banker anymore. "We'll have to find out our new addresses, get someID that's valid in this Reality, find a way to get across

17

DECONTAMINATION
Reality 273
Tempest Season

Reader, with each Reality you become more real to me. I can almost see you. Your presence is palpable, just out of the reach of my senses. Garson says it's Supernatural Life to make a connection like this. It's only natural—in a super way. And we can't harm each other or be untrue to each other or wrong each other. We can only appreciate and support each other. Our connection is an ABSOLUTE GOOD. How about that!

Catterus has paid a visit to all of my family's Alternate Residences—except Amanda's. Amos has been deleting her marriage from the Bystander records every Season so Catterus can't track us down and we'll still have a place to stay. Garson says Catterus was nosing around the Brotherhood Lodge last Reality, trying to find us. The Monks denied acquaintance with us, but I don't know if he believed them. So maybe it's a good thing we're moving out.

Look on the bright side, I say.

We're delighted to discover the Tempest Season is a Light Season, after having to put up with weird Mystic, but the new Season also means we have to move out of the Brotherhood Lodge, which we're not so pleased about. We're being evicted from our happy home.

We're all sitting in the parlor when we hear the new arrivals walk up the stairs. We hear a few muffled voices in the accent of Moonglow, but we can't make out any words. This bunch must be pretty important to displace us.

We're hoping Cooper's anonymous friend can help us find ID's and a safe place to live. When we contact him through the Society Message Boards, all we get is the cryptic note: "Cave in Rock: 8 am."

So at 8 am we're hiking down the path along the Ohio River to Cave in Rock. We come to this story-high hollowed-out place in the rock face fronting the beach—Cave in Rock. The Cave is so shallow it doesn't make much of a hideout—mostly it's a landmark for tourists to visit, but even they aren't interested in it in the Tempest Season.

There's some guy seated inside with his back to us. He's got long straggly black hair, and he's wearing this t-shirt that has a hologram of Cave in Rock on the back. As he turns, we see there's a hologram of the Shawneetown Museum (the old bank) on the front. He's got a bedroll beside him. He looks like a bum. We exchange Nods, and when I notice his hook nose, I recognize him.

"Hey, you're Bungee from the Merchant Season."

He sneers at me. "The journalist," he says. He wags his finger at me. "Don't you mention me in that damn journal of yours."

"I won't," I tell him.

I thought Cooper would line up some high class expert to help us—some professor type or real estate Eloi. Instead, he's sent us a guy who's Survived by scrounging and scavenging like some tunneling vermin you can't get rid of.

Bungee isn't much of one for introductions or any of the other social niceties, but at least he doesn't try to sell us anything. He just hands out these voter registration cards with our names on them.

"These are IDs," he says, "from the current Season."

I give mine a look. There's a red, white, and blue flag in the background with my name, address, district number, and polling place on it. It looks official enough, but how would I know if it's genuine?

"Where did you get these?" I ask.

Bungee regards me with narrowed eyes and pursed lips. He doesn't care much for questions. "I hacked into the Voter Registration Office. Is that okay with you? These aren't forgeries. They're the real deal."

Amanda scowls at him. "But we're going to need picture IDs to get by in this Reality.

Bungee gives her a stare and a snarl. "What do I look like—Member Services? Do I look like I've got the kind of resources the Society offers? You'll get picture IDs each Season when you're Members. Until then, these will get you a picture ID. Just present these at the Vehicle Registration Authority and ask for a duplicate of your driver's license."

"You mean the DMV?" I say. "We have to go to the DMV?"

He gets exasperated when I say that and starts to pace around and gesture at us like he's selling Anachronisms. "No, not the Dee Um Vee, you Tourist. You say something like that, you'll get the Bystanders wondering about you. It's called the VRA in this Reality, the Vehicle Registration Authority. It's on Jefferson Street uptown."

We're staring at our new IDs, wondering about the addresses on them. Bungee doesn't like the looks on our faces.

"And stay out of your Alternate Life," he says. "Send someone else to your address to Decontaminate, before you go Prospecting."

I look up. "Prospecting?"

Bungee gets this incredulous gape on his face, and he inspects us one by one. "Hasn't your Sponsor taught you how to Prospect? What have you been doing for the last three Seasons?"

He's making us all feel like a bunch of dummies, and we shuffle our feet and look at each other, not knowing what to say.

Bungee shakes his head in disgust, his lip curling. He throws up his hands in defeat. We're hopeless.

"We've been Surviving," Amanda growls at him. "We've been living in the Brotherhood Lodge, studying for the Society Exam."

Bungee shrugs and shakes his head. "I guess that's one way of doing it." He stops pacing and stares at us. He wags his finger at us.

"You're planning on going to your Alternate Residences, aren't you?" He rolls his eyes. "That's your big plan, isn't it?"

"Why not?" Amanda asks him. "That's as good a place to live as any. And it's free."

He looks away from us like he can't believe we're not Extinct yet. "Decontaminate first," he tells us. "Send someone else ahead to check out your Alternate Residence before you go there. Do some Archaeology and then Decontaminate."

When he looks at us, he can tell by our faces we don't know what he's talking about, and he lets out a few cuss words from Merchant. "Auditory hellfire, sticky fingers, three dollar bill!" He's flailing his arms now. "Don't you Tourists know anything?"

We're all cringing. It's like Amos dressing us down all over again. Bungee gets another astounded look on his face.

"You're a bunch of Past Lifers, aren't you!" He closes his eyes and scrunches up his face like we're the ones who smell like bums. "Your Sponsor has to spend all of his time singin' at your asses about Past Life, doesn't he?" He cusses some more. "No wonder he doesn't have any time for the important stuff."

He stands there regarding us silently for awhile, evidently trying to decide if we're worth bothering with or so hopeless he may as well start composing epitaphs.

"To Decontaminate," he says, "you remove all personal items from your relative's Alternate Residence so there's no suggestion of Newpast or Alternate Timeline. So it looks like a hotel room." He looks at our faces for signs of recognition. And shakes his head when he sees none. "First you've got to do Archaeology," he says. "Sift through the Strata to find out what your relative's Alternate Self has goin' on. In the worst cases you'll find Fractures—a meth lab or a weapons cache or a stack of summons. And that's your cue to GET THE HELL OUT OF THERE AND DON'T COME BACK!"

He pounds his fist into his palm to emphasize the point. "Look for Traces of trouble—empty alcohol bottles, drug paraphernalia, a dirty run-down appearance. Fault Lines. Again, GET OUT OF THERE. Don't take chances. You don't want to be there when the Bypolice or some furious creditor or rival druglord shows up. If you find bad news, GET OUT." Bungee waves his crossed arms in a mock warning.

"Really good news can be just as bad—a notice of a winning lottery ticket, for example. Bystanders will be at your door constantly. The Alternate's relatives and friends will start crawling out of the woodwork. You don't have time to deal with that stuff, and it's dangerous. You need to minimize your contact with the Locals, and you can't do that if there's too much good news."

He's got that wary stare on his face again, like he's not sure we're listening. But he sees we are—so he goes on.

"It's not just the obvious stuff you've got to watch out for. Look for subtle Traces too—a book of matches, a sympathy card, ammunition, prescriptions in the medicine cabinet."

Well, he goes on and on with the instructions. Zeke even starts taking notes. Of course, Bungee is still dissatisfied with us at the end and looks at us like we're doomed or something. He starts handing out baseball caps to us.

"The Shawneetown Salt Miners," he says. "The Local team in this Reality. The VRA people will make you take off the caps for your ID pictures, but it might help explain why your hairstyle's no good. Or maybe they'll think you're trying to cover up a bad haircut, and they'll feel sorry for you rather than wonder why you have a weird haircut in the first place."

So we put on our baseball caps, and now we do look like tourists. But Bungee's still not satisfied with us. He opens his mouth to start in on our clothes but gives up.

"One more thing," he says. "If you get picked up by the Bypolice or the CTA or Society Security, *you don't know Bungee.* You never heard of him. He doesn't exist. He's just a colorful character who hawks Anachronisms to nostalgic Longtimers at The Common. You don't know him, and he doesn't know you."

He inspects our faces closely. "If you see me on the street, just keep walking. Don't speak, don't make eye contact. You get me?" He surveys us with narrowed eyes. "If anyone asks where you got those voter registration cards, tell 'em they came in the mail. Or you found them in an alleyway. You didn't get them from me. There is no Bungee. There is no Black Market. They fell from the sky."

We're looking at each other, wondering what we've gotten ourselves into.

And then, with no farewell, Bungee turns and leaves us, carrying his bed roll with him. When we start to follow, he waves us off. "Wait until you can't see me anymore. I don't want anything to do with you."

We watch him leave in stunned silence.

"Thank you!" Cartmell calls out to him after a few moments. All of us chime in with the same, but Bungee's moving fast, and he's already too far away to hear us.

So we wait as he disappears from sight. We're feeling anxious, thinking over the predicament we're in. The longer we're in the Timestream, the farther we get from the familiar, and the more dangers there are. We're not ready for this. It's The Common all over again, Bystander version.

What can we do except take his advice? It's all we've got. So we go to the Vehicle Registration Authority on Jefferson Street.

Everyone stares at us at the VRA, but we get copies of our drivers' licenses, except for Cartmell, of course, who doesn't have one. We also pick up a map of Shawneetown to see where our Alternate Selves live. Amanda's Alternate Residence on Emerald Court looks like it's in a nice neighborhood in Omaha, and it's nearest to a public Safe House, so we head out there on a city bus.

The traffic seems heavier than ever. Shawneetown's getting bigger with each new Reality. The Bystanders give us these looks like they're wondering where we come from, but we've gotten used to that. Typical Bystander behavior. Since it's a Light Season, they leave us alone. But this is one of those Gray Seasons in between Light and Dark, so we have to be extra careful.

As we look out the bus windows on our way to Omaha, we notice almost everything's green in this Reality. The skyscrapers are mostly made of green glass and steel, and even wooden buildings are painted different shades of green. It's like that emerald city out of the Oz books by L. F. Baum.

And we're Dorothy.

So we start referring to the Tempesters as "Munchkins" even though they're not short, saying things like, "Dexter, put that Subvocalizer away. What are the Munchkins going to think?" They don't have funny voices either, but they do have sideburns and dress in green clothing. Most of them have red hair— they must dye it. They seem to think we're every bit as weird as we think they are, and they discuss us in low tones. The bus is humming with conversations. From what I overhear, it's mostly gossip.

At Amanda's Alternate Neighborhood in Omaha, we get off the bus and gaze at the cul de sac she lives on. We make Amanda and Pete and the kids stay at the bus stop. They aren't to go inside the house until it's Decontaminated. Barlow stays with them to make sure they follow instructions. The rest of us head for Amanda's Alternate Residence. There aren't many pedestrians on Emerald Court, but occasionally we see a face with red hair peeking out a window at us. They're real busybodies here in Tempest.

Amanda's house is a nice two-story five-bedroom painted pastel green at the end of the cul de sac. We walk up the sidewalk to the front door and find the door's locked, so I take out the burglar tools Cooper showed me how to use, and insert them into the lock and work the pins.

I'm showin' off, you know.

"Uh oh," Cartmell says in a low voice. "Munchkin coming."

Just as the lock clicks, I hear a neighbor's voice, speaking in a Tempest accent. "Hello! They're not home." The pain of every Longtimer: a nosy neighbor. I slide the burglar tools into my pocket with my back still turned to him. Cartmell and Zeke are both smiling and waving to him. They introduce themselves, and I turn and smile. "Dexter Vann," I say. "I'm Amanda's brother."

The neighbor shakes hands with us, and we explain ourselves. We're family, here to house sit for Amanda and Pete until they're back from vacation. He listens to us and seems to go away satisfied. I can't believe how easy everything has been so far, how lucky we've been. And then things start to go to hell.

We can see something's wrong as soon as we enter the house. Traces. All the shades are drawn, and it's dark in there, not like Amanda's usual Alternate Residence. There are no toys scattered around the room. The place is too clean. It looks like some model home. The only thing out of place is a black shawl draped over the back of one of the chairs.

And then I spot the Fracture—a funeral program on the dining room table. We all see it at once and look into each other's eyes, and we put the clues together—why there's a funeral program, a black shawl, and no toys. But before we can inspect the program more closely, we hear a car pull up in the driveway, and Zeke peeks out the shade.

"It's the Bypolice!" he cries.

That frigging Munchkin neighbor called the frigging Bycops on us! We're all moving in different directions now, not knowing what to do. We want to run for it, but we're cornered here at the end of the cul de sac. We can't very well refuse to answer the door because it's unlocked.

"You forgot to lock the door," Zeke barks at me.

"Me?" I say. "Who said it was up to me?"

Cartmell shushes us. "We all screwed up, okay?" she whispers. "What are we going to do now?"

When the doorbell rings, we look at each other in panic. There's only one Bycop, so maybe we can take him out. The only trouble is the neighbor's watching. He's probably got one hand on the window shade and the other on his phone. We're just going to have to bluster through it.

So I try to pull it together, and I go over to the door and open it with a big grin on my face. The Bycop has a green uniform—they all do in this Reality. And of course, the guy has red hair and these long bushy sideburns. We explain ourselves, all smiles, how we're just house sitting for our sister. "House sitting?" the Bycop says. He's not familiar with the term. They don't call it that in this Reality. We're falling over each other, trying to explain, and we show him our IDs, but he still looks dubious at us.

And then I wave my arms and cry, "We don't know Bungee!"

Zeke and Cartmell get neck burns from whipping their heads around so fast to glare at me. And eye burns too, they're so furious.

"Dexter!"

"What?" I say. "It's only a joke. Don't worry, he won't get it." I'm only trying to put everyone at ease with some humor.

Well, the Bycop looks at us like he's never seen such a bunch of odd specimens, and I guess our cover is blown. We just don't act like bereaved relatives. And why would Amanda and Pete go on a "vacation" right after their kid died? We didn't know about it ahead of time, so we never got a chance to come up with a convincing story.

So I can tell the cop's going to take us in and let someone else sort it out downtown, and I know they'll search me and find the burglar tools, which are illegal. And they'll grill us, and when they find out we don't know what we should, they're going to think we're imposters. After all, we don't look like our Alternate Selves. We haven't had time to get our hair done or change our clothes. We were going to take care of that stuff once we had our Alternate Residence Decontaminated. But here we've fouled up at our first stop.

And then the door opens, and Amanda and Pete and the kids come tumbling into the house. "We're back!" they cry. They must have seen the Bypolice car pass them at the bus stop, and they figured it must be after us.

What a relief! They show the Bycop their IDs, and he compares their ID pictures to photographs he finds around the house. Amanda's big on family portraits. She and Pete don't look quite right—no red hair or green clothes, but they're clearly the same people. And Jackson and Jessalyn are spitting images of their Alternates. The only problem is one of them is supposed to be dead. The neighbor told the cop all about it.

It's very confusing and suspicious to the Bycop, but hey, obviously we are who we say we are. He can see the family resemblance. We've all got IDs, and what's he going to do—arrest us for being weird? So what if one of the kids has come back from the dead? Obviously, there was some kind of mixup.

So the Bycop calls the funeral home, but they can't find the body. It doesn't extend into the Present. Its extension is Jackson or Jessalyn, and clearly neither of them is dead. As a matter of fact, here's the kid just fine right in front of him. So he finally gives up and apologizes to us and leaves.

Amanda breaks down in sobs as soon as he goes, and she clutches Jackson and Jessalyn to her and won't let them go.

Oh, brother, what a mess!

Then Barlow shows up and makes everything worse with his stupid questions. We end up having to get Amanda out of there. It's too Contaminated. The specter of her Alternate Life is too overwhelming.

Amanda and Pete change into Tempest styles before we leave and loan us what clothes they can. We find some red hair dye and try to do something with our hairstyles. But still we're a sight to the Munchkins. We look as weird to the Locals as a bunch of flying monkeys in bellboy uniforms as we sit waiting at the bus stop. But

18
DENIER
Reality 274
Tempest Season

I've been thinking about you, reader, thinking about this journal. I know I exist, but what about you? Are you real? Or just someone I've made up? Do you feel real? I guess as long as you're real to me, you have reality. So maybe I'm doing you a favor by composing this journal—by keeping you in existence. And maybe it helps you for us to get together like this. Do you need a friend, too? Let it be me. I'm here for you. I'm on your side.

Garson says you exist, and I believe him.

Well, we finally do it right in this new Reality. We've got our Tempest fashions and our hair styled— with the Tempest curlicues. We make sure Amanda's house isn't in a dead-end street, and we've got an escape plan if anything goes wrong.

We make sure the neighbor's not watching, and we lock the door behind us. Barlow helps us steal a station wagon so we'll have a get-away car. It's parked in the garage of the empty house behind ours.

We do the Decontamination right this time and don't find any Fault Lines or Fractures. Lucky for us, this Reality is not as extreme as the last one. Tempest is Evolving—like every other Season. Everything's not so green, and the Bystanders don't all have red hair. They aren't as nosy either, so we pass as Locals, and they're content to go their way and let us go ours. But we still call them Munchkins.

I guess we're becoming Longtimers. But we don't want to be Longtimers. None of us do. Not really. We want to be who we used to be. We want Reality 250 back. We're afraid to change because we think if we change we'll lose our identity and our home Reality, while if we cling to the past, we'll be able to get it all back.

We're in Denial, you know.

Because we *have* changed. We're changed in a lot of ways. And will continue to change. But we're fighting it. We're fighting it every inch of the way.

I explain this to Cartmell at the breakfast table in the kitchen of Amanda's Alternate Residence in Brownsville.

"Am I clinging to the past?" I ask her. "Is that why I can't find a Strategy? Am I just too stubborn to change?"

I hang my head and look down into my coffee cup, which I'm holding in both of my hands.

I'm continuing to worry that I haven't found my Strategy. I need to make a new start, but I can't see how I can find a career when I don't even have a Strategy. I thought I was becoming a Realizer. What a Traveling Dream that was.

"Don't worry, Dexter," Cartmell says in a soothing voice between bites of toast and apricot jam. "You'll find your Strategy."

"I just can't Adjust to being a Colonizer," I tell her, "like you and Amanda."

Cartmell gives me a startled glance. A twinge crosses her face and then a frown. "I'm not a Colonizer," she says, almost laughing. "And neither is Amanda."

Well, that's news to me. "Okay, you're an Assimilator. What's the difference? You've both got Strategies, and I don't." I pause. "If Amanda's not a Colonizer, then what is she?"

Cartmell grins slyly, glances out the doorway, and then declares in a conspiratorial whisper: "A Controller."

A Controller! Well, I guess that fits. Every Longtimer has to Adjust to the loss of control over their lives caused by the Time Changes. Controllers react by obsessing over those things they can still control, usually other Longtimers.

"Haven't you noticed," Cartmell says, leaning forward and giggling, "how Amanda has started acting like Mom?"

Of course I've noticed, but I didn't realize anyone

else had.

"It's called Replacement," Cartmell says, "substituting someone else's persona for your own in order to handle your stress." This doesn't sound good. I thought Amanda was Stabilizing, but now I'm wondering if she's replaced Denial with another Unadaptive Strategy.

But maybe Replacement's not so bad. Maybe I could try it. I sigh and straighten up. "I don't think that would work for me."

"What wouldn't work for you?" Amanda asks me as she strolls into the kitchen in a light blue sun dress, appearing before us like some CTA Stealth Craft. Cartmell and I freeze for a second, wondering if Amanda has overheard us. She wouldn't like it if she knew we'd been talking about her behind her back.

She doesn't look at me but goes straight to the sink to fill her tea kettle with water. Apparently, she hasn't overheard us. She's just making conversation.

We exchange Nods. "I can't find the right Strategy for myself," I tell her, finishing my coffee and putting down my cup.

Amanda puts her tea kettle on the stovetop and turns the burner on high. "Why don't you be a Colonizer like the rest of us?"

Cartmell and I glance at each other. She suppresses a giggle. "That doesn't work for me," I say.

Amanda looks over at me as she reaches for a mug out of the cabinet. "Have you asked Amos for his advice?"

"He's too busy," I tell her. "You know we never see him."

"We'll see him next Season," she tells me. "He's planning something special to celebrate our first anniversary of life in the Timeflow."

I look aside. "It's been that long already? A whole year? It sure went by fast."

"I guess Cooper's right," Cartmell says, "about Time

being a Trickster." We all have our own personal theories of time.

Amanda reaches for her Irish Breakfast tea bags and places one in her mug. "There's something I need to talk to you both about." She turns to face us, acting solemn all of a sudden like we're in violation of the Time Laws or something.

I just want to groan because I know this talk she wants to have is just more stubbornness and Denial. More trying to turn back the clock so we can pretend we're gonna get back to Reality 250 and everything's gonna be how it used to be.

"We need to do something about Barlow," she says.

Barlow? I can't figure out what she's talking about. Does she mean his continued lack of karma? I scratch my head. "What about him?"

"He's a Denier," Amanda declares.

"Oh, that." She's right, of course. We're all in Denial, but Barlow worst of all. I figure he's just too stubborn to move on.

Barlow hasn't got his karma back—not a lick of it. And I can't understand why. Sure, we're all Dischronofiliated, but none of the rest of us are having the problems Barlow's having. Surely, his Alternate has built up some karma in this Reality. So why isn't it transferring to Barlow? We think his Alternate has moved out of town—could that be the reason? Or is Strange Karma at work here? Strange Karma is one of the mysterious processes involved in Supernatural Life, one of the Nine Transkarmic Elements of Being. I haven't gotten that far in my *Parattak* yet, and Amos hasn't explained it to us. But I doubt if he can explain it— because Strange Karma is inexplicable.

All I know is if Barlow had his karma, he wouldn't be a Denier.

Amanda's glaring at me now like she thinks I'm not paying attention. "You know Amos said we should guard against Unadaptive Strategies if we spot one in ourselves or each other."

I recall him saying that but can't recall him mentioning any remedy for the problem. I thought it was one of those self-correcting things we'll grow out of. Amanda can't see her own Denial. Of course, it's not as obvious as Barlow's. He's Mr. Denial.

"Okay, Barlow's a Denier," I say. "But what are we supposed to do about it? If we confront him, he'll just deny it."

"I suggest we make a family intervention," Amanda declares, "and force him to own up to his Unadaptive Strategy and get him to choose a new one."

A family intervention? I don't like the sound of that. Or the sound of "forcing" someone to change their Strategy. Barlow won't like it either.

"He wouldn't go for it," I say. "He'll blow a fuse. He could get the Panic and turn all Stage Three on us."

"Not if we do it right," Amanda declares. "We'll ease into it and let up if he starts getting too agitated. We'll get a doctor to help us medicate him. It could take a few days, but if we all keep the pressure on, he'll have to face up to his problem."

I'm against it. I don't like the whole idea. I'm not sure it's legal. And I don't think it would work. I'm not going to sacrifice Barlow's freedom of choice and risk his sanity just to satisfy Amanda's urge to control him.

So I tell her, "Amos said we should choose our own Strategy. Barlow has a right to handle his stress the way that works best for him."

Amanda crosses her arms. "Amos told us not to adopt Unadaptive Strategies." Controllers always resist resistance. They have to put down the contras.

"Have you consulted Amos about this intervention?" Cartmell asks, seemingly in innocence.

Amanda's eyes flash like a Time Machine on the fritz, and she gives her little sister a furious look. "You know Amos doesn't have time to keep up with the family or solve family problems. That's why he put me in charge. Are you refusing to go along with me as head of the family?"

I look away from her and cringe. Oh, brother! We don't need manipulation like this.

"Are you loyal to the family?" Amanda asks us. "Or not?"

I groan. She's looking at us like we're a couple Violators planning the Time Holocaust. Then her tea kettle begins to whistle, so she takes it off the burner.

"Barlow needs our help," Amanda declares, "and I think you should be willing to make an effort for him even if it's hard for you."

Okay, maybe Barlow does need to change, but I'm afraid that's not what this is really about. I need to figure some way out of this, or I know the family interventions won't end with Barlow but will go on until Amanda has us all in line. That's what Controllers want.

"At least ask Belinda before you commit us to this," I say. "She knows him better than anyone else. She knows how he'll react and how to handle him. She can decide what's best for him. I'm not willing to go ahead with this unless Belinda's on board."

"Me too," Cartmell says quickly. She's willing to step out of line if someone else is with her.

Amanda regards us silently for a moment, dissatisfied with both of us. She hadn't counted on opposition. She figured this would be as automatic as a Nod. She pours the water from her tea kettle into her mug and watches as the tea diffuses through the hot liquid. "All right," she says. So she takes out her cellular and punches in Belinda's number. Belinda has been living in the Bystander World. Amanda doesn't like it, and there's an uneasy truce between them.

"Where are you?" she asks when Belinda answers on the other end. "We have to meet. To discuss Barlow." She turns her back to Cartmell and me and lowers her tea mug. "Because he's a Denier and we need to help him get past that. Where? Why The Common?" Amanda glances at her watch. "Okay, we can meet you there in forty minutes. The Nevertime Cafe. All right. Goodbye."

Just as Amanda ends her call, Barlow comes shuffling into the room, still barefoot in his pajamas. He's gruff and unshaven and not completely awake. We glance at each other and sneak out of the kitchen as quietly as we can, hoping to avoid disturbing the wildlife.

So the three of us head to The Common for our rendezvous with Belinda. We know Zeke will go along with whatever we decide, and Cooper's off somewhere on a gambling binge. Besides, the four of us form a majority of the family.

Zeke stays home to watch the kids, and I drive us to The Common. Cartmell sits beside me, and Amanda sips her tea in the back seat.

I'm not wild about meeting at The Common. It ranks up on my list of Least Favorite Places right after the Interrogation Room aboard a CTA Cruiser. But who knows—maybe The Common won't be so bad this time. Maybe we won't run into Catterus—or any other Timecrimer.

The Common is in its usual spot on the fairgrounds, but the fairgrounds are in what used to be the Saline District. We cross the field and mount the steps up to The Common's entrance. The guards stop us and ask us a few questions.

"Are you carrying any Anachronisms on your person?" one of them says to me.

I hesitate. "Sure," I say. "I have a Subvocalizer from the Foundry Season. And a Pocket Computer from Compass. A cellular phone from Wilderness and—"

"Stop it," the guard says, holding up a hand. "You're boring me to death. Go on in."

So we go in. People don't stare at us like they did the last time we were here. No one calls us Tourists. Of course, we're dressed differently—in standard Longtimer Casual: jeans and sandals from the Castaway Season and collarless white cotton shirts that everyone used to wear in Overlook. These are the clothes that seem common to most of the Seasons. You can get by in just about any Light Season dressed like this. Dark Seasons, of course, are another matter.

So we turn left and head down the Promenade toward the Nevertime Cafe. The surroundings seem familiar. We're not twisting our heads, staring at everything like visitors to the World's Fair. We walk ahead clockwise, always bearing right in a never-ending arc, past restaurants and hotels and shops.

I suppose the people in the Common look the same now as on our last visit, but not to my eyes. They're more familiar. I can identify which Season a lot of them are from. I see some faces I recognize. It seems like an entirely different crowd.

Even the geography of the place seems less strange. The Nevertime Cafe appears on our left, coming a lot sooner than last time. Belinda isn't there, so we gather around one of the outdoor tables alongside the Promenade. Metal vines painted black form the surface and legs of both table and chairs, like somebody's patio furniture.

A few tables away from us, a man in a white suit, a bow tie, and tinted glasses stands and motions to us. I remember him from our last visit. It's Mr. Sun from the Clockwork Season, an Oldtimer in his seventies. I recognize his pale face and his straw fedora hat. We Nod to him, and he Nods back. He motions us over, so we join him at his table.

"You're Amos Vann's family, aren't you?" he asks us. "I notice the resemblance. Please—have a seat. Amos is a good friend of mine." He indicates the chairs with a sweep of his arm. He doesn't seem as stressed out as the last time we saw him. He's friendlier. He hasn't pulled a gun or threatened us or insulted us or anything.

We hesitate and question each other with our eyes. We don't see any gun in sight, and we don't want to offend the guy or get Amos mad at us. So we sit and join Mr. Sun at his table.

"I'm so glad to see new people joining our ranks," he says, beaming. "That's what the Timeflow needs—new blood."

He meant that a lot more literally the last time we met.

A waiter comes by momentarily, and we order tea and coffee.

"You picked the perfect time to visit The Common," he says to us. "It's usually not too crowded mid-Reality. Of course, you can never tell when the next Change will come along." He gazes into the distance down the Promenade. "I remember when there was no Common and not enough Safe Houses to go around. You had to fight off the Bystanders for a spot onboard. A nasty business that, a nasty business."

That explains a lot, I think to myself.

"Now they turn Bystanders away at the gate," he says, "unless they have a Sponsor with them. And the Society has its own guards. You don't have to count on the CTA for everything. As if you ever could. They've never considered the Longtimers their responsibility, those jerks. Get the Timecrimers, that's all they care about."

Just then our Beepers go off, and the lights along the Promenade begin to flash. The Matinee is over. It's Intermission time.

I can't believe it. Of all the bad luck! This is the last place I ever want to get caught in during a Time Change. But at least we're already in a Safe House. I just hope Barlow, Zeke and Pete and the kids are taking Shelter.

The other customers leave their tables and walk into the Promenade and gaze up at the television screens, but Mr. Sun stays put, so we do too.

He shakes his head at the worried people. "Tourists."

I guess he's right about them. There's no reason to enter the Promenade yet. No reason to head for a Perch early. The foot traffic around the Common picks up right away, and so does the noise level from the chattering voices. We have to shout to hear each other over all the racket.

"I don't know why they get so anxious and loud," Mr. Sun observes. "They're in no danger here. Why can't they just relax?"

He sits, legs crossed, and sips his tea with a placid expression on his face. You can tell he's weathered his share of Changes.

Soon the waiter appears with our drinks. The Fourth Dimensional Television Network broadcast has started, and the Café isn't taking any more orders, but we have time before we need to get to a Perch, so we have our coffee and tea and chat as we eye the passing throng.

We spot Belinda approaching from down the Promenade, and we wave at her to join us. She's got this puzzled look on her face when she sees us with Mr. Sun. I guess it must seem pretty weird for us to be sitting with him. Like rabbits sitting with a coyote.

"There you are," she says when she reaches our table. "Sorry I'm late." She gives us all a Nod, and we Nod back. She's dressed in a silver jump suit, and I wonder if she changed costume just for this meeting.

Belinda's one of those habitually late people. I forgot about that, I don't know why. I guess I assume the dangers of the Longtimer life will make her punctual. Since everybody else has changed, I expect her to change too. Now that I'm almost a Longtimer, I expect change and am thrown off balance by a lack of it. Her face is made up like someone from the Nagara Season with the sandals and the silver face paint and the whole bit. She looks like a Longtimer, but why a Nagaran? And she's speaking with a Raindance accent. What's that all about?

Mr. Sun stands up and greets her with a big grin on his face. It turns out he already knows her—but how? She wasn't with us when we came to The Common last time. They exchange Nods, and Belinda sits down.

"You're looking quite ravishing today," Mr. Sun says to her like he's seen her many times before. We're kind of confused by the coincidence of her knowing him. It's pretty strange.

The waiter comes to bus our table as we exchange greetings. Then Mr. Sun excuses himself and heads for his Perch. Like a lot of Oldtimers who live in The Common, he has his own strap in a reserved section. We're going to have to take one of the public straps.

When we spot our chance, we plunge into the crowd and cross to the inner wall and take hold of one of the straps like commuters riding the 57 from Carmi. The Longtimers around us don't seem as strange or intimidating as the ones we encountered last time. Most of them actually seem familiar. Here a Promise Seasoner, there a Highlander, a few spots over an Oldtimer from Atmosphere. Even those who aren't dressed in their original fashions give themselves away by their haircuts or gestures or accents. Sure, there are a few I can't pinpoint, but overall, I feel right at home. I'm one of them now.

There are a few Voiders in the mix, too, of course, but I know better than to assume they're Travelers. After all, thousands of normal law-abiding people live in the Void.

I anticipate the familiar feeling of null gravity this time. I don't even notice the floor move out from under my feet. I'm too busy Nodding and talking to the Longtimers around me.

A couple Newcomers from the Concordance Season careen through the air, passing us in awkward somersaults and flailing their arms in an attempt to regain control. Toddlers. They'll learn eventually.

Society guards fly through the air with the aid of jet packs and scoop up the loose Passengers before they injure themselves. It reminds me of my own first visit to the Common, and I feel myself blush. Was I actually so naive? Surely I was never such a Newby. It seems impossible now.

We watch the Reports on the Time Change as they appear on the television screens. Once the Common begins to spin, we let go of our Perches and float down to the Promenade in seemingly-straight lines of descent like people sliding down ropes. Actually, we're moving in arcs.

Landing on a spinning surface is always a little tricky—you need to start treading before you touch ground—but I manage it without stumbling. I remember how I twisted my ankle last time and was hobbling around for days afterward.

Once we're reoriented, Mr. Sun tips his hat to us and sets off to attend to his business, and the rest of us return to the Nevertime Cafe, where the waiters are setting up the furniture. It's chained to the floor, but it gets jostled when the cafe and everything else moves to the outer wall.

It takes the waiters a while to set up after null gravity. They seat us as soon as they can, so the four of us sit and talk while we wait for service to begin.

Amanda explains to Belinda her concerns about Barlow and her intention to make a family intervention to force him to choose a suitable Strategy. She makes it sound perfectly reasonable, but that's not the way Belinda takes it. She's clearly not pleased with the idea. You can see the distaste for it push her silver face back and to the side like the odor of rancid milk. She lets out her breath and gives us a dirty look. "I can't believe you're even suggesting such a thing," she says in her Raindance accent. "You can't be serious. This is Barlow, your brother."

"That's why I want to help him," Amanda insists.

"Help him! You'd be killing him if you tried this stupid intervention of yours."

Amanda glares at her and pulls her head back. "We have to do something. He's in Denial—"

Belinda gives us a look of disbelief. She pulls back then leans forward like a boxer coming in to deliver a punch. I'm afraid for a moment she's going to charge us. Her eyes look like a mad bull's.

"That's his Strategy," she insists. "It's his way of Coping. Don't you get it? By using Denial, Barlow's able to control how much change he has to deal with. He can postpone his Adjustments to a later time when he can better cope with them. It keeps him from becoming overwhelmed by all the changes around him. And you'd take that away from him?" She shakes her head at us, her mouth still open. Amanda tries to say something, but Belinda cuts her off. "I can't believe you'd be so callous and cruel. It would be a disaster if you took Barlow's Coping Strategy from him. He'd be instantly overwhelmed. He'd go Chrono in a week. You know how lost he is, you know he has no karma."

Amanda works her mouth, but she can't get the words in gear. She thought she had the situation under control, she's caught off guard by Belinda's explosive repudiation. I guess no one was expecting Martin Luther either, back in 1517.

"I know Denial doesn't work for you or me or the rest of the family," Belinda says. "It would be a disaster for us. But it works for Barlow, and you shouldn't try to take that away from him. It's ingenious, actually, the way he's able to stop change and hold it up until he's ready to deal with it."

Well, Amanda doesn't know what to say to that. We're all stunned by Belinda's assertions. Denial—a viable Strategy? It seems crazy. Completely wrongheaded. But that's Barlow for you. Belinda's right when she claims his Denial has Stabilized him. Precarious as that Stability might be, it's preferable to Disintegration. I know now I couldn't go along with any scheme that might jeopardize my brother's fragile Stability.

"You're just going to have to accept Barlow the way he is," Belinda declares, "Signs and all. I know he's changed since Wilderness. We've all changed. But he's still family, and we need to look out for his best interests rather than trying to force him back into his old mold."

Belinda's nailed it. That's what we really want. To see Barlow return to the way he used to be. We don't like dealing with this strange new self of his. It makes us uncomfortable. We've been thinking about what's best for us, not him.

"At least he has a Strategy," Belinda declares. "Maybe it's not a very good one, but it's his, and it fits him. He's chosen it, and it's chosen him. I envy him. I wish Denial would work for me. Then I'd finally have a Strategy."

Well, what could Amanda say to that? Belinda not having a Strategy! Who's ever seen a more stereotypical example of a Chameleon? Amanda stifles a laugh and just drops the whole thing. We sit there in uncomfortable silence for a few moments—until I break up the wake.

"I hate to rush everyone and interrupt the festivities. But we need to catch the first Ferry out of here. And I do mean the very next one."

I stand casual-like and stretch. The waiter approaches us, but I shake my head and wave him off.

"What's the rush?" Cartmell asks me. "We should listen to the Reports first. Barlow and Pete can watch the kids."

I turn from the table for a moment to yawn and gaze in an unfocused way toward the café's exit. "Stop staring at me," I tell everyone. "Get up. And smile. Contingency Plan Seven. I just spotted one of Catterus's gang pass the café. And I think that was his *second* time by. We need to get out of here quick, or we'll be knee deep in Void

Pirates."

Everyone's looking toward the entrance to the café, so I move to block their view—that is, block the Pirate's view of them.

"Come on," I say. "You, too, Belinda. Get Mr. Sun on the phone if you can. We could use his help."

None of us are armed. I think nostalgically about those revolvers Amos handed out to us back in Guidepost. Those guns are in Society Storage because we don't want to carry them around. We don't share Amos's enthusiasm for shooting down Bystanders. But now I wish we were more like him.

Everyone stands, even Belinda. She's on her phone, chatting with Mr. Sun in low tones.

"Act like I'm telling you all a funny story," I say, smiling as I head to the exit. Cartmell laughs, but Amanda and Belinda look grim. That's their typical response to my funny stories, I guess.

I don't see the Pirate, but of course, he would avoid us. He would make himself as invisible as possible.

"Are you sure he saw us?" Amanda asks. "Maybe it's a coincidence."

"He saw us," I say.

"Are you sure it was one of Catterus's crew?" Cartmell asks.

I don't bother to answer. Catterus has no doubt had a lookout posted at The Common ever since Moonglow, waiting for us to come back.

We hurry down the Promenade toward the Ferry. "Don't look behind us," I tell everyone. "Don't let on we've spotted him." I wish we had Barlow with us. He could deal with this Timecrimer.

When we get near the Ferry, we can see how low the countdown has gotten, so we break into a full run. We scramble for that Ferry like we're heading to Shelter in a Timestorm.

It's your standard Shuttle with 48 seats and standing room for another two dozen. We all crowd inside—it's standing room only now, so we turn to face the door. I can see the Void Pirate rushing after us. He's dressed in the untanned leather pants, vest, and hat common in the Guidepost Season. He's not far away, so he's going to make it to the Ferry in time.

Oh, crap.

He's revealed himself. He has to because he doesn't dare lose us. He's undoubtedly armed. I don't like the odds of the four of us versus an armed Void Pirate.

He's got tattoos on his face like someone from Sideshow, but I don't like what they say about him. Divorce, anger at society, greed, prejudice, resentment, rebellion, law-breaking, reform school, prison, bullying, contempt, revenge. Gang signs—lots and lots of gang tats. He's the one they call "Bones," because he likes breaking them.

He's reaching for his holster as he nears the Ferry. Then I notice Mr. Sun come ambling into his path, all innocent-like. The Pirate collides with him, and they both flip like pancakes and hit the ground. The Pirate rolls across the floor and scrabbles to his feet. He limps forward, but the Ferry door shuts automatically in front of him. He has his D-pistol out and points it at us, but it's too late to use it.

Mr. Sun is gone. I can't even see which way he went.

Warnings are blaring. Red lights are flashing, reflecting off the Pirate's face. Then the Ferry windows turn black with the Void.

CONTROLLER
Reality 275
Tempest Season

At last—I can relax. I appreciate the time you give me, reader. It really makes a difference in my life. Garson says there may be more than one of you, but that's okay because there's more than one of me. Because I'm all strung out across time. A different one of me for each listener or reader. So we've got something special, you and me. Not a physical relationship—a karmic connection. We exist together somewhen in time. A mingling of souls. A hope and a wish.

Momentary. Evanescent.

But *real*.

I hate to give you the bad news, but Belinda just got kicked out of the family, and I think it's for good. I'm not sure we'll ever see her again. I don't think anyone wanted it to happen, and even now I don't understand how it did. The Time Change Stress Syndrome just got the best of us is the only explanation I can come up with. I can't account for it. I can only tell you what happened.

As soon as we get out of the Ferry from The Common and into the new Reality, Belinda disappears from sight. I assume she's gone back to her Bystander life, and I don't expect to see her again—and who can blame her after being subjected to Amanda's criticisms and insults in the Ferry or, for that matter, always.

But as I step out the front door of Amanda's house today, I encounter Belinda walking up the street—like a Time Beacon that's gotten the All Clear and has returned from the Void to its remote perch in the Bystander World disguised as part of the Local scenery. Her silver Longtimer suit and face paint are gone, replaced by the latest styles of the current Reality.

She dropped the Raindance act once we were alone in the Ferry and the Change was over. Her focus switched to Tempest. She didn't intend to return to living with the family, and she disturbed us all with her shocking remarks about the *Parattak*, the Society, and Dr. Morlock. She acted like a Voider rather than her old self, making me wonder if she has two or three new lives in the Sequence rather than just one.

I think I liked her better as a Bystander.

It's reassuring to see her now in the familiar guise of one of the Locals. But I have to squint my eyes in surprise at the quickness of the change. I'm still wearing my Longtimer Casual outfit. I join her on the driveway, and we Nod at each other. "How did you get those clothes so fast?" I ask her.

She shrugs. "I slid on down to the Salvation Army and peddled my Nagara togs for something more jazzy." Jazz. That's the current craze in this Reality. There's a fresh breeze, and I can smell the honeysuckle along the neighbor's white fence as we walk up to the house.

Belinda's wearing a green hunting shirt and tight capri pants. A green beret. Red hair. Sandals. A black scarf. She'll fit right in with the Tempesters of this Reality, who are clannish. If you don't mesh with them, they shun you.

"Dig your duds, doll," I comment, making fun of Belinda's Tempest talk, but she ignores the quip and pushes past me into the house. Amanda lurks inside the door, and I can hear the cool reception she gives Belinda.

"Where have you been?"

"Chill down, sis. Just ramblin', that's all."

The house is dominated by the odor of the roast Amanda is cooking. I can also smell onions—and carrots if I use my imagination.

Amanda's still in the light blue sundress she wore to The Common. She stares at Belinda slightly off-center, taking in the transformation in her clothes and manner like the dress code monitor at school. "From now on, you'll tell me ahead of time if you're going anywhere. No more disappearing on us, if you want to stay in this family."

Another ultimatum. Why can't Amanda see the effect that will have? Or does she?

"No prob, sis. No diff. No arg."

I can tell the dialect is getting on Amanda's nerves. Entirely predictable. So why can't Belinda see that? She knows Amanda hates the Bystanders.

"And no more talking like a Bystander," Amanda says, "or acting like one. You'll be a Longtimer like the rest of us."

Belinda shakes her head. "No can do, peg."

"Stop talking like that. You're a Longtimer just like us, from Reality 250 just like us. You can talk like it and act like it."

Belinda shakes her head again. "You've got the wrong key for this lock, peg."

Amanda's nostrils expand as her anger grows. I think she's going to blow up at Belinda, especially after the fury of her accusations in the Ferry. But then Cooper comes strolling up the path to the front door like a Time Share Solicitor and distracts her.

"Cooper!" she cries, losing all interest in Belinda. She brushes Belinda aside and runs to the doorstep, but I get to him first. As I greet him and shake his hand, Amanda charges out of the house and runs up and hugs him, knocking me aside. Cooper always has been her favorite, I'm not sure why. He was Mom's favorite too.

He's in his usual leather jacket. He's worse than Barlow about blending in with the Locals, yet he fits in wherever he goes.

Amanda's face is lit up with a smile when she pulls back from Coop. "How long are you staying for?" she asks.

Cooper shrugs.

"Well, you're welcome anytime."

We assumed he'd gone off on his own again, so it's a real treat for us to have him back for another Reality. Cooper is free entertainment.

I can see Belinda's face looking out now from the shade of the doorway. Like an Outcaster peering in from the Void. "I thought Rounders like us had to file a flight plan every time we want to ramble."

Amanda glares at her, then turns to smile at Cooper. Belinda scowls and ducks inside. She's never liked Cooper. She's the only one in the family who's immune to his charms. She sees through his lies and excuses. She never falls for his schemes. To her he's just a low life.

The rest of us think Cooper's a lot of fun. Sure, he gambles too much and makes up stories and hangs out in bars and dives. He'll associate with anyone. But he's still our brother, and he can charm the socks off a cat. He's handsome and has a look that seems to fit into every Season.

So I go inside with Amanda and Coop. Cartmell runs out in her yellow sundress to greet him too. We sit in the living room to catch up, even though he Sheltered with us in the Safe House back in Mystic. Of course, we see Cooper more often than Belinda, but she's been with us more recently than him, so Cooper's the newcomer now.

Belinda stays in the next room while we focus all our attention on Cooper. Even Barlow comes downstairs to greet him.

Amanda looks around for Belinda, and not seeing her, stands up, her face turning all Timestorm. "Where's Belinda?" she demands. She walks to the doorway. "Belinda!"

"What?" a voice answers from the next room, after a short delay.

"Are you in this family or not? Get in here and welcome your brother Cooper."

"We just saw him in the Safe House last Season," her voice complains.

"Get in here," Amanda orders her, "and make your brother feel welcome."

Belinda grumbles awhile before she finally drags herself to the living room. Amanda stands with her arms crossed and won't sit until Belinda's seated.

"Why does Cooper get all of the attention?" she declares in a non-Tempest accent. "There wasn't any big welcome when I came home."

"You're not Cooper," Amanda tells her, which is a mistake because I don't think Amanda should show favoritism. She's the head of the family, like Mom or Dad.

Cooper smirks as he sits in a rocking chair with his legs loosely crossed. He seems bored. We're all lined up on the couch and the love seat.

"He comes and goes whenever he pleases," Belinda complains as she enters the room. "How come there's one set of rules for him and a different set for me?"

Amanda grows angry that Belinda is spoiling Cooper's homecoming with her whining.

"Stop it, Belinda," she says. "You're boring him."

"Boring him! Everything decent bores him. What about all the things that bore me?"

It's so strange, hearing Belinda trying to stand up for herself and defy Amanda. Especially after her Moonglow masquerade. But it won't last. It can't. Belinda always crumbles.

"I'm sorry, Cooper," Amanda says, "for Belinda's outbursts. You know how strange she's become."

"I'm not sorry," Belinda declares, crossing her arms and seating herself on the smaller of the two easy chairs in the room. She's behind Cooper, but the rest of us can see her easy enough.

Amanda ignores her and sits on the couch across from me. "Start your story again," she says to Cooper, "so we can hear the whole thing."

Cooper leans forward, his elbows on his knees, and looks into our faces. "Have any of you ever heard the story of Lianna from Raindance?"

No one answers him. Barlow shakes his head

slowly. Cooper glances around at our faces again, and I lean forward, getting interested despite myself. Cooper can always Lever me into a story, because he's a great storyteller.

We wait breathless for Cooper to begin, and just as he opens his mouth, Belinda declares, "I have."

Cooper shuts his mouth and looks over at her like she's an exhibit from Ripley's Museum. "You have?" Belinda squirms on her chair as if dissatisfied with the topic. "Repeatedly."

"Liar!" Amanda thunders, giving Belinda a faceful of fury. "You're just trying to ruin Cooper's story and spoil his homecoming."

Belinda turns sideways on the easy chair and rolls her eyes. "Have it your way," she mutters.

Amanda glares at her from the couch, her narrowing eyes counting off the seconds until she'll exact an appropriate revenge. "Go on, Cooper," she says, turning toward him. "Duh doesn't know anything."

Belinda glares at her upon hearing the old nickname she'd always hated, the one that used to incite her to tears if repeated enough.

"Belin-Duh. Belin-Duh."

Belinda turns away from her and slouches down on the couch so she's looking away from us, her arms crossed.

Cooper seems deflated. "I didn't realize anyone else had heard it," he says in a disappointed voice.

"Well, I have," Belinda says. "And you know it." She squints like it's an act on Cooper's part, and he has some secret motive for telling this story.

"Shut up, Belinda," Amanda growls at her. "Go ahead, Coop. She's just pretending she knows."

"Yeah, come on, Cooper," I say, "tell us the story."

So Cooper looks around at the rest of us to gauge how interested we are, and after making us hold our breath for a few beats, he begins his tale.

"This happened to a woman named Lianna during the Raindance Season."

"Not the Raindance Season," Belinda chides him. "She was from Raindance. It happened during the Moonglow Season."

Cooper nods. "Yeah, that's right, during the Moonglow Season." He pauses and collects himself and hunkers down, his voice growing softer. "Well, this Lianna wasn't your ordinary sort of Longtimer who just wants to Survive in the Sequence. She was able to impersonate the Locals, to convince them she was one of them, and that's exactly what she was doing in the Raindance Season—"

"Moonglow," Belinda corrects him.

Amanda glares at her. "Stop interrupting him. It's a story for god's sake, not sworn testimony."

Belinda slouches farther down in the easy chair till she's nearly lying down, her face red. "Wasn't my mistake," she mutters.

Cooper squints into the distance as if searching the landscape. "Right, Moonglow. You all remember the Moonglow Season."

Amanda's never gotten over Moonglow, and you can see it in her eyes. Belinda doesn't look very happy about it either. It's not a pleasant memory for any of us.

"So anyway," Cooper says. "Lianna found herself in the Raindance Season, so of course she did everything she could to fit in—"

"Moonglow," Belinda mutters through gritted teeth.

Amanda's eyes flash at her, and Cooper stops talking and straightens up, obviously irritated. "Do you want to tell the story?" he asks, twisting around to look at her.

"No!" Amanda cries. "She's awful at stories. Please, Cooper, go on."

"Yeah, Coop," I say, "you can't quit now." We're a rowdy mob, ready to start chanting "We want the story."

Some people think the story of Lianna from

Raindance is in the *Parattak*, but it can't be, of course. You can't find it printed anywhere, because it's one of the stories the Voiders tell. So we're eager to hear it.

Cooper waits to see if Belinda is going to say anything more, and when she doesn't speak or even glance at him, he leans forward again and looks us in the eye.

"So anyway, when Lianna goes out on her own, she finds it's not so easy, making your way through the Sequence all alone, and pretty soon she meets up with a bunch of Finaglers and gets involved in their schemes and Bycrimes."

Belinda squirms on the couch and emits a stifled moan. "What are you trying to pull, Cooper?"

Cooper stops talking and leans back. "I'm just telling Lianna's story."

Belinda side-gazes him. "There weren't any Finaglers when I heard the story."

"There were when I heard it," Cooper says.

"Didn't I tell you to stop interrupting?" Amanda snarls at her sister. The two exchange vicious looks.

Belinda turns away from Amanda and shakes her head at Cooper. "What's the use? Go ahead. It's your story now."

Cooper gives her a thoughtful look then turns back and leans forward. He straightens up again and glances at Belinda to see if she has anything to add, but when she doesn't let out a peep, he bends over and resumes his storytelling look.

"Well, here Lianna was, all on her own in the Sequence, with no family to help her and only her Finagling friends to see her through her difficulties. Moonglow lasted a lot longer than anyone thought it would. And the Bypolice began to catch on to some of the cons the Finaglers were running. So Lianna was picked up in a dragnet with some of her Finagler friends and taken downtown to be interrogated at police headquarters."

Belinda frowns and glances at Cooper in surprise—like she can't believe she's heard him right.

Cooper lowers his voice, speaking more softly and confidentially the further into the story he gets. "Well, this was a pretty tight spot Lianna was in, but she'd been rehearsed about what to do if she ever got arrested by the Bypolice. She was supposed to call the Brotherhood and have them bail her out. Only, Lianna's Beeper went off while the police were interrogating her. She checked her Wristwatcher and noticed it was flashing. There was a Change on its way and no time for the Brotherhood to intervene."

Belinda gasps. "That's not the story of Lianna of Raindance. That happened to Carmen of Veranda. You've gotten the two stories confused."

Cooper stops talking and peers sidewise, all innocent-like. "It's all the same story," he says.

"It is not."

"Will you stop interrupting?" I complain at Belinda. "We're not concerned about the source of the story."

Amanda's so mad she can't speak for a moment. "Go on, Cooper," she growls. "Just ignore her." Ignoring is one of Amanda's weapons. But she likes total onslaught better.

So Cooper takes a breath and starts in on his story again. "Well, the head Finagler had told Lianna that if she ever got in a fix so tight nobody could get her out of it, she should call a certain phone number. So that's what she did. She called the number she'd been given and—"

Belinda groans. "I know what you're doing," she says, turning in her seat. "You're going to take the story and twist it and try to embarrass me by making me look bad."

Cooper gives her a thoughtful glance like he doesn't know what she's talking about. He looks aside and concentrates. Belinda crosses her arms and puts her sunglasses on.

"Come on, Cooper," Amanda calls to him. "Tell us the story."

"Yeah, Cooper," Cartmell says, "Come on."

I'm sitting on the love seat with Zeke, and I scratch my upper lip with my thumb. "What do you care," I say to Belinda, "how Cooper tells the story or whether he gets it right?"

Belinda takes a breath then starts to tremble. She's mad but she's also embarrassed. She takes off her sunglasses. "Because I'm Lianna," she barks at me in a savage voice.

We're stunned. Belinda is Lianna of Raindance?

She confronts Cooper. "And you know it."

Cooper seems genuinely surprised. He's twisting around and doing a double take. "You're Lianna Belda?" he says, blinking in surprise. "Really?" He looks aside, contemplating this new development. He strokes his chin. "But you can't be. You're not from—"

Growling, Belinda puts her sunglasses back on. "People think I'm from Raindance because they can't believe I'm from somewhere as dull and ordinary as Wilderness."

We pull back from her. People think Belinda's from Raindance? And the Voiders are telling stories about her?

Cooper continues to think, giving his chin a good workout. He glances over at Belinda and smiles. "You *tell* people you're from Raindance, don't you? So they won't wonder where you're from. You don't want anybody to know you're from Wilderness."

Even through her sunglasses we can see the lightning bolt glare Belinda gives him. "So what if I don't?" She turns away from him.

Amanda is flabbergasted. "You're ashamed of Wilderness? Why would you be—"

"Oh, can it," Belinda says, taking off her sunglasses and putting them in her purse. They don't protect her from us. They're no shield from her family who's known her all her life. She gives Amanda a resentful glance. "Living in Wilderness was fine for you. You liked being a banker in a one-bank town, where everything revolves around the stupid bank. But some of us don't want everyone thinking we're some uninhibited ignoramus from hickbillyville."

That's what she thinks of Wilderness? That's what she thinks of Shawneetown? That's what she thinks of us?

"Shawneetown ain't some hick town," I tell Belinda. "It's the third largest in the country."

She scoffs at me. "Now," she says, "but not in Wilderness. It should have been a city, but it was just a big town."

The truth hurts, I guess, but I don't agree. Maybe I'm in denial, but I think Shawneetown's a city, an important city and always has been, and it's not a hick town, though I know that's how some of the Longtimers view us. They don't like our accents, and they don't respect our countrified, laid back ways. They look down their noses at us and think they're too good for our sort.

"Go on with your story, Coop," Amanda urges him. "Don't listen to Duh. She's not Lianna of Raindance. She's just trying to impress us by making things up."

Belinda crosses her arms and turns away from her and rolls her eyes.

"Yeah, Cooper," I say. "Tell us the story." I'm really interested to hear it now. It's got some relevance.

Cooper glances at Belinda then squints. He looks upward for a moment, shakes his head as if to clear it, then turns to regard us again.

"Well," he says, gesturing, switching into storytelling mode. "There was this clan among the Night People of Moonglow who sunk into the Dark Ways and took up primitive rituals and black magic and the unspeakable customs of lost and backward religions from the wild, untamed jungle peoples of the Dark Days before civilization."

Belinda's just shaking her head and wriggling her feet now. Cooper ignores her and goes on, his charismatic voice drawing us into the tale.

"And they adopted the barbaric rites of cannibalism and human sacrifice." He pauses to let the horror sink in.

"We all know how depraved those Night People were," Amanda says, trying to gore Belinda's goat.

"It was only one small group," Belinda replies. "They weren't even really Night People. They were a sect that split off from the Luneans. They called themselves 'the Moon People'."

Cooper glances at her in surprise. "That's right," he says. "I'd forgotten that." He gives her another glance, then lowers his voice tuba deep as he turns to look at us. "They were known as *the Moon People*."

Amanda and Barlow and Zeke and Cartmell are really eating it up. Cooper's a great storyteller. I guess it's from all that acting experience. He really knows how to spin a tale. I've got to hand it to him. He's a lot better at it than me, even though I like telling stories as much as he does.

"So the Moon People grab these two Longtimers from the Passion Season. They're out here surveying for the Society and don't know about the Moon People yet. What a way to find out, huh? So the Moon People have this big kettle set up to boil, and—"

Belinda lets out a muffled exclamation. "You're embroidering," she says.

But Cooper just ignores her because he's got the rest of us enthralled like scouts around a campfire, and he's making eye contact and gesturing to show how wide and round the kettle was. "And they start pounding on these enormous drums."

"They were bongos," Belinda says.

"Boom! Boom! Boom!" Cooper's making these huge drumming gestures with both arms, throwing them up and down. And in a deep reverberating voice, he intones, "Bring in the doomed."

And so the Moon People carried in the two Longtimers, all trussed up on spits and planted the spiked ends of the spits in the ground, surrounding them with kindling like two campfire sites.

"They're going to burn them?" Belinda observes. "I thought you said they had a big kettle." She eyes him sideways.

Cooper doesn't look at her. He just scratches under his chin. "First they were gonna roast 'em and gorge on their meat, and then they were gonna boil the remains for stew. Because some of the Moon People prefer barbeque, and some prefer soup."

Belinda's rolling her eyes.

Cooper pauses and gathers himself together and leans farther forward as he readies to deliver the meat of his story. His voice becomes even more dramatic. "Well, just before the heathen Bystanders were about to ignite the fires with a torch and toast the Longtimers, Lianna from Raindance, dressed as a Nagaran, zoomed in on her motor scooter, right into the midst of the horrid festival and disrupted the depraved ritual. The Moon People jumped back from the sudden intrusion as if some mighty spirit had materialized before them.

"At first they were outraged and furious that their secret ceremony had been encroached upon, but as Lianna climbed down from her motor scooter, some of the revelers recognized her despite her silver face paint. Their mouths dropped open, and their eyes shined like two moons.

"'It's Benilda!' they cried, for that was her name among the Night People.

"A hush spread over the Moon People, and many of them sank to their knees, so smitten they were by Benilda Lavan."

Belinda makes a face and fidgets in her easy chair and begins to mutter. "I don't know what story you think you're telling, but it's--"

"'Great Lore-Folk of the Moon,' Benilda intoned in her Moonglow dialect. 'Desist in your hoary practices. Your acts should shine like the moon and twinkle like the stars. Do not dwell instead in the blackness with no end.'

"Well, at first the Moon People were offended by Lianna's condemnation of their necromancy, but the more she spoke, the more she won them over as if she was undoing some deep dark spell that had been cast over them.

"'Don't worry,' she whispered to the captured Longtimers in her Raindance accent, 'I am a Longtimer like you, and I'm here to rescue you.'

"Well, the Longtimers were astounded, for they too had recognized Benilda, Queen of the Night, because she was the most famous celebrity of Moonglow among the Night People. Everybody knew Benilda, and everyone revered her, so to find out she was actually a Longtimer from the Raindance Season astonished them.

"So the Moon People slashed the bonds binding the Longtimers, and the two of them climbed onto Lianna's motor scooter and drove off into the night. Lianna stayed behind and partied with the Moon People till dawn to mollify them and make up for ruining their gory spectacle. What unholy rites Benilda participated in through the wee hours of the dark night with the Moon People, we can only surmise, but the fact is cannibalism and human sacrifice were only two of the unspeakable practices of that unruly tribe. They engaged in others that were not as bloody but just as barbaric and taboo."

Belinda is writhing in exasperation at this point like some sort of contortionist, but she doesn't interrupt. She lets Cooper continue his story.

"Well, it turns out the two Longtimers kidnapped by the Moon People were both Eloi, friendly with the upper crust of Longtimer society. And the select among the Eloi were especially grateful to Lianna of Raindance, so they threw a lavish party to honor her, and all the biggest names of the Society were there, including Jordan Jordan and Eileen Von Otter and Red Phillips and Molly Waters.

"This party, though not as depraved as the Moon People's was as much of a revel and lasted as long into the wee hours before dawn. And at dawn—"

Belinda jerks around in her seat and lets out a cry, giving Cooper a pointed glance. "Oh no you're not," she says. "You're not the only one who can tell stories." She drills him with her eyes. "I could tell a few stories of my own—about Brendan from Regency. They say he was at that party too, because there had been a rumor that Dr. Morlock would attend."

Cooper and Belinda lock eyes and regard each other stonily for a long time without speaking.

"I wouldn't know," Cooper says finally, turning back around. He averts his eyes. "I wasn't there. I got this story second hand."

Belinda turns away from him too, her arms crossed. She's still mad, but not as mad as before.

"Go on, Cooper," Cartmell says. "Tell us the rest."

Cooper runs a thumb down his jaw. "That's all there is," he says. And then he clams up.

Amanda's frowning, glancing from Cooper to Belinda and back. I know what she's thinking. She's thinking Belinda has ruined Cooper's story, cut it short and deprived us of its splendid ending. And by doing that, Belinda's spoiled Cooper's homecoming. Which isn't really a homecoming because we know he'll be off again as soon as he's bored. But that's not how Amanda looks at it, and she's really mad.

"Belinda!" she cries, trying to draw her sister's attention. She's ready to blow up, but what can she say? Cooper's the one who decided to end the story here. He ruined his own homecoming.

It's strange to see Belinda having the upper hand

over Cooper. After all, how does she know any of this? If she's been living only among the Bystanders, how did she hear a Voider story? It's difficult to imagine my sister out in the Void swapping stories with the Outcasters.

Amanda's on her feet now. "Belinda, leave the room. The family needs to have a conference."

Belinda gets up from the couch in a snit. "I was going anyway," she says. "There's nothing more I can do for you people. I need to get back to my own life."

Her own life? Belinda's leaving us? We're so shocked we even forget about Cooper's story.

"Don't go," Cartmell pleads.

"I have to," Belinda tells her.

Amanda's face transforms from outrage to shock to anger. "We work together now—as a team," she says. "We can't have you undermining that. You can't just come and go from this family like some Transient,"

Belinda's eyes glimmer. "Why not? Cooper does."

"Cooper's different!" Amanda yells, standing and putting her foot down. "He blends in. He's one of us. You only try to blend in with the Bystanders, never us. He accepts the family's plan and goes along with it. You try to destroy it. When you come and go, it's disruptive. You injure family unity. If you want to be part of this family, stay. Otherwise—"

Belinda simmers for a moment and glances around at the rest of us before glaring at Amanda. "You can't kick me out of the family. I'm just as much a part of this family as you are, and you can't change that."

Amanda lifts an eyebrow. "Can't I?"

I realize suddenly that she actually can. She's in charge now. We all depend upon her for our Survival. Even Amos depends on her to keep the family together. None of us can afford to cross her. And she can be such a terror, that none of us would want to try. So if she wants to declare that Belinda isn't a member of the family anymore, then, well, I guess she won't be.

Belinda just stands there, gazing at Amanda defiantly. But it's a lost cause. Strange Karma is against her, has been from the very beginning. Belinda could have reasoned with her sister, but she doesn't stand a chance against Strange Karma.

Amanda crosses her arms, ready for a battle of wills.

"If you leave the family again, it will be for the last time," she warns Belinda. "Don't test me."

Which is exactly the wrong thing to say. I suppose Amanda thinks a threat will scare Belinda. But it only scares the rest of us, because we're the ones who will suffer if Belinda leaves. The whole family could go into a depression.

Amanda seems to think Belinda came home only because she ran out of money, but money's never been a problem for Belinda. Dream Life is what brought her here. And Dream Life is what takes her away.

Belinda never talks to us about her Chameleon life. Amanda interprets her secrecy as an attempt to hide the bad consequences she's suffered. But Amanda's the only one who thinks that. She can't resist the opportunity of making an attack on Belinda, even though she should have known it would only drive her from us.

"Who do you think you are—Queen of the Bystanders? You ought to know that means nothing to Longtimers. Because even the most highly placed Bystander is below the lowest Longtimer. Go ahead and leave. You'll be back. You'll come around for another handout. Like a stray cat. And about as grateful too."

But Belinda isn't listening to Amanda. I know she'll slip away soon and disappear, and we won't be able to find her among

20
MEMBERSHIP
Reality 277
Valediction Season

Well, mon ami, we've made it through six Seasons together now, and that calls for a toast. If you don't have anything to drink handy, tilt one back in tribute to me later. Give me a moment of silence and then cheers to you. Rejoice that you're not trapped in the Bystander World like me.

If you're like me, then by now you're wondering "Where's Catterus? Why hasn't he caught up to you yet?" I've been having the same thought, but the answer, reader, is he hasn't caught up to us because we've been careful, and he's no mastermind.

But I'll bet you're getting impatient, and you're itching for a showdown—because so am I. I want to get that jerk and his cronies off my tail. I want to stop looking over my shoulder. But it's not only my family that's prevented Catterus from closing in on us. It's him too. Because he's a big chicken, and he's afraid to meet us on equal terms. He only intends to show up when everything's to his advantage and he can bushwhack us good.

So maybe we'll have to go after him. But first we need to celebrate—because we've been in the Timeflow for more than a year now, and our celebration up on the Society Time Station was no celebration at all. If you've read my journal entry about Reality 276, you know what a disaster that trip was. I just hope Belinda can forgive us for how we behaved. We all need some recreation after we get back.

The family is having its first meeting of the new Season in the Brotherhood Lodge, and we get to spend the night, so it's a party in there. I'm really looking forward to catching up with Garson and Greta and Brother Samuels. This is as close to a home as we've ever had in the Timeflow.

So we're hanging around in the library when Amos arrives with the good news. I've got my ankle wrapped, and the sprain is nearly gone now. I'm leaning against the piano, talking to Barlow when Amos comes striding up to us.

"You passed!" he cries out joyously. "You all passed." He looks like a sports fan whose losing team has miraculously won the championship game. We've passed the Society's Membership Test. In another Season we'll be Longtimers.

It's time to celebrate!

I straighten up and smile. "Who got the highest score?" I ask Amos. I studied for that test until the Cone uncoiled.

It takes a moment for the question to register with Amos, because he's shaking hands with Barlow, who starts whooping. Zeke enters the room from the kitchen to see what the noise is about.

"So we all passed?" he presumes.

"Yes!" Amos cries. "All of you. Every one. Your Sponsorship is over."

"Who got the highest score?" I ask him again.

Amos glances at me, distracted.

"Oh," he says, "Zeke did."

It figures. I would have predicted that. He hardly had to study for the test at all.

"Zeke scored over a hundred percent," Amos declares. "He set a record for the highest score ever made on the test."

Over a hundred percent? How's that possible? Only someone like Zeke could find a way to exceed the top score on that exam.

"Who scored second highest?" I ask Amos.

"What?" He looks at me and then away from me. "It doesn't matter, Dexter. It's not a competition." He won't meet my eyes.

"Who scored second highest?" I demand, getting a little angry. I don't like him putting me off. Okay, so I'm a buzzing little insect that won't go away. I just want an answer.

Amos gives me an impatient glance. "If you must know, it was Cooper."

Cooper!

"But Cooper didn't study. How could he have scored so high?" The only thing he studied was faces in a poker game.

"He got one hundred percent correct, Dexter."

"He must have cheated."

Amos squints sideways at me. "He didn't cheat. Quiz him yourself."

I grumble for a moment. He's so damn lucky, maybe he didn't cheat–or maybe my suspicions about him are correct. In which case it makes sense and doesn't count anyway.

"Okay," I say, "who came in third?"

Amos is shaking hands with Amanda. "It's not a competition, Dexter. You should be thrilled you've all passed."

"He's been a college student for too long," Zeke declares. "He's become competitive about tests."

Zeke's right—about me being competitive. But it's not because of being a college student. It's because of report card time. If you got good grades, you had to tell Mom and Dad. You had to gloat. Because otherwise your achievement would be overlooked. You couldn't count on Mom and Dad to pay attention. They didn't care. They took it for granted that we'd get good grades.

Zeke's the one who broke them of their bad habits. When they had to admit to his teachers that they didn't know he'd skipped a grade, it made them look bad. They couldn't get away with claiming they ignored him for his own good. That excuse wouldn't fly. They had to start paying attention to his achievements so they wouldn't get embarrassed. Zeke would order them around in an off-hand way. You need to do this and this and this. And they'd do it. Because they knew if they didn't, he'd figure out another way to get what he wanted, and that would get them in trouble—and make them look bad.

The rest of us had to brag about our accomplishments. Otherwise, Mom and Dad wouldn't know they'd happened. My older siblings eventually got used to just letting it go and getting attention elsewhere, but I guess I haven't gotten old enough to do that yet. I hate bragging. I really do. But I can't help it sometimes. I'm still trying to make up for those early years of neglect.

I want to brag now about how well I did on the Society test, but Amos is making that as hard as he can. "Who scored third highest on the test?" I demand of him, enunciating slowly.

"You got a ninety percent, Dexter," Amos declares. "That's twenty percentage points higher than what you needed to pass. Barlow here only got a seventy-two." Lower than seventy doesn't cut it because the Society doesn't want any dummies in the ranks. Dummies don't Survive.

Barlow's whooping and grinning like a Tourist after his first Safe House ride. He's been so lost for months now, it's a miracle he passed.

Greta comes into the room, pushing a cart with a sheet cake on it, half white, half chocolate, with butter cream frosting and sparklers on top.

"Who came in third?" I demand over the excited voices of my brothers and sisters. They're paying attention only to the cake, but Amos hears me. He sighs and throws up his arms.

"Amanda," he says. "Amanda's score was third highest."

Amanda?

I frown, and the corner of my lip raises up so high it nearly shuts my left eye. My sister outscored me on the test? She didn't study as hard as I did. She never took the Fourth Dimensional Science course. How did she do so well?

It was Zeke! Because he was her study partner. He switched and let Cartmell partner with Barlow, Pete paired with Greta, and I got left with Cooper, who was never around. Zeke anticipated all the questions and prepared Amanda for them. I knew I would have done better if I'd studied with him instead.

Everyone's lining up for cake like fans at a concert. Garson comes in with cups and a pitcher of milk. I'm at the end of the line behind Amanda.

"Why do you need to have the highest score?" she asks. "What difference does it make? Pete's score was lower than mine, and he doesn't care. Cartmell scored two points lower than me, and that doesn't bother her."

Two points lower than Amanda means three points above me.

Cartmell?

"But she's only fourteen years old," I say. "She didn't study as hard as I did. How could she have scored higher on the test?" She didn't even have to take the test, for god's sake.

This doesn't make sense.

We've moved up in line so we're next to Amos as he eats his cake with a plastic fork. "It doesn't matter, Dexter," he declares, putting down his plate. "What matters is you all passed."

Amanda gets her cake, and Greta serves me a slice, but I'm not paying attention. I wander away, holding my plate.

Maybe Cartmell copied off Zeke's test. Or maybe it was luck, like Cooper. Just pure Vegas luck. That's why she beat me. Or maybe Amanda gave her the answers. But I know that's not it. Because I know there's another explanation, lurking where I can barely make it out in the catacombs of my mind. My intuition knows it's right. I've been missing something, all along. Someone's been concealing things from me.

I look for Cartmell, but she's not in the room. She's hiding like some kid who's misbehaved. She doesn't want me to know. I put down my plate on the piano.

She's smart. That's what it is. Smart like Zeke. Cartmell's a girl genius. Why didn't I see it before? That little sneak. She's been hiding it from us. Except Zeke, of course. And he'd keep her secret. The two of them against the rest of us.

Garson sits at the piano and starts playing "We're in the Money" like he's the one who just passed. He doesn't know what a bummer it is when everyone else scored higher than you. I'm "brother of" again, and I may as well get used to it. So I pick up my piece of cake and wander across the room. I'm still blown away by my discovery about Cartmell. I shake my head and look for a fork.

"So what did you score on the test when you took it?" I ask, coming up to Amos.

He gets this impatient look on his face. "They didn't have the test when I became a Member. It doesn't matter, Dexter. Stop obsessing on your score. You should be happy your brothers and sisters did so well on the exam."

So he *is* from one of the early Seasons.

"Yeah," Barlow says, finishing his second piece of cake on the yellow couch. "Chill out. Be happy for us. Accept the good news." Everybody's celebrating. Barlow grabs Zeke, and they start to dance.

I open my mouth to protest, but all that comes out is "Belinda. Did she take the test?"

Amos becomes exasperated. "For god's sake, Dexter, it doesn't matter. You passed. That's all that matters."

I find out later, when I'm talking to Zeke and I reveal that I KNOW how smart Cartmell is, that she could have scored a 99 percent on the test, but she thought she'd better get a few answers wrong so no one would suspect. I guess she thought I'd do better, but I didn't have a study partner. She's a sly one, Cartmell is.

She's so secretive, keeping her thoughts to herself. Imagine—hiding how smart she is for all these years! It just goes to show how smart she is.

"Just one more Season," Amos tells us, going for a second piece of cake. "And we'll celebrate. Once that's over, you're all officially Longtimers."

Amanda smiles, and popping up suddenly, Cartmell cries out in glee and does a dance with Jackson. Longtimers!

"I'm not waiting another Season," Barlow says, starting on his third piece. "I'm celebratin' now." Everyone joins in with him on that idea, and they're dancing all ding-dong like they just killed the wicked witch. Brother Samuels rolls in a cart with a bowl of punch on it.

I feel glad too, but I'm restless. Celebrate now? And a Season from now? I guess we need to do something to help us feel better about ourselves so we can make the transition to the new life. Amos keeps insisting we celebrate our accomplishments.

Garson's playing "Good Times Are Here Again" like we've just been elected to the Intertime Government, but Zeke interrupts him to give him a piece of cake. I should feel great, but I'm actually feeling low. Because I know once we're Members, we'll all have different jobs and different lives. And that could split up the family.

The family—that reminds me. Amos ducked my question.

"Hey," I say, "What about Belinda? Did Belinda take the test?"

Everyone looks at me like I'm being competitive again, but I'm not. They've all eaten their cake and are going for punch, but I'm still holding my paper plate in my hand like I'm Oliver begging for more.

"Yeah," Cartmell says, sipping from her cup of punch, "where's Belinda? Didn't she have to take the test? You said we all passed."

Amos hesitates, and we know something's up.

"Yeah," Barlow says, "where is she? Didn't she pass?"

We're staring at Amos, and he's on the spot, like the first guy with the Void Race results. He's got to tell us. He hesitates as long as he can, but finally gives in. "Belinda didn't have to take the test," he reveals.

Didn't have to take the test! What is she—in the Void Prison or something? We all start clamoring for an answer, so Amos holds up his hand to quiet us down.

"Belinda's an Eloi now," he says.

An Eloi!

"It's just honorary," he tells us. "But it means she doesn't have to pass the examination." Honorary! Being elected President is honorary. Becoming an Eloi is like winning the lottery.

"You mean she's a Member *now*?" Zeke says. "And a Citizen of Time? She doesn't have to wait another nine Seasons? And she can join the Guilds and live out on the Time Stations if she wants?"

Amos nods. "She has to support herself in the Timeflow like everyone else, so I doubt it's going to make a difference in her life, but, well, it is an honor, and you should be proud of her."

Proud? We're too stunned to feel proud. Garson starts playing "This is my Lucky Day," but we're not feeling lucky—we're feeling we got rooked.

Belinda an Eloi? I never would have guessed she'd be the first of us to reach that status. And she probably doesn't even care, while I know Amanda's burning up inside with envy. She'd give anything to be an Eloi.

An Eloi! How can that be? Maybe there was something to that Lianna from Raindance story Cooper was telling us. But if that's true, then he *has* been posing as Brendan of Regency and he *was* at Belinda's party looking for Dr. Morlock. And that would mean I'm right about him.

That night, before the Ceremony, when I pass the

Chalice Room on my way to the stairs for the third floor, I can hear the voices of Amos and Mr. Yen inside, and I pause to listen like I'm Cartmell spying on Belinda.

"You must feel gratified," Mr. Yen says, "that your charges passed the examination."

"Yes," Amos says. "I never thought they'd make it. I never thought they'd all Survive this long."

"They are a strong-willed bunch," Mr. Yen declares. "That bodes well for their Longevity. You under-estimated them."

"They are smart," Amos admits. "And stubborn. They can be resourceful. I think they can Survive on their own."

There's a pause. "You know," Mr. Yen says, "when you first came to me and told me your intention to Sponsor nine people at once, I thought you had gone Chrono."

Amos chuckles. "Ten people," he says.

"But really only nine." I guess Mr. Yen is discounting baby Jessalyn. "You know that's nearly unheard of, like someone finding their way back after Drifting off the Plane. It's been more than a year since anyone attempted a task so difficult. For all of them to Survive is, well, it's unheard of. And for them to not only Survive but pass the Membership Examination on the first try--"

"I know," Amos says. "They're exceptional."

"You know your achievement has impressed the Elders," Mr. Yen declares. "And the news of your triumph has reached the Scion. It reflects well on your ability to lead. Great advances are in store for your career. Much will be expected of you."

I hear someone coming down the corridor, and I straighten up and begin to walk again, stiff from crouching next to the door for so long. I try to act nonchalant, but I know I'm as obvious as a safecracker wearing a stethoscope.

Cartmell comes running up beside me. "Dexter," she

says in a hushed voice. "You know you're not supposed to eavesdrop." She wags her finger at me.

I huff at her. She's always spying on the rest of us and trying to overhear our conversations. She has to know what's going on in the family. She's a regular one-girl intelligence agency.

"What did you overhear?" she asks me eagerly. "Come on, spill it."

I laugh. "If you're so smart, smartie, why don't you figure it out?"

"Oh, come on," she says. "I don't have all Season."

I decide to tell her before she starts bringing her interrogation tactics to bear on me.

"I guess Amos set some kind of record by Sponsoring all of us at the same time."

"Oh that," Cartmell says. "Cooper told me about that weeks ago."

I frown. How did Cooper find out about it? That guy has so many connections! He's always got the inside story.

"Amos never thought we'd make it this far," I tell Cartmell.

"Neither did I," she declares.

But I don't' believe her. She's been just as oblivious as the rest of us. In between Time Changes none of us have worried much about our Survival. We've been too focused on our Past Life. Of course, Cartmell doesn't have as much

21

REINCHRONATION
Reality 278
Valediction Season

I celebrated your birthday today, reader. I know I got the date wrong, but who says your birthday celebration has to happen on the day of your birth? I lighted a candle in a cupcake. I know you'll do the same for me on April 22nd. That's when mine is. And don't worry—Catterus won't show up like he did today. Just you and me and maybe Garson.

I wish you could meet Garson. I think you'd like him. But all I can do is tell you about him.

Sometimes Garson's sharpened teeth can make it seem he's smiling when he really isn't. This is one of those times. He calls me on my cell this morning (interrupting your birthday celebration) and suggests we meet at the old Westwood Cemetery, where Mom and Dad are buried. It seems like an odd suggestion, but you know how strange my life has gotten, so I say, "Sure, why not?"

So I take the subway into town to the Acheron Station. I'm wearing a black gown like everyone else in this Reality. It's a Light Season despite the weird fashions, so no one really cares that I've got on cowboy boots. They attract attention, but I wear them anyway because they seem appropriate for a visit to Boot Hill, which is what we've always called the old cemetery.

When I get there, Garson is waiting for me at the wrought-iron gates. The rest of the cemetery is surrounded by a dry rock wall. This is where the oldest graves in Shawneetown are located, where the Vann family plot is. We may all be in here one day.

Garson guides me to my parents' graves in the back—I know the route well—but when we get there, I discover a new grave where Mom and Dad's used to be. It has a simple rounded gray stone marker that reads:

BARLOW VANN
Beloved Son
Football Champion

Barlow's dates are on it, including his death thirteen years ago. Now I understand what Madame Bela meant when she said "Someone die will." No wonder he doesn't have any karma. His Alternate Self has been dead this whole time.

"How long has this grave been here?" I ask Garson.

He shrugs. It wasn't here last time I visited the cemetery—but that was back in the Wilderness Season, before we were in the Timeflow. The date of Barlow's death is near the end of his first year in college. He was already the star of the football team by then. I guess all the karma he accumulated more than a decade after that is gone. That's a lot to lose—a third of his life.

No wonder my Alternates are different from me. They had to finish growing up without Barlow's influence. I would have ended up a lot moodier, I guess, a lot more private and solitary. I mull that over as I stand there next to Garson. In his Monks' robes he fits right in with this Season's fashions.

"Where are my parents' graves?" I ask without looking at him.

He shrugs. Sometimes he doesn't feel like talking, probably because so many people find him hard to follow.

I don't feel like talking either. So I just stare at Barlow's grave some more, thinking this is a preview of the inevitable real thing.

I'm not the same after that. I can't concentrate. I keep thinking about the past. So I wander over to our old house in Karbers Ridge. I know—I should stay away from it. It's Past Life. But I'm so weirded out I figure things can't get any worse.

I discover the old homestead is still there on Maypole Street—a simple whitewashed frame house the shape of one of the hotels in Monopoly, with a screened-in porch on one side and a garage on the other.

The weird thing is Mom and Dad's old copper-colored Hudson is in the driveway. I walk over to it and glance inside at the tan seat covers and dashboard. It looks just like I remember it, only smaller. Everything seems smaller than it was when I was growing up.

The lawn's freshly mowed, and someone's cultivated the garden. The house looks like it's been whitewashed. What the heck? Has Amos been over here sprucing things up? Or Amanda? It looks like someone lives here.

So I go and knock on the front door. I start to feel pretty silly about that. Why am I knocking on the door of a house that's been deserted for three years? (We kids still own it, but none of us wants to sell it—or live here). So I grab the doorknob and turn it and find it's unlocked. I push it open and step inside.

I'm greeted by a familiar odor—the smell of home. Every house seems to have its own characteristic scent. This one's a robust cooking smell—like roasted flowers. I'd forgotten all about it. It really takes me back. I feel like a kid again, and I'm expecting to hear the yells and excited fast-moving voices of my brothers and sisters, the raucous melody of our old home.

But there are no voices. I hear other sounds. First, the ticking of the grandfather clock. There it is—right in the front hall where it always used to be. It stopped working the day Dad died, and Amos never could get it fixed. But here it is, ticking away just like in the old days.

The next sound I hear is the purring of a cat. Mom's cat Tabby comes waltzing by, like some ghost, and rubs up against my boots. Tabby's long dead, too. I look around—there's a rug on the wood floor. All the old furnishings are here.

What the heck is going on?

As I turn, I detect other sounds, but they're drowned out by the deep chiming of the grandfather clock, as if it's a Time Machine whisking me back to Wilderness.

I step into the sitting room and almost collide with Mom, who's bustling on her way to the front door. She stops and frowns at me in surprise, but she's not as shocked as I am.

"Dexter!" she cries. "What are you doing home? I wasn't expecting you until Thursday. Did you leave for Thanksgiving Break early?"

I look—and then I look again. She seems the same as always, white haired, as tall as me, not as husky as Amanda but strong and stern-looking. She's dressed as always in a simple dress. No Valediction robes for her. She couldn't care less about the latest fashions. Her brown eyes blink at me a few times.

A whole herd of memories comes stampeding at me from out of the past and tramples right over me. My first bicycle, my first trip to the Dentist, lying in bed while Mom takes care of me while I'm sick, picking out a freshly cut Christmas tree from a corner lot, opening presents on Christmas morning. I realize it's not just Reality 250 I'm pining for—I miss my past. And with Mom returned, I've gotten a bit of my past back.

When most people talk about their love for their parents, they mention all of things their parents have done for them and how grateful they are. And I could list what my parents have done, too: brought me into the world, fed me, clothed me, raised me, gave me shelter, cared about me, taught me to be self sufficient, to have high standards for myself. And a lot more.

But love isn't gratitude. Love is a yearning inside that won't go away. A yearning for another person. And that yearning can only be satisfied by hearing, seeing, or feeling that person. You never get over that. Your parents are important to you your whole life, even after they're gone.

And when they come back from the dead—

"Oh, Mom," I say, overcome with emotion, "I've missed you."

She's baffled at first by my tears, but then she seems to figure it out. "Dexter—you're homesick. You haven't been homesick since you were a freshman."

Homesick is an understatement. Whensick it's called.

My past still has me in its grip. Pulling my sled behind me by a rope as I trudge up a snowy hillside, having a snowball fight with Barlow and Cooper, riding in an overheated school bus on a frosty morning all suited up in a parka, scarf, and stocking cap, Mom's serving us steaming mugs of cocoa at the breakfast table after we've shed our snowy outer layers.

Mom and I hug, and I realize how long it's been. I haven't been hugged by anyone since Wilderness, more than a year ago.

"What are you doing back so soon?" she asks, pulling away from me.

I don't know what to say. That I've come from the Neverbeen?

"I was just over at Barlow's grave."

She flinches, and a dark shadow seems to fall over her face. "He would have been nearly thirty now. A doctor or a lawyer." She closes her eyes. "He would have made us proud."

Doctor or lawyer! Unemployed head case is more like it. I'm glad I don't have to tell her what's really become of him.

Mom turns around. "Moses!" she calls out. "Moses, Dexter's come home." She listens, but there's no reply. She frowns. "Cartmell! Get down here. Your brother's back."

She walks over to the curving staircase and looks up it. "Where is that girl?" she muses. "She should have turned up by now. She usually doesn't miss a thing."

She's not here. Not anymore.

"I think she's over at Amanda's," I tell Mom.

"Amanda's!" Mom frowns at me. "What would she be doing over there?"

"She'll be over here soon," I tell her. "All of the family's coming."

"Tonight? I haven't finished thawing the turkey. I haven't made the stuffing yet. Or the green bean casserole."

We hear the complaining tone of the dryer. "I'll be right back," Mom says. So she trundles off to attend to the laundry.

I take out my cell phone and punch in Cartmell's number.

"I'm at the old homestead," I tell her. "You need to get over here right away. Mom and Dad are here. They've been Reinchronated."

Cartmell gasps. She starts to jabber, but I don't have time for it, so I say, "Just get over here. Bring Amanda and Zeke with you—but don't bring Barlow. And don't tell him. Because he's dead. I don't have time to explain."

I cut off the signal and punch in another number. It takes awhile to get an answer, and I pace in a little circle while I wait. Soon I hear Amos's deep voice on the other end.

"Yes?"

"Amos, it's Dexter. There's been a development. I'm at Mom and Dad's house. They've been Reinchronated."

No gasp, but I can hear Amos's deep breaths. He doesn't seem surprised. These are breaths of wariness.

"I know," I say. "I should have stayed out of my Alternate Life."

He exhales. "Mom and Dad aren't Alternate Life. They never change." There's an edge of resignation in his voice, like he's run into a recurring problem.

"Then this has happened before?"

"Many times."

Many times? How long has Amos been in the Timeflow?

"How many?" I ask.

"Never mind." Another big issue he wants to avoid.

"You don't sound excited to hear they're back," I say to him.

He pauses, then says in a gruff voice, "I'm jumping for joy. Just like you. But you need to prepare yourself for how you're going to handle it when they Vanish again. You need to be ready for the grief. It's a whopper."

The grief? I hadn't thought of that.

"You need to prepare yourself," Amos says, "for dealing with them. It's never easy."

He's thrown me again. "Because they're Alternates?"

"Because they're Mom and Dad," he barks at me. "You know what they're like."

Stubborn. Obstinate. Full of expectations. I was so glad to find them alive I'd forgotten how difficult they can be.

"I'll be by there later," Amos tells me. "I have some things to take care of first. Call your brothers and sisters. They're going to want to know about this. You'll all have to take advantage of this opportunity as soon as you can."

I'm grappling with Amos's mater-of-fact attitude. "You make it sound like this isn't going to last."

"It isn't." He grumbles for a few moments. "Their Reinchronation won't last out the Season. They might not even make it to the next Reality."

We're going to lose them *again*? *Not again.*

Amos hangs up on me, and I'm left standing there in the front hall with a silent phone next to my ear. So I click it off and slide it into my pocket. I'm preoccupied and only casually gazing out the window when I spot someone across the street.

Is that who I think it is?

I walk over to the window for a better look, but it's fogged up because of the cold and wet. So I open the front door for a better view.

I see Catterus standing on the lawn of the house across the street, looking right at me. He's dressed all in black with a black lacy dress coat and a tri-cornered hat. All the Void Pirates like dressing the part. They think it legitimizes them, makes them romantic figures in a business that's grungy and mean.

Our gazes lock for a few seconds. Then a truck goes by in the street, blocking my view and making splashing sounds in the drizzle, and once it lumbers out of the way, Catterus is gone. I can't see him anywhere.

So I leave the house and ease the door shut behind me. I walk up to the street and look both ways. I can't see anyone in either direction. Where did he go?

Was I just seeing things?

The drizzle has gotten thicker—and I'm starting to feel wet, but I cross the street anyway. Why—I'm not sure. What am I going to do if I find him? Say, "Aha!"? Have some kind of confrontation?

I need to protect Mom and Dad.

There's a hedge surrounding the house across the street. And a fence behind the hedge. Between them would be the perfect place to hide. So I cross at the driveway and walk between the hedge and the fence around the side of the yard and toward the back. I can't see Catterus anywhere.

I'm getting nervous. The drizzle isn't the only thing making me wet. I'm beginning to sweat. I wish I had Barlow with me. He's got nerves of steel, and he knows what to do in a situation like this. At least, he used to. But we can't bring him around—because he's dead, you know. Mom and Dad couldn't take the shock. He'd put them back in the cemetery for sure. Because there's no way to explain his existence in terms they'd understand.

They're Rejectors, you see. They won't listen to anything out of their comfort zone. They're set in their ways. They've got brittle views, and the experience would only break them rather than bend them to a new outlook.

As I continue farther down the passageway between hedge and fence, the path grows darker. I'm in the shadows on the far side of the house now. No Man's Land. It occurs to me that coming after Catterus is dangerous and could be a huge mistake. It could get me killed. But I'm committed to my plan of action, and really the only threatening thing I've encountered so far is the darkness. And the weirdness.

As I round the corner at the back yard, a figure steps from an alcove in the fence behind me, and I whirl around to confront him, suddenly alarmed. I expect the Void Pirate, but it's not Catterus. It's someone in a leather jacket and jeans, with perfectly styled hair and expensive leather shoes.

"Hello, little brother," he says. He's got his hands in the pockets of his jacket. "What brings you here?"

I don't know what to say at first. I'm taken by surprise. What is Cooper doing hiding in this hedge? I sputter for a few seconds. "I just saw Catterus," I tell him. "Standing in the front yard. He disappeared, and I came in here to look for him."

Cooper nods. "I was afraid of that." He purses his lips. "There have been reports. We'd better get over to Mom and Dad's." He gestures for me to go first, and we walk back the way I came.

"I couldn't see where he went," I say. "Maybe into the Void."

"Nah. We have a Cruiser patrolling out there. The Fourth Dimensional routes in and out of here are sealed up."

When we come out from behind the hedge, we look around but don't see anyone up or down the street.

"Let's go check out the back yard," Cooper suggests.

So I cross the street with him and walk down the driveway past Dad's old Hudson and along the side of the house between our hedge and the garage.

"We'll have the area secure pretty soon," Cooper tells me. "We should have anticipated this. Catterus is bound to be watching the phone books in each new Reality, looking for our Alternate Selves' addresses to pop up. He'd spot our parents' names right away."

"Does he intend to kill them?" I ask.

"Nah, he's just looking for the bunch of you."

I think that over. "Well, he found me," I say. "Why didn't he do anything about it?"

Cooper glances at me like I'm asking for trouble, but I'm just trying to figure things out. I'm an Analyzer, you know. Surely that's my Strategy. As close as I've come to one.

"Catterus wants to take you all out at the same time," Cooper tells me. "And not leave anyone behind for retribution."

That sounds like the Catterus I know.

"But what about you and Amos?"

He grunts. "I wasn't there when you crossed him, and besides, we're already on his enemies list. We're on a lot of lists. We don't have time for retribution. He's going to let the Syndicate deal with us."

As we round the corner of the house into the back yard, I can see the locust tree and the big elm I used to climb as a kid. And then we hear a voice behind us.

"Hold it right there—or I'll shoot."

So we stop and turn our heads toward the voice, and there's Dad, holding his shotgun aimed at us. He's tall and clean shaven—not as tall as Amos and Amanda and Barlow, but over six feet. His gray hair's so thin he's almost bald. What really strikes you about him, though, are his penetrating blue eyes, clear as a couple ghosts. They can make you nervous, those eyes, like they're staring right through you.

A new flood of memories washes over me. Walking through the woods with my twenty-two—hunting with Dad and Barlow, skating on a frozen pond, sitting in our motorboat at the lake, holding a fishing pole, waving at Mom while I'm water-skiing behind Dad's boat.

I can feel the yearning again, the yearning for Mom and Dad, the yearning for my past. It's what I came from. It's who I am.

He lowers his gun barrel and regards us. "Hello, boys," he says. "What are you doing back here?"

I look over at Cooper for an answer. The truth is too impossible to fit. Our lives have outgrown their clothes.

"Looking for you," Cooper says smoothly. He was always good at coming up with a cover story. He's the best bluffer you ever met. "Why the gun?"

Dad holds it tucked under his armpit now as he eyes us. We're dressed pretty odd, in his view. "There were some trespassers out here earlier," he tells us. "I saw them from the bedroom window. Big palookas. Troublemakers. So I got my shotgun."

Dad likes hunting big game. He's a real show off.

Cooper nods. "Doesn't look like they're here anymore."

Dad has always been territorial. Barlow had to argue with him to get him to take down the "Trespassers will be shot" sign. Dad can be a very generous person, but not when it comes to property. He likes to choose his companions, and he doesn't care for intruders.

"Let's look over the place anyway," he suggests. He's going to do it himself regardless of what we want.

So we walk around the other side of the house with him, but no trespassers. Just as we reach the front yard, half a dozen police cars pull up, their lights flashing, and a mob of cops climbs out. That's one of the perks, I guess, of being the lawyer for the police union.

I give Cooper a sarcastic glance. "I guess we don't need to worry about Dad's safety."

"Nope," he says. "You're the one we need to worry about. We'll have to pull you out through the Fourth Dimension, in case Catterus is tracking you. We don't want him following you home to Amanda's Alternate Residence."

The police search the property but don't find anyone. Cooper and I figure Catterus and his gang are gone. They've high-tailed it out of here. I guess he was just trying to prove he could find us—that we're not beyond his reach, that eventually he's going to get us, and he'll have his revenge.

Yeah, but maybe we'll get him first.

So Cooper, Dad, and I head inside the house, which is now full of cooking smells. There's a turkey in the oven and a pumpkin pie. I guess we're having Thanksgiving dinner early, and Mom's going to cook something else on Thursday.

Mom makes a big fuss over Cooper. He's always been her favorite. Then my other brothers and sisters start to arrive. Amanda's the first. She's all dressed up like she's meeting dignitaries. Mom and Dad don't seem to notice. She's just a kid to them. Mom starts ordering her around, and Amanda follows after her like a dutiful daughter. Mom puts her to work in the kitchen. She's got company, and that means a big meal must be prepared.

Zeke and Cartmell arrive next, and they're jumping for joy at seeing Mom and Dad again.

"What's all the fuss for?" Mom asks, frowning at us. "What's gotten into you? You act like you haven't seen us for years."

Three, to be exact.

We look back at her with shining eyes. It's not every day someone comes back from the dead.

So Zeke and Cartmell follow Mom into the kitchen to help, but they keep getting in Mom's way, so she kicks them out of there, and they join us in the sitting room.

There's suddenly a ponderous knock on the front door, and we all freeze in our seats. Dad's in his office, and through the doorway I can see him reaching for his shotgun, which is propped up next to his desk.

This can't be Catterus, though. It has to be one of the cops, because there's still a bunch of them outside. They've posted guards all around the house.

It can't be Amos. He wouldn't bother knocking. He'd just barge right in.

"Oh, no," I say. "It's not Barlow, is it?" I look at Zeke and Cartmell. "You didn't tell him, did you?"

They look back at me innocently. They seem as surprised as me. So I go to the front door and open it.

A woman in a black Valediction robe is standing on the porch. She's not only got on the robe but also the dark eye makeup they like in this Season. I can't figure out what one of the Locals is doing here.

"Yes," I say. "Can I help you?"

"Knock it off, Dexter," she growls.

It's Belinda.

She pushes her way past me into the house. I have to take a few steps back to try to adjust to this new development. I'm completely at a loss. "How did you know?" I sputter. I didn't call her—I don't have her number.

She just glares at me. I guess Amos must have called her.

"Where are they?" she demands.

Zeke and Cartmell and I exchange glances. This is going to be awkward, after her getting kicked out of the family and Amanda putting a gag order on us. I don't know what to say to her. But I've got to try, at least.

"Belinda, it's so good to see you. I'm sorry about what happened up on the Society Station—"

She shoots me one of Amanda's dirty looks. She doesn't care to be reminded about the cold reception we gave her on the Station in the Void. I don't think she's forgiven us for that, except for Zeke, of course, who saved the day.

She looks over at him now.

"Mom's in the kitchen," he tells her, "with Amanda."

So Belinda turns toward the kitchen, her face reflecting her mental preparations. She and Mom have never gotten along.

She takes a step, but Mom comes striding into the sitting room, wearing her apron, oblivious, in everyday mode. She stops when she sees Belinda—then looks away.

"Mom," Belinda says, stepping toward her. But Mom has this sullen look on her face, and she turns and leaves the room without a word.

Belinda reaches after her, but Mom's gone. She's mad at Belinda about something. Mad at Belinda's Alternate Self, that is. She doesn't know this is a different Belinda. I don't think Amanda said anything. Her feud with Belinda is the farthest thing from her mind now.

I notice Dad standing in the doorway of his office with his arms crossed. He's wearing khaki slacks and a green plaid hunting shirt. "What did you expect?" he says to Belinda.

She glances over at him.

Dad's giving her his fed-up-with-us look. "Did you think she would welcome you back after what you did? How do you expect her to act?"

Belinda turns to look in the direction Mom has gone with a far-off expression on her face. "Like she loves me as much as I love her."

Dad lets out a harumphing exclamation and walks back into his office and shuts the door.

Rejectors. They're never easy to get along with. Everything is a violation of their rules. Everything's got to be done on their terms.

Belinda's the same way, of course, when it comes to the family. She'll go out of her way to mix with the Bystanders. But she expects *us* to accommodate *her*. Like she's the Queen or something—which I guess she is, now that she's an Eloi. But we're too proud, too much like Mom and Dad to cater to her. There's a little Rejector in all of us, I guess.

I'm trying to come up with something to say. I think we all are. That's when Amos shows up in a weird orange suit from some Lost Season and walks right in the door, into the middle of our confusion. He glances at our faces with a puzzled expression. He doesn't understand what's just happened.

I guess Dad must have been watching out his window when Amos pulled up front. Because he opens the door to his office and looks around at us until he spots Amos. He frowns at the transformation in Amos's style and dress. He looks Amos up and down like a drill sergeant during inspection.

"Come in," he says. "There are some things we need to discuss." It's not a request. Dad turns and heads for his desk. My parents view Amos as the only adult among us, but he's not their equal. There's still a pecking order.

So head bowed, he sighs and steps into Dad's office. He doesn't know what Dad wants. We don't get hints from him ahead of time. He only keeps us informed of what he's thinking when he feels like it, and this isn't one of those days. Maybe Dad's going to chew him out. Maybe it's something else. Amos marches in like a prisoner to his cell and closes the door behind him.

Facing Catterus doesn't seem so intimidating now. Void Pirates are a cinch compared to this.

22

REJECTORS
Reality 279
Valediction Season

I've been thinking, reader. What caused my parents to be Reinchronated? It's Strange Karma come to me through Supernatural Life. But what was its cause?

Could it be you? Is your karma coming across time and shaking things up? If so, you've affected me, too, reader. You've given me confidence. Not to change my parents—no. They're a lost cause because they can't change.

You've given me the confidence to Sponsor Quint a fourth time. This will be my final chance with him, so I've got to make it count. I've been afraid to try up to now, afraid of how I'll feel if I fail. But now I believe I'll do my best, and if I fail, it won't be my fault. It will be because Quint is a lost cause like my parents and can't change. You've given me the resolve to *try*—to Sponsor him one last time.

Quint has always been curious about the Brotherhood. We all were when we were kids, but when I tell him I'm a member of it now he gives me a look like there's something wrong with me. Because we've always thought the Brotherhood is for weird old geezers who don't have anything to do but gab about the past and perform silly rituals.

As we walk up the hillside toward the Lodge, he gives me a suspicious glance, as if he's trying to figure out how I've turned into an old geezer and whether I'm as weird and useless as everyone else in the Brotherhood. He's dressed like the other young people in the Valediction Season—in suspenders and a jersey and clunky black leather shoes. It seems strange to me that I don't identify with Bystanders my age. I feel years older than them, and I look it too.

I can tell Quint's trying to figure out what's happened to me since he went off to college four years ago. He still takes me for my Alternate Self. He hasn't caught on that I'm a whole 'nother person from a distant Season. He's not able to think in those terms, because I've just started Sponsoring him. He thinks I'm Sponsoring him to join a lodge. The word "Longtimer" is meaningless to him.

Once we walk up the steps to the house, we're greeted by Brother Samuels who is standing on the porch with his hood down. "Is this our new Initiate?" he asks me, smiling upon Quint.

Quint gives me this startled look, like I'm rushing him to sign up for something he wants no part of. "Not yet," I tell Brother Samuels. "He's still checking us out."

Brother Samuels Nods and opens the front door for us. He's a tall, plump man with large hands, a flattop haircut and pale skin. His history is a complete mystery to me. I know he must predate Wilderness, but I've never been able to figure out When he comes from. I wonder if he recognizes Quint. He's seen him during my three previous attempts at Sponsoring him. He's the only blond-haired kid we've ever brought over.

The Society permits each person to be Sponsored only four times. If you can't catch on after four tries, the Society deems you a hopeless case and refuses to waste any more of its resources on you.

Quint is a hopeless case.

Of course, officially, Amos is his Sponsor, and I'm only acting as his agent, but I don't think Amos and Quint have ever met.

As we enter the Lodge, Quint looks around at the tunnel-like hallways. The Lodge's corridors have carved wooden arch-work at intervals along the way. Walking down them can seem like heading down a mineshaft.

"Where are we going?" he asks me.

"To Room 999," I tell him. "It's the Lodge's public Safe House." I've told him what a Safe House is, but I doubt he remembers because he Rejects everything I say.

"A Time Machine," I tell him, "that Travels a few instants in Time in order to escape Time Changes."

He gives me a look to let me know he's getting tired of hearing all that malarkey. I resist telling him how tired I am of that look of his. I've been seeing it for six Seasons now.

Once we reach Room 999, we turn and enter. It's not a big room. There are a few padded chairs inside, bolted to the floor. Portholes behind drawn curtains. A television screen for Fourth Dimensional Network broadcasts. Quint glances around and gives me an impatient look. "This is it?" he says. "This is your Time Machine?" He looks like I'm trying to sell him the Tri-State Bridge.

I can tell by his tone of voice that he's irritated. I forget sometimes it doesn't look like much. I'm still remembering my family's eager celebrations here back in Wilderness after our first few rides. I guess Quint thought I would take him to one of the fancy parts of the Lodge like the Library or the Sanctuary or the Chalice Room.

"You brought me all the way here," he says, "to show me this?"

"It's not as ordinary as it looks," I tell him.

I'm interrupted by the appearance of one of the Monks, come to repair the television. I give him a Nod then return to explaining. But Quint can't take his eyes off the Monk, and interrupts me after a few minutes. "That guy's got tattoos all over his face." Quint looks more than disturbed. He's disgusted.

I glance over at the hooded Monk. "Oh, that's Garson," I say with a smile. "I thought he was weird, too, at first. Don't worry, you'll get used to him."

But there are some things you never get used to—like Rejectors.

Quint gives me his malarkey look again and raises his arms in disbelief. "Why are you hanging out with people like this?"

Amanda asked me the same thing last Season when she saw me with Quint. And she's the one who has more reason to ask it, because I'm closer to Garson and her than I am to him. He used to be my best friend, but now he's a stranger.

Garson's my best friend, and Quint's the one who looks odd to me with his strange Valediction jersey and suspenders and cowlicky haircut. He looks so strange, like no one I've ever known. But I don't want to tell him what a freak he is. He and the other Bystanders. I care enough to spare his feelings.

"When the next Time Change starts," I say, "the Beacons we've set up Downtime will send out a Signal as the Change approaches. My Beeper will go off, and my watch face will flash, and we'll have twenty to sixty minutes to get to a Safe House. It will take us into the Void of the Fourth Dimension, where there's no—"

Quint gives me another annoyed look. "Oh cut it out with all that science fiction crap." He doesn't realize he's just showing what a Rejector he is. All of the Rejectors hate what they call science fiction. They don't like anything that deviates from their own narrow view of the possible. He never used to be a Rejector back in Wilderness, but he's been one ever since. He used to love reading science fiction. He couldn't get enough of it.

Quint's already fallen so far in my estimation he can't plummet any further. He has no clue what a Bystander he is. He doesn't realize that I detest him even more than he detests me. The only difference is I'm willing to forgive him.

"What has happened to you, man?" he says to me in his Valediction speak. "What are you doing in this creepy lodge with all these creepy people?" He shakes his head and backs up from me. "I came along because I didn't get it. I couldn't figure you out. I thought you'd have some explanation, but you just keep giving me all this weird crap." He gestures at my clothes. "Look at you.

What's with the cowboy boots and dungarees and vest? You look like some kind of hick. I didn't want to say anything, but it's not cool, man. It's not cool at all."

Quint's about to leave. I can recognize the signs since I've been through this before. I've failed again. If I could just sit down and reminisce with him, we could connect. The problem is we can't reminisce—because we have different pasts. I remember Reality 250, and he remembers 279. We don't have any shared experience. We have different world views, molded by different environments. We're too Dyschronic. As I said, it's hopeless—and I'm going to have to face that.

"This isn't going to work out," I tell him. "I know that. We're too different. But I still remember the friends we used to be. And I want to honor that friendship."

Quint's quiet, and he's not looking so skeptical. I've managed to connect with him in a small way.

"I know the Brotherhood isn't for you," I tell him. "I just wanted to do something for you But I can't. You're going to have to do it for me."

He doesn't look suspicious anymore, but he's frowning. "Do what?" he asks.

I've never given up on Quint before. I feel like a mercy killer, but that's better than how I usually feel when I finish with him. "I want you to do all the things you've ever wanted but have been putting off," I tell him. "I want you to do them now, in the next few days." At least he'll end his life on a happy note.

He stares at me for a few seconds. "You mean, like a bucket list?"

"Yeah, a bucket list. I want you to live to the fullest *now* like there's no tomorrow." Which there isn't. I look him in the eye. "Can you do that for me? For old time's sake?"

He looks at me like this is the first sane thing I've said all day, like he can't believe a lunatic like me would say something so reasonable.

"Okay," he says. "Yeah, I can do that, man. I was

going to do it eventually—so why not now?"

It's not going to save him—but it's the best I can do.

"Why don't you come do it with me?" he says. He looks at me like the old Quint, the one who wasn't a Rejector.

I'm tempted to forget the Time Changes and run off on some wild adventure with him and be friends one last time. That's the Danger. That's what could Wipe me Out of Time. Danger Number Seven from myself, from my own infatuation with Past Life.

I shake my head. "No," I say. "You go on without me. Take someone special. Do it up right. Make this count."

Quint starts to smile. "You're all right, Dexter. You're not such a weird old geezer, after all."

And that's as close as we get before we call an end to our friendship. I get to say one last goodbye before we part ways forever. He gives me a wave and walks down the corridor out of sight. And that's the last I see of him. I feel like I've said goodbye to my past.

I remember the time the three of us, he, Harley and me, went to the prom together in high school. A triple date, six of us crowded into one car, passing a bottle of Wild Turkey on the way to the after party, laughing and whooping it up.

I remember when we graduated and ran outside and threw our caps into the air and cheered, glad to be on our way to bigger and better things. And he said to me, grinning. "You know, we should be bawling instead of cheering. We're going to miss the great times." And he leaned close to me and said. "But we'll be friends forever, you and me. Nothing's going to change that."

And I believed him. I still do.

And I remember—but what's the use? It's all a bunch of Past Life. Nostalgia and that pathological stuff. Signs of Attachment, barricades to living in the Present. I could never understand what was so wrong with reminiscing, but now I wish my memories would just leave me alone.

I've been feeling sad for a long time since Quint left. I still do now. But losing him this time was easier than the last three times. He's become more difficult with each Season, more of a Rejector. And they say, "Once a Rejector, always a Rejector." I should have Sponsored Harley first, but it's too late, because Harley's Extinct.

Brooding over my failures, past and present, I walk into Room 999 and belt myself into one of the chairs like I'm getting ready for Emergence. Then I go limp. I'm too exhausted to sit up.

Garson's screwing on the back of the television set. He pulls back the hood of his robe and looks over at me. "That Quint was?" he asks.

I look at him, surprised—I didn't know he was still here. I stretch and sit up. "Yeah."

"Best your friend?"

"Used to be."

He nods and starts packing his tools in a metal toolbox. "Never a chance to Sponsor my got any I friends of," he says. "My short so Season was because. People scares now them, me look to at." He rubs the side of his neck like he has a cramp. "Can't them blame I. No normal look I don't to anymore even myself."

Being from Sideshow must be pretty hard, being shunned by both Bystanders and Longtimers. Of course, I may as well have been from Sideshow in Quint's view. To him I was just as much a freak as Garson.

Quint's personality seems to change more with each passing Season. He becomes less like his old self, and Sponsoring him becomes more hopeless. I've failed sooner this time than on the last three attempts. But it hurts less this time. I can almost accept it, not because I feel less friendship toward him but because my attachment to the Longtimers has grown so strong. I have new best friends now.

It's going to be hard telling Brother Samuels that my

Sponsorship didn't take. He'll be disappointed because everyone roots for a Sponsor. It's a tough job, because you can't do it right without becoming attached. That's the whole point, after all, to forge human links and create a sense of community. I just hope Brother Samuels doesn't lecture me or try to comfort me for my loss.

While I'm still thinking things over, I spot Amos entering the room with my parents, and I wish I could hide. I notice Garson put his hood back up. Mom and Dad have been Reinchronated in this Season, and they won't Endure long. They couldn't understand why we were making such a big deal about them when they came back into Existence. They had no idea they'd been dead. Their death's in the Neverbeen.

They look pretty much as I remember them—but not exactly. I wonder if my perspective's flawed, or if they *are* different in this Reality. Dad's a little hunched over now. Mom's always been an inch taller—she looks a lot like Amanda, though she's white haired and wrinkled. Dad's gray too, and his face has a weathered look, and his hands are gnarled, but his blue eyes seem the same, searching like spotlights.

"This is Room 999," Amos tells them. "This is where you come when there's a Time Change."

Dad glances around the room, obviously bored, like he's looking at real estate he doesn't intend to buy. He's more interested in the television being repaired. Mom keeps looking at Amos and doesn't pay attention to Room 999.

"This is nice, son," she says to him.

Garson picks up his tools and excuses himself with a Nod toward Amos. Amos Nods back.

I wish I wasn't in the room, because I know Mom and Dad will lose interest in being Sponsored once they see me here. They'll assume the Lodge is a place where the kids hang out, and they won't want to come here.

"Well, hello, Dexter," Amos says after he notices me.

"What brings you to the Lodge? We usually don't see anyone so young here." We exchange Nods.

Dad harrumphs at that, because he just saw Quint leaving. Kids hangout. His verdict is rendered.

"Hello, Dexter," Mom says. Dad nods at me, but not in a Longtimer way. Being with Amos is a treat for them, because they consider him an adult. I'm still just a kid in their eyes.

"Shouldn't you be at school now?" Dad asks me, like I'm neglecting my paper route or something. I stifle my response, because I don't want Amos to feel I blew his Sponsorship. The only school I go to now is a course in Fourth Dimensional Science.

"This is my day off," I tell them. Of course, that creates exactly the wrong impression, because now they think the Lodge is where I spend my free time. My hangout.

Amos tries to distract Mom and Dad from me by continuing his tour. "This is where you need to come," he tells them, "whenever your Beeper goes off. Just drop whatever you're doing and come straight here. Park anywhere. Just make sure you get into this room before twenty minutes have passed."

"But what if we're doing something important?" Mom asks.

"Nothing's more important," Amos reminds her. "Your Survival depends on getting here on time."

"But what if I'm at Bridge Club?" she says.

"I can't interrupt a trial," Dad tells him. "Or my golf game."

Amos sighs in frustration. They're hopeless, of course. They always are. He's explains everything to them, but they just take it like he's telling them the rules of some game the kids like to play. He told me he'd like to get a Longtimer their age to Sponsor them. But no one wants to Sponsor someone who's already failed their first three tries. And Mom and Dad wouldn't be likely to pay attention to someone they don't already know.

"Well, thanks for showing us around, son," Dad says. "But it's time for us to be getting back." He holds out an arm toward Mom. She'll ignore it if she wants to stay.

"Thank you for showing us around," she says. "I'm so glad you joined this Lodge. Your father's met so many important people that way. And I don't know what he'd do if he wasn't a member of the Crusade. He'd have to play on the public courses."

"It's not all about golf," Dad protests.

"Yes, it is," she says. "You said so the last time you wrote a check for your membership."

Dad would argue the point, except he's ready to leave. "Come along, Mother," he says, still holding out his arm.

Mom takes a step toward him. "You shouldn't be spending so much of your time with us," she tells Amos. "You should find yourself a nice girl."

"I have," he tells her.

She stops, suddenly interested, and Dad drops his arm. "Why haven't we met her?"

Amos is hesitating now, I'm not sure why. "You haven't met Joanne?" he asks them.

I can't tell if he's referring to a Longtimer or to someone from the past. Or maybe he just made up the name.

Mom smiles. "No, but we'd love to meet her."

"She'll be here," Amos tells them. "Twenty minutes after your Beepers go off. Don't be late."

I'm not sure if Mom and Dad believe him. They know he's trying to trick them into coming back. But they also know he'll bring Joanne to meet them if he can manage it. Mom and Dad are capable of catching on, but like all Rejectors, they refuse to try. Sponsoring them is like beating yourself with a hammer. In the end all you have to show for your effort is a bunch of bruises.

Mom takes Dad's arm, and they exit, waving

goodbye to me. Amos collapses onto the couch and puts his face into his hands.

"Planeless Darkness!" he cries. "I'd rather try to turn a bunch of Day People into Night People."

I know what he means. "Why is it so hard," I ask, sitting next to him, "being a Sponsor?"

He sits up straight after a moment and sighs. "It's only this hard with Rejectors."

"Yeah," I say, "but why do we keep trying to Sponsor these Rejectors?"

Amos looks at me and considers the question, then looks away. "I guess it's because we're stuck in our Past Life."

I'm surprised to hear him say that. He's lectured the rest of us so many times about Past Life, I'd begun to think he didn't have any of his own. I'd always thought he was Sponsoring Mom and Dad for our benefit. I never realized he has his own motives. Or an Attachment to Past Life.

"Wasn't that Quint I saw leaving the Lodge?" Amos asks me. "I thought you already Sponsored him three times."

"I thought you already Sponsored Mom and Dad four times."

Amos pauses and adjusts his glasses. "This counts as their first time since they've been Reinchronated."

I nod like it's the same with me. "I got Brother Samuels to Sponsor Quint this time." Amos knows I'm lying, that I signed him up as Quint's Sponsor without telling him. And he knows I know he knows. But he also knows it's useless to lecture me, especially about Over-Sponsoring. He can see I got stung, and he knows what that feels like. I think we've both had all we can take of that subject right now.

There's a long section on Sponsoring in the *Parattak*, explaining its purpose and who to Sponsor and when to do it and how to go about it. What to say, what not to say. And how to handle it if you don't succeed. "If you cannot tolerate the prospect of failing as a Sponsor," the *Parattak* says, "you should not Sponsor. Because every Sponsor fails at least as often as he succeeds."

> Sponsorship is a sacred trust and should be undertaken only with patience and reverence. Survival of the Initiate is its aim but not its guarantee. Sponsoring can be a test of the Sponsor as well as the Initiate. Failure is an opportunity for growth. For learning lessons. For a more harmonious Adjustment. Never view Sponsorship as a complete failure, even if your Initiate perishes, for the undertaking is meant to further the development of the Sponsor as well as the Initiate. It is a test of your own fitness, a lesson in your own shortcomings. You must learn that lesson and move on. Never let Sponsorship endanger your own safety. It is vital to keep your Focus and your Direction regardless of the outcome of your Sponsorship. Do not ever let a failure in Sponsoring affect your resolve.

I don't think I'm going to read the *Parattak* for awhile. I think I've had enough.

I need to talk to Cartmell tonight. She always seems to know what to say to cheer me up after my failures with Quint. She understands me, I guess, and knows why I keep Sponsoring him, knows how I feel. So I'm about to stand and get out of there when Barlow shows up at the door to Room 999.

We've told him about Mom and Dad, and he's agreed to stay away from them. He's been trying to Sponsor one of his cop friends, and he's come to tell Brother Samuels the Sponsorship is over, because the guy doesn't know who Barlow is anymore. And I guess Brother Samuels must have told him that Amos and I are in Room 999. Or maybe he spotted Mom and Dad leaving and figured it out for himself.

"What's going on?" he asks us, giving us a Nod.

"Nothing anymore," I tell him, Nodding back.

So he comes over and sits down beside us. And there we are—See No Past Life, Hear No Past Life, and Speak No Past Life. Then Barlow says, "It's hurts seeing Mom and Dad and not being able to speak to them."

We both look over at him.

"It's not as bad as you think," Amos tells him. "Life is easier when you don't start speaking to them."

In the end Amos is proven right. Come the next Reality Mom and Dad are in the cemetery again. We all revisit the old homestead, but it's empty and dark, the lawn unmowed, the garden overrun with weeds. Their furnishings are gone, and so is the Hudson. It rains all day.

The grief is a whopper.

We have Brother Samuels perform the Ceremony for the Re-Dead from the *Parattak*. We stand around their graves with umbrellas in the rain. I still miss them.

Amos says they'll probably be back. The grief will come back too. I feel like I've been hit by a truck and been thrown forty feet. I'm glad to be alive, but I don't need any more reminders of my mortality.

I saw Ramon Sanchez today. We passed in the street, but he didn't recognize me. He was dressed in a suit and pushing a baby carriage.

23

VOID PIRATES
Reality 280
Valediction Season

Amos sent along the news this afternoon that another Time Change is on its way in a few hours, a big Season-Ender. Today will be the end of Valediction. This is good news because the end of Valediction means we've Survived seven Seasons. In three or four hours we'll officially be Longtimers.

Longtimers!

Of course, no Time Change warning is entirely good news. Our Membership is not going to come easily. We know we're going to have to earn these last few hours in Valediction, especially after Amos tells us about Catterus. The Terror of the Void has found out where we live and has sworn vengeance on us for our offenses against him in The Common. He's coming after us this afternoon.

The fleet's off chasing Void Pirates with the CTA, and the Intertime Police are engaged in a raid on the West Coast. So we've got no defenses. We're as vulnerable as a bunch of hapless Bystanders with a Timestorm bearing down on them.

These last few hours of our Initiation are likely to prove the most difficult we've ever spent in the Timeflow. We can feel dread like a blanket of humidity in the air as we sit in the dining room of Amanda's Alternate Residence in Stonefort. We're targets.

We're doomed.

I think I've figured out now what happened back in the Sayonara Season. The Time Syndicate hired Catterus to take us out. We had become such a thorn in their side that they had to do something about us. So they brought in Catterus. That's why Amos called it an "old rumor" that he had been hired to kill us.

But this time Amos has been bringing us along more slowly. He's letting us Adjust before he sends us against the Syndicate. So there's been no hit put out on us. Catterus's revenge is being fueled by his own guilt. We must seem like a bunch of ghosts, returned to wreak vengeance on him.

We're all pretty nervous as we wait for our fate in our house in Stonefort. We fidget and look at each other uneasily across the dining room table. When the back doorbell rings, we jump even though we know who it is—at least we hope we do. Because Amos told us he'd send over a couple of his agents to act as our bodyguards.

After the doorbell, the room gets really quiet. I'm closest, so I go into the kitchen to the back door and look through the curtains, and Zeke follows me to peek through the window shades. Zeke doesn't recognize the two guys in raincoats outside, but I know them well enough—it's Bert and Ernie, the two guards from the Flatiron Building who gave Barlow and me such a razzing back in Wilderness.

I just open up the door and turn my back and walk away. I'm not going to welcome those two jerks. They obviously feel the same way—they're both scowling, and they keep their hands in their raincoat pockets as they shuffle inside. They don't have any greeting for us either. They don't even Nod.

The day is so dark and cloudy, it's almost like night. The rain has let up, but the concrete streets are still dark and damp. Our visitors are wet but not dripping. They drag a cave smell inside with them.

Bert, the tall skinny one with the sallow skin, gets a particularly sour look on his face when he enters the house, nose first, and gets a whiff of us. He and Ernie walk through the doorway and stop in the kitchen, glancing around.

"What's wrong?" Ernie asks Bert. Ernie's the short and stocky one with the pasty face and blond hair—unkempt, uncombed.

Bert gives the air another sniff. "They don't smell right," he says. Ernie glances at us through the doorway into the dining room from the kitchen. We're all wearing Longtimer Casual and giving them a stony stare. We're not much of a welcoming committee. No hello. No greeting. No nothing.

Ernie returns his gaze to Bert as if discounting our presence. "So what do they smell like?" he asks in a low tone.

Bert's lip curls, and his scowl deepens. He sniffs a few more times. "Longtimers," he growls. I know what he means—Longtimers get to smelling a bit like Safe Houses after awhile—vacuum sealed air with metallic overtones.

He's disgusted because he can't stand the idea that we might have changed, that he might owe us some respect. He can't bear the idea that we're acceptable, and he's disappointed he can't hate us like before. Of course, Ernie's no bundle of joy either. They're both Uptimers who predate us in the Timeflow and therefore have no use for us.

To tell the truth, we're acting no better than them, maybe because we're so tense due to the death sentence Amos has just given us. We don't have room in our brains for hospitality, not for Ernie and Bert.

Amanda takes a dislike to them immediately. She doesn't like having to open her house to a couple strangers, especially not these two, who are a living challenge to her authority, an insult to her leadership, a suggestion she can't protect the family herself. She'd almost rather it be Catterus at the back door. At least she wouldn't have to deal with someone new.

She leaps out of her chair and blocks the dining room doorway before our guests can advance, and she leans against the molding with her arms crossed and her brows lowered. We were having a family meeting, but Bert and Ernie are not invited. I suppose it says something about our state of mind that we never ask them their names or thank them for coming over to help us.

Pete and the kids are at the kitchen table, finishing up their lunch. They're done eating, but Jackson's still gripping his apple juice sippy cup in both hands and watching the new arrivals with big eyes underneath brown bangs.

Bert and Ernie keep their raincoats on. It's dark and blowing outside, so Pete goes over and closes the back door and locks it. This December 24th isn't cold—the weather's more like Halloween. But these are trickers, they're no treat for us.

They regard each other with a reluctant roll of their necks, wipe their shoes on the mat and glance sideways.

"Is this all of them?" Bert asks. "How many do we have to babysit today?"

That really sets Amanda off, and she uncrosses her arms and gives them one of her knife-in-the-face looks.

"*Sit down!*" she barks at them, making them both wince.

So they sit—at the kitchen table with the kids.

Amanda returns to the dining room, and we go back to our meeting. "Where were we?" She looks around the table.

"We were discussing whether we should go into hiding—" I say.

Cartmell shushes us. "I hear something."

We freeze and listen.

"Kill the lights," Amanda orders. Barlow leaps for the fuse box and slams the breaker off, and the house is plunged into shadows.

We're holding our breath, listening to the blowing wind, but there are other sounds, too: slamming car doors, footsteps. My eyes quickly adjust to the dim light coming in the windows. I can see Bert and Ernie have drawn their side arms, and Zeke is peering out the window shade.

"It's the Bycops," he says. He hesitates and takes another look. "And Catterus is with them."

I peek out the window and recognize him right away. He's wearing his long gray coat and has the pale face of a Voider. He's hatless and without a headband, and his uncombed hair sticks out in clumps like some leafy vegetable on his head.

The Void Pirate must have made up some story—anything to get the Bycops out here. They'll round us up and detain us for a few hours, he'll disappear from sight, and we'll be far from the nearest Safe House. That's his plan—maroon us in Valediction so we get Wiped Out of Time.

But we aren't going to let that happen. Not today. We're ready this time. Amanda doesn't bother to ask if the front door's locked. She knows we'll never make that mistake again. She just says, "Evacuation Plan A," and we scramble.

We grab our backpacks and bags from the hallway and begin to step toward the side of the house single file. We always keep our stuff packed up and accessible. We're ready to go at a moment's notice. We've rehearsed all of the scenarios.

When Bert and Ernie are the last two in the kitchen, Amanda says to them, "If you don't need a babysitter, just stay there. But if you want to Survive, follow us." Turning on her heel, she leaves them. They hesitate only momentarily before falling in line.

A booming voice reverberates through the windows of the house. "This is the police," one of the Bycops announces on a bullhorn outside. "Come out and give yourselves up. We have the house surrounded."

We glance at each other. Scenario Twelve. The Bycops have a cordon around the house. Are we going to have to switch to Evacuation Plan B?

The Bycops know better than to try to break in. We have our booby traps set up. Besides Bert and Ernie,

Barlow's the only one of us who's armed, but the Bycops don't know that. Once they saw the lights go out inside the house, they knew they'd lost the element of surprise. So storming the house is no longer their prime option.

I can see why Amos carries a gun. We ought to be carrying, too—but we don't like the extra weight. We want to Travel light. I swear, come next Season I'm going to start packing. And I realize Cooper's probably been packing this whole time. No wonder he wasn't afraid of the gangers back in Wilderness. He could have blown them away at any moment. He was probably wearing body armor too. I just wish we had some now.

Once we reach the east side of the house, Zeke peeks out the slot in the secret door he has constructed. Just as we suspect—the house is not literally surrounded. The Bycops are guarding every door and window and escape route. But there are no doors or windows on the east side of the house, where we are. There's just a wall and six feet of shade between the house and a seven-foot high stockade fence. They don't know about our secret door. So the Bycops haven't bothered to place anyone on the east side, and we can still use Evacuation Plan A.

Even in broad daylight you have to look closely to realize there are two identical fences running alongside each other on the east side of the house—ours and the neighbor's. Ours begins halfway up the house's east side behind some bamboo, and there's a three foot gap between the two fences. So all we have to do is exit through the secret door and walk through six feet of shadows and then between the fences as they curve along the back property line. And we do so quietly, single file.

If there hadn't been any gap, we would have come up with a way to scale the fence or go under it. If the Bycops had us actually surrounded, we would have resorted to Evacuation Plan B, which involves climbing up into the attic and onto the roof. We have an Evacuation Plan C too. We have plans for every contingency we can think of. The Munchkins aren't going to catch us with our pants down ever again.

Once we get to the corner of our property, the neighbor's stockade fence ends where it runs into the other neighbor's identical fence, but we squeeze through the gap between fences, and we're in the back yard of the deserted house behind ours. The owners left on a surprise Hawaiian vacation when they unexpectedly received plane tickets and hotel reservations in the mail, reservations made on a credit card that will never have to be paid off.

We walk across the yard single file under a pear tree beneath the menacing dark sky. We can hear an indistinct voice over a bullhorn and the sound of breaking glass behind us in Amanda's Alternate Residence as the Bycops shoot teargas canisters into the house to smoke us out. Feeling smug, we make our way to the garage of the deserted neighbor house, and Zeke trips the latch we've installed on the door. Inside the garage is the station wagon that Barlow's customized for us, with specialized shocks and a hemi engine. Our getaway car.

Naturally, Amanda has a seating chart for the station wagon. Guests go in the back seat beside her (of course, Belinda or Cooper or Amos were our expected guests). Pete and the kids sit farthest back, Zeke and Cartmell in front of them. Barlow's our getaway driver, and I'm riding shotgun—literally. There's a shotgun in the front seat.

Now the Bycops are storming Amanda's Alternate Residence. They don't have a clue where we are. So we all climb into the station wagon and take our places. I'm holding the shotgun up front, and Pete's got Barlow's revolver drawn in back. After starting the engine, Barlow hits the garage door remote, and we watch as the garage door slowly rolls upward in front of us like a curtain, revealing a gray avenue.

It's so dark outside the street lights have come on even though it's only three pm, and we can see pools of light at intervals down the street in both directions. There's not much to see. The street's deserted, and the wind has died down. There's no movement, no sound on the street. It's a cemetery out there. We can hear something from our house behind us, but the noises are too faint for us to sort them out.

We're thinking about what's ahead of us, not behind us. Where's Catterus's gang, we're wondering. He's with the Bycops, but where are they? We don't know Catterus has left our house and joined the roadblock at the entrance to our street.

Looking carefully both ways, Barlow closes the garage door behind us and edges the car down the driveway, its motor panting heavily as we roll ahead and creep into the avenue. One end leads into darkness between the staggered pools of light. At the other end a blaze of light illuminates the side of the police barricade across the intersection: half a dozen cop cars and just as many cops, including Catterus.

Barlow draws in a deep breath. "I've got this," he says to us. We look into each other's eyes but don't say a word. We know what he means. The old Barlow's back—the one we used to know in 250. His Alternate Self has been Reinchronated, so his karma has returned, and he's his old self again. We can hear it in his voice and see it in the set of his jaw. We're going to Survive, after all. If Bert and Ernie weren't here, we'd be celebrating already.

Barlow eases the car into the street so it faces the side of the barricade. He's challenging the Bycops like this is a bullfight.

"You're going the wrong way," Bert cries. "They've got that intersection completely blocked off. Don't go that way. You've got an easy shot out of here in the other direction."

He's right, of course. But I'm not about to give him any credit. I just turn and look over the front seat at him.

"We don't do things the easy way," I tell him. "We're Vanns. We do things OUR WAY." I give the shotgun a pump and nod at Barlow.

To punctuate my remarks, Barlow begins revving the huge hemi engine he's installed in the station wagon and turns on his brights. The cops begin to scramble at the end of the street, looking like ants in an overturned hill. They drag the barriers around to face us.

"What are you doing!" Bert cries. Ernie lets out a strangled moan. Then Barlow hits the gas, and the tires squeal, burning rubber, and we peel down the street full throttle, pedal to the metal—like someone's thrown the checkered flag.

"You can't break through there! Those cars are three deep!"

He's right, of course, but Barlow doesn't listen. In seconds we're barreling down the avenue, approaching the roadblock at sixty, seventy, eighty miles an hour, and Bert and Ernie are squealing and bracing themselves and holding an arm up in front of their faces. And then Barlow says, "Now, Zeke," and everything turns as black as if we'd plunged into an ocean of oil.

I turn on the dome light and see Ernie lower his arm and look around. He panics for a moment as he realizes he's rising off his seat. "This is a Safe House!" he cries.

Bert already has his seatbelt latched, and he cusses. He gives us an accusing look. "Where did you get a Dimensionalizer?"

Zeke shrugs. "I built it myself." He's showing off again, but this time I don't mind.

I count off the seconds to the Uptimers' inevitable question. "How did you do that?"

Zeke just smiles and doesn't bother to answer. He's just insulted them, but the dummies don't realize it. So I answer for him. "It's not so hard—if you understand the science involved."

But Bert and Ernie are not impressed—and not happy about being thrust into the Void without warning.

"You can't operate a Safe House without a license," Bert declares. "You can be arrested."

I chuckle at that. "Oh, this isn't a Safe House," I tell him. "It's got no rocket engine or guidance system. It's not pressurized or airtight. We've leaking air like a sieve. In fact, we're going to have to return to the Three Dimensional World in about—" I look at my watch. "Three, two, one—"

Bert jerks his head around to stare at Zeke, and Zeke smiles just before he jams the control Lever forward. Dim scenery appears all around us, and the tires chirp as they hit the pavement with a jarring thump, jostling us. We're still moving down the street beyond the roadblock, but Barlow jerks the steering wheel around and slams on the brakes, and we spin around and stop, facing the back of the barricade a block away.

The wind has the tinny smell of rain, and the windshield gets splattered by an occasional drop. The sky alternates dark and shiny silver like a can of sardines.

Barlow revs the engine a few times to get the Bycops' attention, as if preparing to charge again. The cops scramble to pull the barricades around so they're blocking us. They crouch behind them, weapons drawn.

Bert is fuming. "You've passed the barricade. Now get us out of here. What are you waiting for? We've got to get to a Safe House!"

Sounds like good advice, but of course, it's not. "All the Safe Houses nearby have been disabled," Zeke announces, looking at his phone. Now we know what Catterus's gang has been up to and why they're not here. "The closest one that works is all the way downtown."

"Figures," Barlow says. He's not surprised. Has he counted on this all along?

Bert's shaking. "Well, let's get going," he says. "It'll take more than an hour to get downtown, even longer if the traffic's bad."

But Barlow doesn't care. He's got his own plan. So I give Bert a smile and load another shell in my shotgun, and Barlow taps the gas pedal so we coast forward till we're a couple car lengths from the barricade. He pulls the emergency brake and opens his car door. Bert and Ernie are too astounded to react.

As Barlow steps out of the car onto the pavement, every eye is upon him. The Bycops have just seen him run a barricade by disappearing and rematerializing on the other side. He's escaped a police cordon and eluded a manhunt, and now he's left the protection of his vehicle and he's standing right in front of them, unarmed and unprotected but clearly not afraid. So the cops stand there staring at him, wondering what is going on.

But Catterus knows what's going on, and he recognizes Barlow, and he's full of rage, remembering how Barlow tripped him up and made a monkey of him in The Common. He doesn't have time to find a weapon, so he charges Barlow, but Barlow's ready for him and grabs him and flips him around and bends him over the car hood and slaps a pair of cuffs on him—like he's done this maneuver a hundred times, which he has.

And that says it all. The Bycops know Barlow's a cop. It's undeniable. They can recognize one of their own. And they know Catterus is a crook. They've dealt with people like him before dozens of times. So it dawns on them pretty fast what's going on, except for the Time Travel part, of course.

Then I hear one of the cops exclaim in a startled voice, "That's Barlow Vann!" And a murmur runs through the crowd. Clearly, he's a legend. *Finally—a Reality in which Barlow graduated from the Academy!* No wonder he's got his karma back.

It dawns on me what Barlow's Strategy is. He's a Hero. The problem is the Time Changes robbed him of that by turning him into a refugee. But now he's back. Big as ever.

Barlow holds up a gold badge. "Special Services," he announces to the crowd. And suddenly Ernie is fumbling and searching his pockets and cussing. Barlow picked him clean without him noticing. A trick he learned from Cooper, of course. We've all picked up some tricks from Cooper.

"There's a price on this man's head where I come from," Barlow tells them. "And I need your help to take him in. I could use an escort downtown."

The cops glance at each other and start to move, shoving the barricade out of the way and climbing into their cars. They don't need any persuading. They know speed is what we need. And they're a speed franchise.

Barlow hustles Catterus into the back seat of our station wagon between Bert and Ernie, and Amanda joins Zeke and Cartmell behind them. We're ready to go as the Bypolice cars start to file out, their red lights spinning on top.

We get out of the neighborhood like a rocketing Timecraft and head southeast, sirens blasting, and it's smooth cruising. We get downtown in record time. It's like a jaunt around the block rather than some long drawn-out journey.

The Bycops drop us at the Ixion Station of the Shawneetown subway, so we scramble down the stairs past the popcorn vendors and buy our tickets and slip through the turnstile and down more steps into the Catacombs beneath the city.

The subway platform is teeming with Bystanders, holiday shoppers carrying presents and shopping bags. It's so crowded it seems like rush hour. Only a few shopping hours are left before Christmas Eve. The Locals are all dressed in colorful festive robes for the holiday. A kaleidoscope of rainbow patterns. Amanda orders us into position, and we stride ahead in a wedge formation, Barlow at the point, Bert and Ernie dragging Catterus behind him with Pete and the kids in back. We look more like a tank advancing than a family, and the Bystanders scatter ahead of us.

When we check Room 999 at the end of the platform, we discover it's already launched. "The Safe House topside is gone too," Zeke announces, staring at his phone. This is a pattern we've seen before, and we're not much liking our Déjà Vu.

"Where's a Safe House with plenty of room, that isn't going to launch early?" Amanda asks Zeke, fixing him with her eyes. We all know the answer to that one: The Common, of course.

"In this Reality it's in Riverside Park," Zeke declares. All the way down toward the river. Near Lethe Station. So we head to the platform to catch the subway train heading southeast.

A train pulls up just as we reach the first loading slot, and we're able to flow into the first car since the crowds are waiting farther down the platform. Pete and the kids sit down—with Barlow and Catterus in the seat behind them. The rest of us grab straps near the door, like paratroopers ready to jump.

Instead of moving, the train emits an alarm tone, and the out-of-service banner appears on the display at the front of the car. A voice over a loudspeaker informs us that due to a blockage of the tunnel ahead of us, this car is out of service, and we need to exit the train.

So now we know what Catterus's gang has been up to in the last thirty minutes. Sabotage. They're tracking him, and they intend to prevent us from getting him into the Void before they can intercept us. They mean to ambush us. They must be heading our way right now.

I glance at my watch. Just a few ticks more. All we've got to do is Survive for another couple hours, and our Initiation is over. Then we'll be full Members of the

Society of Time with all of the benefits. We just need to get to a Safe House before the Time Change. But that isn't going to be easy with the trains out of service and murderers on our trail.

I start wondering what we're going to do when Catterus's gang catches up with us. Besides Bert and Ernie, we've got only the one gun—Amanda made me leave the shotgun behind in the station wagon. Of course, even if we were armed we'd be no match for the gang's D-Weapons. We don't stand a chance if they intercept us and we get into a battle. Our only hope is to stay one hop, skip, and jump ahead of them.

Amanda orders us to climb to the next level where the pedestrian walkways are, but they're swarming with holiday shoppers, so progress is slow toward the next station. There's a Christmas smell in the air of gingerbread and candy canes.

"I've got this!" Cartmell says suddenly, and she disappears into the crowd. I want to go after her, but there's just too much foot traffic for me to follow, and besides, it's useless to try to prevent Cartmell from carrying out one of her schemes. They usually involve some major complication like her disappearing from sight just when we need her at our side.

Amanda notices her absence right away. "Where's Cartmell?"

"She took off," Zeke tells her.

"Well, why didn't you go after her?"

Zeke looks at me. "That's Dexter's responsibility," he says, squirming off the hook. I give him my thanks-a-lot look.

Amanda glowers at me, but I'm not going to let her blame me. This isn't *my* fault. "You know how impossible she is when she gets some fool idea in her head. I can't find her in this crowd. She's just going to have to take care of herself."

Amanda is not pleased with that answer, and she gives me her knife-throwing eyes. Cartmell's disappearance means another delay while we stand around, waiting for her to reappear. And no one wants that, because the clock is ticking, and the Time Change warning could come at any moment, reducing the time we have left to less than an hour, with Catterus's gang still hot on our trail.

But it's not long before we spot Cartmell heading toward us. She's riding on one of those golf carts the city has for the disabled and the elderly—only this is no golf cart. It's fully motorized, and it seats twelve.

The driver pulls up beside us, and Cartmell tells him to stop. "Here they are," she says.

The little sneak. But I'm not mad this time. This time she's hit the jackpot. But it's kind of rankling to me—because now Amanda and Zeke and Barlow *and* Cartmell have done something to save the family, but I've done squat. I'm just riding on their shirt tails. I'm just following along in their wake. I'm "brother of," tagging along.

"Sorry," the driver says when he stops the cart. "I can take only the disabled party. Which one is it?"

"My brother Barlow," Cartmell informs him.

So Barlow starts limping forward, really piling it on, looking all pathetic and fragile and old like some grampa with bursitis.

"I'll have to see your disabled certificate."

"I have it right here," Barlow tells him, bringing up his fist.

Pow!

The driver goes flying onto the ground. The Bystanders are staring. "Nothing to look at here, folks," Barlow announces to them in his cop voice. He holds up Ernie's badge. "I'm with the police. Just move along." Then he says to us in a hurried tone. "Climb on. This is going to be a bumpy ride."

So he hops into the driver's seat. We scramble aboard, Zeke and me riding shotgun, Bert and Ernie on either side of Catterus and the rest behind them. Barlow guns it, and we're off to the races.

Barlow lays on the horn, but some of the Bystanders are too slow or too stubborn or too oblivious to get out of the way, so the cart knocks them aside, right and left, out of our path. It feels like riding in a speedboat over high waves—bump, bump bump, and it sounds like driving down a road with cracks at uneven intervals—thump, thump, thump. Some of the Bystanders don't get back up right away—but who cares? They're *Bystanders*! Their lifespan's just a couple hours now. And ours will be too if we don't knock them out of the way.

Barlow swerves when he can—to save time, not to spare the Bystanders, but it's still rough going, especially for the Locals. Some of them give out a squeal when we hit them, some yell at us, some start to squawk, but there's no slowing us down. Hell, it's a lot better than trying to run through this crowd—and a whole lot quicker. We plow through the shoppers like an express train, passing the Persephone and the Sisyphus Stations and continuing down the Hades Line, but at the Acheron intersection Barlow suddenly slows to a stop because he's spotted something ahead.

"Void Pirates," he says.

I look up and around. They're on the walkways above the tunnel, and they're staring at us. They're holding rifles with twisted double barrels made of shiny gold-silver alloy, and they've already got us located because of the beacon implanted inside of Catterus. He probably swallowed it and will eliminate it in a few hours so no one else can track him.

From the glint of light, I can see the Void Pirates aiming their D-rifles at us. But the one they call "Skull" has a bull horn and uses that first.

"We have you in our sights, Barlow Vann. Give up Catterus, and nobody gets hurt."

Barlow jumps out of the cart and grabs Catterus and holds him in front of him as a human shield. The Pirates open fire, and we duck for cover. Pale yellow fireballs zoom across the cavernous chamber like comets, each shot resounding like the "oomph" from a tuba. A network of lightning bolts etches itself over Ernie's body when he's hit, and he disappears from sight, knocked into the Void.

The Bystanders are numb with shock. Someone screams, and they start to run. The Void Pirates won't fire at Catterus, but they don't mind aiming at the rest of us. A few Bystanders get knocked into the Void by the fire, and the rest of them scatter for cover, but we scatter with them. Each of us grabs a Bystander for a shield. Mine's a red-robed old lady who starts squawking in her Valediction-speak like someone pulled her string. But I ignore her. I'm watching the Pirates up on the walkways, sighting us like a bunch of guards on prison walls.

Half the gang's up there, including Skull, Bones, the Weird Sisters, and the one they call "the Psychopath" and a few others I don't recognize. But Catterus's second in command Dorca Del Rio isn't here. She must be back at the Timecraft, coordinating the operation, maneuvering squads to intercept us regardless of the direction we turn. There's probably a bunch on its way from behind us right now.

That means Skull's in command on the ground here in the Catacombs. He's the gaunt one, cadaverous, his face scarred and his eyes hollow. He's as close to resembling the walking dead as you'll ever see. Of course, his companions are no beauty pageant either.

The guys are all shirtless, wearing red and white bandanas and white pantaloons tied by a sash with a D-Pistol or cutlass beneath it. The Weird Sisters have on black lacy tops and pointed hats, and the Psychopath is wearing clothes in clashing colors so loud it hurts your eyes to look at him. They're all carrying a Dimensional Weapon of some sort.

It's time for me to step up and share everything Cooper's been telling me about D-Weapons with the rest of the family. So I do.

A D-gun projects a limited field. It can't Void an object bigger than a man, so if two people cling to each other, they won't be knocked into the Void, not if they're full sized adults. The Electric Net has to completely surround your body, so if you have your feet firmly planted, or if you hang onto something firmly rooted, you won't go into the Void. The problem is trying to keep your grip when you get hit by a D-charge. It almost always knocks you backward, and that lets the Net surround you. A running target is easier to Void than a stationary one, so we're standing still.

We're actually doing the Bystanders a favor by holding onto them, although they don't see it that way. Two precise hits in a row from the same angle are what it'll take to Void us, but we're not going to stand around and let them take a second shot. I just hope the Pirates don't have any D-grenades.

They're too far away to get a really good shot at us, but only a good shot will take us down. And with a double target, they'll have to hit us twice in a row to knock us into the next Dimension.

One of the Void Pirates descends to the ground and tries to flank us, but Barlow draws his gun and drills him between the eyes. The Bystanders run for cover as the Pirate splays out on the ground. Barlow's a crack shot, and he used to routinely win the department's shooting contests, though he had to leave all his medals and trophies back in Wilderness.

The Void Pirates on the walkways are too distant for Barlow to hit accurately with a handgun, so he saves his ammunition. After seeing their crony get taken out so easily, none of the other Pirates tries to climb down and come after us. If two of them shoot at the same target at the same angle, they could dispatch our Bystander Shields—but we'd just grab another—causing a standoff.

Someone should have called the Bycops by now, so we know the gang must have done something to distract or delay them. We can't depend on them to get us out of this mess.

"Let Catterus go," Skull declares through his bull horn. "And we'll let you go."

But we're not budging, because we know they'll Void us once they have Catterus. So it's a stalemate— until the Pirates come up with a new plan.

"People of Shawneetown," Skull declares over his bull horn, "we mean you no harm. We only want the ones who are using you as shields. They have kidnapped our friend and are holding him hostage. If you can separate them from their shields, we will eliminate them and you can go free."

While he's saying this, I catch sight of something at the edge of the walkway. A female Bystander in a green robe is walking down one of the ramps next to the escalators, looking around in bewilderment, just arrived and not understanding what's going on. She's carrying a Christmas present with purple giftwrap covered with lollipops. The strange thing is I recognize her.

It's Marcy. I swear to god it's her. I recognize her blonde hair, her flawless complexion, and that distinctive pinched nose. I'd know her anywhere.

I let go of the old lady Bystander and wave my arms. "Marcy, take cover!" I hear the oomph of a tuba.

Marcy hesitates, unsure what to do. There's a look of recognition in her eyes.

And then a D-blast hits me full in the chest, knocking me back. I feel electric charges all over my body, biting me like I've fallen into a herd of rats. A tingling spreads across my skin, tickling my short hairs. I try to plant my feet, but I feel the coldness of the Void lapping at my scalp. My hair is floating free in nothingness, and my eyes are plunged in darkness, and I can't breathe, and my ears no longer hear a sound, and my face begins to freeze—but before I black out, I feel something around my legs, something pulling on me, pulling me back.

It's Barlow. He's let go of Catterus and grabbed hold of me before the Void can completely claim me. And he drags me behind the cart.

Catterus tries to run for it, but Bert trips him up and grabs hold of him. The Pirates fire, sending Bert's Bystander shield into the Void. But Bert ducks down behind the cart, too, dragging Catterus with him.

Seeing another Bystander Vanish has a dampening effect on the crowd. They're not going to try to mess with us, not after seeing what happens when we let go of our shields. So it's back to a stalemate.

When I regain consciousness, I find myself lying on the pavement with Barlow sitting on me. I look around for Marcy, but I can't see her anywhere. I want to find her, but Barlow won't let me up.

"Take it easy, brother," he says. "Your system's had a shock."

He means the Void, but to me the shock was seeing Marcy.

Less than two hours. We just need to last for a couple crummy hours in the Timeflow, and we're free. Why does everything have to be so hard? There you are just trying to make it through this life when, boom, all of a sudden there's Bycops storming your Alternate Residence and Void Pirates all over your ass trying to neutralize you. Give me a break! Timely Rogers, why does this have to happen *now*? Can't things ever go smoothly in this Void-sucking, Byshucking, Stormducking, sonuvalucking, brother-effing Timeflow? What next? What the truck now?

And then our Beepers go off, and our Blinkers start flashing. I look down at my display. The Time Change is coming in sixty minutes. I groan, and I kick my feet and let out a scream of protest, and everyone's staring, but I don't care. This is too much, just effing too much.

The Timecrimers are all looking at each other and gesturing. They're not any happier with this development than I am. They're pointing at their watches and looking at each other with panicked expressions on their faces. A few of them are arguing. Bones is waving his arms, and Skull is pacing in frustration. They're having a cow up there. Even from where I'm laid out I can tell that. It's really something to see.

Finally Skull lifts his bull horn and renders his verdict. "Sorry, Catterus," he announces, "You know how it goes."

"No!" Catterus yells. He tries to stand up, still handcuffed, but Bert pulls him down. The Void Pirates turn and run for the exits like a bunch of commuters late for work. They have to get to their Safe House in time just like us, and evidently it's not close by.

Catterus has a sick and angry expression on his face. Barlow climbs off me, and I sit up, feeling my body for injuries. "Too bad, Catterus," I say to him as I stand. "But it's for the best."

He glares at me. Now I'm on his list with Barlow. We all are, I guess. "This way we all get to Survive," I tell him.

He growls back at me, "Tell that to Cyrus Lee." When we don't register the name, he adds, "The guy you shot in the head."

Jeez, what does he expect? That we won't fight back? Has he forgotten what they did to Ernie?

We release our Bystander shields, and everyone relaxes. The tunnel begins to buzz with voices again. We head to our cart and start to clamber on, when Amanda gestures to us and points to the lower level. A train is approaching the station. We can hear the rumble and then feel it. The subways are running again! So we hop off the cart and run down the steps to the platform and crowd into one of the cars.

Life has returned to normal. Finally. And for once we have enough time to get where we're going. And no gang committing sabotage to slow us down.

Catterus is not a happy Traveler, though. No, not him. He's about where I was right after our Beepers went off. When I was in Voidlock, he was feeling all Light Seasony. Now it's the other way around. So I try to say something to soothe him.

"Well, at least the Void Prison is better than the Void."

He looks at me all Timestorm with Godheads in his eyes. Death Sentence. Double Death Sentence.

Yeah, right, like I haven't already been knocked into the Void once tonight and had Marcy taken away from me yet again. He thinks he's going to top that? Good luck.

I look over at Barlow and notice he's grinning like I've never seen him grin before. Zeke is laughing. So is Cartmell. Even Amanda is smiling. And I realize we've done it! We've really done it. In a few more minutes we'll be safe. And we'll be Longtimers.

Longtimers!

We've proved something today—proved we can Survive. And more. We showed everyone what we're made of. I guess I didn't do much, but heck, I participated in the contingency planning. I'm a Vann, not just brother of a Vann.

We're *Longtimers,* by Ingersol. No one can dispute that now. No one can take away what we accomplished.

And we've got Catterus to boot.

It's celebration time.

Barlow lets out a cheer, "Woohoo!" like he's Homer Simpson. We're grinning like idiots, except for Bert and Catterus, of course. I guess Bert's not so pleased with us for celebrating right after the loss of Ernie. This is a grim moment for him.

But not for us. The reward on Catterus's head is enormous. It's not enough to make us Eloi, but it'll pay our Society Fees for the next year or two. We'll get to relax and take our time while we become Citizens. We'll be able to afford to live up on one of the Stations in the Void—or down in the Catacombs. No more dealing with stress or Bystanders. No more scrambling to Survive.

When we reach Lethe Station, we proudly file out of the subway train in formation and head topside, shouldering the Bystanders aside as a unit, like we're still on our race cart. Bump, bump, bump. Barlow and Bert hold Catterus on either side as we advance.

Riverside Park's just a couple blocks away. We've got loads of time. Nearly forty minutes when we spot The Common in the distance—the castle of Camelot on the misty horizon. Our goal is in sight.

But it's not all lit up as usual. It's dark as a haunted house. Something's wrong. Because there's a problem.

I'm scratching at the underside of my arm and looking around at my brothers and sisters making sure this isn't some hallucination. They're looking around too—and none of 'em are smiling. Barlow starts cussing, and Cartmell stamps her foot.

"This ain't fair," Pete says. "This ain't right."

"What the hell!" Barlow cries. "What is it *now*?"

There's a cordon of Bycops blocking the path up to The Common with barricades and Bypolice cars all over the place. We just groan and droop. Not again! We thought we'd left that behind us in Stonefort.

We had an understanding with the Bycops. Why are they doing this *now*? Besides, how did they know where we were going? Even Catterus didn't know. How did they get here ahead of us? Who sent them? Are we going to have to escape all over again?

Or does this have nothing to do with us?

We send Bert ahead to check it out, and when he returns, he signals us to come forward. Once we reach the scene of the crime, we get ushered into this tent that's been set up as a crisis headquarters, and we see Amos sitting on a campstool, talking on the phone with his Flatiron buddies all around him.

What the heck is going on?

J.B., the uniformed guy from the lobby of the Flatiron building, fills us in. "It's the Moon People," he says.

The Moon People! Are you kidding me? Moonglow is *over*, and the Moon People got eliminated with everything else, so how can he be saying the effing Moon People are causing this?

"They fled to the Void as soon as Moonglow ended," he tells us, "And turned to Piracy. They've been raiding the Plane ever since. And now they've captured The Common and everyone in it. They mean to tow it into the Void, sell it for salvage, and fill their meat lockers with Longtimer steaks."

What the Flow! Moon People? Don't make me laugh. Come on. You can't be serious. Moon People? Now?

But he is serious. "They've been raiding everyone and everything across the Plane, including other Void Pirates. Catterus is their mortal enemy, him and the CTA. They've been making fools of the CTA, leading them on wild goose chases all over the Void. The fleet's a whole parsec away. So they can't rescue us from this. I don't envy the Elder now. Disaster and ruin is what this is. A Dark Season, a Dark Season all around."

The Moon People? I still can't get over it. I just shake my head. Of all the Strange Karma! How is this possible? I just can't believe it.

Moon People.

How am I ever going to get over this? This can't be. This is inexplicable.

When Amos gets off the phone, he motions us to him and regards us sternly. "There aren't enough Specials for everyone, so some hard choices are going to have to be made. We'll have to draw straws for the remaining spots. And I can't spare you from the general lottery."

Can't spare us? We're in jeopardy too? Because of Moon People?

Amanda's got this look of outrage on her face. We're beside ourselves. We just went through hell to get here—and now he's telling us it might have been for nothing? We didn't fight our way here just to be Wiped Out because of some Safe House shortage.

"This ain't fair, Amos," Barlow growls.

"Yeah, Amos," Amanda says. "You're our brother. You're supposed to look out for us."

Amos presses on the crosspiece of his glasses and scowls at us. "I'm the Elder of the entire region, not just your brother. I can't play favorites in this. You'll join the lottery with everyone else."

We start to moan and groan, that is, everyone but me. I'm still lost in astonishment. The Moon People! I can't believe it. I shake my head. But I've got to speak, so I step forward.

"I've got this," I say to Amos. He doesn't hear me at first. I guess he's too focused on how to deal with this mess. So he goes on with the bad news. "There are more than four hundred Longtimers in need of Shelter nearby, not to mention those held prisoner by the Moon People. All tolled, we could lose two thousand Citizens."

"I've got this," I tell him again.

It takes a moment for what I've said to register with him. He stops talking suddenly and stares at me like I'm a little green man declaring "Take me to your leader."

"What did you say?"

I scratch the back of my head and wrinkle up my face. The Moon People! Of all the luck.

"I have this."

Amos adjusts his glasses. He knows what it means. He knows I wouldn't say it if I didn't mean it. He knows what's at stake. But still—the whole thing is so unbelievable.

The Moon People!

"You have a plan for dealing with the Moon People?"

I close my eyes and grimace. This is not what I wanted. This is not how I envisioned myself making a contribution to saving the family.

"Yes," I say, "yes, unfortunately, I do."

Amos is astonished. He doesn't know what to think. He doesn't know what to say.

"Dexter really does have a plan," Cartmell exclaims, jumping up. "You should listen to him."

"Yeah." Zeke starts to laugh. "It's brilliant, Amos. It's so outrageous it might even work."

The plan was hatched during one of our late night contingency sessions at Amanda's Alternate Residence in Stonefort. It was late, and we were getting tired and giddy. So just for fun we started thinking of the most absurd contingencies we could come up with, and I said, "The Moon People." Everybody started laughing. And then everybody started spinning these ridiculous scenarios and far fetched plans, each more elaborate and outrageous than the last.

And I won.

My plan was the most absurd and outrageous of them all. We laughed and laughed about it. We never thought we'd actually need a contingency plan for the Moon People. We thought they were Extinct. I wasn't serious. It was all just for laughs, though I admit mine is the most workable, the most potentially effective of all the weird scenarios we spun that night. I never thought we would actually use the plan.

The Moon People. Really? It's not a joke? Then, yes, I do have a plan.

Amos looks from Cartmell to Zeke to me. He doesn't ask for details. He doesn't ask for proof. He just says, "What do you need?"

I rest one of my elbows in my palm, and I rub my chin. Cartmell hands me a jar of Nagaran silver face makeup, so I don't need to add that to the list. "A Nagaran tunic and a motor scooter," I tell him. Amos gestures to his people to get it done, but I'm not finished. "And oh, yes, I'll need Catterus."

Amos frowns at that. He doesn't know we've captured Catterus and brought him in for the bounty. So we fill him in.

"Can you guarantee he won't escape?" Amos asks me. "Can you guarantee you can return him to custody?"

I shake my head. "He'll probably get away. But that's better than losing The Common and everyone in it."

Amos looks down and nods in agreement. "All right. Let's do it. Let's get this problem solved." He doesn't ask for the details about the plan. He trusts me. And I'm grateful for that because I wouldn't want to try to convince anyone of the merits of this crazy plan. I don't know if I could keep a straight face if I tried to explain it to anyone. It's a long shot. And now I'm wondering if it's even possible to pull it off.

I guess Bert reads the uncertainty in my face because he scowls. I didn't even know he was in the tent. "This is lunacy," he says. "He can't do it. No one can reason with those lunatic Moon People. It's folly to even try."

That really sets me off, digs into my inner Amanda. So I go over and give him a shove. "The only person here who can't do this is *you*." I give him another shove, before he can react to the first. "But I can. Because I'm a Vann." And I shove him again, and he falls over and has to reach out to steady himself so he doesn't land on his back. But he knows better than to get back up and face me again.

But I give him one last cannonade. "I can do it, and I'm going to do it, and it's going to work."

Amos's assistant brings forth a Nagaran tunic and a motor scooter. So I take off my shirt and pull on the tunic. I'm already wearing Nagaran sandals. Cartmell holds up a mirror while I apply the silver face makeup. It smells like peppermint.

"Where's Catterus?" I demand.

Barlow drags him forward in handcuffs.

"Whatever it is, I'm not doing it," Catterus says. He frowns when he sees me in makeup. I look like the Tin Man.

"You'll do it," I tell him, "or we'll turn you over to the Moon People."

He turns white. He's heard of their unspeakable practices. "The Moon People! What are those Farbs doing out here?"

I signal Barlow to take off the handcuffs.

"You're my servant," I tell Catterus, "so far as the Moon People are concerned. You'll do whatever I command. Don't look me in the eyes. Don't look the Moon People in the eyes. Don't speak. You're just window dressing to convince them I'm somebody important. So don't pull any funny business. Because if this doesn't go down just right, you're going to be in their bellies before morning. Got it?"

Catterus looks around at us. "This is insane. You can't negotiate with those cannibals. They're savages. It will never work."

I walk right up to his face. "It'll work if we make it work. They're idiots. We can make monkeys out of them—if you play your part."

Catterus regards me steadily for a few moments. He doesn't like me, and he intends to kill me when he gets the chance, but there's a growing respect in his eyes.

"A con game," he says. He looks around at my family. "You're a bunch of con artists, aren't you? You conned the Bycops, you conned the Bystanders, and now you've conned the government into supporting your game." He nods. "Okay. So you're going to con the

Moon People too. And now you want to con me into helping you. I've got only one question. What's in it for me?" Catterus is trying to turn the tables on us. He thinks he can negotiate.

"Your life," Barlow growls.

If there's a Safe House shortage, Catterus is going to be left behind. Execution by Timestorm, it's called. His only hope is if we get The Common back.

"And your freedom," I tell him.

Barlow blinks at me, his jaw hanging open. "You're not going to let him go!" Barlow's turned white. Bert doesn't look too happy either.

I don't say anything.

"Oh, come on," Barlow says. "He's a killer. He's a Pirate. He's as dirty as they come—" Barlow's really worked up, and he's gesturing with both arms and pacing in front of me.

Amos clears his throat. He has to do it twice to get Barlow's attention. "There's something I haven't told you," he says. Everyone turns to look at him. He regards Barlow and me in turn. "Your brother Cooper was in The Common when it was taken by the Moon People. They're holding him captive too. I don't know if he's still alive, but I'm willing to bet he is. He needs your help. And letting Catterus go is the price we have to pay."

Amos stares Barlow down, and Barlow clams up. But he doesn't move, so Amos has to unlock the handcuffs.

I climb onto the motor scooter. "Coming, servant?" I ask.

Catterus sneers and climbs on behind me. "This better work," he says, "or you're going to die in the worst way anyone's ever died before."

"You too," I remind him.

I gun the engine and take off like a shot, right between the police barricades and up the sidewalk into Riverside Park. I haven't been here since Barlow and I took our stroll back in Wilderness. The afternoon is still dark and looks more like 6:30 than 3:30.

The tree branches are casting subtle shadows over the landscape as we zoom past on our motor scooter. The Common isn't hard to find. We could see it from the street, but it's obscured by trees until we climb uphill into a broad meadow in the center of the park.

Suddenly, The Common looms ominous and silver-black before us like some dark-sided moon. Reflections of flames flicker along the silver walls of the lower levels. The Moon People have built a bonfire, and they're chanting and dancing around it to the beat of drums. Some of them have adorned their faces with colorful war paint, but most of them are stark white. They look like ghosts dancing around that fire. Their shaved heads and faces are coated with luminescent makeup so each head shines like a glowing moon.

Their captives are tied up on stakes around the blaze. I recognize a few of them. There's Mr. Sun and Bungee and Mr. Yen, but I don't see Cooper. Guardians of the Moon cross their spears ahead of us as we approach, so I slow down and stop before them.

"Take off your shirt," I order Catterus under my breath.

"What?" he says, "I'm not going to—"

"Just do it." I'm channeling Amanda again. So he takes off his shirt.

I stop the motor scooter and climb off. "Now kneel," I tell him. "In the dirt."

He hesitates, so I shove him down on his face with my sandal and place one foot on his back. I can tell he's cussing and uttering death threats under his breath, but I don't let that distract me. "I hate you. I hate you more than your brother. I'll get you. I'll get you all."

The guards recognize Catterus right away, and when they see me subjugating him, they're impressed. I've got their attention. They can see I'm a man to be reckoned with.

"Greetings, Children of the Moon," I say to them in a perfect Moonglow accent. Even I'm surprised by how flawless it is. "I am Tredex, brother to Benilda, the Queen of the Night. You can address me as King."

Their eyes fill with awe, and they begin to simper and bow. The King of the Night!

"I need to parlay with your Monarch on this Eve of the Daymoon. We have propitious dealings that must be discussed."

The guards quickly dispatch someone to fetch the Monarch, and the rest of them gather around me, goggle-eyed. They've all heard of the Queen of the Night—but to actually meet the King! They will be telling stories of this for the rest of their lives.

Soon a procession approaches us, complete with palm fronds and moon banners, representing all phases of the moon. The Nobles among the Moon People attend the Monarch in this royal parade. His loftiness is brought in on a highly decorated palanquin with a curtained coach atop it. The eight bearers take pains to lower it slowly so it touches ground gently.

I order Catterus on his hands and knees, and I sit on his back and cross my legs and inspect my fingernails. The Monarch of the Moon People parts the curtains of his palanquin and emerges into the torchlight. He is fabulously dressed in the crimson robes representing the harvest moon. The hem of his robe is lined with small skulls. I can't tell if they're actual baby skulls or not.

The Moon Monarch isn't as old as I expected. He's spry and carries himself like an acrobat. He looks like he could leap right over me up to a second floor window.

Most remarkable, though, are his sleepy smiling eyes. They give him a wry expression even when he isn't smiling. He has a small moustache, too—I didn't notice it at first because it's covered with luminous white makeup like the rest of his bald head.

He's grinning as he approaches me, and I get the feeling he genuinely likes me. Me, Dexter Vann, I mean Tredex, King of the Night. I realize I'm grinning also—and Ingersol-be-damned—I like him too. I can't help myself.

His subjects are watching us in eagerness, as if they're yearning for us to become boon companions and unite our two kingdoms in friendship. It makes me feel like I really am a king.

I stand, and we Nod to each other. His attendants rush forward with a throne, and the Monarch gets seated. I sit on Catterus's back and cross my legs. The Monarch recognizes Catterus, of course, and he likes what he sees. He's pleased with the use I've found for his arch enemy. It implies I've conquered the entire gang.

"Greetings Supreme High Holy Bat," I intone, channeling Cooper. "I have come to negotiate a trade that will be much to your advantage. The moon will shine brightly upon you for Seasons to come after—"

My words are cut short by the sound of a motor scooter. I whip my neck around, fearing that Catterus has made off with my ride. But how could he? I'm sitting on him.

It's some new arrival, and the guards don't attempt to stop or slow the rider down. I'm wondering if it's one of Catterus's gang, but the guards would have never let them in. They would have sounded a general alarm. So I train my eyes on the scooter's rider. It's a woman in a Nagaran ceremonial dress. I'm worried for a moment they've brought in an actual Nagaran to identify me. She's got silver face paint, and when she stops and takes off her helmet, I recognize who it is.

I stand and approach her, trying to get my words in first. "Greetings, Benilda, my sister," I say in a Moonglow accent. "It is I, your brother Tredex, King of the Night."

Belinda is obviously taken by surprise. She had no idea I was here. She's come on her own to try to save the people of The Common. She climbs off her motor scooter and shakes her hair behind her. "Greetings, Monarch," she declares. "Greetings, brother," she says to me. We do the Dance of Recognition common among the Night People—a swivel to the left, a swivel to the right, I bend up, she bends down, I lean right, she leans left, she bends up, I bend down. We touch elbows and Nod.

The Moon People are eating it up. Both the Queen *and* the King of the Night! Together, right in front of them. This is spectacular.

"Your Holiness," I address the Monarch, "I wish to petition you to transfer your hostages and your great prize The Common to me."

The Moon Monarch is clearly surprised. There can be no doubt now of my royalty. No commoner could possibly suggest a course of action so brazen. The Monarch is speechless for a moment. He almost laughs.

"What could you possibly trade that could equal these prizes in value? I will not surrender such wealth just out of respect. How would you pay for such a treasure? I am truly curious. You intrigue me."

Belinda's eyeing me, apparently wondering the same thing. She's come just to negotiate for some of the hostages. I'm going for the whole shebang.

"I agree the trade will not be an equal one," I tell the Monarch. They are expecting me to say that—but they're not expecting what comes next.

"What I offer is far more valuable than the paltry prize I'm bartering for. You will want to give me much more once you see the priceless treasure I have to offer you."

They're rapt with attention. There's amazement in their eyes. Even the Monarch is impressed. They trust the word of the King of the Night, and they're going to expect me to deliver on my promise and produce a treasure greater than any they've ever seen, greater than the whole combined wealth of the Common.

I start to wonder what will happen if I don't deliver? What if my offering is deemed unworthy? If I've miscalculated—will that end the deal? Will they still let Benilda make her plea? Will they negotiate any further—or will there be some dark punishment for disappointing them? Have I just turned Belinda and me into cannibal chow? There's only one way to find out.

So I dig in my pocket, and I produce my treasure.

The most sought-after Relic of the Lunean religion: the light blue plastic ring out of a cereal box that I stole from the Bystanders back in Concordance. A simple plastic band with a depiction of the Moon as its setting.

An exclamation of awe runs through the crowd as I hold it high for all to see, and they fall to their knees. They all know what it is. It's legendary. For the Luneans, it's the Ark of the Covenant, the sacred stone of Mecca, the Holy Grail. Its value to them is beyond belief.

I tried to throw it in the trash back in the Safe House before the Mystic Season, but it floated back out. I figured maybe that's a sign. So I decided to keep it. As a souvenir.

The Monarch's eyes are as wide as moons, and he's clearly trembling as I stroll forward and place the ring on his finger. A solemn moan runs through the prostrated crowd.

I hear someone laughing, only for a couple seconds. I'm not sure anyone else caught it. It's coming from the Longtimer tied to the nearest pole. His belly's shaking, and he's sniggering. I look up and realize it's Cooper—he's in disguise, and I hadn't recognized him. He's been watching the whole time.

There are tears in the Monarch's eyes as he regards his new pride and joy. He holds it up to the crowd, and they gasp and coo in awe.

"How can I ever thank you?" his Holiness says to me in a choked voice. "This is a priceless treasure for my entire tribe. All the wealth in the world could not equal this. I will be in your debt forever."

"Consider it a gift," I tell him. "And make me a gift of The Common and its contents."

His face lights up in gratitude. "So it shall be." He can hardly keep his eyes off the ring. So we stand, and he reaches forward and grabs my forearm, and I grab his, and that seals the deal. He gets a plastic bauble, and I get The Common and all of its passengers. It hardly seems fair.

But which of us is getting the raw deal?

The Moon People don't bother to pack up. They just pile into their Tow Barges and disappear into the Void. And as soon as I think to look around for Catterus, I can't see him anywhere—he's completely disappeared, just like I figured he would.

Amos and the Longtimers come tearing into the park in a convoy of vehicles to get The Common operational again. His agents are all over the place, looking for Moon People who might've been left behind, but they don't find any.

We've got fifteen minutes left in Valediction. Of course, that's more than Cooper and I had at the end of Concordance when we stole our rings. That's right—he's got one too.

I pull out my pocket knife and go over and start cutting his ropes.

"Well played, little brother," he says. "You don't have the Nagaran look quite right, but hey, you're supposed to be from Moonglow, right? You do a tolerable Moonglow."

High praise from Mr. Expert in Everything.

"Of course," he adds, "I had the situation completely under control."

I smile. "Obviously." I finish with the ropes and collapse my pocket knife. "Big 'ol brother from 250."

He's rubbing his ankles and wrists now. "I decided to let you and Belinda be the heroes this time," he says. "You can thank me later."

"You didn't want to blow your cover."

He starts to nod—then stops himself and grins.

"What was your cover, by the way?" I ask. "I don't recognize the getup."

He steps forward and gestures nonchalantly, his arms crossed, his hand stroking his cheek. "Oh, no cover. Just a temporary change in style."

Yeah—the style of the Promontory Season. And nobody in their right mind would want to follow their fashions without some ulterior motive.

But I let it drop.

He looks like a clown, really, with the white grease paint on his face and the white and blue checkerboard shirt he's wearing. The Promontorians were real suckers for the harlequin stuff. He doesn't look as bad as some, but the baggy purple pants don't help or the green elf moccasins with the curled toes or the crimson fool's hat hung with little bells.

He looks ridiculous.

Amos comes up to us. "Good work, Dexter. Are you all right, Cooper?" He tries to pretend Cooper's not in disguise. Hah!

"Fine and dandy," Cooper says. We're soon joined by the rest of the family, all of us together for the first time in Seasons.

"Cooper, is that you!" Cartmell exclaims. The rest of them goggle at him like he's the elephant man or something. "It's the Promontory look," he says. "It's not that strange." It is if you haven't lived through that Season—and Promontory was more than a hundred Realities ago.

Amos has ordered a Special for us, a huge rescue helicopter that doubles as a Safe House with a propeller on each end. It's like an airliner inside with rows of triple seats on either side and an aisle between them and a window for every other row. We take off vertically so we can enter the Void midair.

Everybody else loads into The Common—all the Longtimers are saved—and it launches with minutes to spare. I don't know what Amos said to the Bypolice. Who knows—and who cares?

Well, in short, I'm a hero now. The government's given me the Medal of Valor. This is the first time it's been awarded to a Non-Citizen, much less a Newcomer. Of course, I'm not a Newcomer anymore by the time they give me the medal. I'm a full Member of the Society of Time with all the rights, resources, and privileges of Membership.

I've done it. Finally. And I've finally made my contribution to the family effort.

Now, if I could just find a Strategy—

I've filled up a whole Volume with these journal entries. So I guess getting a Strategy's going to have to wait until the next Age.

I embellished a little in my Moon People tale, I admit, in the style of Cooper. I think it makes the story better, though, don't you? But it happened mostly that way. Close enough, for government work.

I'm in tight with the Monarch now. "How much do you think the undying gratitude of a Moon Monarch is worth?" I ask Cooper as we ride in the Special.

He ponders the question. "I have no idea," he says.

I guess it's worth something, though I'm not sure it's worth any more than the Medal of Valor or that plastic ring from Concordance. It's the experience that really counts. Each time we Survive, we learn to Adapt a little bit better.

I can see now why Amos kept drilling us for so long, warning us about all the hazards we might face and what to do to escape them. At the time his lecturing seemed obsessive and annoying, but I can see why he kept hounding us, why he had to keep pounding the lessons into our heads over and over. It makes sense now. It all seems worth it.

The roaring of the Timestorm is so deafening, we can't hear each other shout. I can feel its hands on us, shaking the copter. I can't hear any voices until we enter the Void.

Everything turns black outside, and the noise stops, except for the sound of the propeller blades that are still turning in the darkness. I check to make sure everyone's all right. The whole family has made it, but I notice in the seats across from us there are Newcomers dressed in red and green and yellow and violet Valediction robes, rising off their seats and fumbling with their seat belts and looking around all google-eyed and hang-mouthed. So I jostle Cartmell with my elbow and say, "Take a look at those Tourists over there!"

My whole family turns to stare at them and starts to laugh. Newcomers are such idiots. They're like a bunch of drooling babies, and it's hard to put up with being around someone so stupid. I can smell this bunch too. They smell of pine room deodorizer, and it's really off-putting, especially because they're not even aware of it. I just want them to go away to Newcomerville.

I remember dimly that I was a Newcomer once—but that was a long time ago, back in the Dark Ages. The Fourth Dimensional Television Network news broadcast springs to life on a television screen on the helicopter's ceiling. It depicts the Timestorm, and the Newcomers' eyes are glued to it, but none of us bother to watch. We've seen it all before. We're just waiting for the early Reports about the Anachronisms and new customs of the Sunset Season. As I look around at my brothers and sisters, I think, "We made it." With all the odds against us.

"We really are going to Survive," I mumble out loud. And that makes me smile. We just Survived our seventh Season. Our probation period is over.

We're Longtimers now.

And I've just finished my first journal entry! And that's an accomplishment in itself, don't you think?

24

LONGTIMERS
Reality 281
Sunset Season

This Age is coming to an end. And that means we'll be separated for awhile, you and me. Out of communication. I'll miss you, dear reader. I really will. But hang in there. I'll be back. We're Longtimers—so we've got to stick together, be there for each other. In the meantime:

Watch out for Timestorms.
Keep your Blinker and Beeper close at hand.
Don't get stuck with any Bystander dollars.
Take your Realities one day at a time.
And most of all, read my journal entries.

You've probably been wondering what happened after my last entry, after I left you out in the Void during Intermission. I don't blame you for being curious.

Well, our descent into the Three Dimensional World begins with the appearance of vapors in the Void ahead of the helicopter. I'm lucky I've got a window and can watch, but Cartmell and Amanda are crowding in to look, too, their faces near mine, and I can smell their jasmine perfumes.

The vapors ahead of us get lighter and thicker in color. And the rotors above us grows louder and our ride bumpier. The vista brightens to a view of cotton-candy clouds while the rotors drone so loud we can't carry on a conversation without shouting.

In addition to the jolts, I feel pushed down into my seat, and I realize gravity has returned. Gaps appear in the cumulus ahead, and I can see something glittering and twisting below us, a green ribbon shimmering against a pink horizon: the Ohio River at sunset. I glance at my watch to find it's quarter past five. My arm's heavy now—weightlessness is gone.

Ahead in the distance: the Shawneetown skyline. Spires of silver reflect gold shafts of light. The storm clouds are gone, and the vista is magnificent, the buildings standing at attention in perfect formation before the spotlight of the setting sun. The sound of the rotors takes on an ooh and ahh that I realize is coming from the voices of passengers who are watching out their windows.

The buildings of Shawneetown loom like giants as we descend—giants of glass and steel. I can see the tallest buildings first, and I don't recognize all of them, just the Roebuck Tower and the Posey, all silver instead of green or blue. I can't identify much else until we get closer and I recognize the Raveller and the Wrigley Building and the other classics. I feel the pride of a returning native. My eyes become misty and bright, and I realize *I love Shawneetown!* It's the greatest city ever.

We're rocking in our seats as we plummet through air pockets, so it feels like a wagon ride over dusty trails, bumping up and down. The rotors drone, the buildings fly by as we approach the ground. As we pass over them, I catch sight of the portico and five fat pillars of the old Shawneetown Bank building, yellow like a brick of cheese. We begin to slow and turn as we descend.

I recognize the turret of the Brotherhood Lodge and then the third story. The second and first floors swing into view amid a cloud of dust. The noise of the rotors screams in our ears, and we feel a jolting bump. The whine of the blades rises but begins to wind down, and the air around the helicopter clears, and we can see that we've landed on the front lawn of the Brotherhood Lodge.

Everyone begins unbuckling before the announcement comes to take off our seatbelts. A din of metallic clicks and voices. A lot of passengers are standing up. The Newcomers across the aisle from us are jabbering like a bunch of Monkeys. And twisting and jumping like Monkeys, too. I see Amos is still sitting, belted in, but he's beaming.

We've made it—we've really made it. Cartmell and Amanda and I trade hugs. The Void hostess is thanking us and giving us exit instructions. Everyone's grabbing their luggage. The hubub of voices grows louder. And then we hear the sound of the hatch cracking open, and the cabin floods with the last rays of sunset as the door opens and descends. I can see steps unfolding with wire balustrades.

I grab my backpack from the overhead compartment, and Amanda gets her suitcase. Cartmell's got her Hello Kitty pack, Zeke his laundry bag, and Barlow his duffel. We're ready to bivouac in this new Season, ready for our next posting in the Timeflow.

Soon people start moving forward and down the steps. The rotors above us are turning slowly, creating a strobing shadow as we descend. Solid ground feels so strange and hard as I climb down—a shock of firmness after the weightlessness of the Void. Each footfall is like a quake to my skeleton. Dinosaur steps. I'm walking, then running up the sidewalk, almost bouncing off the pavement toward the familiar building, painted white in this Reality but bathed in the orange of the setting sun.

The sunlight gets dimmer, and the air grows colder in the winds of sundown as we climb up to the porch. Garson and Greta and Brother Samuels are waiting for us, giving us hugs and a homecoming greeting. The porch lights are on, and the Monks have lighted candles. It's as bright as a birthday cake.

I'm so glad to see Garson's colorful, friendly face, his hood on his shoulders. How could I ever have found him strange?

"Home welcome you, Dexter," he says. "Glad made it so I am you." It's so good to be here. We hug and shake hands. How could I ever have considered the Lodge a forbidding place?

Inside the entry hall, all the lights are on, and it's brighter inside than I remember it. For the first time it seems like a family's residence, like Christmas homecoming, and I half expect to see Mom and Dad.

We pile our coats on the rack. We're all hugging and shaking hands. We're even greeting the Newcomers, who are looking around the Lodge in awe. They probably know it only as a haunted house.

We move down the corridor to the library, finding it decked out in banners that say WE DID IT! and CONGRATULATIONS, and I realize it's set up for our party to celebrate our Membership in the Society and Amos's election to Elder. The furniture is antiques with needle point on the cushions rather than the yellow and red vinyl chairs we're used to. But it still feels like home.

There's a hooded Monk at the far end of the room, gesturing to me as I enter. So I cross the wooden floor and follow her through a doorway. Before she lowers her hood, I've figured out who it is. We enter the banquet hall with only one overhead light on. The room's larger than the library, and in the shadows I can see tables with white tablecloths and a sideboard covered with silver serving trays.

I can smell roasted chicken and duck and dressing and rolls and the sweet aroma of freshly baked fruit pies—peach, cinnamon apple, and pumpkin. I'm overwhelmed with a rush of holiday spirit. I give Belinda a hug and look at her in the dimness. Her face has no tattoos or jewels or face paint. It's just her, and I'm so glad she's not trying to be someone else.

"Remember, Dexter, back in Moonglow when I told you that every Reality is a new chance, every Season a new start? And you can be anyone you want to be?"

I laugh. "Yeah, I remember that."

"Well," she says, "I'm a new person, and I'm coming back to the family. And I can't wait to start living together again." She sheds her Monk's robe to reveal a silver Longtimer suit below it. She looks like Myra Case or Jordan Jordan now. I'm eager to get to know the new Belinda.

I hope she's right about us living together. We're staying at the Lodge for a few days, but then we'll have to move out, and no new living arrangements have been made. I do hope we can stay a family.

Belinda is misty eyed as she embraces me. "I wanted you to be the first to know."

Another light goes on overhead, and I hear a cry, and Cartmell runs into the room. "Belinda, you're back!" She's so excited. She's hugging Belinda and doing her little dance. What a holiday this is!

A third light goes on overhead, and in the dimness across the room I see the outline of a large figure walking toward us in the wide-open, easy-going gait of Wilderness. "There you are," his voice purrs. He encircles Belinda with an arm.

Cartmell and I stare into each other's faces. Barlow and Belinda are together again. After six Seasons of being on the outs, those two are cozy now. They've always been close and affectionate, just short of lovey-dovey, close enough to be annoying but not to make you wonder. They were inseparable until Moonglow. I never have found out what changed. But now it's back to best buddies.

It seems like madness—magical and strange. Well, I guess they're entitled to a new start. The whole world seems brand new. I have my doubts about whether their closeness can last, but hey, we live in a world where nothing lasts, so why worry about it? You've got to live in the present. That's all you've got.

Another light goes on overhead, and I catch sight of Cooper creeping into the room and peering into the serving dishes. He pulls a few stuffed olives out of one and pops them into his mouth. He's chewing and smiling, and he replaces a serving lid as he catches sight of me approaching.

"Hey, little brother," he says. His disguise is gone. He's in his jeans and leather jacket. No white grease paint. No elf shoes. He's wearing Wilderness duds like me. I've changed into my old clothes, too.

"Hey, big ol' brother from 250," I say back at him. I catch the scent of strawberries and incense as I sniff the air. "When abouts have you been since Mystic?" I ask him. "How did the what-do-you-call-it stunt work go in where-do-you-call-it now?"

"California," he says. He grins. "That's where they grow strawberries, you know."

"Sounds exotic," I tell him. "I'd like to come and see it sometime."

He Nods and puts his arm around me. "I'll have to take you with me one of these days." He looks at me with a twinkle in his eye. "Now that you're all grown up."

I laugh and realize that Cooper still has another hors d'oeuvre in his hand. He pops it in my mouth, and I taste a pastry shell with a savory bacon and cheese filling. I try to talk with my mouth full as I chew.

"I'd like to see some of these movies you've been making."

"So would I," he says. "So would I." He takes his arm off my shoulder and spreads his hands in a gesture of regret. "But they've all been Wiped Out by the Time Changes."

I'm misty-eyed now. "What kind of movies were they?" I ask. "Spy movies?"

He crinkles up his face. "Oh, no. Travelogues mostly, with a lot of special effects."

"And adventure?" I say, "And stunt work?"

He smiles and shakes his head. "You make it sound romantic. It's really just a lot of hard work. Sometimes interesting, though."

"Tell me about it."

He laughs. "I'd like to," he says, putting his arm around my shoulder, "if it wasn't just so gol-darned secret. Movie studio contracts. Confidentiality agreements and all, you know."

I nod like an insider.

Then another light comes on above us, and I turn to see Amanda entering the room. She walks up to her sisters and says, "Welcome back to the family, Belinda. You're looking good, Cartmell."

Belinda's all smiles as she leans on Barlow. He looks more relaxed than I've seen him in seven Seasons.

"Everything's back to normal!" Cartmell exclaims.

Amanda rolls her eyes. "There's no such thing anymore." I'll have to side with her on that one.

The Newcomers and the Monks wander into the room next, adding color to the broad hall. The rest of the lights come on overhead as Amos enters with his guests. All eyes turn his way. This must have been what it was like when a magnificent potentate would enter the room in ages past—a Pompey or a Caesar, the Conqueror returning in glory from Gaul. This is what it's like to be in the presence of Greatness. Amos enters in his perfectly tailored suit from the Triumph Season, a glorious uniform from a war won with honor. He struts in to a standing ovation, holding his arms high to acknowledge his beloved companions.

Zeke sidles up to me from out of the crowd and murmurs, "He comes from the Second Era in the Hotshot Season." This is one of those obvious things he has figured out. I want to hear more, but it will have to wait.

I watch shining Amos cross the room, gripping the arms of comrades and admirers, everyone reaching out to touch and be transformed by the hero.

Garson and Greta and Brother Samuels spread throughout the chamber, distributing flutes of champagne to all of the guests. They too are family now. We raise our glasses in a toast to the Great Man and the Great Family, the Vanns. Amos stands on a chair to give his speech.

"I want to congratulate my brothers and sisters on their stupendous achievement—seven Seasons of

Survival." A cheer rings out, and glasses clink, and I taste the cold gold liquid sparkling as it dries my taste buds and glitter-chills down my throat.

"I am so proud of my brothers and sisters today," Amos declares. "But it was not entirely out of brotherly love that I Sponsored you. I have plans for you. Big plans. I need capable, courageous, honorable, and trustworthy people to carry out the grand designs of tomorrow. You are not simply my loved ones—you are the heirs to the Kingdom of Time, the Protectors of the Aeons, the leaders of the new Chronotastic Era."

Another cheer breaks out, and Amos climbs down from his chair so we can start spreading our congratulations personally in groups of two and three and four. Good cheer spreads across the room.

What are the great plans Amos has for us? What is his vision of the Chronotastic Era? I want to find out. I want to live it and live in it. But it will have to wait until next Season.

Zeke comes up to me and hands me a certificate. I've completed my training in Fourth Dimensional Science. He has one for himself—and also one for Barlow. Now we're qualified to apprentice as Dimensionalizer Repairmen.

Amos is distributing our Membership cards and Identity Rings to us as he mingles his way through the crowd, giving and receiving congratulations.

"Amanda, what are we going to do?" Cartmell asks. "Where will we live? How will we Survive? How are we going to make it in the Bystander World?"

Amanda doesn't seem concerned. "I've got some ideas," she says, "And I'm sure Amos has some suggestions." She draws Cartmell to her for a hug.

I can't wait to hear these new ideas and start putting them into practice. I want to live—to the same full extent I'm living now, at this celebration. I want my life to be a celebration.

Our future appears glorious. Sure, there will be a lot of hardships, a lot of risks. But I think we're up to the challenge.

We've done it. We've Survived. We had to accomplish a lot to get this far. How much becomes apparent when I look over at the Valediction Season Newcomers, a family named Lopez. Amos invited them to our Celebration, and they accepted gratefully. They're still in the Tourist phase—all geegawing and rubber necking with cries of joy and surprise and stares of wonder. They prance around in their colorful Valediction robes like they're flaunting how clueless they are. They dress like graduating seniors without the mortar boards, but they act like freshmen. Were we ever like that? I guess we must have been. We're jaded now in a lot of ways—but not about our future.

The Lopezes regard us with awe. I've never seen somebody so impressed. They're so ignorant of what's ahead of them, they don't know what questions to ask. They follow us around like puppy dogs and hang on every word they overhear. They're so eager.

I shake my head. How did we Survive if we were ever like them? Jordan Jordan is their Sponsor, and she's come to our celebration too but spends most of her time herding her Newcomers, trying to teach them Manners without bringing them along too quickly.

Mr. Yen is here. And Tate. And Shadow. Yes, even Shadow. He wears Longtimer Casual now. He doesn't act or dress like one of the Night People. He blends in, but Belinda doesn't have much time for him, so he spends his time with Garson and Gretta and parties till dawn.

I guess this is the event of the Season because even Myra Case and Molly Waters and Red Phillips are here— not in any official capacity. They're acquainted with Amos, and they know the Spotters, so of course they're friends with Belinda. She seems to have more friends in the Timeflow than the rest of us, and it's so strange to think of what an outcast she used to be. It's strange to think of what we all used to be.

There's something I haven't told you, haven't told anybody. The Valediction Season wasn't the only time I've seen Marcy. I saw her in Tempest too. I spotted her in a subway train just before the doors closed—and she looked like she recognized me. And she wasn't any Munchkin, either. I think she's a Longtimer. She's out there. I tell you she's out there. And one of these days we're going to meet.

When Amos makes his way to me to give me my Membership card and Identity Ring, I say to him, "How does it feel to have a family that's finally Survived all the way to the Membership stage?"

He raises his eyebrows as he pins my Membership card to my shirt pocket, but he's not as surprised as I expected that I've figured it out.

"It feels Right," he says. "I knew you could do it. It's the way things ought to be."

Spoken like a Conqueror.

"How many times did you Sponsor us?" I ask him. "Before it finally worked out?"

He gives me this weary kind of smile. "Fifth time's the charm."

That sends me back on my heels. *Fifth* time! "But I thought the Society will only let you Sponsor someone four times."

He looks askance at me. "We're Vanns," he says. "No Restrictions Apply." He adjusts his black frame glasses. "You underestimate how important this is, how important my plans for you are. Not just important to the family but to future generations."

I let that sink in. Future generations? People I've never met? And may never meet?

"For the future readers of your journal. This is their celebration too."

My readers? I'd almost forgotten about you. I get up on my chair and draw everyone's attention. We raise our flutes one more time.

Reader—this one's for you.

Afterword
NEW JOURNALS DISCOVERD!
By Professor Simon J. Worthy

There is more to Dexter Vann's story—a lot more. Volumes more. Hundreds of journal entries spanning years. Each adventure more astounding than the last. This is only the beginning.

I have chosen to title this volume of transcripts QUANTUM TIME THEORY. That is my choice and not Dexter Vann's, though I will defer to him should he step forward. A company called Chronoversal Export has offered to publish these accounts and supplied an author to take the credit. I can hardly serve as editor and also claim authorship, though obviously Dexter Vann is the real author.

Or is he?

I have acquired 24 more journal entries, covering a period of time not long after that depicted in this book, and I intend to publish them under the title THE CHRONICLES OF NEVERBEEN. The writing style is undeniably Dexter Vann's. They can have been composed by no one else. These 24 journals also tell a story, a story I wager you will want to read. I estimate there are enough journal entries out there for another nine or ten books, though I have not authenticated them yet.

What's more, there are gaps in what we already have. The recordings suggest Dexter Vann was in the habit of making an entry for every Reality he experienced. I don't know if this is true. If it is, there are missing transcripts—holes in our account—of his first seven Seasons in the Timeflow. 31 Realities pass during his tale, so there should be 31 transcripts, not 24 to cover this time period.

Collectors have contacted me to let me know they have some of these missing manuscripts. I intend to purchase them so I can put them on a web site and publish them at some future date.

Whether these accounts are fictional or real you must judge for yourself. I would prefer to have the recordings themselves rather than transcriptions. I want to see the box they came in. I would like to see the Subvocalizer they were recorded with—and perhaps a Dimensionalizer too. But sadly, all we have at present are the transcripts.

Are they truth or fiction? I'm not willing to render a verdict until all of the evidence is in. And the evidence keeps mounting. More and more transcriptions are being found, singly and in bunches. I am in negotiations to purchase them all.

I have discovered more material than can fit into this book—not just the missing chapters but also fabulous curiosities, including photographs, artworks, interviews, surprises, teasers, pleasers, and more. Extras of all varieties—the equivalent of a whole additional volume. I am putting it on the web for free at two different sites:

nedhuston.com
ridethetimemachine.com

There is too much even for the web site, so some treasures will have to be posted for a limited time and switched out for others each month. To receive a listing of all of the Extras and the dates they will be available— and also the dates of the publication of future volumes of THE NEVERTIME CHRONOLOGY—sign up for the Chronotastic Newsletter for free at the web site.

If you hunger for more, Book 2 of THE NEVERTIME CHRONOLOGY, THE CHRONICLES OF NEVERBEEN, will be out in 2017. But there is already more online— hours of material with more being added monthly.

So what are you waiting for?

In Memoriam

Brendan Carver, Regency sales representative

Paul Dougherty, Landslide driver

Ernest Felton, Evernight Intertime agent

Rollo Gerard, Tempest policeman

Ferdinand Gomez, Wilderness professor

Wilbur Hays, Guidepost ghost hunter

Martin Hoffer, Guidepost security guard

Obadiah Jones, Guidepost, ghost hunter

Jym "Marauder" Kinkaid, Hari Kiri pirate

Cyrus Lee, Fogbank pirate

Alston McNamara, Concordance bank president

Quint Palmer, Valediction student

Junius Pollard, Castaway assassin

Harley Porter, Wilderness student

Marcus Quartus, Nevertime Elder

Felipe Sanchez, Wilderness unemployed

Abraham Smeckler, Moonglow haberdasher

Riley Spender, Wilderness unemployed

* Barlow Vann, Wilderness student & football star

Edwina Vann, Valediction housewife

Moses Vann, Valediction lawyer

* Jackson Vaughn, Tempest child

    * Survived by Longtimer Self

Glossary
The Terminology of the Longtimers

Characters in this novel use words from the vernacular in their usual sense. They also use jargon and slang unique to the Longtimers and Bystanders. These terms are capitalized in the text and defined here. This is not a complete compendium of Longtimer terminology but includes only terms used in this book.

4DTN (n) Fourth Dimensional Television Network

42nd Directive (n) a law to prevent Longtimers from revealing things to Bystanders

Accommodate (v)/**Accommodator** (n) a Nonadaptive Coping Strategy—Accommodators aim to satisfy and please Bystanders

Accords of Nevertime (n) the agreements that created the Society of Time, the Central Time Authority and the Intertime Government

Adjust (v)/**Adjustment** (n) fitting in with a new Season, Reality or environment in Time

Aftermath (n) the changes that come after a Timestorm

Age (n) a set of seven Seasons

Alter (v) to Change something

Alteration (n) something Changed in Time

Alternate Life (n) one of the nine Transkarmic Elements of Being: the life of your Alternate Self

Alternate Residence (n) the residence in the Present of one's Alternate Self

Alternate Self (n) a Bystander version in the Past of a Longtimer in the Present

Alternate Timeline (n) the history of a vanished Season or Reality

Anachronism (n) something that Existed in a past Reality but not the current Reality

Analyzer (n) a Coping Strategy that uses analysis as a coping mechanism

Annihilation (n) being Wiped Out of Time

Apprentice (n) a Longtimer who is allowed to learn a profession controlled by a Guild

Archaeology (n) the study of one's Alternate Life

Artifacts (n) items unique to a Season

Assimilator (n) a Coping Strategy that relies on relationships to help with coping

Attachment (n) obsession or dependence upon memories, customs, values, items or people from the Past

Beacon (n) a warning device in the Past that sends a signal to the Present when a Time Change approaches

Beeper (n) a device that beeps to warn Longtimers of an approaching Timestorm

Big Time, the (n) life as a Citizen of Time with all of its serious requirements and responsibilities

Blinker (n) a device that flashes to warn a Longtimer that a Timestorm is on its way

Brotherhood (name) the Brotherhood of Time

Brotherhood Lodge (name) the house used by the Brotherhood of Time

Brotherhood of Time (name) a quasi-religious and charitable organization that helps Longtimers across Time. It is served by Monks who perform rituals for the Society and who study and venerate a holy book called the *Parattak* and who practice the rites and rituals of a religion called Timeism

Bycops (n) slang for the Bypolice

Bycrimes (n) crimes against Bystanders

Bypolice (n) Bystander police

Byshucking (expletive) a Longtimer curse word

Bystander (n) a person who Exists only in a particular Reality and has never used a Safe House

Bystander World (n) the society of the Bystanders in he Present

CTA (n) the Central Time Authority

Calendar (n) slang for *year*

Catacombs (n) the Shawneetown underground, where the subway, tunnels, canals and pumping stations are

Central Time Authority (n) a law enforcement group that fights Timecrime, especially in the Void

Chamelon (n) a Coping Strategy that involves blending in

Change (n) a Time Change

Change (v) to change something in Time

Change Barrier (n) the force that keeps short-range Changes from reaching the Present

Change in Time (n) Time Change

Changeworld (n) the world created by Time Changes

Chroniac (n) one who has gone "Chrono"

Chrono (adj) Longtimer slang for "crazy"

Chrononaut (n) a person who legally Travels through Time for science or exploration

Chronophobia (n) fear of things related to time, especially fear of strange Longtimers and unusual Seasons

Chronoverse (n) everything, including all possible or hypothetical universes, parallel or other dimensions, all times past, present, future or otherwise, all places real or fictional

Citizen (n) a Citizen of Time

Citizen of Time/Citizenship (n) a Longtimer who has belonged to the Society of Time for at least 15 Seasons

Colonizer/Colonizing (n) a Coping Strategy for dealing with change—a Colonizer tries to recreate a familiar environment

The Common (name) a Time Station that also functions as a Time Ferry. It spends half of its time in the Three Dimensional World

Cone (n) slang for the Time/Space Continuum, so named because of its shape

Conqueror/Conquering (n) a Coping Strategy for Dealing with change— Conquerors try to make their environment Adjust to them

Contaminated (adj) full of indications of Alternative Life

Contamination (n) the spread of elements of the Longtimer World to the Bystander World or vice versa—or the spread of elements of Alternate Life to Current Life

Controller (n) a Coping Strategy in which one deals with change by trying to control one's environment or companions

Coping Strategy (n) an approach to living that helps a person cope with change; there are many different Coping Strategies

Council of Nevertime (n) a gathering of important Longtimers in the history of the Timeflow when the Intertime Government was founded and Seasons began to be officially named and numbered

Counterstrike (n) a law enforcement/military maneuver meant to undo the effects of a Time Change

Cruiser (n) a large Timecraft outfitted with weaponry for battle

D (adj) Dimensional

D-Charge (n) the charge from a Dimensional Weapon

D-Grenade (n) a Dimensional Grenade

D-Gun, D-Pistol (n) a hand-held Dimensional Weapon

D-Weapon (n) a Dimensional weapon, capable of changing the direction of Reproduction of matter in Time so an object/person will leave the Three Dimensional World and enter the Void

Dark Days (n) the years before the Nevertime Season

Dark Men (n) members of the Lunean religion who worship the new moon

Dark Season (n) a Season that is unlike previous ones

Day People (n) one of two groups of Bystanders during the Moonglow Season. The Day people are picky and obstinate. They operate primarily during daytime

Daymoon (n) a full moon during daytime

Decontamination (n)/**Decontaminate** (v) the process of eliminating all traces of Alternate Life from a residence

Deep (the) (n) Protospace in the Fourth Dimension outside of the Plane and the Pathway

Déjà vu (n) a repetition of an event from a former Reality

Deny (v)/**Denial** (n)/**Denier** (n) a Nonadaptive Coping Strategy—Deniers refuse to accept or acknowledge change

Deteriorate (v)/**Deterioration** (n) the process by which the changes in a person or Reality become less integrated and consistent so that the rate of change speeds up, ending in insanity

Dimension (n) One of the four directions of movement--back-forth, up-down, right-left, Past-Future

Dimensional Weapon (n) a weapon that changes the Fourth Dimensional direction of matter so its reproduction enters the Void or The Deep

Dimensionalizer (n) a device that changes the direction of matter's Reproduction so a Time Machine or Safe House can leave the Three Dimensional World and enter the Void

Direction (n) motivation to Survive

Directive (n) a law passed by the Intertime Government

Disappear (v) to no longer Exist in either the Past or Present

Dischronofiliated (adj) disoriented and disturbed as a result of changes, especially changes in Time

Disintegration (n) the process in a Longtimer of becoming more and more Chrono

Do-Overs (n) slang for Time Changes

Downtime (adj) closer to the Present or the present

Dream Life (n) one of the 9 Transkarmic Elements of Being: daydreaming, believing in illusions, or believing only what you want to

Drift off the Plane (v) leave the Plane and enter uncharted Protospace where there are no beacons for guidance

Dropout (n) the moment of leaving the Three Dimensional Universe

Dyschronic (adj) not compatible with elements of another Time or Season

Eden (name) the first Season, years before Nevertime

Elder (n) a high level official in the Intertime Government

Electric Net (n) the field projected by a Void Rifle to surround an object and make it propagate in a new direction

Eloi (n) the elite rich upper class of Longtimers

Emergence (n) the act of entering a new Reality

Endurance Fallacy (n) one of the fallacies of False Life, the belief that a certain Reality or custom or practice is going to last

Endure (v) remain in the Timeflow or the Timestream

Escapist/Escaping (n) a Coping Strategy that uses entertainment to cut down stress

Exist (v)/**Existence** (n) to have existence literally in the Past or the Present or the Void

Extension (n) Extension in Time

Extension in Time (n) matter across Four Dimensions

Extinct (adj) without Existence in Time, neither in the Past, the Present, or the Void

Fault Lines (n) problems in one's Alternate Life

Ferry (n) Time Ferry

Finagle (v)/ **Finagling** (n) **Finagler** (n) conning the Bystanders for profit

First Reality the (n) the very first Reality, when the Time Machine was invented

Focus (n) will to Survive or focus on Survival

Forecaster (n) a news anchor on 4DTN broadcasts

Four Dimensional World (n) the Fourth Dimensional universe outside of the Present

Fourth Dimension (n) a spatial dimension that includes the Three Dimensional World (Past and Present) as well as the Void (the Future, Protospace, the Plane, the Deep). When using this term, often Longtimers mean only the Void

Fourth Dimensional Science (n) the science devised to explain Time Travel, the Void, etc.

Fourth Dimensional Television Network (n) a television news network that operates in the Void to provide news for Longtimers

Fourth Dimensional World (n) the Void, specifically habitations on the Plane or in the Deep, including the Pathway

Fracture (n) a dangerous event or circumstance in one's Alternate Life

Future (n) Voidspace (including the Plane) located spatially ahead of the Present.

Godhead (n) a small and dark cloud at the front of a Timestorm that rains down lightning bolts

Gray Season (n) a Season between Light and Dark

Guild (n) an association of Longtimers that controls entrance to and membership in a profession unique to the Timestream

Hibernation (n) Longtimer slang for the Interval, especially if spent in a Shelter

In Memoriam (name) a list of Longtimers Wiped Out of Time during the last Time Change or Era

Inner Sanctum (n) the center of the Brotherhood Lodge

Intermission (n) slang for the Interval

Intertime Government (n) the government elected and supported by the Longtimers

Intertime Police (n) the police force of the Intertime
Government
Interval, the (n) the time between when a Time Change starts
and ends

Jikki (n) a form of black magic practiced during the
Moonglow Season

King of the Night (name) a fictitious leader

Landfall (n) arrival in a new Reality
Lifeline (n) one of several technological devices (Beeper,
Blinker, Wristwatcher, Cellular) that help keep
Longtimers safe
Light Men (n) members of the Lunean religion who worship
the full moon
Light Season (n) a Season similar to previous Seasons
Live Off the Land (v) slang for stealing from the Bystanders
Local (n) a Bystander
Lodge (n) the house used by the Brotherhood of Time or a Safe
House Resort for Longtimers
Longevity (n) length of time a Longtimer Survives
Longtimer (n) technically, anyone who is not a Bystander.
More specifically, it is used to refer to anyone who is
not a Bystander, Timecrimer, Newcomer, or Tourist.
Longtimer Casual (n) a fashion that will blend in with most
Light Seasons
Longtimer Law (n) Time Laws
Longtimers Anonymous (n) a support group for those who
are having difficulty Adjusting to changes
Lost (adj) Wiped Out of the Timestream
Lost Seasons (n) the Seasons before Nevertime, starting with
Eden, followed by Babylon and ending with Limbo.
No one knows how many there were
Lunean Fortune/Lunean Treasure (n) alternate names of the
Lunean Relic
Lunean Relic (n) a religious relic valued by Luneans
Luneans (n) followers of a moon worshipping religion that
began among the Bystanders but spread to Longtimers

Manners (n) the customs of the Longtimers

Matinee (n) slang for the current Reality

Member/Membership (n) in the Society of Time

Membership Examination (n) the test that a Newcomer has to pass in order to become a Longtimer

Mobile Safe House (n) a Safe House which is also a land, air or sea craft

Monk (n) a member of the religious order of the Brotherhood of Time

Moon Monarch (title) the leader of the Moon People

Moon People (n) a cannibalistic sect that split off from the Luneans

Moonball (n) a decorative ball representing the moon

Moonbird (n) owl

Moonglasses (n) sunglasses

Munchkins (n) the Vann family's nickname for the Bystanders of the Tempest Season—later, Bystanders in general

Neverbeen (n) non-existence, never having existed, including people, places, and things that have been Wiped Out of Time

Nevertime (n) the name of Season 1, the first official Season but not the first Season ever

New Town (name) an upscale area of Shawneetown northwest of downtown

Newbies (n) slang for Newcomers

Newcomer (n) one who is being Sponsored to become a Longtimer

Newpast (n) the past of one's Alternate Self

Nexus (n) a turning point in Time where a sequence can branch off in different directions

Night People (n) one of two groups of Bystanders during the Moonglow Season. The Night People operate primarily during night time. Their appearance and culture vary greatly from the Day People

Nod (n & v) a short bow done by Longtimers to acknowledge each other's losses

Oldtimer (n) a person who has been a Longtimer since the early Seasons

Oldspaper (n) a newspaper for Longtimers, distributed mainly but not exclusively in electronic version

Opportunist (n) the Coping Strategy of one who makes no plans but Adjusts to changes and circumstances as they occur

Originating Point (n) the place (coordinates) where a Time Change began

Outcaster (n) a Voider who doesn't fit in with common Longtimers

Pangeans (n) a fringe group among the Longtimers dedicated to its own secret agenda

Panic, the (n) a stage of frenzy that ends in a Longtimer becoming Chrono

Parattak (name) a holy book prized and studied by Longtimers

Past (n) a place in the Three-Dimensional World that can be visited by Traveling in a Timecraft. It Exists spatially before the Present. It correlates with the past known by the current Bystanders but not the past known by the Longtimers

Past Life (n) one of the nine Transkarmic Elements of Being, an attachment to one's past and past expectations

Pathway (the) (n) an area of protospace surrounding the Time/Space Continuum in the Past

Perch (n) a place to keep still during Dropout

Pilot (n) one who pilots a Timecraft

Plane (the) (n) the three Dimensional Area of the Void where there are human settlements and Buoys for navigation

Posterity (n) the inhabitants of the Post-Change World

Pre-Dawn (adj) before Reality 1

Prefect (n) a minor appointed official in the Intertime Government

Present (n) a place in the Three-Dimensional World at one end of the Time Solid, the present of the Longtimers and Bystanders

Promenade (n) the broad circular strip in The Common for Longtimers to walk or congregate

Protospace (n) the nothingness surrounding the Three-Dimensional World. It fills the Void, although pockets of the Void may also include space, particularly in the Plane. It is different from space, which has dimensions and contents and is not nothingness. The laws of physics operate differently in Protospace than in Space

Public Safe House (n) a Safe House for all Longtimers

Quantum Time Theory (n) A theory of time invented by Time
  Traveling scientists. It asserts the universe is a
  discontinuous four Dimensional solid with the big
  bang at one end and the Present at the other,
  constantly growing as the Three Dimensional Universe
  is reproduced along the Fourth Dimension.
Queen of the Night (name) a celebrity among the Night
  People, Belinda's nickname in the Moonglow Season,

Range (n) an estimate of how far back in Time a Time Change
  has occurred
Realignment (n)/**Realigned** (adj) a change in Rehistory
Reality (n) a period of Time starting after a Time Change and
  ending with the next Time Change
Reality 1 (n) the first Reality to be numbered and designated
  by the Council of Nevertime; not the same as the First
  Reality
Reality 250 (name) The Reality that the Vann family comes
  from
Realizer (n) the Strategy of being yourself; the Strategy of
  someone who needs no Strategy because they are so
  well Adjusted
Rehistory (n) Altered History or the study of Altered History,
  past, present, future, or hypothetical
Reinchronation (n) when a Bystander who was Extinct comes
  back into Existence
Reject (v)/**Rejector** (n) a Nonadaptive Coping Strategy—
  Rejectors refuse to Adapt or believe
Relic, (the) (n) the Lunean Relic, a revered relic in the Lunean
  religion
Replacement (n) an unadaptive Coping Strategy: replacing
  your Persona with someone else's
Report (n) a news story about a new Reality
Room 888 (name) a variation on Room 999
Room 999 (name) code name for a Safe House

STA (name) Stability Through Action, a fringe group of
  Longtimers in favor of Changing the Past to improve
  the Present; as a political group they are legal, but

388

what they advocate is illegal. They seek a change in the law

Safe House (n) a Time Machine that can move a short distance through the Fourth Dimension but cannot Travel into the Past

Scion (n) the leader of the Intertime Government

Season (n) a culture in Time lasting one or more Realities.

Season-Ender (n) a Deep Time Change that ends a Season

Second (n) a distance (186,000 miles) across the Fourth Dimension

Sector One (n) a division of the Earth that includes Shawneetown, IL

Self (n) a continuing version of an individual, Unchanged by Timestorms, with the same DNA and the same evolving personality and memory

Seven Dangers (n) the seven dangers that threaten a Longtimer's Existence: Timestorms, Bystanders, Timecrimers, Time Travel, other Longtimers, Bankruptcy, and Self (depression, insanity, etc.)

Seven Hazards (n) the Seven Dangers

Shelter (n) Safe House

Shuttle (n) a short-range Timecraft that operates between Time Stations and the Three Dimensional World

Signs (n) symptoms of the Time Change Stress Syndrome

Slice (n) a discrete version of the universe along the Fourth Dimension

Society (n) the Society of Time

Society of Time (n) Longtimers who have joined to form a civilization of people who Survive Time Changes

Society Station (name) a Time Station in the Void

Speed of the Universe (n) the speed at which the universe is reproducing itself across the Fourth Dimension— 186,000 miles per second

Sponsor (n)/**Sponsorship** (n) someone whose official role is to help guide a Bystander into becoming a Longtimer

Sponsor (v) the action of training and guiding a Bystander into becoming a Longtimer

Spontaneous Creation (n) the theoretical process by which movement and new matter are created as the universe duplicates itself along the Fourth Dimension

Spotter (n) a Longtimer whose job is to explore a new Reality and make Reports of it

Stabilize (v) when a person or Reality ceases changing at a rapid rate and stops Deteriorating or Transforming

Stealth Craft (n) a Timecraft that cannot be detected by radar

Storm (n) Timestorm

Stage Three (n) also "the Final Stage" when one goes Chrono

Strange Karma (n) an inexplicable force that affects Longtimers. When Strange Karma operates, Effects can come before causes

Strata (n) events and artifacts of one's Alternate Life

Strategy (n) Coping Strategy

Subvocalizer (n) a device that allows one to make a recording without speaking out loud

Survive (v) to exist unchanged from Reality to Reality

Syndicate (the) (n) the Time Syndicate

Terminal Velocity (n) the greatest speed that a Time Change or signal across time can reach under normal circumstances

Three Dimensional Universe/World (n) the three dimensional solid consisting of the Past and the Present

Threshold (n) the boundary between the Three Dimensional Universe and the Fourth Dimension

Time (n) the Past, the Present, and the Future

Time Bank (n) a Time Station and bank which is in the Void as often as on the ground in the Three Dimensional World

Time Change (n) a change made in the Past, which propagates forward and changes the Present as well as all the Past between the location of the Change and the Present

Time Change Stress Syndrome (n) a mental affliction in Longtimers caused by too much stress due to constant change

Time Ferry (n) a vehicle for transporting people from the Three Dimensional World to Stations in the Void

Time Holocaust (n) a term referring to the deaths of billions of people as a result of the Time Changes

Time Laws (n) the set of laws, enacted by the Intertime Government, that apply to Longtimers

Time Machine (n) a device for travelling through the Fourth Dimension through Time (Protospace and space), not time (duration or a cause-effect chain)

Time Problems (n) problems adjusting to changes in Time

Time Share Solicitor (n) one who sells time-share apartments on the Time Stations in the Void

Time Solid (n) the physical universe, consisting of the Past and the Present

Time/Space Continuum (n) the Three Dimensional Solid consisting of the Past and the Present

Time Station (n) a habitation located in the Void

Time Syndicate (n) a group of Timecrimers and Travelers who cooperate in carrying out activities in Violation of the Directives set down by the Intertime Government

Time Travel (n) to Travel across or through Time, from Present to Past or Past to Present or to the Future

Time Traveler (n) one who Travels in or across Time

Time Traveler's Guide to the Chronoverse (title) a guidebook for Longtimers

Time World (n) the culture and experiences of the Longtimers

Timecast (n) a news broadcast made from the Void of the Fourth Dimension to the Void or the Three Dimensional World

Timecraft (n) a Time Machine with a rocket engine that makes it capable of Traveling through the Fourth Dimension

Timecrime (n) crime committed in the Void or the Past or in furtherance of criminals operating in the Void or the Past

Timecrimer (n) anyone who violates the Directives laid down by the Intertime Government, specifically Void Pirates and those who Travel without a permit (Travelers)

Timeflow (n) the Longtimer Society across Time

Timely Rogers (interjection) a phrase used to express surprise or frustration

Timeship (n) a long-range Timecraft

Timestorm (n) a storm caused by a Time Change. A Timestorm ravages across the earth, changing everything in its path, killing all people and creating new ones in their place

Timestream (n) the Past, Present, and environs as they propagate across Time

Timesucking (expletive) a Longtimer curse word

Timewhacking (expletive) a Longtimer curse word

Toddler (n) a derisive term for a Newcomer

Tourist (n) a Newcomer who hasn't yet Adjusted to the Timeflow, or one who seems to lack the proper seriousness about Adjustment

Trace (n) an indicator either of Alternate Life or of Vanished History

Transform (v)/**Transformation** (n) the process by which the changes in a person or Reality become more integrated and consistent so that the rate of change slows down

Transkarmic Elements of Being (n) nine possible stages of being (some mystical) that are experienced by Longtimers: Past Life, Alternate Life, Dream Life, Present Life, Future Life, Hidden Life, Supernatural Life, Afterlife, and Essence

Travel (v) Travel in Time

Travel in Time (v) to move across or through the Fourth Dimension from the Present to the Past or from the Past to the Present or Future

Traveler (n) one who Travels in or across time, to or from the Past in Violation of the First Directive, which forbids Changing Time

Trickster (n) a Coping Strategy that involves the use of trickery in order to Survive and Adapt

Trip (n) a journey through the Fourth Dimension

Type 2 Safe House (n) an early model Safe House

Unadaptive Strategy (n) a Coping Strategy that does not help one to Adapt

Uptime (adj) earlier in time, from a Vanished Season or Reality predating yours

Uptimer (n) a Longtimer who entered the Timeflow before you

Vanish (v) to no longer inhabit the Chronoverse as a Longtimer or a Bystander

Violater (n) one who violates the Directives

Visit (v) to Travel through Time to a place in the Three Dimensional or Four Dimensional Universe

Void (n) the area of protospace outside the Three Dimensional Universe, consisting of the Plane, the Deep, and the Pathway

Void/Voided (v, adj) to send someone into the Void

Void Asylum (n) an insane asylum in the Void for crazy Longtimers

Void Pirates (n) gangs who commit piracy in the Void

Void Prison (n) a prison in the Void where convicted Timecrimers are kept

Void Rifle (n) a long range Dimensional Weapon

Voiders (n) slang for people who live in the Void

Voidship (n) a very large Time Machine that can Travel deep into the Past or Travel far across the Void

Voidsucking (expletive) a Longtimer curse word

Wabash Canal (name) a canal that connects Shawneetown to the Great Lakes or Mississippi River through a series of canals and navigable rivers

When (n) a place in the Present or Past

Whensick (n) homesick for the past or for a former Reality

Wild Man (n) a Longtimer from the Wilderness Season

Wilderness (name) a Light Season in Time right after Compass and right before Moonglow—the home Season of the Vann family

Wiped Out of Time (phrase) no longer Existing in the current Four Dimensional Universe

Wristwatcher (n) a wristwatch whose face flashes when a warning of an imminent Timestorm is broadcast

Made in the USA
San Bernardino, CA
21 March 2017